THE NAPOLEON JOB

THE NAPOLEON JOB

NICK THACKER

CHAPTER 1
NAPOLEON

7:18 PM | **December 1, 1805**

Austerlitz, Austria

"Gentlemen," he began. "Do mind this hill. There will be a battle upon it, and each of you shall have your place."

He looked up from the great wood table at his marshals. They each nodded curtly. He pushed his lips together in a thin line. A battlefield smile; the best they could hope for from their *Grand Commandant*. He had led them this far, he had confidence he would lead them through the next storm.

And there was always a storm. There was always another battle, another fight. His marshals, the best of them at least, understood this. There was, for Napoleon's France, no 'ultimate goal.' If dominating the entirety of the western world was accomplished, it would only be an accidental bonus of the true goal: the journey of conquering.

He had served as emperor of the French for about a year now, but his track record of victory had already begun to precede him. His men were proud, yet humble. Confident but loyal to their leader.

The victory would play out just as he had strategized; he was sure of it. It was not for his sake then that this meeting was taking place, but for his marshals. They needed to be as true to the plan as he; they needed to understand the risks involved and maneuver accordingly.

He turned to the man standing at his right. His most trusted aide. "Have we the numbers we were hoping for?"

The man nodded. "Yes, Commander. 75,000, prepared for battle. Fully stocked and well-fed."

Napoleon nodded. They were not the numbers he had been hoping for, but it had been a year since the French Army had crossed the Rhine with his 200,000 troops. They had expanded their territory greatly, leaving detachments around Austria and the scattered nations surrounding. To prepare for the new Russian threat, Napoleon had navigated to this location, near the hill upon which his next victory lay.

"And they have no knowledge of our true capabilities?"

The man shook his head. "My scouts have returned with news that, to the best of their knowledge, the Allied commanders have not changed their perspective. They believe we are hurt, still limping from our retreat."

Napoleon nodded once again, his brow furrowing. It was a calculated retreat, pulling back to feign a weakness, one that he had sold well, thanks to his hard-earned political talents of acting and subterfuge. He never liked to pull back from an easy victory, but he knew that the greater war was far more important to France's success than a single battle.

He had also purposefully weakened the right front of his army, hoping to invite the Allies to attack at that point on Pratzen Hill, hopefully cutting off Napoleon's communication line with Vienna. Instead, he had moved the center and core of his army to a position adjacent to the hill, hidden and out of sight.

"Commander," another voice from across the table said. "We are to attack after they reach Pratzen Hill, yes?"

He nodded. He had already explained this.

"And if we fail... if we lose Pratzen Hill --"

"The hill is not the victory, but merely the battleground," he snapped. "We feign a weakness to invite an incursion where *we* want it. That is the point. Pratzen Hill *will* be taken by the enemy, but I assure you, men, it will later be *retaken* by us."

There were murmurs around the table. He knew they were skeptical. It was hard not to be. They were tired, overworked, fearful of the inevitable failure. Every army failed — that was historical fact. At some point, Napoleon's march would come to an end.

But not yet. Not today, not tonight.

Not tomorrow.

He understood not only his strategy and the strategies of his opponents — he knew his opponents themselves. He knew their inner thoughts, their desires, their histories and their understandings of the battlefield. He knew what they knew, and that was why he knew his strategy would work.

He turned to Legrand, whose forces would be bearing the brunt of the Allied attack tomorrow at first light. "General," he said, "are your men prepared?"

"Of course, Commandant," Legrand answered without hesitation. "They understand the precarious situation they will put the rest of the Army in if they fail. And they will not. We will hold the flank."

Napoleon moved on to the rest of his marshals in attendance. Davout's Third Corps would be marching from Vienna, but he trusted this man more than the others, and he knew Davout would arrive on time. When he finished discussing final plans and tactical changes, he retired and returned to his private tent.

There, he took stock of himself. He was weary, but excited. Nervous, but cautiously prepared. He was not shaking, he was not unsteady.

He took in a deep breath and prepared his letter to Josephine. Perhaps it would be his last, though he suspected it would be one of many more to be penned by his hand.

He sat at the desk and gathered his thoughts. In staring down at the blank page, he noticed the rigid body of the saber tucked against the side of the tent and the desk.

Napoleon stood and reached for it, bringing it close. In the absence of most of his worldly possessions, this singular item had given him peace and comfort when confusion and chaos began to reign supreme.

He pulled it from its sheath, admiring the bluish-gold steel, the elaborate markings on it, and the sheer craftsmanship of it all. He let his fingers fall over the five embossed roses on the hilt, knowing the power they held within. It was a truly remarkable piece, and though it had not been originally intended for battle, he had worn it during raids and skirmishes, and he planned to do so again tomorrow.

It was *his* sword, and it was the one most cherished by the great commander.

CHAPTER 2
BILLY

10:26 AM | **March 7, 2021**

Imrali, Turkey

The prisoner stood on the edge of the cliff looking out over the water. It was a sheer two-hundred-foot drop to the roiling, churning waters below, but it wasn't even a straight shot. Jagged boulders and edges jutted out from the side of the cliff, ensuring that anyone unfortunate enough to fall — or anyone insane enough to jump — would have a rough way down.

Billy Beckham smiled. It reminded him of the carnival games he used to try to win as a child. His parents would take him once a year, and he would save his allowance for months so he would have enough to play all of the games. Even though his father told him over and over again that they were all rigged — that they were designed to be either impossible or extremely difficult to win — Billy couldn't help it. He was infatuated by the way the ball bounced around as it fell through the vertical shaft on its way to the bottom. The tiny rubberized metal sphere would bounce and dance around and over the wooden ledges, eventually finding its way into one of the six chambers at the bottom of the glass-front case. One of the chambers would offer a prize, the others nothing.

He had never won. His ball somehow always found a way in one of the outside chambers.

Billy took a step backward and turned around, imagining that the carnival game reference was a metaphor for his life. *I never won. Never won nothing at all.*

He took a deep breath, wondering if it would be better to just jump off and end it all right then and there. Surely it would be quicker. Surely he would beat the twenty-nine years of the thirty-year sentence he had still facing him.

An American by birth, William Beckham had been in the wrong place at the wrong time when traveling through Turkey and had ended up with a bag of drugs on his person.

Okay, so he had been in the wrong place at the wrong time *and* made a few wrong decisions.

He had claimed to not know where the drugs had come from, but he was missing that crucial element when it came time to explain himself: an alibi.

He had merely wanted to have a good time his last night in Istanbul. The friends he had met — or at least the people he had been calling friends — had finally taken him to a secret spot, where he had been promised an incredible time.

The party had been fun enough, but at some point someone had slipped something into his drink. He awoke the next morning, already locked up and behind bars.

He hadn't had much money before the trip, and twenty-eight-year-old Billy had not known any lawyers. As such, he had been at the whim and mercy of the Turkish judicial system, which had decided to make an example of him. He bounced around the system for a year, expecting to be held back and eventually released, made a mockery of, held out to the western world in the tabloids as an example of white privilege. He would, after much grief, head home.

Unfortunately, Turkey was not interested in sending him home. He had been handed a sentence that had shocked him.

Thirty years without bail.

It wasn't the first time an American had gone astray overseas and ended up in another country's prison system, but it was one of the few times that the country's court system had gone the extra mile to deliver an unnecessarily cruel sentence. He had wondered if it was even real — if he had accidentally, somehow, pissed off the wrong person. But he'd had no lawyer or money to hire an investigator.

If he had been sent to Imrali because of someone's nefarious reasons, those reasons were still a mystery to him.

His hands were un-cuffed, his legs free, and he lifted his eyes up from the rocky earth and stared back down the hill toward the Imrali island prison in the distance. There was a small courtyard in the center of the complex, but this was the first time Billy had been outside the prison walls since his arrest, and certainly the first time he'd been outside without walls around him or shackles on his hands and feet.

He looked toward the cloudy sky, trying to find the pinpoint of light that represented the sun, hidden behind folds of fluffy water. He thought he saw it, then tried to use that information to determine what time of day it was. The trouble was, he couldn't remember if he had to calculate for how far they were from the equator or not, and if that were the case, he had no idea what that meant for the calculation...

"Billy! Over here!" the voice had come from a man, Taavi, whom he had befriended over the past year. He didn't particularly *like* the man, and he felt the feeling was mutual, which was ironic, as he had explained to Billy early on that his name meant 'adored.' Still, Taavi was the only person he'd met so far who spoke English. Billy had not yet picked up enough Turkish to get by, but thankfully everything in the prison was scheduled and regimented. He didn't need to learn Turkish to stay alive here — if he wanted, he didn't need to think or speak or even wonder anything at all.

He walked toward Taavi's voice, joining him and three other prisoners who had been taken out of their cell block earlier. They had been put in handcuffs, then marched out of the back door and toward these cliffs at the edge of the island, where the cuffs had been removed. No one had been told what was happening, but there had been enough armed guards marching next to them the whole time that Billy knew this was some sort of planned exercise. More than likely the Turkish government had told the guards to give them all a bit more sunshine and exercise, so they were begrudgingly letting them out to play for an hour or so.

He looked at the guards now, recognizing for the first time that they weren't all wearing the uniform of the prison's main security force — black and khaki, with a tiny yellow logo emblazoned somewhere on it. Some of the new guards wore black pants with tight black shirts. Their weapons seemed different, as well, though Billy had no idea why.

Billy didn't waste much energy worrying about it. Truth told, he probably wouldn't have needed a guard watching him twenty-four hours a day. They were on a remote island off the coast of Turkey, and the only thing here on Imrali was the prison itself — no homes, no roads, no other inhabitants at all. They were ten miles of open water from the nearest shore. A boat came twice a week to drop off supplies and mail for the inmates, but that was it.

He had yet to receive a letter from anyone back home. His parents had passed away five years earlier, his mother right after father, from early onset cancer, though he couldn't remember what type. He remembered not feeling terribly sad when that had happened, though he did wish his father were still around. It would be nice to talk to the old man, to ask him about the carnivals and the relatively safe, fun times they had when Billy was just a boy.

Somewhere along the line his old man had checked out from parenting, or from life in general, either because his job at the power plant had gotten too busy, or he had found out about his cancer diagnosis, or something else altogether. Billy never knew. His mother did her best, but she ruled with an iron fist, and he had very little interest in softening his heart for the hardest woman he had ever known.

He was now completely alone in this world, and he probably would be until he died. It was a fact he had come to accept. As crazy as it had seemed before his sentencing, he wondered if it was all that bad.

Free food, free entertainment, free everything. For thirty years.

Sure, most of it was crap — the 'fresh' food was ten minutes away from going rotten and the only entertainment was the monthly movie they would allow the prisoners to see, but inevitably it was a movie from America that he had already seen fifteen years ago. Perhaps he could get into chess — there were prisoners who spent hours each day across from each other, a board between them.

He walked over to where Ramon was standing, falling in line next to the other four prisoners. The guards circled them, each brandishing an assault rifle but with the point of it aimed down toward the ground.

"Any idea what's going on?" he asked.

Taavi shook his head. "Exercise?"

Billy smiled. "Standing in line next to you isn't much exercise, friend."

Taavi scowled, but didn't respond.

The guard in front of the line began barking orders in Turkish. Billy had no idea what any of the words were, but he recognized his prisoner number being called and looked up at the man. The man repeated the number, staring straight into Billy's eyes.

Billy heard the slight lilt at the end of the string of numbers, and realized it had been a question. He cleared his throat. "Uh, yeah. That's me." He recited his prisoner number for good measure and the guard nodded and continued down the line, checking that he had the right people in front of him.

Billy caught more movement from the corner of his eye and noticed another man walking toward them. He was not a prisoner, nor was he a guard or someone Billy recognized. He was not wearing the uniform of a guard — either the standard one of Imrali or one matching these new uniforms. Instead, he wore a suit — navy with dark pants and fancy leather shoes. An absurd choice, considering the weather today, but Billy had a feeling this man did most of his work indoors.

The newcomer walked briskly toward the group, not looking up or stopping until he was standing directly next to the guard who had checked off his list.

He didn't speak, and when the guard finished with his list and verified that all five prisoners were accounted for, Billy watched the new guy reach into his pocket and pull out a small, round object. It was about the size of a postage stamp. He held it out in front of him, examined it, and then looked around, finally passing the thing to the guard. The guard did the same thing, then turned and asked a question to the man in Turkish.

"What did he just ask?" Billy asked under his breath.

Taavi answered. "Is the test ready?"

Billy suddenly felt weak at the knees. *A test? What sort of test? And why all the formality?* If these guys were testing some sort of new vaccine, some new medication — something he knew the Turkish government allowed to be tested on prisoners — they would have simply been brought into one of the prison labs or another space inside Imrali.

What test needed to be done way out here, on the cliffs?

CHAPTER 3
SAUL

7:12 PM **| March 9, 2021**

Hever Castle, Kent, England

The room was lit by dozens of tiny sconces on the walls, their fronts frosted plastic hiding fake candles. Three chandeliers — also boasting fake candles that almost looked real if the eye didn't dwell — hung from above. The almost-dim, mysterious effect was completed by off-white LED track lights running down the length of the space in three neat and tidy rows to match the rows of chairs that had been set out.

The effect was remarkably accurate. The space looked and felt just like a Tudor castle, and had been decorated with items and artwork that reflected the period. There was even an axe-wielding knight's armor in the corner, on a hardwood circular pedestal.

Saul Brodeur looked around quickly, not actually moving his head but simply flicking his eyes left to right in a constant one-two motion, taking everything in as well as checking for signs of anything new. Any new entrants to the room, anything that had not been in his peripheral gaze the moment before.

One-two. Left, right.

It was a practiced motion, one he repeated involuntarily, listening forward but watching all around him the entire time.

The place was well-constructed, built to the highest standards and kept healthy and structurally sound over the years. As well it should — it was, in fact, a Tudor castle. Anne Boleyn had spent her childhood there after her father had inherited it in 1505, but original construction had begun over two-hundred years earlier. It had eventually fallen into the care of William Astor, who sold it to Broadland Properties Limited, who had set it up as a hotel, meeting space, and auction house.

While the garish additions such as the LED track lights and the flickering fake candles behind each of the sconces were a nice touch, he would have preferred the original, dimly lit and damp interior of the castle. Almost none of them were as bright, warm, and inviting as the movies made them look. He had always loved castles, the mystery and intrigue and countless stories the walls could tell, if only they could talk.

And while this place was certainly no bastardization of a castle — it was *real*, after all — he would have preferred a bit less interior design.

At the same time, he understood that he was not the target clientele for this sort of event. He, instead, was a soldier in a room of civilians. A prophet in a room full of laypersons. A hardened steel weapon in a room full of soft, hollow caricatures.

The man to his left grunted, the woman next to him breathing in short, steady rhythmic breaths. He was in tune to each of the individuals around him, analyzing but not focusing on each of their tics and quirks. He needed to know them, he needed to understand any potential threat from any potential direction.

All the while, his entire active focus was directly in front of him. A woman, seated in the third row from the front, and in front of her, on the podium. The man there spoke rapidly down toward the audience, a trained professional. He spoke the commands and requests with a practiced finesse.

"Do I have one-point-seven-five, one-point-seven-five, asking again do I have one point —"

He paused for a moment, noticing the paddle that had been raised.

Saul looked at the sign that had just lifted to his right as well. He flicked his eyes there and then back up at the auctioneer behind his lectern.

"One-point-seven-five! We have one-point-seven-five, wonderful. Do we have two million? Two million pounds for the fine water-color-on-canvas. Two million, asking for two million. Do we have two million? Going once..."

The auctioneer waited a few more seconds, asked again, and then smacked this tiny gavel on the top of the lectern. "Sold for one-point-seven-five million! One-point-seven-five pounds for the watercolor, to a Mr. Edgar Rauthson of Lancaster. Sir, your painting will be delivered by method of transportation of your choosing, if you would just find our team in the Hall of Exhibits after the auction closes."

Saul watched as Mr. Rauthson nodded his approval, and the auctioneer immediately continued. From the auctioneer's left, Saul saw two tuxedo-wearing auction house employees wheeling out a large cart, upon which was a velvet blanket covering a small, shallow object. He swallowed and straightened his back, feeling the anticipation and excitement. *This is it*, he thought. *The object I have been waiting for.*

The auctioneer began his prepared speech. "Next up, we have a once-in-a-lifetime opportunity: for the first time in many decades, one of the world's most famous swords — and certainly the world's most valuable sword — is up for auction by a private collector who has been lending the sword to the Museé de l'Armée in Paris. This sword, known as the Sword of Austerlitz, rode on Napoleon Bonaparte's side into battle in 1805, and in many skirmishes after. The most famous Battle of the Three Emperors took place near Vienna in the winter of 1805, and it was this sword that was said to calm Napoleon's nerves."

He saw that people around the room were excited, just as he was. He also knew that no one, save for the woman in the third row, was prepared to bid high enough to actually win the thing. For them, this would be nothing more than entertainment — a sideshow to lend legitimacy to the main attraction.

For him, however, this *was* the main attraction. This was the entire reason for his attendance. The entire reason for his charade, for his donning the uncomfortable clothing of the rich and feigning ties to ancient lords and kingdoms in order to gain entrance. He had clinked his glasses against those of modern-day duchesses and dukes, and he had rubbed elbows with London's elite. It was sickening, but was part of the job.

Now he had the opportunity to end this phase of the project and begin the next. He said a silent prayer that this phase would end swiftly and smoothly, tonight, without needing to extend into tomorrow.

He was prepared to offer ninety-five million pounds in order to acquire the object of his employer's desire, but not a pound more. Another few million and alarm bells would be set off in the tabloids. His mysterious and discrete employer would receive unwanted and unwarranted press attention for outbidding arguably the sword's rightful owner.

He stared at the back of the head of the woman in the third row. He had chosen this position carefully, jostling for this particular chair after the hors d'oeuvres had been served and the drinks emptied and refilled a final time. By placing himself directly behind her, she would have to turn fully around in order to see who exactly she was up against. It was a small yet important power-play.

The bidding began. The auctioneer held up the gavel and cleared his throat after his short presentation. "And now, the bidding shall begin. We will start with the highest opening price of the evening, the previous sale price of the sword, in today's dollars, that it was last sold for. Bidding shall begin at fifty-million pounds."

There were gasps and small utterances around the room, and the man smiled. This was all expected, this was all part of the game. The auction house would take their cut, the castle that had been rented and decorated for the occasion would receive their cut as well, the new owner of the sword would be able to take their prized possession back into whatever great hall would become its home for the next few decades, until a new collector with even deeper pockets came calling.

The woman's paddle rose. The man saw the auctioneer give her a slight nod. It was all as expected. "We have fifty-million pounds from Miss Delacruz."

Miss Delacruz. He smiled. It was an alias, a name meant to throw off anyone not paying close attention.

But anyone in this room would absolutely be paying close attention. *Everyone* here knew who she really was. *Josephine Campbell.* Everyone here knew about the family ties to Napoleon. Miss Delacruz-Josephine-Campbell was purchasing a birthday gift, something her unsuspecting husband would cherish above most things. It was an elaborate gift, but it was nothing to a family with riches such as theirs.

"We have fifty-million, do we have sixty-five million? Asking sixty-five million pounds for the sword carried by Napoleon Bonaparte, his prized —"

Saul raised his paddle and the auctioneer saw his number. He frowned, for a moment not understanding. Then he cleared his throat once again and nodded, curtly.

"Indeed. We have a bid for sixty-five million, from a Mr. Lacroix, who is..." he read the card on the lectern. "...Visiting us from the north." It was another alias, but this one was sound. Saul knew it was vetted, planned and tested against scrutiny. No one here would know his actual name and employer, and no one here would know his actual motives.

The man to his left shifted and grunted again, and the woman next to him — the man's mistress, Saul knew — began to breathe a bit quicker. This would be the most exciting thing they had seen all weekend. *What a disgusting charade.*

"Sixty-five million to Mr. Lacroix, do we have seventy-five —"

The woman raised her paddle once again, a bit higher this time. More confident. Saul was not concerned — there was always a backup plan.

As soon as the auctioneer spoke, Saul raised his own paddle once again and spoke. "Ninety-five million," he said.

The auctioneer's eyes widened. "*Ninety-five million pounds*, we have ninety-five million from Mr. Lacroix. Ninety-five million for the Sword of Austerlitz. Do we —"

The woman raised her paddle, this time standing up from her chair. She turned around slowly, swinging her head back and forth and trying to find the 'Mr. Lacroix' in the audience. She didn't know who it was she had been bidding against, nor would she recognize him from anywhere, but her eyes did seem to linger on his own for a moment before she turned back around the auctioneer.

She took a breath and spoke softly. "One-hundred twenty-five million." She stood there for a second, letting it sink in for the audience around her, then sat down in her chair.

The auctioneer audibly gasped. "*One — one-hundred twenty-five million pounds*," he whispered, his neck bent into the microphone. "Miss Delacruz bids one-hundred twenty-five million pounds for the Sword of Austerlitz, the prized possession of Napoleon Bonaparte. Do we have another bid? Asking one-hundred fifty-million?"

The man grinned from the side of his mouth, his eyes narrowing as he looked over the throngs of rich and elite art collectors. A few were looking back at him, the shock registered plainly on their faces, but he didn't pay them any attention. He kept his eyes straight, looking at the back of the woman's head.

She was beautiful, petite and looking quite a bit younger than he had imagined, perhaps in her mid-forties. Her hair was pulled back tightly and whipped up into a decorative shape atop her head, no doubt the cause of much concern for whoever she had paid to do it.

The auctioneer slammed the gavel down and cheers erupted from the audience. Their fair damsel had won the day against the villainous tyrant who had come to swoop her husband's prize out from underneath her.

It was a shame, really. Saul did not want to extend this night any longer — he had a fine bottle of wine and a hot bath waiting for him back at the hotel room — but this was the job. She had made her choice, and while surprised, he was not shaken.

The game would move to the next phase, and then it would end. There was no other option. He would win, just as he always did.

The woman could enjoy her victory for the moment. In another moment soon to come, the sword would finally be his.

CHAPTER 4
BILLY

10:29 AM | **March 7, 2021**

Imrali, Turkey

Imrali prison had been established in 1935 as a place for Turkey to keep track of convicted criminals without having to spend much on security. Prior to Turkish ownership, Imrali had been a small Greek settlement since the days of Pliny the Elder. The island offers a natural moat: on three of its four sides, steep cliffs arc up to a plateau on top. The rocks at the bottom dissuade anyone from trying to climb down, as the intensity of the ocean swells and barnacle-covered stones hidden just beneath the surface rip through any clothing and skin in seconds. The waters around the island are infested with a dozen different species of shark as well.

In 2007, Imrali prison was closed and sold off by the Turkish government, but at some point in the future a private owner had reopened the place and had gotten it back into working order. Billy knew the name of the company — *La Guerre International*— as it was emblazoned on shirts of the security guards and in a few places on signs in the cafeteria.

He had never heard of the company before coming here, and

from what he had been told, the prison had supposedly been closed after being sold and replaced by a modern, expensive office complex.

Billy knew that was all a lie — he was living in a prison that had clearly been built almost a hundred years earlier — but he was in no place to argue. Whatever *La Guerre* had done to persuade the Turkish government to continue sending prisoners to them had worked, and Billy had yet to see anyone from any official government capacity set foot on the island to check in.

The suit-wearing man stepped forward and turned his back to Billy and the other prisoners and addressed the guard. Half of the guard's face was revealed, and Billy watched it to try to read his expression. He got nothing useful out of the examination, and after a minute the suit walked back and took up a position about a dozen feet away.

As if on cue, all of the other guards backed up a few paces as well.

Billy's heart began to pump a little faster. *What's going on? What are they all afraid of?*

And why am I still standing here if whatever they're about to do is going to be dangerous?

He had had no illusions that the Turkish prison system was even remotely as modernized as the US one, but he had at least hoped that the cruel environment was simply due to a lack of funding or just some arcane judicial practices.

He had hoped that it wasn't like this by design.

Now, Billy was starting to suspect that the place he had been sent to was not really a prison, per se. Or at least not an 'official' Turkish one. Had he ended up here by accident? Was he really supposed to be in some jail cell somewhere on the mainland?

He opened his mouth to speak but stopped himself when he saw the guard lift the small object and hold it up to the light. He tried to see what it was, but the man was too far away. It didn't matter anyway.

The guard removed something from the top of the object then

turned it over in his hand and pushed something on the back of it, like a small, hidden button. Then, nonchalantly, he tossed the object toward the prisoners.

Billy watched it bounce on the rocks and skitter to a halt in front of the man in the middle of the line. All five leaned in and tried to see what it was. The man on the far right even kneeled, bringing his head closer to the object. He heard Taavi whispering in Turkish with the man next to him, but no one else spoke.

Billy felt his neck tighten, as if his muscles were suddenly having a spasm. He tried to move it, but then felt his jaw go tight as well.

What the hell?

He moved a step to the left, just as something began visibly pouring out of the object. He couldn't see anything, but he heard a slight hissing sound as whatever was inside was rapidly expelled and pushed into the air, like a tiny aerosol can.

It didn't last long, and ten seconds after it had started leaking, the hissing died away and stopped.

He looked toward the other prisoners, but as he did so his neck froze into place. He tried lifting his arm up to rub it, but about halfway up his shoulder and elbow hardened as well, as if frozen in place.

He was frantic now, feeling his heart pounding even harder. Working overtime.

And then even his heart seemed to slow down. He felt the fear set in at that point, knowing that somehow he had been poisoned with something. That something was blocking him out of his own body. His mind raced. *What is this?*

The man in the suit watched on from behind the guard, his face a mask. The guard seemed surprised, his eyes wide and his mouth open. The other guards were murmuring, and Billy could almost hear them, but it seemed as if even the air around him was being sucked away, as if he were being put into a vacuum. He felt himself trying to scream, but then realized it was just his throat constricting and closing in. He forced himself to take a deep breath, pulling it in through his nostrils just before they, too, froze and stopped working.

His chest heaved as the air entered his lungs, the force of it pushing his ribs out and against the impactful weight of whatever it was closing him down.

Within a few more seconds, he was completely frozen. His breath was tight, held in and not allowed to escape, and he felt the panic of knowing he was being slowly asphyxiated set in.

I'm going to die like this, he realized. *Whatever they've done — whatever this man has done to us — it's gonna kill us.* His entire body, internally and externally, had been frozen around him, trapping his mind inside. But he would run out of breath long before the starvation or thirst set in. He knew he could hold his breath one, maybe two minutes under pressure, but he had not been prepared.

He had not been given a warning, and the breath inside of him was going to cause his lungs to explode. He tried to gasp, feeling the sensation of it working but knowing that nothing had actually physically moved.

Then the panic ratcheted up another notch when he realized that he still could not take in or expel air. The oxygen inside his lungs was beginning to sour, and he desperately needed to blow it out and suck in fresh air.

But he couldn't. His arm was locked in place, halfway up his side, his neck turned and arched downward as he looked toward Taavi. His eyes still worked a bit, but they too were stuck inside their sockets, unwilling to cooperate. They were slightly out of focus, but he saw Taavi and three other prisoners, all blurry, all frozen in shock as well, including the kneeling prisoner at the end of the line.

Just at the bottom of his peripheral vision he could see the object on the ground, its tiny round orb shape empty and dead. Was it going to do something else? Was there anything more to this insane experiment?

CHAPTER 5
BILLY

10:30 AM | **March 7, 2021**
Imrali, Turkey

Another ten seconds passed, and the man in the suit walked over and plucked the orb from the ground. He did not look up at the prisoners, did not look at Billy. He simply turned and walked away. As the suit approached the guard, whose mouth was still open, a slight shake to his head, he leaned down and whispered into the shorter man's ear.

The guard seemed to be confused for a moment, but then gathered himself and nodded. He answered in Turkish, what Billy understood as the equivalent of the word *okay*.

Billy was now screaming internally, a silent and inaudible scream that only he could hear. He was banging on the doors of his mind, trying to get it to cooperate with the rest of his body, trying to get it to *do* something. If he fell, perhaps he could get his chest to fall hard enough to push the air out and be replaced by another life-giving breath...

Perhaps...

And then his arm began to move. He felt it in his fingers first, a tingling sensation, like he'd just slept on it for too long. It continued up his elbow and then to his shoulder and suddenly his arm dropped back to his side. His neck was next, followed by his toes and feet and legs. After another ten seconds, his body was mostly loose again, the tingling post-paralysis sensation covering him from head to toe. He felt his hair tickling the top of his forehead.

He gasped for air, a motion that actually took place this time — and felt his lungs once again replenished. He took a few more sharp breaths, holding them in and letting them out, and sucking in the sweet elixir of life as he did so. He stumbled, putting his hands on his knees and dropping to a squat. The others did the same, except for the man at the end who simply lay down on his back and heaved his chest up and down, his eyes straight up into the murky clouds.

Billy looked up. He saw a dot in the sky — a drone?

Billy had no idea what that was. He had no idea *why* it was. It didn't matter. It was all over.

He was alive.

He felt the involuntary relief of knowing that he was alive and yet in no better a situation than he had been ten minutes prior.

He looked around again, then noticed something odd — the guards had moved back into position around them, forming a tight circle around the group.

They had obviously stepped back when the weird gaseous mixture had been released into the air, but once it dissipated or died or whatever had happened, they pushed forward again.

Only this time, their weapons weren't lazily pointed toward the ground.

They were all pointed toward *him*. They were pointed toward the *prisoners*.

He heard one of them mutter something in Turkish, and a few grunts around the circle as they answered the leader.

The guard who had thrown the object toward them took a few steps back as well, letting the circle close around Billy and the others.

Finally, after another few seconds, the leader of the group of black-clad security guards barked an order.

Their weapons began to fire.

Billy immediately felt the hot lead flying through his body, tearing through flesh and bone with every impact. A couple of rounds burst out through his stomach, having traveled through nothing but organs and tissue. They were firing with their weapons pointed slightly down, aiming for the lower part of the prisoner's torsos, so as not to hit the guards on the other side of the circle with their crossfire.

Billy fell to the rocky earth, still in shock. There was pain, but it was like someone else was experiencing it for him, like his body had simply checked out and his mind was no longer accepting feedback. He now understood the test.

He understood why they had been brought out here.

He opened his mouth a few times, but only blood came out. His eyes stayed open, even as the life drained away from him. He wondered what it would be like to die; he wondered what the other side looked like.

His vision became more blurry and then darkened completely. He thought he was still alive, even as the pitch black surrounded him. He couldn't feel anything at all anymore, couldn't feel the pain or the shock or the surprise.

But he felt like his mind was still moving, still trying to put things together.

Just when he thought he was finally gone, he saw a flicker of light in front of him.

Somebody's standing over me. He couldn't see anything, couldn't actually make out any shapes, but he knew it was one of the guards. He felt himself being dragged, being pulled over the rocky dirt and slightly uphill. He wondered if he *was* already dead — if this was something in the afterlife pulling him toward some version of the pearly gates. He didn't deserve that though, he had never been a member of any organized religion, nor had he ever had any spiritual encounters.

Billy was about to try to squeeze his eyes closed for good, to try to make the black nothingness return, when he felt himself pushed a bit harder, still being dragged but now also being pulled along by two forces, one on each side of his body. He remembered the cliffs, remembered looking out over them and wondering what the fall would feel like...

Imagining falling down like the tiny ball in his carnival game...

He wondered what the end would be like.

And then, with a final heave from both guards at his side, he felt his body being pushed over that same ledge.

The end.

It seemed he was about to find out.

CHAPTER 6
REQUIN

11:00 AM | **March 7, 2021**
Imrali, Turkey

The man known to his associates only as Requin looked through the glass wall down into the space beyond. His office sat on the top story of the two-level complex, and he had made sure the glass wall on this side of the room could be immediately shifted from clear glass to opaque frosted glass with the push of a button. Most of the work he did in this office was paperwork, research or otherwise, and therefore was not secretive in any way. But there were times when he wanted to close the space to prying eyes from down below, just in case one of his employees or laboratory techs decided to look up and see who their boss was meeting with.

Today was one of those days. To anyone watching on as he shut off the view into his office space, it would look as though he were simply preparing for a meeting about *La Guerre's* latest development. The boss had meetings. This was nothing out of the ordinary.

To Requin, however, this meeting represented far more. They were preparing for the final phase of the project he had spent the better part of three years working on. They were preparing for the *public* phase of the project.

While it would have been easy enough to have his team set up a secure server to compile his notes, plans, and goals digitally, he also knew anything that involved a computer could be hacked.

The ultimate computer — the human brain itself — could be hacked, and he had proof of that downstairs. So there was no way he could trust a computer created by the human mind to be anything less than unsecured.

He turned from the glass just as his appointment entered the room from one of the doors on the opposite side of the office. This door led directly to an elevator, which led directly to the helipad above. He had built his headquarters beneath a prison built on a rock floating in the sea. The island, Imrali, sat near the coast of Turkey, and the purchase had so far proven to be an effective location for his compound.

Sold to him in 2007, he had done everything he could to keep the building of the two underground levels a complete secret. Since his company was considered by Turkish authorities merely a research company, he had left the barbed wire fences up along the property borders — no one would question them, since his research was expensive, secretive, and important. He had one wing of the prison intact, but had begun converting the other wards into offices for his growing staff. In addition, he had the towers at each of the four corners of the main prison facility converted into offices as well.

The place was neither just a prison nor just a corporate head-quarters. It was a bit in between — there was certainly a laboratory and office beneath the surface of the island, but there was *also* an active Imrali prison complex aboveground. Further, the prisoners here were no longer part of any government detention system, but instead had been acquired through black-market exchanges and flown here via helicopter. Their paperwork back on the mainland would just show them as diseased, victims of a brutal and barbaric Turkish prison system, and since the only type of prisoners who were brought here were ones who had no family or friends, those with no ties to their prior life, there was never any risk someone might come snooping.

It was a perfect arrangement: he had plenty of subjects for any experimentation his laboratory needed to pursue for their research. And since his team had recently made quite a breakthrough in their latest project, having a ready-made source of humans for their trials had proven especially handy.

Since his main operation existed beneath the surface in the underground levels, there was plenty of room to grow, and there was plenty of room for his space to one day host the *real* owners of the place, should they need it. They had helped him pull the necessary strings to purchase the island, and they had fronted the money for his company to make the acquisition.

He had been a member of *The Faction* for over a decade, and he had risen through their ranks quickly, no doubt due to his professional success as the owner of a profitable research and development corporation.

The man he was meeting with crossed the room and the pair shook hands. Requin smiled. The man standing in front of him was wearing a blue suit coat with dark pants, the colors slightly off but the overall effect one of modern sophistication and a telling sense of fashion design. Requin knew it was no longer true that one had to have matching coat and pants. To finish out the ensemble, the man had donned bright tan leather shoes and a matching belt.

Requin had never met the man — Stinson — in person, but he carried himself with respect and an air of importance. He already liked this man. A representative of *The Faction,* this was a rare thing indeed: meeting another member — a man of a higher rank in the organization — face-to-face. *The Faction* rarely risked meeting in person, opting to keep their dealings digital and subtle. He had heard whispers that some at the highest levels of the group met regularly, but no one knew when or where.

Stinson was a trained specialist, like many of the Faction's operators. But unlike the others, Stinson's speciality seemed to be everything. The man was ex-military, trained in many things useful to The Faction.

He offered the man a seat, and joined him by moving back behind his desk and taking his seat in his own chair.

"The mining incident went well," Requin said.

Stinson nodded. "It was simple, really."

"Good. And I have heard no reports yet from upstairs," Requin began. "I trust that means the experiment went well?"

The ma seated across from him nodded. "Perfectly, I would say," he answered. "The acid performed exactly as we had anticipated — it is not terribly strong, but in a tight, controlled space, it is more than adequate. Your work here has been exceptional."

Requin nodded slowly, trying to take the compliment in stride. "Yes, my technicians have worked hard to get us to this point. I believe they will be able to deliver the final result in a matter of days."

"Very well," Stinson said.

"I have a special task force working out the details as we speak. We are beginning to replicate the acid compound for mass production, and I've got another team working on enhancing the effects, if it is possible."

"Good," the man said. "*The Faction* is pleased with your efforts here. We are close."

"Indeed," Requin answered. "The twins are active now as well — I will keep them updated with your progress in Mexico, as these next attacks must be timed well."

"Perfect. I must return, but please keep us informed."

Almost as soon as he had entered, the representative from *The Faction* had left the office.

CHAPTER 7

BEN

12:26 PM **| March 8, 2021**

Chugach Region, Alaska

"Okay, okay," Ben said, trying to talk through the laughter. "Do you remember the first time we saw you?"

Reggie's eyes widened, mock surprise plastered on his face. "What — you mean the first time I saved your ass?"

Ben groaned in laughter. "You rolled in like a Panzer tank, lighting up the place — *literally* — and pretending you were some mercenary army."

Julie and Sarah laughed along.

"I *was* some mercenary army," Reggie responded. "I turned around the work lights from a nearby construction site and then flicked the power switch. It lit up the entire insides of that hotel."

"I remember," Julie said. "We were already almost dead from the explosion, and then you came in and blinded us."

"*I* remember coming in and saving your butts. *All* your butts. Lot of butts were saved that night." Reggie placed the glass of water back on the table with his prosthetic arm. He had lost the real arm in Peru less than a year earlier. "Ben, you got anything stronger?"

"You know I do," he answered.

Before he could stand up, Julie placed a hand on his. "Why don't you let *me* pour these?" she asked.

"What, you think I'll over-pour?" he shot back.

She raised an eyebrow at him as she stood up and headed to the cabin's small kitchen, and Sarah jumped in. "Last time you two went at it, we ended up in Antarctica with our plane shot down."

Reggie roared in laughter. "That general didn't even want us there," he said. "He only sent us because *his* bosses didn't want to send the entire US Army. I was only playing with him a bit."

"You were wasted."

He shrugged as Ben chuckled. "Well," Reggie argued, "if he would have given us a heads-up, we wouldn't have had as much to drink."

"*Or* we would've had *more*," Ben added.

Julie returned with two rocks glasses that looked barely full. "Aw, come on, Jules," Ben said. "It's mostly ice."

"There's *plenty* of whiskey in there, dork. Besides, if we're going to spend the night reminiscing, we should at least have you two sober. You're the glue of this operation, anyway."

"The glue?" Reggie asked. "I'm the *butt-saver*, remember?"

"Yeah," Ben said. "And I'm the fearless, Captain America-looking leader. I'm the guy the entire world looks to when there's a problem."

Sarah and Julie shared a glance.

"What?" he asked, taking a sip. "You think I *wanted* this job? I was totally happy working at Yellowstone when Julie here ripped me out of my cozy, camping lifestyle."

Her jaw dropped. "Really? I pulled you out of an active volcano that was spewing a deadly virus into the air. If I hadn't have shown up, you'd be either dead or thumbing a ride between National Park privy-cleaning duties."

"Privies aren't too bad," he said. "People don't poo as much when they're camping."

Reggie's face twisted into a disgusted expression. "Gross, man. Hey — if we *are* reminiscing and stuff, we need Mrs. E. Where is she?"

"And we should wait for Freddie to get here, too. He'll want to see the place and hear all the war stories before bedtime, I'm sure."

"His plane just landed," Ben said. "Sent me a text a few minutes ago. 'Grabbing a ride, should be there in an hour.'"

"It's always two hours from that airport," Reggie said.

Julie smiled. "Yeah, and I think Mrs. E is still working. Her husband's been doing double-duty trying to get us cleared from that Antarctic thing."

"That 'Antarctic thing' would be a much bigger thing had we *not* gone down there," Reggie said. "The United Nations should probably just learn to accept help every now and then. I mean, we're not asking them to thank us publicly or anything. The UN should just hire us outright, you know. That terrorist attack at that mine, for example — we could have help stop it. I'll tell Mrs. E to —"

"Tell her what?" a new voice rang out. The kitchen and dining room was really a single space, but the new addition to Ben and Julie's cabin was a hallway and conference rooms, as well as a two-story living quarters space, that abutted up to the back of the kitchen. Mrs. E appeared in this doorway and stepped into the kitchen. "Just got off the phone with my husband."

"Oh?" Reggie asked. "And does the mysterious Mr. E finally want an in-person meeting?"

To date, Mrs. E's husband had never shown his face in person to the group. He appeared through television and computer screens, always soft-spoken and articulate, wearing the same clothing. To Ben's knowledge, the man suffered from some sort of debilitating disease that had him mostly bedridden, save for the few hours a day he was behind his desk.

He and his wife had amassed a fortune building a multinational conglomerate of communications companies, providing satellite technology and services for many nations around the world. He was a fair, benevolent benefactor for the group, and it was through his efforts that the Civilian Special Operations had been established in the first place.

"No," she said, striding into the room. Her six-foot-five frame was nearly too big to fit in the kitchen, but she walked as though she hardly noticed. "He *does* want a meeting, however."

Ben cocked an eyebrow. "Oh? Has he found us a new mission. Is it the mining attack?"

"Oooh," Reggie said. "If not, I'll bet it's in the Caribbean. I *love* the Caribbean. Best beaches in the world, man."

"You've *been* to the Caribbean," Sarah said. "I remember that one *vividly*. You almost became a saltwater crocodile's breakfast."

He smiled sheepishly as Mrs. E continued. "No," she said flatly. "It's not a mission, and it's not related to the terrorist attack at the mine in China."

"Okay, when's the meeting? Usually he just emails and we —"
"Now," she said.
"Wait," Ben said. "*Now?*"
She nodded.
"What's this about, Mrs. E?" Julie asked.
"I'll let him tell you himself. But it is urgent, and since we're all here..."

Ben and the others stood up in tandem. Reggie took his drink with him, Ben left his on the table, a water ring already forming around the base. He looked at Julie, but couldn't read her expression.

He didn't have to guess what she might be thinking, however.

There aren't a lot of urgent meetings that are about really good things.

CHAPTER 8
SAUL

9:12 PM **| March 9, 2021**

Kent, England

"The Sword of Austerlitz," Saul said. "Crafted by Martin Guillaume Biennais, of Paris, a famous goldsmith of the time."

The woman's eyes were bulging out of her head, the effect not helped by the fact that her hair seemed to be pulling them out as well. It was just as tightly wrapped and coiffed as it had been at the castle, save for a single strand of blonde that was caught on her eyebrow.

There were tears in her eyes, but to her credit she had not started bawling.

Yet. Saul knew the tears would fall. He was even more excited to see them, to learn if his prediction — that she would sob in a quaint, controlled manner — would come true.

He had been in this position before. It was one he neither liked nor disliked. It was business, it was the job. He had been told to get the item, he had been given instructions and parameters, and whatever means necessary to get the job done that successfully completed the mission would earn him his fee.

"Do you see the blue in it? He began with folded steel, heating it over charcoal until the silver gives way to the blueish hue. A marvelous specimen, too. The gold foliage Biennais added only brought out the blue coloring."

She didn't nod, didn't pull her eyes away from him. If she was listening, she gave no acknowledgment whatsoever.

He cocked his head sideways and held the hilt in one gloved hand, the sheath in another. He pulled the sword completely out.

She swallowed.

Ah, so she is concerned for the safety of the piece.

"Rest assured, I will be taking very good care of the sword, Miss Delacruz. Just as the auction house has, so will I."

She didn't respond.

"And while we are on the subject of the auction, we may dispense with the pleasantries now. I know you are not Miss Delacruz, nor is there a single Spanish-blooded marriage in your family. Why choose that alias?"

Again, no answer.

"No need to reply," Saul said, now starting to pace the room with the sword in hand. He walked over the great area rug in the woman's dining hall, or living room, or whatever the rich people called this place. "I know your family's history."

It was a beautiful setting — unlike the castle, which was a good attempt converting a dark, damp space into one more inviting — this woman's home had been *built* to look inviting. Everything from the crown moulding to the carpets and rugs and drapery screamed luxury, and yet it was all bright and floral, light yellows and whites with a hint of sea green.

If she had done it, he was impressed. But he had a feeling the decor was just one of many things she outsourced — she had the money for it, thanks to her husband. Whatever the man did, he was successful at it.

Saul had another feeling, however — that her husband hadn't done anything other than be related to Napoleon. The riches came with the name.

"Your husband," he continued. "He is out of the country, yes? And he leaves you here alone?"

He strode up to the great armchair in the center of the room, the only one with space between the arms and the seat that he could get a rope wrapped around, and he leaned down, catching a hint of the woman's perfume.

"He leaves you *unattended?* It does seem dangerous, no? To leave a damsel such as yourself —"

"There will be workers here," she gasped. "Soon. So whatever you do to me —"

"They are coming tomorrow, Miss Delacruz," Saul said quietly. "I know their schedules as well as I knew yours. For the time being, it appears that we are alone. *Together.*"

Now she began to sob, the tears falling with a rhythmic precision. Larger than he had guessed they would be, denser and heavier. It was not a good look on her, and he was slightly disappointed.

Her chest rose and fell as he looked down over her shoulder, and he couldn't help but notice her beauty. He licked his lips. She pulled against her ties, the ropes cutting into her wrists. He had bound her arms only, not worried about keeping her legs in place. But it was part of the reason he was standing behind her now — he didn't want to take the chance in approaching her from the front.

"It is truly unfortunate that I must leave so quickly after meeting you. I appreciate your discretion in bringing the sword into your home, and I appreciate your cooperation."

She spat, suddenly and unexpectedly. "I will tell," she said. "I know your face — not your name, but —"

"My name is Saul," he said, smiling.

As he spoke, he could almost smell the fear rising from her. *She knows, now. She understands.*

She understood the consequence now of bidding against him, of trying to win the sword from him. A short-lived victory.

And she understood why he was so quick to offer his name. A

single name like his would not be enough for indictment, nor would it be enough to find him in the first place, but he had not hesitated in offering it.

And she knew why.

The sobs came more rapidly, her chest and head now bouncing up and down with each pull. He stood there for a minute, appreciating the moment, taking his time with it.

"W — why?" she whispered.

He looked up at the vaulted ceilings. The display of wealth in every direction. It would be easy enough to explain away his actions as those of a modern-day Robin Hood. That he was merely 'redistributing the wealth.' Taking from the rich to give to the poor.

It was an admirable reason, but it was the wrong reason.

He sighed. It was not a Robin Hood situation. With his employer, it never was.

His employer did not *need* the sword. He simply *wanted* it.

Saul was taking from the rich to give to the richer.

"Because," he answered, sliding the sword fully out of its sheath. It glistened in the light, the delicate and ornate design dancing, moving. He pulled the tip of it back, resting the blade on the top of the chair. "My employer is paying me to give it to him."

"That's your reason?" she asked.

"That is the only reason," he said.

He balanced the tip and aimed it for a final second, then plunged it forward, steeply and thoroughly, slicing through a bit of the chair's fabric top.

And through the back of the neck of the woman strapped to it.

CHAPTER 9

BEN

12:32 PM | **March 8, 2021**

Chugach Region, Alaska

Mrs. E was already seated behind the conference room table. Ben was surprised she'd gotten here so quickly, since she had only moments ago left the kitchen.

Whatever this is about, it's serious, he thought. Her husband was a man of habit — he went to bed at the same time every day, woke up at the same time, ate the same meals daily. For all Ben knew, he was a robot. So whatever it was that had shaken him up enough to call for a meeting after dinner time — and a few hours later in the rest of the country — was a big deal.

"Have a seat," she said as the others filed in. "I will bring him up on the screen, just one second."

Ben watched her tap at the tablet and glance up at the blank whitewashed wall on the side of the room. When the CSO had decided to expand Ben's tiny cabin into its headquarters and base of operations, he was glad they had at least built multipurpose rooms. This one, while normally serving as their conference room, was also where he and Reggie had installed a pool table, currently hidden beneath the veneered conference tabletop.

In fact, the screen Mrs. E was now working to project on could also be hooked up to a standard television, which meant they could enjoy sports or an old action movie while Ben decimated his best friend in a friendly game of pool.

"What's this about, E?" Reggie asked, seated across from her and next to Ben. He had his hands up and behind his head, clasped together.

She didn't answer verbally, instead pressing one last button on a tiny remote control and then looking up at the screen victoriously. A massive image of her husband, wearing his trademark turtleneck and glasses, appeared onscreen.

His skin seemed paler than normal, Ben noticed. He watched the man's subtle facial cues to determine if everything was okay.

Mr. E swallowed a few times, frowned, then blinked and began to speak. *"Thank you all for meeting at such a late hour,"* he began.

Reggie snickered — it wasn't even past eight in the evening. Sarah smacked his shoulder and told him to shut up.

"I wanted to get your take on a... situation."

"It's the Caribbean," Reggie whispered, a smile on his face. "I *know* it's the Caribbean."

"Reggie, shut up," Julie said.

"It appears an interested party has brought suit against the Civilian Special Operations."

"An interested — brought suit?" Ben asked. "What does that even mean?"

"It means we're being sued," Reggie answered. "And they're interested in ripping us apart at the seams."

Mr. E nodded, clearing his throat. *"I am afraid Gareth is correct. There is an International corporation seeking damages. They have filed suit in the appropriate American jurisdictions, but the core of their business is overseas."*

"What?" Julie asked. "Who is it? How can they seek damages if we didn't even *damage* anything?"

"Well..." Reggie began, stretching out the word. "I mean, there *was* that time in Egypt. At the Sphinx — I mean, technically, we weren't the ones adding bullets to the ruins, but I guess a case could be made —"

"It is not an Egyptian corporation," Mr. E said. *"This corporation is based primarily in Italy, but it has a large operation in Switzerland."*

Ben's heart sank. His fears were realized. He knew exactly who Mr. E was referring to, and he did not like it. He squeezed his eyes shut, dropping his head.

"You know?" Julie asked him.

All eyes in the room looked to him.

"No," he said. "I didn't know about this. But I have a feeling I know which company is suing us."

"The name of the corporation itself goes by a few names, but its arm in Switzerland that is seeking all three types of damages for incidents related to the general period that Harvey was in the country."

"What?" Julie asked again. "He was there on a *humanitarian* assignment. He *helped* Eliza, he stopped what they were —"

"I understand," Mr. E said. *"And yet they are seeking special damages for direct economic loss — their building, equipment, laboratories, for example. And punitive, as well as general damages for the pain and suffering caused by —"*

"Pain and suffering?" Reggie yelled. "That's bullshit! Ben was *shot at*, nearly *died* trying to save Eliza and that other girl, and — for God's sake — they were *torturing monkeys."*

"Apes," Ben corrected. "Gorillas and chimps. And the girl's name is Alina. She's back in college this semester, I believe."

Julie placed her hand over his. "You don't seem too upset about this," she said.

He shrugged. "I'm with Reggie. It's a bit of baloney, in my opinion. And I'm pretty sure Mr. E's got a plan in place already, or he wouldn't have bothered to call."

"I do," came Mr. E's reply, *"and yet I am not sure that any plan of mine will suffice."*

"What's *that* supposed to mean?" Sarah asked.

"There is a legal team I keep on retainer. They are already preparing the general defense and will provide me with details in the morning. But Harvey — I must admit — they are unsure as to how this will play out."

"Unsure?"

"Yes. These cases have the potential to become world news, just for the sheer fact that a company in one country is suing one in another. Add to that your... somewhat celebrity status... it may become a hairy situation."

"So, I'd have to, like, testify?"

Mr. E nodded. *"Most likely, yes. I do not believe we will be able to handle everything through arbitration, and it may come to a jury. If that is the case — and again, I will know more tomorrow — it may be tied up in court for some time."*

"How long we talking?" Reggie asked. "A few months?"

"The proceedings would not even begin *for a few months,"* Mr. E said. *"They would not end for a few* years.*"*

"Holy crap."

"Indeed, it is not a good situation. I wanted you all to be aware that I am taking every precaution, and I am asking that you do as well. Do not engage with any press that may get wind of the case, and — I do not have to remind you — stay away from social media, news, that sort of thing."

"Of course," Julie said. "That's not a problem. But what about us? What about work?"

"I am afraid the work must pause for the time being."

"Wait a minute," Ben said. "'Pause' as in 'stop working?' No more cases?"

Mr. E hesitated, then looked directly into the camera. *"Yes. I am afraid that is exactly what I mean. An indictment like this will come* with great scrutiny from international courts of law as well as United States regulatory bodies. My ties to the military have been enough to keep us out of trouble thus far, but they will not go near an incident like this."

"Okay," Ben said. "Okay, we can get through this."

"I don't know if we can, Harvey," Mr. E said. "I truly hope so, but the CSO exists to serve a purpose. If that purpose is not fulfilled — if we cannot even take on new projects, fulfill new missions — then there is no CSO."

CHAPTER 10
NAPOLEON

9:15 AM | December 2, 1805

Austerlitz, Austria

The great emperor stood over the body of the fallen Austrian soldier. The man had fought gallantly, if not rashly. Napoleon never enjoyed killing — it was a necessary means to an end.

An end, he felt, that may not ever arrive.

Bonaparte dismounted his horse and stepped over the fallen Austrian. The cavalryman had flown in from the north, sneaking wide around the battlefield to come up behind Napoleon's position, a tactic that had nearly caused the French leader's demise.

It was a surgical strike, a popular tactic for the armies he often faced: a few cavalry scouts would be sent around the flanks of the enemy positions, hoping to find a commandant or battlefield leader, then work their way in to make the kill. Most of these attacks were suicide missions, but for some — like this man — the assassination attempt was nearly successful.

He shook his head, disgusted at the needless death and destruction. He wished for peace, ultimately, and hated the price of it. There were stirrings that a treaty would be requested by his enemies, if only he could remain victorious here at Austerlitz.

Napoleon's ruse had proven effective — his army had feigned weakness, withdrawing to a position near Pratzen Heights, a veritable stronghold that was too enticing to ignore. By purposefully removing his army from the Heights, he signaled to the newly bolstered Austrian army that he was even weaker than they had originally thought, and all that was needed to defeat the *Grande Armée* was a decisive attack.

Napoleon had orchestrated that attack for his enemies, as well. He had pulled back his right flank, giving them an easy target. The Russian and Austrian armies had pushed ahead, focusing their might on that open, seemingly vulnerable chunk of space that would lead directly to Napoleon's core.

Napoleon's best battlefield commander, Marshal Davout, would lead the Third Corps to fill in the ranks and close the open wound in his army's side after a long, fast march from Vienna. He trusted the man to accomplish his task — everything relied on his success.

He walked up to the soldier, a company officer, who was running up the hill to Napoleon and his station, expecting a report from the front lines near Pratzen. It was risky sending a man of this rank, but it meant one of his marshals needed to get information to him, and it needed to be trusted.

"Commander," the man began, breathless. "We — we are falling."

Napoleon cocked his head to the side. *How can this be?* "Explain yourself."

"The Allied forces have pushed back Marshal Soult, and gravely wounded many of our cavalry there. Soult is fighting with his back to the wall."

Napoleon took in this information, allowing it to fill the gaps of space in his mind between what he had expected the outcome of this attack to be and his ultimate hope of how it would turn out. The reality, he now knew, was something a bit different.

He needed Soult to hold his ground — only by pushing the

Allies back at Pratzen Heights would he have enough manpower to offset the forces thrown at his right flank, and then proceed to decisively crush the Austrians and Russians. He could not afford a defeat here, nor could he afford anything less than total, complete dominance.

It meant too much to France. It meant too much to *him*.

He sucked in a breath of air, feeling the stirrings of power growing within him. He let it rise up, the anger mixing with the anticipation and optimism, creating a torrent of desire that would guide him, lead him. He would tap it often, using it to then lead his men, to lead France.

He had never questioned the feeling. It had been with him always, from when he was a young man at the academy to when he had to return to Corsica to help with his father's failed mulberry venture. It had been with him during all of the battles and wars to date, lent him the strength to persevere against all odds.

And those odds, it seemed, were still stacked against him.

He nodded once to the *Capitaine*. "Very well," he said. "Return to battle. I will be with you."

He turned to the men gathered around him, who were already tightening the cinch straps on their horses. He did not need to deliver any more order — they all knew what would happen now.

There will be a battle, and each of you shall have your place.

That place was near Pratzen Hill. They needed to prepare for what was to come — they needed to prepare the backup plan.

He put his hand on his side as they began to descend the hill, feeling his *other* source of strength riding there with him, on his belt.

The sword's hilt clanged against the buckle of the saddle as they picked up speed, but Napoleon felt the five pewter roses beneath his gloved fingers. He could almost sense the power they held, could almost feel the victory taking place before it had even happened.

CHAPTER 11
JULIE

12:38 PM | **March 8, 2021**

Chugach Region, Alaska

Julie looked around the table. The group had moved back to the cabin's kitchen, a cozier and more comfortable spot for hanging out, and now a more comfortable spot for discussing something she never thought they'd have to discuss.

Reggie and Sarah looked surprised as well, but Ben seemed generally sad. His hair was disheveled, his sleeves rolled up to his biceps, with the flaps of the buttons hanging out and dangling around his forearms.

"You okay?" she asked him.

"Yeah," he said. He looked around the room. "Hey — I just want you all to know that we'll take care of you. I mean, I'm not sure what Mr. E's planning as far as salaries and stuff goes, but —"

Reggie laughed. "Come on, dude. We *all* are getting paid out our ears for this stuff. Even if — and it's a *big* if — Mr. E has to put us on furlough, or whatever, we've got savings. We're fine."

Ben nodded. "Still."

"It's not going to happen," Julie said. "Mr. E's not going to stop paying us just because someone's suing us. I'm not worried about it."

"Yeah," Sarah said. "It's not about the money, Ben. I mean, this is our *job* now. Sure, I'm still a professor, but you guys — it's what you *do*."

"Not anymore," Reggie said.

"Don't be melodramatic," she said. "We're going to be fine. Mr. E's got a legal team that's good enough to get him through far worse. We just need to lay low, figure out why they're suing us, build a counterargument, and then we're back in business."

"Screw that," Reggie said. "We're supposed to just roll over and die because some asshole overseas wants to take us down?"

Julie sighed. "They're not *no one*, Reggie. They feel like we meddled in their business and deserve retribution for that. And they're far from the only ones who can make that argument."

"But look at what they did!" Reggie said. "What they were doing to those animals. *And* the people — they're a company that doesn't deserve to exist."

"But they have a right to their voice," Ben said. "And they think we came in there and played international police when we have no right to do so."

"That doesn't mean —"

"*But* that's not why this is happening," Ben said.

Everything in the room seemed to halt, and Julie found herself leaning in over the table, watching Ben. Waiting.

"What are you talking about, Ben?" Sarah asked. "There's more to the story?"

Ben nodded. "When I came home from that trip," Ben began, "Julie was asleep. It was late, and I remember sitting right here and reading a headline about EKG and what happened. Tennyson, something Tennyson. That's the guy's name who owns the company. He put his grandson in charge of the operation in Switzerland."

"Yeah," Reggie said. "That guy was a freak."

"Freak or not, his granddad wasn't too pleased about what happened."

"How do you know?"

"It was in that article I read. He said something like, 'I'll do whatever it takes to get back at whoever did this.'"

Julie shook her head. "And that's you. That's us."

Ben nodded. "Yeah, that's us. It's my fault, though. If I never would have gone over there to help Eliza —"

"Nonsense, Ben," she said. "We're in this together. What happens to one of us happens to *all* of us. *Together.*"

"She's right," Sarah said. "It sucks, but no one's blaming you. And who knows — maybe Mr. E's legal team will be able to brush things under the rug and we'll get back on track quickly."

"*Or,*" Reggie said, "maybe we forget about all that legal hoopla and go after this son of a —"

"Stop," Ben said. "That's going to cause more trouble than it's worth. The old man is just pissed we got the best of his grandson, that's all. The world needed to know about what EKG was doing there, and now they do. No one's going to bring that on us; that'll hold up in court no matter what. It's just a pain in the rear that we have to deal with it."

"Which is why we *should* deal with it," Reggie continued. "By taking matters into our own hands and —"

"And *what,* Reggie?" Ben snapped. "Kill the guy? Shoot him? Threaten him with something? How's that going to look for the case? How's that going to help us?"

"Doesn't matter," Reggie said.

"Of course it matters!" Ben yelled. "We knew this was coming, right? We knew *something* like this was bound to happen. Something was going to give — we can't just keep playing vigilante cop around the world."

"But Mr. E set this thing up so the US military would have our backs."

"And that's just *our* military, Reggie," Ben said. "And it's not even really the *whole* military; it's just a few guys in suits. Sure, there's not going to be a congressional committee we have to answer to, but we also can't just operate however we feel like operating, without consequences."

"So what are you going to do?" Reggie asked.

The others around the table shifted. Julie wondered if Mrs. E was still debriefing with her husband, or he had gone to bed and she had retired for the night. She hadn't come back with them after the meeting.

"I'm going to do what Mr. E said," Ben said. "We're *all* going to do what he said. We need to lie low for a while, get some order about all this. We can use the time off. What about the Caribbean? You said you wanted a vacation, right?"

"No, Ben," Reggie said. "I said I wanted a *mission*. I want to *work*. To save the world, buddy. What we always said this was about. I don't want to 'lay low' for *any* amount of time. I don't want to tuck my tail between my legs and run for the hills or any other dumb analogy. I want to *move*. I want to *win*."

Julie watched the interaction. Both men were stubborn, but unlike most stubborn people, their stubbornness was born out of strength, out of experience. They both knew what they were doing, and they both thought they knew what was best for the team.

But only one of them was the leader of the CSO. It wasn't a democracy — there was no vote. Mr. E had told them what to do, and Ben was on the same page.

Reggie must have realized this, as he suddenly softened and sank a bit into the chair. For Ben, this must have been an unfortunate setback. But for Reggie, she knew he'd see it as a personal failure.

"We're going to fight this, right?" he asked.

Ben looked at all of them in turn. "We're going to do what we can."

4:40 PM | **March 8, 2021**
Santa Maria Reef, Cozumel, Mexico

Jessica swam closer to a stack of spiny coral laying in front of her. She had seen some type of tang dart out to examine her, then run and hide when it discovered she was not a smaller potential meal but instead a much larger potential threat.

She kicked by wiggling just her toes, knowing the flippers she was wearing would translate into a much larger motion and push her the necessary six more inches toward the reef.

It was an incredible sight to behold, both from above and below the water. The entire area of the San Francisco and Santa Maria Reef was a veritable oasis above and below the surface of the sea. Jessica and her new husband Sean had come here to get married, opting to stay an extra week after their friends and family went home, and were now on the last day of their honeymoon. It had been an unbelievable experience. *Perfection*, as Sean had said.

And it had been. Every moment, every memory they got to make together.

They had been gifted a resort-hosted excursion called *SNUBA*, which was a combination of snorkeling and scuba diving. Participants wore a scuba mask that covered their eyes, mouths, and noses, but rather than connecting to a tank strapped directly onto their backs, a small hose extended all the way up to the boat, where a tour operator and professional managed their mixture of compressed air and nitrogen. It was a safe, easy alternative to scuba diving, and it did not require participants to go through extensive and expensive training.

Their resort boasted the largest SNUBA experience in the world — a double-decker boat that could host over a hundred partiers at once and about a hundred divers in the water at a time. The hoses from all the divers in the water now snaked over the sides of the boat like tentacles, making the vessel look like some sort of waterborne centipede. She could see the others around her, diving in each of their designated spots, each spaced about a dozen feet apart. They had been instructed to be sure to not swim too close to one another, to prevent their hoses from being tangled.

Her husband was ten feet to her left, absorbed in pulling some sort of massive shell from the ocean floor.

She frowned. They had *also* been instructed — numerous times — to not touch anything while they were down here, but she knew Sean had never been great with following instructions. He believed instructions were designed for the lesser intelligent — not for a capable guy like him.

She smiled around the air hose tucked between her lips, shaking her head. *What an idiot.* She almost wished he would be caught by one of the dive instructors; that he would get scolded and embarrassed in front of everyone on board for messing with the delicate ecosystem here. For as much as Sean liked to tow the line and push his limits, Jessica preferred the rigidity and structure of rules. She was not one to disobey authority, never one to question the experts.

She turned back to her own mini-adventure: trying to find the beautiful fish that was playing with her. She saw its tail poking out from behind a brain-shaped coral and swam gently over the area, careful to not let her movements disturb any sand and blur her vision.

CHAPTER 13

FREDDIE

12:40 PM | **March 8, 2021**

Chugach Region, Alaska

Freddie felt like a kid again. The excitement was palpable, real. He felt giddy, as if he were embarking on a brand-new journey with brand-new boots that were hardly broken in.

And he *was* embarking on a journey, only this one would require far more than just new boots.

As the newest official member of the Civilian Special Operations, he was now part of an elite group of civilian soldiers who had done the things he had only dreamed about. Long before he had become an *actual* soldier, he had hoped to travel the world, beating up the bad guys and notching his belt with cool stories about it.

After his stint in the United States Army had left him with a bit more of an understanding of how the world really worked, he was excited to be doing the thing the military had only given him a taste of.

He stepped out of the small car he'd hired and walked onto Ben and Julie's property. It was marked from the highway with only a small sign, but the sign's lettering had long since worn off. He thanked the driver, paid him, and then took in a deep, sharp breath.

It was cold, and the air tickled his sinuses, but that was to be expected this time of year in Alaska, especially at night. As the driver turned and crunched over fallen pine cones to get back on the highway, Freddie cinched his bag tight over his shoulder.

He had told the driver to drop him off at the end of the half-mile-long road so that he could walk in the rest of the way. He loved the outdoors, and so he'd been elated to learn that Ben and Julie actually lived in a cabin out here.

He was doubly excited to find out that the CSO's headquarters were here, too. He wasn't sure what company policy was on over-staying his welcome, but he hoped they wouldn't mind if he crashed at their place for a few days.

Or weeks, or months.

He smiled to himself as he started walking. *This is going to be a blast,* he thought. *I can't believe I actually made it in.*

He wasn't sure how the others had 'made it in,' or if they ever even had a tryout — he'd just met them all a couple of months ago on the opposite coast, in preparation for a trip they'd taken to Antarctica.

They'd barely survived, and there were two soldiers he'd brought along who *hadn't* survived. It was still unbelievable to remember, and even though he'd seen troops die in the field, this had been far worse. They hadn't expected any real resistance while there, and certainly not the kind they found.

Freddie followed the dirt road down about halfway to the house, listening to the pines swaying and shaking as they redistributed the weight of the early season snow amongst their branches. He kicked a pinecone a few paces, then lost it in the woods when it collided with another in its path.

And then he heard something else.

A new sound; one that wasn't natural.

An engine, he realized. *From a large vehicle.*

And it was getting louder.

Freddie wasn't sure if Ben was expecting a delivery, or if the trucks even came out this far, but he was pretty sure it was a bit late in the evening for something like that. He pulled off the road and found a spot just past a copse of trees that would act as a good hiding spot.

As the truck approached Freddie was able to get a good look at it. White, standard box car one might use for moving or delivering boxes. No branding on the sides or front.

The driver was mostly concealed behind the headlights' bright wash, and Freddie ducked back as they swept over him as the truck drew closer.

Interesting, he thought. *Wonder what he's up to.*

As the truck got even closer to Freddie's position, he could tell the driver was in a hurry. The movements of the truck were erratic, as if the driver couldn't be bothered to slow down and take things carefully. As the truck veered past Freddy, he kept himself concealed but turned around the other direction and followed it.

He waited until the truck was nearly out of sight and began to run. Since he could move at full-speed while still staying hidden in the trees, but the truck had to move over the bumpy gravel more slowly, he was able to keep up with it.

The last quarter-mile ended abruptly, with a large clearing proudly displaying Ben and Julie's cabin, and the magnificent stone structure of the CSO headquarters attached to it.

But Freddie's eyes weren't focused on the buildings. He saw the driver pull to a halt just shy of the CSO building, park, then open the door to the truck. He didn't bother shutting the door after he stepped out.

He jumped to the ground, looked once at the cabin and CSO building, then turned back toward Freddie and began to run.

Oh, this is not good, Freddie thought. *This is not good at all.*

He pulled his phone out, careful to keep the bright screen out of view from the oncoming driver. He typed out a quick text message and then turned off the screen and shoved it back in his pocket.

The driver was getting closer, but he was already huffing and puffing. He was following the road, likely going back to the front entrance of the property as well.

Freddie had to hope his text message would get through — there was no time to waste. He needed to move to where he could be most useful to the group, and that meant trying to figure out why this guy had dumped a truck, still running, onto Ben's property.

And he knew of no better place to start his investigation than with the man himself.

CHAPTER 14
STINSON

4:43 PM | **March 8, 2021**
Santa Maria Reef, Cozumel, Mexico

Stinson pulled his muscular body out of the water and up onto the deck of the boat. The massive floating monstrosity was really nothing more than a party barge that had been converted for use as a specialized SNUBA vessel. The lower area housed the main apparatus and hoses for the SNUBA adventures, while the flat upper deck was now a tiki bar, complete with lit torches zip-tied along the railings.

He had signed up and paid for this trip only a day ago, the last person to enroll.

An expert scuba diver, Stinson had not needed any instruction or guidance from the crew, but he suffered through their presentation anyway. Most of the idiots on the boat had been drunk or in some stage leading up to inebriation, but he — like always when actively on a job — was sober.

He had a mission. He would accomplish that mission today, and he would get his reward. The Faction required loyalty, but it also appreciated members who used their training and skills toward its goals.

Stinson had plenty of training. He had built up an arsenal of skills over his time as a special forces soldier. He could fight anyone, anywhere, anytime — and there weren't many people he knew who could best him. The fact that he was alive was proof of that.

One of the boat crew — a scraggly young man who looked to be no more than a teenager — ran over to him, breaking his own rule about walking on deck.

"Can I help you, sir?" The crew member said in broken English. His voice was surprisingly deep. Perhaps the kid was in his thirties but had not been blessed with a body that matched his age.

Stinson shook his head, marching toward the SNUBA station in the center of the main deck. He had scoped out the boat last night, snuck onto the docks and into the boat. He now knew the layout better than the captain. He knew how long it would take to complete this phase of his mission.

Assuming, of course, I don't get any pushback from the crew.

"Sir!"

Stinson rolled his eyes. The kid was not going to leave him be, apparently. Stinson turned and crossed his arms in front of his chest, putting on an expression that should have told the guy exactly how much he wished to be interrupted right now.

"Sir, if there is something I may help you with..."

"I'm good," Stinson said. He wished the guy would just leave. He needed him to go to the top deck, where the other three crew mates were drinking and smoking while they waited for the tourists underwater to finish their adventure. Getting messy down here would delay him, potentially set him back.

Stinson had studied the schedules for this boat; he knew the crew that would be taking them out today and knew their habit of getting everyone safely in the water for their hour-long snorkel adventure and then completely ignoring them.

They had promised the divers that they would be carefully regulating and maintaining the proper air mixture, but Stinson knew that was a lie. As soon as the tourists were all in the water, the crew would then go upstairs and get a little sunbathing in while it was quiet. He even heard a radio booming some sort of Mexican rap music, and one of the men laughing.

The guy in front of him must have drawn the shortest straw — it must have been his job to check on everyone else. He just stood there, staring at him.

Stinson sighed. He couldn't let this affect his schedule, so he would need to do it quietly and quickly. Efficiently.

With one stride he closed the distance between him and the kid and saw the startled look on the guy's face as it registered the attack.

Not that it mattered — anything he would have tried would have proven to be too late. Stinson had his arm around his neck and was behind him in an instant. He held tight, suffocating him, feeling the bones in the scrawny guy's neck crunching around as his body's involuntary reactions fought against suffocation.

He held him there for a little less than a minute to be safe, then released him, letting him splay out onto the deck. He didn't worry about the body, even if someone else came downstairs too early and saw what he had done, there would be no time to stop him.

Time to complete my mission.

He walked back over to the SNUBA system, gently humming as it pumped and filtered air through the hundred hoses. He found the rounded, curved side of the white-plastic tank and the intake manifold. This, he twisted off, breaking the plastic joints around the screws that held it into place.

He checked for suction with a flat palm, then walked over to a shelf tucked in a life jacket closet. It took a second, but he found the items he had stashed there last night during his surveillance run. He found what he was looking for, then walked back over to the intake.

He shoved the tiny capsule he had retrieved into the open hole, holding it there between a thumb and forefinger. Stinson squeezed it, allowing the pressurized interior to pop, then start pushing out the powder inside of it. The intake manifold pulled in the air and the powder with ease, and Stinson envisioned it floating through all of the SNUBA system's internal compartments and chambers, through any micron filters, the powder aerosolized and now being dispersed down into each of the one-hundred hoses streaming off the sides of the boat.

He allowed himself a few seconds of relief before moving to his next task. The first phase was complete. His job was almost done.

He left the intake valve wide open and walked around to the other side of the device. He looked around for a moment, then found what he was looking for. An extra SNUBA diving hose, coiled and ready in case of failure or repair. He picked it up and walked back over to the intake hole, then shoved the hose into it, twisting as he did so.

It was a loose fit, but he had stashed a roll of duct tape in the cabinet the night before as well, for this exact reason. He grabbed it now, pulling off two long strands of tape and wrapping them tightly around the hose and intake mount. Satisfied, he picked up the coiled section of hose and walked back to the side of the boat.

He heard footsteps above, shuffling around on the top deck. He wondered if one of the men were coming down to check on his crew mate, or if they were just refilling their beverage.

He waited a moment, then tossed the hose into the water.

12:45 PM **| March 8, 2021**

Chugach Region, Alaska

Ben pulled his eyes up from his empty whiskey glass on the table and looked across at Reggie. "I'm really sorry, man," he said. "I wish there was more we could do. I really do."

At first Reggie didn't answer. Then they locked eyes for a brief moment, and finally Reggie spoke. "You can," he said. "*We* can. There's *always* more we can do, Ben. I'm not just going to roll over and play dead."

Ben was about to argue with his friend when he felt his phone vibrate in his pocket. He pulled it out, wondering if it was Freddie trying to let him know that he was delayed. Perhaps he was running late for some reason and would be another hour or so getting in. Strange, as the man should have been here by now.

As Ben pulled the phone out and thought through the plausible scenarios, he saw the screen and the message.

His blood ran cold. His subconscious was screaming at him, but only after he lifted the phone up read the message slowly did he fully comprehend the words.

Get out now.

That was it. No explanation, no further instructions. And it *was* from Freddie. The man had sent a text message to Ben from somewhere close enough to know that there was danger nearby.

No, that's not right. Ben looked around the table and realized that Freddie had sent the text message to *all* of them. Reggie was still staring at Ben, but he noticed that Sarah and Julie both had their phones out, equally confused expressions on their faces.

"You get it too?" He asked.

Julie nodded. Sarah looked up at Ben. "What we do?"

Ben was already standing, preparing to move. "We get out. Now."

Reggie didn't ask for clarification, nor did he stop to check his own phone. He threw himself backward from the table and nearly jumped over it getting out. He pulled Sarah along with him, his long legs making quick work of small cabin space, reaching the doorway first. Ben and Julie met near the living room.

Reggie was already opening the front door and pulling Sarah out, and Ben felt a slight squeeze on his hand as he brushed up against Julie's side.

"I'm scared," Julie said.

Ben nodded. "Me too. But whatever it is, we'll know soon enough," Ben replied.

Freddie was not the kind of man who would play a trick on them, and certainly not one that completely lacked humor. But, then again, he didn't really know the man well. They had met briefly before embarking on their trip to Antarctica, where Ben and the others discovered him to be a reliable and loyal teammate. After their mission, and after standing up to his uncle, a general in the United States Army, Ben and the others had welcomed Freddie into the CSO with open arms.

Tonight was going to be his first official day on the clock, joining the group for meetings and training beginning at dawn tomorrow.

All that had changed with Mr. E's announcement earlier that evening, and now it seemed it was going to be changing a bit more. *What's going on?* Ben wondered, allowing Julie to press him forward and down the front step of the cabin. He quickly ran through a list of the items they should have brought with them. His 'bug out' bag, for one, which was stocked with enough food to keep him alive for a month, and all of them for at least a week.

It also had some small necessities for hunting, trapping, and fishing, so that food wouldn't even become a problem, as well as emergency blankets, protein bars, matches, and a handgun with enough ammunition to get through a scrape.

But that was back in the bedroom, under the bed where it lived. Ben hadn't had time to grab anything, and besides — he had no idea why they were leaving anyway, other than heeding the warning of a man's text message. As much as he hoped they wouldn't be caught without equipment, he really hoped they wouldn't be hiking through the Alaskan wilderness this time of year anyway.

Ben and Julie left the cabin and followed Reggie and Sarah in a straight line across the open field that served as the cabin's parking lot, front porch, outdoor meeting space, makeshift football field, and whatever else the space needed to be. As he moved, he noticed something from the corner of his eye.

Strange, he thought. *That wasn't there before, and it shouldn't be there now.*

It was a truck — all white — like a moving truck or the kind used for deliveries.

He wondered if Mr. E had ordered some communications equipment or was expecting some sort of work order delivery.

But why would the man have scheduled it to arrive this late? Surely no company was running deliveries now? And surely Mr. E had long since gone to bed?

No, Ben thought. *This has to be related to whatever it is Freddie's trying to warn us about —*

He didn't have time to finish the thought before the truck exploded.

4:45 PM | **March 8, 2021**
Santa Maria Reef, Cozumel, Mexico

The fish saw her and darted away, coming to a stop behind another similar-looking coral. She started to move that direction when she noticed motion from the corner of her eye.

She turned back and looked at Sean, who was waving frantically at her.

Jessica frowned. She pulled herself upright a bit, upset that he had pulled her away from her tang, but he wouldn't stop waving.

She felt the muscles in her back tighten, her legs stiffen.

Weird.

She kicked with her feet, noticing that it was taking more effort than it had before, and the kick had not propelled her as far this time. She tried using her arms to pull her closer to her husband, but they too were feeling tight.

In front of her, Sean had stopped waving, his eyes transfixed on her, his body not moving.

He was floating, his hair and swim trunks the only things on his body still moving.

It was surreal — Sean floated in front of her like some sort of underwater statue, watching her drift toward him slowly but not reacting. Suddenly she felt her throat constrict, her neck muscles now seized by some invisible force. She could hardly breathe, even though the tube was still in her mouth. She frantically tried to grasp at her face, but her hands were like rocks. They floated upward but wouldn't come any closer at her will.

She suddenly couldn't move a muscle in her body.

Jessica's body floated closer to Sean's, now only a few feet away. She wanted to reach out to him, to pull him toward her, but neither could move.

What the hell is happening?

She used all of the energy in her body and forced herself to take in a single, small breath of air. It would have to do. Her lungs barely expanded and her chest fought through the pain of exertion.

But it was enough. It was air, and as long as she could hold it...

Suddenly the air changed. It felt damp, humid.

She heard a gurgling sound from somewhere up above, and then realized what was happening.

Her eyes couldn't widen any more, but she felt the internal panic.

Just as the water hit her mouth and exploded into her lungs.

CHAPTER 17
BEN

12:53 PM **| March 8, 2021**
Chugach Region, Alaska

Ben didn't even have time to register the explosion in his mind before the shockwave hit him. It picked him and Julie up off the ground and flung them toward the woods like rag dolls.

Reggie and Sarah were already there, but they were pushed deeper into the woods as well. All four CSO members were thrown back a dozen feet, deeper into the pine forest around Ben's home. Ben landed in a heap of wet, snowy leaves, but there wasn't enough of the white stuff to help cushion his fall. He felt his elbow smack against the trunk of a tree, his ribs stretching and grinding from the immense pressure of catching his entire body as it rolled on. He felt the wound on his side reopening, the one he had gotten from the plane crash in Antarctica, and he tried to put a hand over it to prevent it from bleeding.

He came to a stop and took a few careful, testing breaths. He was alive, and mostly unscathed. Thankfully they had been far enough away from the blast that they had only ended up with a few scrapes.

He hoped.

He needed to find Julie. He needed to find the others, to see if they were okay. He looked up, leaning his upper body against the pine trunk and looked around. As the leaves and debris fell to heaps on the ground around him and his eyes began to focus better, he noticed the others, scattered around the area.

They were all okay. Reggie was mumbling some string of obscenities under his breath, Sarah was rubbing a sore spot on her arm, and Julie was to his left, sitting up in the middle of a small clearing.

Ben looked back toward the cabin, frowning.

There was no cabin left. Actually, there was only *half* of a cabin left. The newest addition to the CSO headquarters — the stone building that used to sit adjacent to Ben's cabin — was completely gone. Piles of stone and twisted metal construction reinforcement shot upward, twisted and burning. Rebar reached up to the sky like the curled fingers of a buried monster. Smoke was pouring out of the half of Ben's cabin that still remained, and he could see the logs on the front side of it smoldering, some of them already lit and engulfed in flames.

No. How could this happen? he wondered. They had been targeted — *he* had been targeted. The truck had been full of explosives, driven here purposefully, specifically focused on taking out Ben and everyone he loved.

The dining room and kitchen area where Ben and the others had just been sitting only moments before was completely gone. Just a pockmark on the earth, nothing but a black smudge left to commemorate its prior location.

"What the —" Reggie began.

Julie screamed, interrupting him. "Mrs. E!"

Ben's head swirled as he realized what she meant. He felt sick. Nausea overcame him suddenly, and he turned to his right to heave. Nothing came up, and he coughed and tried to breathe for a few seconds before sitting upright again and looking at Julie.

She spoke through bursts of tears, her face red, sweat pouring from her forehead. "Mrs. E," she stuttered. "She was... She was in —"

Julie couldn't finish the thought. Ben stared straight ahead, focusing on the cabin, focusing on the pile of wreckage next to it. The truck no longer existed, the CSO headquarters was devastated, and most of the place Ben had called home was utterly destroyed.

"She's — she's got to be in there somewhere," Reggie began. "If we can just —"

"She's gone," Ben whispered. "She's gone. There is no way she could —"

"You don't know that!" Reggie yelled. "You have *no idea*! We have to go and check. If we can just get up and get moving, there might be a way to..."

Reggie tried standing, but then gave up as he realized his knee had been twisted the wrong direction during the explosion. He groaned in agony and slumped back down against the base of a tree. Sarah crawled over to him, weeping, placed her hand on his leg, then curled up next to him and put her head on his shoulder. He breathed slowly, surely, his eyes never leaving Ben's.

Ben saw the brutal anger there. The devastation. Reggie was like a well-trained dog — he was extremely effective and useful, as well as loyal, but he was instinctual. He was capable of snapping, of ignoring every order given to him and simply *driving* toward his goal without a care for anyone or anything else, including his own safety.

Ben knew what it meant to see his friend like this. He was already planning the retaliation, already planning the vengeance.

Julie was the only one standing, but her hands were on her knees and she was panting, still breathing heavily. "Maybe he's right," she said. "Maybe we can look, just to see if she got stuck beneath a piece of rock or something. If we all can move together, we might be able to get her free and —"

Ben shook his head. "We will look, of course. I promise. But, Julie — all of you — I need you to be prepared for the worst. You were with me when that thing blew up. You saw how far away we were when it happened. You saw what it did to us, even out here.

And look at the headquarters building. It's *flattened,* guys. I just don't think there's any way —"

"There's *always* a way!" Reggie screamed.

Ben sighed. He didn't want to fight. He didn't want to argue with his best friend, or his wife, or anyone else. He was done. Unlike Reggie, Ben needed time to process something such as this. He needed a plan, to build himself back up into the resilient person he knew, deep down, he could be.

He pulled his phone from his pocket and looked down at it. Somehow Freddie had known about it. He had predicted it, and then he had saved them from it.

Not all of them, unfortunately, but he had saved Ben and his wife.

As he reflected on it, the phone began to chirp.

Freddie. Ben held it up and showed the screen to everyone else, then pulled the phone up to his ear and connected the call. Mr. E had installed a tall cellular array on the roof of the CSO headquarters building that was designed to locate and strengthen the signals from the nearest cell towers.

That, of course, was now long gone, so Ben and Freddie would have to rely on the spotty connection that existed out here on this side of the highway.

"Hey man," Ben said.

"You guys okay?" Freddie's reply crackled a bit, but Ben could at least hear him.

"Yeah, thanks to you." He didn't tell Freddie about Mrs. E. He couldn't. He would find out her fate with the rest of them, soon enough. No need to get him upset.

"What the hell was that? "Ben asked.

"It was a bomb, but I'm pretty sure you put that much together already."

"We did."

Freddie paused a moment and Ben heard shuffling on the other end of the line. After a few seconds, the young soldier's Southern drawl returned. *"Well, sorry I couldn't be there. I'm close by, though, and I've got someone here who we might want to bounce some questions off of."*

"Yeah? Who's that?"

"Well, why don't you come over here and talk to him yourself?"

CHAPTER 18
STINSON

4:53 PM | **March 8, 2021**
Santa Maria Reef, Cozumel, Mexico

He felt nothing as the hose had slid into the water, and filled. He felt neither joy nor disappointment. He had killed before, and he would kill again. He had been a mercenary, a soldier for hire, even a soldier under the employ of a government. All of those jobs had left him feeling unsatisfied.

Even the deaths by his hand — ones he believed had been deserved — left him with the feeling that something was missing.

The Faction had changed that. It had changed everything. When he had first heard about the group, first heard about what it was intending to do, he had balked. For every secret group that claimed a multi-centuries-long history, there were ten others that had fabricated every aspect of their story. For every group claiming to have members ranging as far back as the time of Aristotle, there were a dozen more intent on convincing the world they had celebrities among their ranks.

He didn't believe any of them. They were all, in his book, frauds and lunatics. He assumed The Faction was no different — that they were just another organization bent on some twisted justification for terrorism and toppling the power structure.

He had not believed they had an *actual* plan to replace that power structure with something better.

But he had still been intrigued. He had allowed himself to be recruited, to be interviewed and questioned by members of The Faction until they had deemed it necessary to fill him in on some of the details. Details of their true history, of their actual membership. They had proven this to him, and he had overcome his doubt and began to trust their veracity.

Then they gave him details about their long-term plan. What they were attempting to pull off, and how. When they did that, he had been convinced.

At every step of the way, The Faction had kept their word. They meant what they said, and he now believed they could pull it off. He was a member, and he would be until the day he died.

Stinson stepped back from the deck, hearing the shuffling footsteps now turned to pounding as they made their way down the stairs. As the man descended, he heard his voice calling out, yelling something in Spanish, no doubt surprised to see him standing there.

The same voice ratcheted up in volume a bit as the man saw the hose that had been attached to the intake.

Stinson turned and faced the newcomer — a massive, overweight man wearing sunglasses and swim trunks. It was the captain, whom he had met briefly upon boarding this morning. The man's brow was furrowed and angry, and he started walking past Stinson, heading for the SNUBA system.

Stinson didn't need an invitation. He struck out with the base of his fist, cracking the man's nose and sending shards of it up into his brain. The captain collapsed immediately onto the deck, dead.

He didn't have time to waste. *Time to finish the mission.*

He jumped over the large man and ran upstairs to where the other two crew members were still partying. The two crew mates were lounging on the far side of the deck, open bottles of beer in their hands. Their eyebrows both rose up their foreheads as they saw him.

The man on the left began to stand, and the other muttered something in Spanish. Stinson continued walking, not slowing or speeding up, even as the man now made his way toward him.

Another second passed and the lanky crew mate was on his back on the deck, his head in Stinson's hands. He had tripped him and brought the man to the ground, careful to wrap his arms around his neck first, cradling the skull.

He snapped his neck quickly, efficiently.

The other man yelled and dropped his beer. He was slightly larger, and it appeared to Stinson that he was out of shape, and when he tried to stand, he slipped on the deck. He slammed to the floor, a slight whimper escaping his lips.

Stinson moved toward him. The man skittered backwards, crab-walking across the few feet of deck remaining, then twisted his body between the two sets of rails.

Stinson was almost on him, but he knew the man had a chance. As he got to where the man's chair was, he saw the crew member push himself with a heavy thrust of his upper body, sending him through the rails and over the edge. He fell, headfirst, toward the water, but didn't make it all the way.

At the bottom level, his head cracked against the side of the boat. The man let out a grunt as he slipped upside-down into the water.

Stinson sighed, knowing he should jump in and find the man, to see if he was still alive.

He quickly changed his mind. *Doesn't matter.* Playing cleanup for this mission was a secondary priority. He accomplished every-thing else he had set out to do, and he wanted to get back to the resort and enjoy the rest of the evening. If he spent time looking for a single unconscious body out of the hundreds that were down there, it would be dark by the time he got back.

He turned and walked to the opposite side of the boat. He descended the staircase, stood on the bow of the vessel, and dove off.

It was a two-mile swim back to shore, but his body had been through far worse. The water here was shallow, and there were sand-bars between here and the resort's jetty. He would make it with plenty of time left for a sunset and a stiff drink.

CHAPTER 19

JULIE

1:05 PM | **March 8, 2021**
Chugach Region, Alaska

Julie watched the two men in front of her as they jogged. It wouldn't have been apparent to anyone but her, but she'd known both Ben and Reggie long enough to know what was happening.

They were competing, trying to outpace each other without flat-out taking off into a sprint. They were racing, trying to be the first to reach Freddie, who had given Ben his location about two hundred yards from the cabin, on the only road in and out. He would be impossible to miss, especially since he wasn't going to be alone.

Ben and Reggie would each try to beat the other man there, and Julie had a clear idea of why. Reggie would most likely start with his fists raised, taking flesh off the attacker's face and knocking him unconscious before ever stopping to think about asking him a question.

Ben would take the more reasonable approach — he'd ask the man questions, try to get him talking, see if he was, in fact, the driver of the truck that had just taken out his home.

Ben was mad — Julie knew that, as well — but he wasn't going to be rash about it. Reggie, however, would allow his emotions to take over. He would not be able to prevent it. In his mind, Mrs. E was gone and this man was responsible.

Julie and Sarah hiked behind them, silent. Julie saw Reggie moving with a slight limp, obviously working through a minor knee or leg injury of some sort. Ben was moving steadily but breathing rapidly, no doubt stressed, scared, and upset.

As they reached the first rise in the dirt road leading away from the cabin, she saw Freddie's massive frame come into view. He was standing over a man who was kneeling on the roadway. She couldn't tell if the man had his arms tied or if he was just holding them down in front of his body.

Reggie and Ben picked up their pace, and Julie tried to keep up. She saw Reggie break into a run, sprinting the final distance to the two men waiting in front of them. Ben couldn't keep up, and he fell back as Reggie arrived.

Reggie slowed, but even from here she could see his arm and hand raised above his head. He was getting ready to swing, to hit the guy in the face.

Freddie was suddenly there. He took a step to his right and appeared in front of Reggie, standing between the kneeling driver and the large soldier. Reggie tried to dodge, but Freddie was bigger and could more easily stand in the way. He brought his arm up as Reggie brought his down.

The two men clashed, Reggie's fist hitting Freddie's outstretched arm and harmlessly bouncing away.

"What the hell, man?" Reggie asked.

Freddie shook his head. "That's not how we handle things, brother," he answered.

Ben arrived at the scene, with Julie closing in. She saw the driver's face clearly now. It was dark, brooding. He wore glasses, and his eyes were sunken into his head, giving his brow a furrowed look. His hair was dark as well — either brown or black, and large curls fell over his forehead and ears.

He was looking straight up at Reggie, his eyes riveted. His mouth was straight, his lips tense.

"Are you kidding me?" Reggie asked. "Who the hell are you to tell me 'how we do things?'"

Ben put his hand on Reggie's shoulder. "Calm down, bud. Just take a second to chill out."

"I'm not going to *calm down*, Ben. I'm going to —"

"I want to kill him, too," Ben shot back. "Trust me."

"And that's not the group I joined," Freddie said, still addressing Reggie. "You attack him now, he ain't gonna tell us a darned thing."

Julie nodded. "He's right, Reggie."

"But he —"

"We *know*, Reggie," Sarah said from behind Julie. "We're all pissed. Trust me. But he's our best chance at figuring out what this is about, and if there's any possible way he'll talk, we need to figure it out."

"Mrs. E could still be alive," Ben muttered. "Hey — why don't me and Sarah go over to the cabin, at least poke around. If she is still in there somewhere, we may not have much time."

Julie and Freddie nodded. Reggie's eyes were fixed on the driver's. Ben pulled Julie aside before he left. "Keep him calm," he said. "We don't need any more explosions tonight."

She nodded and turned to the others. "Ask him a few questions, and then we'll wait for the cops. We have nowhere to keep him, and we can't do anything the police can't do."

"That's not true," Reggie said. She tensed, but he didn't make a move against Freddie.

"What happened?" she asked the newest member of their team.

"I saw the truck coming over the road. Ducked into the trees and watched. He parked, but left the engine running and the door open after he jumped out."

Julie nodded. "Then you sent the text?"

"Yeah," he said, running a hand through his buzzed hair. "Sorry I couldn't call. I wasn't sure there would be good enough connection, but I'm glad it got through."

"Yeah," Reggie said. "We are too, trust me." He paused, then looked at the driver and back up at Freddie. After a moment he nodded, rubbed a wrist over his nose, then extended his hand. "Sorry, man. I wasn't trying to attack you. I just…"

Freddie shook his hand and pulled him close, embracing him. "Hey, brother, I get it. Trust me. Take your time."

"No problem. Just need to keep my head screwed on straight. I'll be okay." He turned to Julie. "If it's okay with you, I probably should extract myself from this particular situation. Mind if I go help Ben and Sarah?"

She nodded. "Of course not. We'll handle this."

Julie had a feeling the man was not just a hired delivery driver, but someone who had been trained and prepared for this exact sort of thing. He was lucky the CSO was not interested in torture and interrogation, but she had a feeling he had been trained for *that* sort of thing, as well.

"Who are you?" she asked.

Freddie's shoulders were tense, the deltoids popping outward as he readied himself against whatever the man might try. But the man didn't move. Didn't speak.

"Who are you working for?"

Freddie and Julie waited for a minute, each taking turns asking him the same two questions. He didn't offer a response, nor did he even shift his focus from one person to the other.

Julie heard the sirens in the distance. She had guessed correctly, that someone from one of the neighboring properties had seen the explosion and called it in to report it, and the Anchorage police station just up the road was already on their way.

The driver heard it too. He turned his head to the side, listening. Then he turned back to Julie and looked directly at her.

"You are dead," he said. "All of you. Dead."

BEN

1:07 PM | **March 8, 2021**

Chugach Region, Alaska

"Ben, over here," Reggie said.

Ben heard the shakiness in the man's voice. Sensed it, really. It was just... different somehow. He'd never heard Reggie like this, had never experienced his best friend's softer side to this extent.

And that could only mean one thing.

"You found her," Ben said. It wasn't a question.

He worked his way free of the rubble he had been climbing around in and pulled himself up onto the flat, sloping slab of concrete — a wall that used to separate the cabin from the main CSO building — and looked around.

The area had already been cleared; the previous owner of the cabin had felled a copse of trees where he had wanted his cabin, and then had opted to build the structure a bit further back, against the protection of the pines behind, leaving a relatively vast open space in front of the cabin's front door. He had also cleared the dirt road, adding gravel and working the sides up into a short curb, and then built the small one-bedroom building. After finishing, he had been forced to sell the place, and Ben had been in the position to put an offer on it.

The cabin came with about a hundred acres of land, and that land curved around from behind Ben and then spread another half-mile south, the same direction the cabin was facing. He had explored every inch of it, converting the best parts of the natural features into things like outdoor gyms, a shooting range, running and hiking trails, and other recreational spaces.

Still, standing upon the fallen wall, Ben's view revealed to him exactly what he loved about this space: nothing but trees, in every direction.

Except, of course, when he looked *down*. Down was devastation. Down was ruin, dismay.

He carefully walked to the edge of the cracking wall and jumped over an open area that was still smoldering from some unknown object burning beneath it. All the possessions he and Julie had owned had been suddenly and remorselessly split in half — the half that lay beneath this wall, charred and still burning, and the half that sat in their bedroom, still in perfect condition and having no idea of the destruction that had occurred one room over.

He walked slowly toward Julie and Sarah, who were also nearing Reggie's location close to the back of the CSO headquarters' layout. It would have been the recreational room, the conference room that could be converted to a gaming and relaxation parlor.

Ben sucked in a breath when he realized what that meant. *She was meeting with her husband*, he thought. *She was talking to him, ignoring the text message Freddie had sent, when the bomb —*

"Ben, come on," Julie said. She had her hand out, waiting for him to arrive. He had stopped inadvertently at the edge of the pile of rocks and concrete, subconsciously not wanting to commit.

He reached her hand and pulled himself up and onto the pile. They walked, hand in hand, until they found what Reggie was looking at.

His best friend had pulled back a few large stones, revealing the face and upper body of Mrs. E, her eyes blackened, her nose bruised and bleeding. She was not moving, and her only remaining arm was extended up and above her head, as if she were simply sleeping beneath a blanket of stones.

Julie sniffed, and Sarah sobbed quietly. Ben turned and found Freddie at the edge of the clearing near the road, still watching over the driver, whom he had moved closer to the cabin. Not to be confused with a civilian who might make a mistake, Freddie had drawn a massive 50-caliber pistol and was holding it about a foot from the man's head, standing just behind him and to the side. A position, he had explained, that was the optimal one: it was far enough away that the subject could not easily get the jump on him, but one that constantly reminded them of the presence of a severe threat, just off their right side.

Freddie nodded, and Ben returned the motion. He didn't speak. Freddie would know why the team had all gathered here; why they were holding hands and looking down at a section of debris on the ground.

Ben wasn't sure what to do with Freddie — the man was clearly helping them, but he couldn't expect the kid to want to stay there forever. The police were just getting to the scene — Ben could hear them approaching on the dirt road to his left — so he had told Freddie to wait and answer whatever questions he could.

There was no reason the police couldn't know about what had happened here. He wouldn't assume the cops could actually *do* anything, but there was no reason to keep them out of the loop. Ben's business, and that of the CSO, was legitimate and on the books, and even though it was hardly a comfort, having their report filed through official channels would help them receive the recompense from the insurance company.

So he'd told Freddie to keep watch over the attacker until the police arrived, then to explain their story from his perspective. They would want Ben's and the others' stories as well, but there would be time for that. Now, he needed to focus on keeping his team in one piece.

As he thought the words, he couldn't help himself. He cried, the tears beginning to fall before he even knew they were coming. Heavy, salty tears, one at a time, as if moving lethargically for his benefit.

He sniffed and rubbed them back with his wrist, then looked up at Reggie, who was staring at him.

They exchanged a glance for a few seconds, and then Ben spoke. "It's her."

No one responded. It wasn't a question, nor was it information anyone was confused about.

"Do we — do we say anything? Or should we wait?"

Julie squeezed his hand. "We'll wait," she said. "We need to get sorted first. There's... there's a lot to do. Let's just let the police and the work crews do their — thing." She choked on the last word, and Ben turned to grab her.

They embraced, and then Reggie and Sarah were there. The four hugged, most of them sobbing and trying to navigate the arms and hands and faces to press the tears back and try to pretend they weren't crying in the first place. Ben didn't care who thought what, he just wanted to make it all go away and go back to an hour ago, before they had gotten the message from Freddie.

Reggie pulled himself back from the group suddenly, and Julie and Sarah and Ben were left with a cold, empty space where he had been. Ben looked up and questioned the man silently. Reggie shook his head, and started walking away.

"Reggie," Sarah pleaded. "Where are you going?"

He didn't stop. He walked faster, heading toward the edge of the collapsed building. He jumped off into the clearing, still moving toward Freddie.

"Reggie," Ben shouted. "Stop."

Reggie didn't stop.

"*Reggie*," Ben said. "That's an *order*. Stop moving, now."

CHAPTER 21

NAPOLEON

8:24 PM | **December 2, 1805**

Austerlitz, Austria

Napoleon entered the tent and noticed movement. He turned to greet the woman standing to his right, her hands clasped in front of her, waiting patiently. He was exhausted, and wanted nothing more than to wipe the sweat, grime, grease, and blood of battle off of him. His clothes needed to be removed so they could be handed off to one of the aides for cleaning, and he had many countless tasks to begin, not the least of which was a full debrief and overview of his victory here at Austerlitz, to be sent back to Paris. He had scores of letters to write to his marshals as well, and he wanted to pen a few messages for his own private notes.

There simply was not enough time to engage in the more *human* desires. This woman was beautiful, and in a way she reminded him of... *No,* he thought, immediately interrupting his own thought process. *She is not Josephine. No one is Josephine.*

Nevertheless, he straightened his back, arched his eyebrows, and put on his most endearing smile. "What is your name?" He asked the woman.

She was young, probably still in her early twenties, and she had the shapely body to prove it. Unlike some of the hired mistresses his men had delivered to him during their journeys, this woman was a fine specimen, unbroken by the ravages of time and the men who treated her as nothing but a doll for their pleasure. Still, he did not find his primal desires awakening as he looked upon her. She was simple, plain — a feature he normally would have preferred in the finer sex — but whether it be the battle he had just won and its inescapable post-victory adrenaline high, or the fact that he still struggled with defeating his own demons, he was not interested in any physical activity with this woman tonight.

"My name is Patricia," she said. Her voice was steady, soft and petite, a voice that matched her frame. The French had a bit of a Parisian accent to it, but it also carried with it an air of confidence, one of trained experience. She either was not new to the act of battle-field mistressing, or she had been to one of the Parisian finishing schools early in her childhood. Napoleon guessed it was the latter — he could always tell a prostitute from a refined lady. There was always something strikingly raw about a woman who had learned from the world itself rather than through the fine sieve of organized women's education.

"And where are you from, Patricia?" Napoleon asked her.

She answered without hesitation. "I am from Essex, near Cochester."

Napoleon raised his other eyebrow and did not try to hide his surprise. *They are setting me up with a woman from the enemy,* he realized. *Curious.*

"I am currently at war with England — you do realize that?"

"Yes, sir," she said.

"Are you a spy, Patricia?" he asked, bluntly.

At this, her face registered shock. "I — I am not..." her mouth opened and closed in fear, her eyelids fluttering and her brow beginning to break out with a sweat.

He held up a hand and let out a slight chuckle. "I am merely playing with you, my dear," he said. "My men, like I, have a bit... of a sense of humor. We have won a decisive victory here today, and I fear this is their way of playing a kindhearted joke on their leader."

The woman relaxed a bit and nodded, but he could still see the strain on her face.

"I assure you," he continued, "I am not the type of man to dwell on feeble slights, especially when they are delivered with grace. Nor am I the type of man to take out my anger on the actual gift."

"I *am* English," she said. "In that I was born there. But as you can tell from my French, I have been a citizen of France for the better part of my life."

Napoleon nodded. "Think nothing of it, my dear. What, exactly, brought you here tonight?"

He knew it was a question that would throw off any female mistress of paid employ, so it was usually a quick way to tell whether or not the woman in question was in front of him by force or by will.

"I... I was told you preferred companionship after your battles."

"Indeed," Napoleon said. "And yet, it is one of the greatest ironies of man that we can be in only one place at a time. A battlefield is no place for a woman, and a bedroom is no place for a man."

"I have known many men whose place seems to be quite suited to the bedroom," she said with a smirk.

Napoleon couldn't help himself. He laughed. His exhaustion was beginning to break through the cracks of his hardened outer shell, and he allowed himself to sit in the ornate wooden chair across from the woman still standing in front of his bed. "As you say, Patricia," he said. "I merely meant that staying at home and attending to the mundanities of keeping house is no place for a respectable man."

"Very well, sir, I was simply trying my hand at humor."

"It does suit you well. Which, again, reminds me: how is it that a woman of class and education such as yourself finds herself here, at the site of a terrible battle?"

CHAPTER 22
SAUL

11:11 PM | **March 9, 2021**
Location Unknown

Saul entered the massive space and couldn't help himself. He looked around, admiring the walls, the ceiling, the floor — they all matched, and they were all exactly the same: empty, devoid of light or decor, and smooth to the eye as well as, he assumed, to the touch.

Slate, he realized. An interesting and luxurious building material, and no doubt one insanely expensive to acquire here, and one he knew was difficult to work with.

Another show of luxury, he thought. There was no *reason* to have constructed interior walls of slate, and although it looked nice, it was unnecessary and didn't offer anything to the structure itself. But this particular luxury he didn't mind. It wasn't gaudy, and it wasn't over-the-top. There was something classy about it, as if it were out of the way enough to only be noticed by people like him, people who appreciated design and architecture to specifically seek out these details.

He then noticed the finer features — the gently coved recesses in the walls, mirroring each other on both sides of the room, the doorways that matched, and the desk itself that had been hewn from the same style of stone sitting across the gigantic space. A deep, rich, matte-gray construction that said everything and nothing all at once.

"I see you admire my office," the man said, rising from behind the desk.

Saul swallowed and took another step into the room. He had been in positions like this many times before, the moment when client met contractor. The moment when the room told him what he needed to know — was this client one who cared about things like power, or did they have no idea what really mattered in delicate transactions such as this. Did they seek that power but do it in a way that was overt, classless, cloying?

Or, in the rarest of cases like the case he found himself on now, did the client's personal space reflect everything needed, nothing more and nothing less, to signal to Saul that they were both knowledgeable about these sorts of things and simultaneously confident enough to not care.

And yet it was not a room of arrogance. It had been born of necessity — the client needed a space to work. But that space had to reflect an air of importance without coming across as pompous.

He nodded, smiling. "I am, indeed."

"You are a student of the schools of architecture?" his client asked.

This time, Saul shook his head. "No, certainly not. I would never claim to be gifted with the intricacies of such an art."

"And yet it is those just like us who the art is intended to please."

Saul gently lowered his head, a nonverbal allowance of victory. "Absolutely. And in that regard, I do humbly allow myself a modicum of satisfaction in understanding more than the layperson."

The client held his hand outward. "Please, sir, join me. Shall I fetch us drinks?"

Saul bowed his head as he entered the space. There were two armchairs in the center of the room, facing one another, each with a side table and lamp next to it.

"Thank you, but I must decline. I do not drink on the job."

"Regrettable, but admirable. You are Saul?"

Saul nodded again. "And you are Lord Tennyson?" he asked.

The man smiled and extended his hand. They shook, and Tennyson sat at the chair on the right side of the space. Saul sat, then leaned forward and began.

"Your prize is with your security team, just as you requested."

Tennyson cocked an eyebrow.

"*And* I have informed Mr. Grayson of your private security detail that it is with Mr. Abrams, and not with Mr. Radford."

Tennyson looked impressed. "You do live up to your reputation, Mr. Saul."

Saul accepted the compliment with grace. "I appreciate an iron-clad contract and a clear description of parameters. After that, it is my utmost pleasure to accomplish those... *peculiar* tasks my clients request."

"So I assume you would be willing to continue with the second project?"

"Of course," Saul said. "Your brief detailed the first project but alluded to two more, each of which may take between one and two weeks."

"And you have the time for this mission?"

Saul had been in this seat before. He knew the true question being asked. *You do not need the money from side projects during your employ with me?*

"I do not." It was true, direct, simple. If the slate-covered surfaces of this room told him anything, it was that this client would appreciate simplicity and clarity.

"Very well," Tennyson said.

Saul began to rise from his chair when his client held up a hand. Saul frowned, but sat back down.

"I appreciate that you are ready to get started," Tennyson said.

"But I thought it more prudent to explain the next project in person. It would be faster, at least for me."

"That is fine," Saul answered. "I still require a written contract, and I hope that will be no problem."

"It is already written, but I would rather ensure you understand the details face-to-face."

"Of course."

"The sword," Tennyson began, jumping in immediately. "It is in the condition described?"

"Perfect in every way. Properly cared for, properly maintained."

"Good. I need you to move it for me."

"Move it? As in, take it from here?"

"Yes."

"But it is already under your protection and watchful eye," Saul said. "Where would you have me take it?"

"The specific location will be in the contract. But I need it to be somewhere far away from here."

"I don't understand, Lord Tennyson," Saul continued. "Why have me bring it here, just to then carry it across the world to somewhere new?"

He hoped it did not come across as invasive, as questioning the man's motives. But, in a sense, that was absolutely what he was doing. He of course did not ever need to know the full extent of his clients' ultimate goals, but understanding a bit of their motivating factors often helped him perform his own role better.

"I can appreciate the confusion," Tennyson said. "And I apologize, but you must understand that finding someone as gifted as you has been rather difficult. Consider this a test of the quality you promise."

"Of course," Saul said.

"Rest assured, I do not intend for you to jump through hoops to gain my employ. You will be paid — and paid well — for your completed projects. That rate will only increase the longer we work together. For this next project, I need you to move the sword because I need it to perform another task for me, before it enters my collection."

"What task is that?"

"You used the sword on the baroness, and then cleaned it and prepared it, correct?"

"Meticulously."

"Perfect. In that case, the deed is half-done."

"The deed?"

"Yes, Mr. Saul. I need the sword to take on the life of its first owner. I need the sword to perform one more final duty, for the good of everything I have been working toward most of my life."

"Okay..."

"You have already used the sword for its designed purpose. Now that it is proven to work correctly, I need you to use it on one more person."

"I see. That implies that I will need to *persuade* another person to have a meeting with me."

"And that is the second project I will have you complete," Tennyson explained. "All of the details — where this person will be located, how best to find them, how best to complete the third project — will be in the brief my team is preparing."

"And you have the person in mind on whom you would rather it be used by?"

Tennyson looked directly into Saul's eyes. "I do."

CHAPTER 23
FREDDIE

3:10 PM | **March 8, 2021**

Chugach Region, Alaska

But Reggie didn't stop. Freddie watched him moving toward him, moving toward the man that had killed their friend. He had never met Mrs. E, but from what Reggie had told him, she had taught most of the group what they knew about hand-to-hand combat, including Reggie. While none of the CSO crew had been an active-duty soldier, Reggie at one point had been. He knew the Army regulations and training manuals in and out, and had even taught them in a different setting back in Brazil.

But Mrs. E had been able to teach him in a way that was fresh, different. She had brought something new to Reggie — a much more hands-on, practical approach. Her art was Krav Maga, something the Army didn't usually train with. Her method of teaching was something Reggie had explained as 'something between Cobra Kai and a kitten' — it was harsh but loving, hard but soft, and *always* effective and brutal.

Freddie had laughed about it, telling Reggie he couldn't wait to meet her. He had an image in his mind of a hardened, tight-muscled, brooding small woman who could just as easily snap his neck as she could climb him and twist it off while riding on his shoulders, but the picture he'd seen of her said otherwise: she was a *massive* human being — standing nearly as tall as Reggie and Freddie, with biceps nearly as large, and a shaved head and sparkling eyes that were almost as welcoming as her martial arts skills were forbidding.

Reggie continued on, closing the distance between himself and Freddie and the driver. Freddie couldn't exactly move toward Reggie to cut him off, nor did he feel comfortable taking the gun away from the back of the driver's head and moving it toward his new teammate.

Besides, he knew Reggie would see right through it — Freddie was not about to shoot him.

"You're disobeying orders, brother," Freddie began.

"This ain't the military, son," Reggie snapped.

"Still, Ben's in charge here, right? I thought —"

"You're gonna need to step out of the way, Freddie."

"I — I can't do that. I was told to —"

"You were told to *watch* him," Reggie said. "I heard the order. That's it. No more, no less. So I suggest you *watch* as I bash this guy's skull in."

"Reggie..." Freddie said, leaning on the two syllables. He felt like he'd been put in a difficult place. *'Between a waterless crick and an empty canteen sorta place,'* his dad would've said. Only this time, it wasn't just a parable or idiom. He was struggling with what to do: defend the man who had literally blown up one of his teammates against one of his new teammates, or allow Reggie to disobey Ben's order.

Thankfully, Ben was jogging over. He only needed to hold off the large ex-Army sniper for a few more seconds, and Reggie didn't look like he was going to go for Freddie's throat.

"Just relax, okay? We're going to get this —"

"I'm relaxed, brother," Reggie said. "I'm *completely* relaxed. You know what? I've never felt more relaxed in my *life*. Ask Ben — he should be here any second, chasing after me. I'm pretty calm, right? I'm not going to do anything rash."

"I — I thought you were about to try to tackle me, and steal my piece."

"First of all, I don't *need* to tackle you, big boy," Reggie said. Freddie gritted his teeth. He knew Reggie wasn't trying to insult him. He was struggling, trying to work through what he'd just been through. "I could take it in a second, without even —"

Reggie lunged forward, grabbing toward Freddie's wrist, but Freddie had anticipated the move. It was the same one he'd learned, the one that had been ingrained in him. He offered his opposite shoulder to Reggie, who slammed his jaw into it as he reached Freddie's side.

The man let out an *oof* of a groan and then pulled back, his plan foiled.

Ben arrived. "Knock it off, Reggie."

"Don't tell me to knock it off."

"What?" Ben asked. "You're going to kill Freddie, then me? Then this guy? Then what? You'll have to take out Jules and Sarah too."

"I'm just — I need to —"

"You need to *chill*, man. All right?"

Reggie didn't respond.

Julie and Sarah reached the spot where Freddie and Reggie were scuffling, and Freddie pulled back to his position and made sure the driver was still there. The man was sitting on the ground, his hands on his knees, calmly looking at the CSO members, snickering.

Freddie wished the orders Ben had given him had been a bit *looser* — the guy on the ground needed a few swift kicks to a few red-alert areas. But he held his ground, straightening his back and pulling himself up, bringing the pistol back up to the man's head.

"What you want me to do, Ben?" he asked.

"Nothing. Just... just let me figure this out."

"I already *figured* it out, Ben," Reggie said. "We need to —"

Ben held up a hand and sucked in a breath. His face had suddenly changed, his entire demeanor different. Freddie frowned. *Weird.* He'd never seen Ben like this, he had never seen the de facto leader of the Civilian Special Operations actually *look* like a leader.

Sure, the man was charismatic, likable in a malleable, 'aw shucks' sort of way — the kind of leader Freddie liked, but also knew wasn't the most effective. He had assumed the leadership of the CSO was something that jumped from person to person, each man or woman serving a term before passing the baton.

He, apparently, had been wrong.

He moved his head slightly, giving the others the impression that he was intrigued, but didn't speak.

Ben moved forward until he was in the center of the group. He frowned, turned a slow circle, then crouched down to meet the driver face to face. He pulled the man's chin up, then stared into his eyes.

"Who are you?" he asked.

The man didn't answer.

"You've got one more chance," Ben said, softly.

The man looked at Ben, smiled, and then spat.

CHAPTER 24
FREDDIE

3:114 PM | **March 8, 2021**

Chugach Region, Alaska

Ben stood up, wiped his mouth, and then looked at Freddie. "I'll give you the special 'welcome to the CSO' speech later. Right now we've got more important things to deal with. Namely, I want you to become accustomed to the leadership style we've built."

He noticed that Julie seemed confused. Sarah's eyes were still red, but she had stopped sobbing. Even Reggie seemed to be interested in what Ben was about to say.

"Give me your pistol," Ben said.

Freddie hesitated, but then handed over the piece.

"Peacemaker?" Ben asked, turning it over in his hands.

Freddie nodded. "Same make, different model. Kind of a throwback. My old man gave it to me."

Reggie shifted, then spoke. "Ben, what the hell are we —"

"Shut up, all of you," Ben interrupted. "Listen to me. Right now. Here's the deal: I didn't sign up for this shit, and neither did you. The CSO *happened* to all of us. Somewhere along the line, we all decided it was good for us. We're not here to rehash any of that, but know this: I have *no* interest in becoming some weird cult dictator, okay?"

No one spoke.

"I'm not here to give orders, and I'm not here to tell you each what to do at every step of the way. Most of the time that's not a problem — I'd rather take orders from you, anyway. I don't always know the right thing to do before I do it, and I know for a fact you all feel the same way. But that's what makes us strong, that's what makes us a team. We aren't the military — we don't have strategists and tacticians and then a whole line of bureaucracy that's determined the best mode of operation and objectives for us.

"What I'm saying is this: I want us to operate the best we can as a team, and that means I trust you. *All* of you."

Reggie's jaw clenched and unclenched.

"I trust Jules with my life. Sarah, you too. Reggie, I don't even need to *tell* you that, man. You're the guy I'd have at my side *any* day."

"You too, man."

"Right," Ben said, barely acknowledging what Reggie had said. He immediately turned and gave the pistol to Reggie.

"Wait —"

"What —" Reggie began.

"Reggie, you've made a decision. It's not good or bad, but there are both of those elements in it. It's not for me to argue with, and it's not for the others to argue with as well."

Freddie moved back, distancing himself from the driver.

Ben continued. "We all handle things differently, just like we all work through things differently. The next few days are going to be a test of that, and I'm not kidding when I tell you it's going to be a challenge. But I *trust* you, and I *love* you. Even you, Freddie. You've saved our ass before, and you'll do it again."

He paused, took a breath, wiped his eyes. Freddie looked on, appalled. This man was unlike any other military commander he'd served for. He was vulnerable, but there was no lack of strength. There was no lack of self-assurance.

It was... refreshing.

"Reggie," Ben said. "I'm going to call Mr. E. I need to tell him about his wife. That's on me, and it's my responsibility. It's what I can do for us, right now."

Reggie nodded.

"Is there something *you* think you need to do for us, right now?"

Freddie watched the man's face, and saw Reggie's nostrils flare, then clench his jaw again. He nodded. "Yeah. I think so."

"Okay," Ben said. "Then I'm signing off on it. Right now, and forever more. You have my trust, and you have my approval."

"I understand," Reggie said.

Ben turned and immediately took Julie's hand and began walking toward the remains of his home. Sarah stood by, watching Reggie.

Reggie didn't hesitate. He looked at Freddie, nodded, and then raised the pistol.

He aimed it at the driver's head. The man's eyes widened, clearly not understanding what had just happened.

Reggie pulled the trigger, and the man's head exploded outward, the shocked expression permanently affixed to his face. He fell back, crunching against his own body on the way down before collapsing into a heap.

Freddie tried not to react, but the sound was deafening. He popped his ears, waited a few seconds, then looked from the dead, bleeding corpse on the ground to Sarah, whose hand was over her mouth.

And then to Reggie, whose face was a blank canvas. He couldn't read anything there; if Reggie was feeling something — anything — it was not reflected in his expression. He just stood there, watching the carnage of the driver's head imploding in on itself and falling backwards, as if he were doing nothing more than swatting a fly.

And then he looked up and turned his empty gaze to Freddie.

"Welcome to the CSO."

CHAPTER 25

BEN

3:37 PM | **March 8, 2021**

Chugach Region, Alaska

"You hid the body?" Ben asked.

He looked at his best friend, hoping this was all a dream, hoping this was some cruel joke, and they weren't *actually* trying to hide from the police the fact that they had just murdered a man on Ben's property.

Of course, that man had also just murdered one of their own only minutes earlier, but it wouldn't change the fact that the local authorities would have more than a few questions for the CSO team.

Namely, who did Ben and his team just kill? And why? What was he doing there? Why did he blow up half of the house and the head-quarters building?

And since those same local authorities had never been told who the Civilian Special Operations team was, nor had they been alerted to the fact that their business was actively operating out of a lowly cabin in the woods near the Chugach region just southeast of Anchorage, they would no doubt want to bring them all in for ques-tioning. It was cryptic, and since multiple deaths had now taken place on the property, they'd be rightly concerned. If the team wasn't arrested, they would at least be detained for a few days while Mr. E threw his legal power behind bailing them out.

So, in short, Ben had decided that their best option was to get rid of the evidence. He didn't feel that they were guilty of any wrongdoing, but he just didn't have time to argue that point with the police who were about to arrive on scene.

As such, he and Reggie had discussed it. Reggie had told him that he and Freddie would take care of it. Ben didn't ask any questions — he just turned and left and had prepared for the call he needed to make.

That had been ten minutes ago, and Ben was surprised to hear the task had already been completed.

"Like I said," Reggie answered. "It's done. They'll never find the body unless they bring dogs, and they would have no reason to do that right now."

Ben still hadn't made the call, instead deciding to stand with Julie and Sarah as they processed through some of the emotions they were all feeling. When Freddie and Reggie returned, Ben had stepped back toward the tree line where they were now, and got his update.

"Still," Ben said. "We need to have a plan. There are going to be insurance claims, and shortly after that they're going to want to start rebuilding. I'll have to be here, as well as a bunch of adjusters and corporate types — not to mention all the contractors and construction workers at some point. Someone's bound to wander around, right?"

Reggie was already nodding. "Yeah, I know man, this is not a permanent solution. The body is underneath some rocks and leaves for the time being. It won't fully decompose for a while, and even then, all of his clothes and stuff will remain there for years. Any trained dog will be able to find it in a few minutes, or if somebody stumbles into the wrong place."

"So what's the long-term plan?"

"Freddie and I will come back with shovels —

"You're not going to bury the body. He doesn't deserve to be —"

"Slow down, buddy," Reggie interrupted. "I never said anything about burying any bodies. The shovels are to help us dig up some land to make a fire ring — sort of like the one we made in the clearing behind the house last summer."

Ben knew exactly what he was talking about. The previous summer, Reggie had led them all through some outdoor survival training, the sort of thing the man used to do when he owned his bunker and some land in Brazil.

"We'll burn it," he continued, "but it's not going to be a ceremony. It's going to be gasoline and a match. He deserves less than that, but we just need to get rid of the evidence and do it the right way. We'll also burn the spot he was laying in, and rough up any ground between there and where the fire pit will be to throw off the scent."

"That works," Ben said, nodding along.

"Ben, it's a long shot someone's going to come looking for him — he was probably just a grunt for hire. I doubt his family is going to know he was on his way here to blow us up, or if he even had family."

Outside, Ben was calm and collected. On the inside, however, he was reeling. He was seething, wanting to exact revenge on whoever had done this.

Whoever had ultimately called the shots and decided that he and his team — not to mention all of his worldly possessions and professional equipment — should be destroyed, buried beneath piles of concrete and stone.

He gave Reggie his approval, but he wanted to destroy the evidence himself. However, he didn't want to do it with something so formal and elegant as fire.

No, he wanted to use an ax. Or a blunt object. He wanted to hack and destroy.

"You okay?" Reggie said suddenly.

Ben blinked a few times, registering that his friend asked him a question, then nodded abruptly. "Yeah," he said. "Yeah, I'll be all right. It's going to take some time, but you heal from this sort of thing. You always do."

He and his friend looked at each other for a long moment before Reggie swallowed and cleared his throat. He kicked the dirt in front of his feet and stood up straighter. "True," he said, finally. "That's true, but it doesn't mean you ever really forget. You never really let it go."

Ben nodded. He couldn't help but think of his parents. His father, brutally attacked by a grizzly bear, later dying in a hospital. And his mother, suffering and finally expiring in her home after contracting a deadly virus.

He thought of the others as well — the ones they had lost on their missions. The previous leader of the CSO, a man he had been honored to serve with.

That man's death had been exceptionally hard to swallow, especially considering that Julie had been the one to pull the trigger.

He knew that she too would be struggling through her own ghosts. He needed to be there for her — he needed to be there for all of them — but he was just old enough and barely wise enough now to know that he needed to be there for himself as well.

But all that had to wait. Right now, he had a job to do.

He needed to call Mr. E.

"You going to call now?" Reggie asked.

Ben nodded. "Yeah, I guess."

"Need help?"

"No," Ben said. "I don't think there's anything you'll be able to do."

Reggie stared into Ben's eyes for a few more seconds, tears welling in them. Then he stepped forward and grabbed Ben in a bear hug, squeezing him tight. Ben was stunned at first, but then he pulled his hands up as well, embracing his friend.

"We're going to be fine," Reggie said. "*You're* going to be fine."

"I know that," Ben said. "It's just that sometimes..."

"Sometimes what we *need* to do isn't exactly what we *want* to do."

Ben took a deep breath, then nodded slowly.

"Yeah, that's pretty much it exactly."

CHAPTER 26

BEN

3:46 PM | **March 8, 2021**

Chugach Region, Alaska

Ben walked along the path that used to lead out of the back of his cabin, when his cabin still existed. Now, there was just a black, charred scar where the back door used to meet the small square concrete slab of his patio. The path, however, continued on into the forest as if nothing had happened. He stepped over the area gingerly, as if trying not to harm it anymore, then pulled the phone out of his pocket.

He knew there was a bit of cellular service here, as he used to make calls from this spot long before the CSO had built its headquarters building and attached it to his home. He scrolled through his contacts and found the number he was looking for — a cell phone number Mrs. E had given them long ago.

He had never used it, and to his knowledge, no one else had, either.

The meetings they'd had with Mr. E in the past had all been pre-scheduled, using videoconferencing software one of Mr. E's companies had developed. He wondered if the number even worked.

He pressed it and brought the phone up to his ear. After a few seconds, it began to ring. The connection sounded strong, and there were no dropouts.

After one ring someone picked up. *"Hello?"*

Ben swallowed and tried to moisten the dry inside of his mouth. "Hello. Hey, it's Ben. Harvey. Sorry, Harvey Bennett."

"Harvey?" the voice asked. *"This is...unorthodox."*

Ben knew the man did not have to add anything to that statement. This number was for emergencies only — there were no exceptions. Mr. E knew that, and he knew Ben knew that.

Which meant he would already know something was wrong.

Ben blew out a breath of air and tried to gather himself. There were still tears in his eyes, but he wiped them back with his wrist. "Hey, Mr. E. I — I needed to call you."

"Harvey, please. Just tell me, what happened?"

"A bomb. An explosion, here at the house. At the headquarters."

There was a pause, then Mr. E returned. *"Hmm. I did get an email alert from our satellite imaging overhead that there had been some sort of infrared anomaly in that area. I had planned to look at it tomorrow morning."*

Ben suddenly realized that the man must have been talking on the phone with his wife when the explosion had gone off, when their transmission would have been cut. Or, if they had been video conferencing, he may have seen something onscreen.

"Thank you Harvey," Mr. E continued. *"I will send an email to our insurance company tomorrow, and I will get on the phone with the legal team here — "*

"No," Ben said. "That's not... that's not why I called."

There was a longer pause this time. *"Then for what reason have you called this number?"* Mr. E asked.

"There was a message — a text message, sent to our phones. Freddie sent something, and we all got it. We were in the kitchen, and then got the text and left the house immediately. But —"

"But my wife was talking with me."

"Yes," Ben said, the tears returning.

"I see," Mr. E said. *"The connection did drop abruptly, but I did not think to check the timestamp of the anomaly."*

"Mr. E," Ben said, finally mustering the courage. "She — she did not get the message, and she did not get out in time. Sir, she's gone."

The next pause felt like an eternity. He looked around at the picturesque wilderness environment in which he had made his home for the past four years. He didn't want to turn around, to see the utter devastation. He wanted *this* direction — the perfect serenity of the evening forest in front of him — to be the truth.

He saw a bird take flight in front of him, landing on a branch just yards away. It looked at him, examined him with a cock of its head, then took off with a small chirp. He had not yet seen or heard any other animals in the area since the explosion. At first, his ears had been completely overwhelmed by the blast, leaving him momentarily deafened. But when his hearing returned, there were hardly any other noises around.

The animals would stay away for a few more hours, at least until the most daring of them advanced back toward the cabin and declared it once again safe.

"I see," Mr. E said.

That was it. No emotion, no real response. Perhaps the man had to process things a bit — Ben certainly would have needed to.

"Harvey," the man continued. *"Thank you for calling me. I know this has been difficult."*

Now Ben frowned and looked down at the screen in disbelief. The call had not been disconnected, but Ben couldn't believe how emotionless — how robotic — the man was. True, Ben had never known Mr. E well enough to understand his personality — if he even had one — or his quirks, or his nuances. They had only ever interacted through a screen, and it seemed that taking the visual context clues away made the man come across as even colder, even more detached.

Ben pulled the phone back up to his ear. "Mr. E, what would you like me to do?"

"*Yes,*" he replied, *"taking action will be a good distraction from what has taken place. If you can send me any pertinent details, I will begin the investigation as to the cause of the explosion tomorrow morning.*"

Ben squeezed his eyes shut. *Now, for the kicker.* "Mr. E — I hate to tell you, but the explosion was not an accident. There was a truck; someone came just before Freddie sent us the text message, and then..."

He couldn't finish the sentence, but he felt there was no need to. He had done his task, he had delivered the news. Mr. E would grieve in his own, strange way.

Ben waited, and after a few more seconds, Mr. E spoke a final time. *"I see. I will be in touch."*

And then the call disconnected.

CHAPTER 27

NAPOLEON

8:47 PM | **December 2, 1805**
Austerlitz, Austria

"I had no choice in the matter, sir," Patricia answered. Her voice was honest, true. "I was assigned to you. But I have wanted to meet you for some time. What I've read about you, at least the parts I believe, have made you out to be an incredible man, one worthy of the title and role you have been given."

"I certainly like to think so," Napoleon answered with a smile. "But I suppose my legacy has yet to be determined. Please, have a seat. I am exhausted, and all I want is food and wine and rest. I hope you will indulge me at least that much?"

"I am here for your pleasure, sir," Patricia said. She walked over to the opposite chair and sat, daintily, on the very corner of it. Something about the way she sat, perched there with her chin up and her hair beginning to fall around her eyes, reminded him of Josephine.

"And yet the only pleasure I can imagine experiencing at this moment in time is that of gluttony." He turned around to the matching wooden work desk that had been set up against one flap of the tent and grasped the decanter of red wine and poured two glasses. He never understood how these sorts of delicate items found their way to a battlefield. They were as fragile as the woman sitting in front of him, and yet his aides had taken great care to ensure all the favorite comforts of his home life had been transferred to his wartime one.

He passed along the glass and she took a careful sip. He copied the action, enjoying the sweet, bright bouquet of aromas that stung his palate. It was one of the finest wines he had ever tasted, and he had been sure to bring enough along to last him months on the road. The greatest irony about it was that it was not a French wine at all but a Spanish one, a Madeira.

"This is very good," she said.

"Indeed. Tell me, Patricia," Napoleon said, leaning toward her. "These things you have heard — these things you believe — what are they?"

She paused for a few seconds, examining the legs of her wine as they drizzled down the sides of the glass, then looked back up at the leader of the French Army. "They say you courted Josephine, that you still fancy her."

He cleared his throat. He had not at all expected her to mention *her* name, nor in such an abrupt, unbecoming way. "I — I am not sure who you have heard that from, Patricia."

She coolly and calmly balanced the wineglass between her fingers as she watched Napoleon adjust in the chair. He felt slighted, tricked. No one in the past decade had ever gotten this close to him without proper vetting. No one had ever come into his tent and claimed to know his business.

He could have her killed — perhaps *should* have her killed.

And yet there was a question here. Something nagging at him, pulling his thoughts in a different direction...

"Josephine has moved on," Napoleon said. "She no longer loves me."

"She is your wife, sir. And she *does* love you," Patricia said. "She wants you back. No more adultery. No more mistresses."

"And who are you to be delivering her messages?" he asked. "You speak for her?"

Without waiting for the rest of the question, she nodded. "I do, in fact, speak for Lady Rose."

He had not heard the name she used to call herself by for many years. After their marriage, Marie Josèphe Rose Tascher de La Pagerie had simply adopted the name Josephine, how most of the country and world knew her. The empress had devoted her name and life to Napoleon, but she had — on more than one occasion — devoted her bed to other men.

This woman, Patricia, must have the ear of Napoleon's estranged wife. He had never met many of her handmaidens or court help, but that did not mean his wife had not found one or two she could trust with intimate details.

"Why?" he asked. "Why would my wife care now — now that I have succeeded here?"

"It has nothing to do with your success, sir."

"Then what? Surely she is lonely without me around the halls. She cannot find companionship?"

Patricia shifted, then put her glass of wine on the edge of the table next to her. "Sir, she has told me to find you. At all costs. She wants you to know that she wants you back. She *needs* you back. She understands what you are doing here and does not intend for you to rush your work. The empire requires you here, and she understands that. But she needs you to know something."

"What something might that be?" Napoleon gripped his own wineglass tighter, feeling the cool crystal against his fingertips. He could not know exactly what Patricia's news could be, but there were only a few things worth making the journey for.

As she spoke, Napoleon forced his eyes to stay riveted on the beautiful young handmaiden. He wanted to believe what she was saying. Wanted more than ever to believe it, but it seemed impossible.

"Empress Josephine wants you to know that she is with child."

CHAPTER 28

JULIE

7:15 AM | **March 9, 2021**
Anchorage, Alaska

The next morning came abruptly. The CSO team had moved to Anchorage and found an inexpensive hotel to stay the next few nights. Julie knew that Mr. E would easily have sprung for the finest accommodations Anchorage could offer, but they weren't on vacation. They needed a bed and little else; any extra luxury would only make them feel guiltier for what had happened.

And after Ben's conversation with Mr. E, she knew it would be better to just leave him alone. He would already be going through enough after hearing about the loss of his wife in the brutal attack from the day before. Julie rolled out of bed and tried to sneak into the bathroom without Ben hearing her. He groaned and muttered something, but stayed asleep.

In the bathroom, she took a minute to gather herself. She would eventually need to shower and prepare for the day, but first, she felt like she needed to assess herself and assure herself that she was going to be okay. She blinked a few times, wiping the crust of sleep away from her eyes, then yawned. She had hoped to sleep in, but it seemed as though the gruesome explosion and long hours conversing with police and fire department officials had taken its toll, and her anxiety and restlessness had won out over her mental and physical exhaustion.

She yawned again, knowing that they would have time to take a nap later that day if need be. In fact, now that she thought of it, they didn't have a plan at all. She supposed, if she wanted to, she could simply go back to bed and sleep the rest of the day away. Perhaps starting over tomorrow would give her enough of a break.

No, she thought, *Reggie and Sarah will be downstairs getting an early start.* She knew they were both light sleepers, and because of Reggie's stint in the military and Sarah's career as an anthropologist and university lecturer, both were early risers. She assumed Freddie would be, as well.

While brushing her teeth, she flicked through the latest news and updates for her area, the world, and anything in-between that had happened to land onto her phone's RSS app. Finding nothing noteworthy — and no articles as of yet about the explosion at her house, she clicked the phone off and prepared to take a shower.

Then she heard a slight knock at the door. She smiled, shook her head, then turned around and opened it. "Ben, you don't have to knock. We *are* married."

Ben shrugged. "Sorry, it's just, I guess I've always been in the habit. Having a little brother and wanting a little bit of privacy... You know."

"What's up?" She asked. "I was just about to jump in the shower."

He looked at her, still wearing the sleek nightgown he had gotten her as a gift a few months ago, then at the shower, then back at her. He arched his eyebrow.

"Not even a chance," she said quickly. "I have a bit of a headache, and it's going to turn into a rager if I don't get some coffee and food in me immediately. And besides..."

"Yeah, I'm feeling about the same as you, actually. And after yesterday —"

She cut him off by holding up a hand. "Let's not talk about yesterday. There will be plenty of that later, but for now, let's just start out like it's a normal day."

Ben looked up at the ceiling and then down at the floor, leaning from side to side. It was obvious something was wrong.

"Oh, crap," she said. "What happened now?"

"Well," he started, "I wish you wouldn't have said we should start out like it's a normal day, because I'm afraid it's not going to be." He pulled his own phone up and held it out so she could see the screen. "I just got an email. It's from Baden Tennyson."

Her eyes widened and her blood ran cold. "*Baden Tennyson* sent you an email? What the hell does he want? What does it say?"

He swallowed, then answered. "Well, actually, I didn't read it yet. I checked my phone when you got up, and just saw that there was an email, then I saw who it was from. I thought... maybe it would be best for us to see it together. I have a feeling it's about —"

"Don't even say that," she said quickly. "He's suing us, but that doesn't mean he's the one who's trying to *kill* us, too." She sucked in a breath. "Okay, don't read it. I'm going to jump in the shower real quick and then we can go meet up with the others. They'll want to see it as well, whatever it is."

Ben nodded, then tossed the phone on the bed and moved toward the duffel bag next to the bed, starting to get dressed. They hadn't packed much, as neither had wanted to go into the part of the bedroom of their cabin that was still standing. Neither had wanted to discover how much of their belongings had been burned and scorched, and how much remained. Reggie had gone in for them and retrieved Ben's duffel bag he kept under the bed, which had a change of clothes in it for each of them. But since he and Sarah had been staying with them in the new CSO headquarters, all of their travel items and suitcases were gone. They would have to go to the store later anyway, so Julie had just decided to go with them.

Freddie was the only one of the group who still had a full complement of clothing and hygiene accessories, since he had just gotten off the plane and was about to get to their place last night before the attack.

"There's something else," Ben said, throwing on the shirt he'd been wearing the day before.

She flicked her eyes toward him and took a deep breath. "Great, do I even want to know?"

"No, but you need to know."

"Okay, what is it?"

"The email," he said. "There's an attachment. A video."

CHAPTER 29
BEN

7:22 AM | **March 9, 2021**
Anchorage, Alaska

Ben and Julie found Reggie, Sarah, and Freddie all gathered together in a booth in the diner that was attached to the hotel. The restaurant was nothing fancy — just a simple breakfast place that offered a small selection of lunch and dinner items as well — but it seemed warm and well-lit, and — most importantly — all of them had cups of steaming hot coffee in front of them.

Ben's stomach growled as he approached, and Reggie pushed a fourth and fifth cup over in front of the empty seats. Ben grabbed his and took a sip before even sitting down, and thanked Reggie.

"You guys doing okay?" He asked. He hadn't come up with anything useful or helpful to say, but he also didn't want to walk up to the table and not say anything at all.

Reggie shrugged, and Sarah just stared, shellshocked, down at her coffee. Freddie nodded slowly. "Yeah, I guess we are. Best we can hope for, I s'pose."

Ben nodded. "Yeah, I know the feeling. We're going to figure this out, I promise. You have my word."

"What's to figure out?" Reggie asked, his tone bitter. "Asshole came in blew up your house, blew up our CSO headquarters. I think *that's* pretty straightforward, don't you? What's to figure out?"

"Reggie —" Sarah began.

"No, man," Reggie continued, addressing Ben directly. "We need to go after those guys. We need to get the punks who planned this whole thing. Tennyson, whoever he is working with, all of his henchmen. They're out there somewhere, still planning our demise, and we're here with our heads in the sand."

Ben let his gaze fall to the table, noticing that Julie did as well. A waitress approached but saw the tension at the table and quickly turned and left. He would have to order food in a few minutes. Apparently it was time for him to spill the beans.

"Speaking of Tennyson," Ben began. He watched as the others at the table perked up. "He sent me an email."

"Uh, what?" Reggie asked. "He sent *you* an email."

"What's it say?" Freddie asked.

Ben shook his head. "Haven't read it yet. Wanted to make sure we all saw it. Together."

He pulled the phone out, opened his email inbox, and clicked the title. Before he placed it down on the table he saw the subject line.

>> *Now that I have your attention...*

"Well, shit," Reggie said. "That's a damned fine way of introducing himself."

Freddie was shaking his head, his fists balled on the table.

Ben read the email aloud. *"Mr. Bennett, I would normally hope that this email finds you well. In this particular case, I imagine you are not well. Not as well as you could be."*

"Guy's an arrogant mother—"

"Keep going," Sarah said.

Ben continued. *"Regardless, there is a matter for which I require your personal presence. A request, of sorts. If you would be so kind as to be at the address listed below — tomorrow evening, please. Shall we say 6:30 pm, local time?”*

Ben flashed his eyes down the screen and saw the address.

“That’s London,” Freddie said.

“And he wants you there *tomorrow* evening?” Julie asked. “What the hell for?”

Ben didn’t respond, but he continued reading the message aloud. *“I am a man of my word, though I have found through much experience that others may not be. Therefore I have taken the initiative to provide you and your team some incentive. I ask that you come alone, and I ask that you do not share the contents of this email with anyone outside of your team.”*

“Well, that’s kind of him,” Reggie said. “At least he knows we work as a team.”

“Yeah, but he wants Ben to come alone to England,” Julie added. “I’m not okay with that.”

“He wants him to come alone to the *meeting* place,” Reggie said. “No chance in hell I’m staying here while Ben gets himself into another bind.”

Ben flicked his eyes up, unable to keep the anger down. It had been boiling beneath the surface since yesterday, and something about the way Reggie was talking made it explode upward. “Oh?” he asked. “You going to come with? Save my ass again? Prevent one of us from getting blown up?”

“The hell does that mean, man?” Reggie asked, pushing his coffee away. He started to stand up. “You want to discuss something with me?”

“Reggie, stop it,” Sarah said, pulling his arm. “Ben, what’s the ‘incentive’ he’s talking about? If he wants you to come meet him that badly, what’s he got on us to ensure you’ll be there alone?”

Ben nodded and scrolled down, finding the video file downloaded and ready to play. It was small — likely only a few seconds long. He held his breath and clicked it.

The screen turned sideways and became a full-screen view of a room. It was dim, too dark to see much detail in the background.

But in the foreground, everything was crystal clear.

"Is that —"

"Eliza Earnhardt," Ben whispered. It was the red-haired woman he'd met in Switzerland, the one who had requested the CSO's help in bringing down Tennyson's company, EKG. They had been successful, ultimately, at stopping the sickening animal testing that had been going on in Grindelwald, but it had come at a massive price.

To see her face again, especially like this, gave Ben anxiety.

Onscreen, Eliza began to speak. She looked directly into the camera, directly at Ben it seemed. She had been crying, and it seemed that she had her hands tied behind her back. She cried as she spoke, her sobs rocking her body back and forth.

"Ben — if you get this message — please. They are going to hurt me. They might... they might kill *me. I don't understand, I don't know what I did, or what you did. But please, hurry. Do what he says, or it mean —"*

The video cut off.

"Holy crap," Freddie said. "You know her?"

Ben nodded but didn't respond.

"Rewind it," Reggie said, softly.

"You see something?"

"Yeah." He watched Ben pull the scrub marker back to a location at the middle of the video, then released his finger. "Right there," Reggie said. "What the hell is —"

He stopped himself, and Ben saw why. While Eliza had been talking, her body gently moving, the lighting flickered with her motions and revealed a bit more of the room. She was wearing a sweater, a tiny gold chain around her neck. The light glinted off of it. It also revealed that there was something hanging just above Eliza's head.

Something that made Ben's heart sink even further.

"Is that —" Julie started, then stopped. Ben saw the coloring of it glinting in the light. Almost blue, gilded with gold-looking designs up and down the face of it.

"I think it is," Sarah said. "My God. It's a *sword*."

CHAPTER 30

GALBRAITH

9:19 AM | **March 10, 2021**

Interpol Office, London, England

Peter Galbraith glanced up at the drop ceiling of his tiny, cramped office. It was smaller than it looked from the outside — and from the outside, it looked small — but at least he *had* one. He had spent the first five years of his job at the International Criminal Police Organization either getting coffee for the higher-ups or wishing he could get coffee for someone because the real job was even more drab. Most of the mundane tasks he had spent those five years doing had been done from a desk in Manchester, where the main Interpol office in England was headquartered.

Two years ago he had accepted a promotion, but had to move to the large cubical farm in the center of the main floor in the London branch office. It had come with the possibility of rapid advancement, a perk which had proven true about a year ago when he had accepted the position of *Director of Local Intelligence — London.*

While this office was only a shade larger than his old cubicle, it was certainly better. He had been given a role that had him acting as supervisor over a few other people in the office, which meant that while he was still in the office most days, every now and then he got to actually go into the field. Even then, most of his work was spent talking to witnesses and victims, preparing an official report for the media, and then writing up the boring debriefs for his department heads. It was not much different from what he would imagine the role of chief of beat cops in a London precinct would be.

He had originally chosen this role because of the allure of getting to travel — of chasing down international terrorists and bringing them to justice. He wanted to be a modern-day Jason Bourne, and he wasn't afraid to admit it. He kept himself physically fit as well, though the last five years in the cubicle and the one year in this office were not helping with his workout regimen. That said, he knew he could outrun and outlast any of his coworkers, though it was admittedly a low bar.

He sighed, taking a long breath and holding it in. On his agenda in a few hours was to touch base with his supervisor over lunch, which no doubt would be one of his famous scheduled hour-long meetings that inevitably would last at least two or even three, effectively prohibiting either of them from getting any actual work done in the afternoon. To make matters worse, his boss had zero personality or interests besides a love for food. A self-declared foodie, the man would choose for the meeting location whatever restaurant had most recently been reviewed in the *Evening Standard,* but then spend most of the time ranting about why the reviewer was an idiot.

At least it'll be a free meal, Galbraith thought. *Hopefully he chooses Italian. I could use some Italian food.*

He shifted in the old creaky office chair and turned back to his computer screen. He checked email for the thirteenth time that hour, then flicked over to his browser, where he had open all of the local and regional news sites, as well as a few general continent-wide European channels. Interpol worked with local law enforcement to find criminals who were outside the jurisdiction of a single city or even country, so keeping up with the most recent continental news was a requirement for the job.

In his mind, Interpol was supposed to be the European version of the American military: nowhere was off-limits, no one was on too high a pedestal to topple it over, and nothing was out of the question. They could go anywhere, do anything, and be the world's "good guys."

In reality, however, Galbraith had discovered that Interpol was merely a resource organization — meant to provide on-the-ground support — rather than an actual policing organization. Sure, they had a lot of tech bells and whistles, and there certainly were field agents, but these gadgets and secret agents were the exception, not the norm. While he tried to keep abreast of changing trends and continue training on whatever the latest technology was, the truth of the matter was that he most often felt chained to his desk.

He didn't want a vacation — he wanted a break from his vacation-like lifestyle. He wanted *action*. He wanted to do something, to *be* something.

He heard the sound of an email dinging into his inbox, but frowned when he didn't see anything. Then he realized that it was from his phone, which meant it was an email that had been sent directly to his personal account, not the one at Interpol.

He pulled out his phone and opened the email app, then couldn't help but smile when he read who the sender was.

The Faction.

He began to read the email, his eyes widening and his mouth beginning to water.

>> *You have been tapped.*

>> *Our interests in America and Geneva seem to have aligned. There will be a meeting in London, one which Interpol would be justified in attending. Details to come, but expect further clarification no later than 6 PM this evening.*

The sender's email address had been obfuscated using rerouting and IP masking, and, as always, there was no byline.

The Faction was a secretive organization, and for good reason. It was part of the appeal, part of the reason he had joined their ranks and sworn loyalty to them. He had wanted something more than what Interpol was offering, and when The Faction had begun to express interest in his expertise and experience, he had jumped at the chance.

While Galbraith thought the interests of The Faction pure, he knew many would take issue over their *methods*. It didn't matter — officially, The Faction did not exist. According to Interpol intelligence, it was a myth — a pipe dream cooked up by some of the more eccentric terrorists they had interrogated. Most gave up only a little information — a source, a mention of an attack somewhere in the world, whispers of a group intent on enacting a New World Order around the globe — but most Interpol agents and staffers denied any veracity to these claims. Nothing substantial had ever surfaced that proved The Faction's existence.

Galbraith knew the truth, however: The Faction was real, as he was an active member.

CHAPTER 31
RAOUL

9:21 AM | **March 10, 2021**

Campo de' Fiori, Rome, Italy

Raoul checked the canister inserted onto the base of his home-made flamethrower as he stepped into the square. The weapon was heavier than he remembered, and he wore it awkwardly. He had not quite gotten comfortable with the feel of it slung over his shoulder. He looked left and right, double checking that no one had yet noticed that a flamethrower-wielding young man had just walked into a public area in downtown Rome.

The piazza was called Campo de' Fiori, and he had dined here a handful of times while attending university at the *Accademia Nazionale di Santa Cecilia.*

In the center of the rectangular square, standing in his permanent pose of defiance facing the Vatican, was the statue of Giordano Bruno, a philosopher and astronomer who was burnt at the stake for heresy in 1600.

A poetic end for a heretic, Raoul thought. *Much like the poetic end for the heretics here today.*

It was a bustling square today, with many tourists and locals colliding in a frenzy of activity — the people buying fresh food for tomorrow's meals at the outdoor produce stands, the out-of-town shoppers looking for the perfect souvenir, and business owners conversing with one another outside their shops. To his left, the café on the corner was serving espresso the way it had always been served, before the American version of frozen, blended coffee-esque beverages had blown up and changed the world of drinks.

He smirked at the patrons sitting in their chairs, sipping their lattes and reading the paper. *Sheep,* he thought. *All trained to think what the people in power want them to think.*

He was here to change that. He was here to make a point. Not for these people — they were already gone — but for those who would watch the events about to take place here over and over again on one of the myriad streaming sites or news channels around the globe. It would be aired constantly for the next 24 hours — maybe 48 if they got lucky and nothing else terribly noteworthy happened around the world for the next couple of days — and he could almost hear the newscaster's voice: *the video you are about to watch may be disturbing...*

Of course, the stations would show the video anyway, as it would make them a lot of money. People wanted to see the destruction, wanted to feel the visceral reaction to terror, and the companies that owned the news stations would serve it to them in heaps, piling it on well after they had been fed.

He knew how it worked. The power structure required money. They required a lot of it, and they had built a world that had trained everyone to believe that money was the most important economic structure.

He had studied economics in college, even gotten a degree in it. He was smart, more than capable of holding a job and becoming a career economist. Sitting behind a desk all day, researching and writing papers that would be published in economic journals that a dozen people would read...

But he had never wanted any of that. No, Raoul was interested in more. That's why he had joined The Faction. That's why he had worked his way into an interview, proving that he had the intellectual prowess of the best and brightest.

He was not just some dumb revolutionary — not just some flat, one-sided radical.

He wasn't interested in terrorism, but in what it promised: a better world. A world not governed by money, but by power. Even better, power that had been *earned*. Deserved.

A meritocracy.

Raoul took another step into the square and heard a scream. It had come from the café to his left. Apparently, an old woman there was not interested enough in the daily paper she had in her hands, and couldn't keep her head down. She had seen him, seen the weapon slung nonchalantly over his shoulder.

He made a *tsk* sound with his mouth but continued walking, ignoring her screams and shouts as others tried to see what was bothering her. He knew his destination. He needed to be at least ten more steps into the middle of the square, where he would join forces with the three other young men who had been sent by The Faction.

He had only been given a snippet of the mission — that was The Faction's *modus operandi*. Afterward, long after the dust had settled here, he might be allowed to understand more of their grand plan. But right now, it didn't matter — he trusted The Faction, knew that his goals and their goals were aligned.

As smart as he was, Raoul had no problem playing the role of foot soldier for a bit. Building and wielding a gun was not his desired career path. But he didn't mind doing it. He knew it would eventually lead to a far better world than the one they were all sharing now, and he knew he wouldn't have to do it forever. He knew that The Faction required proof of one's loyalty before advancement. It required proof of his trust.

The scream was joined by another, and then another, now coming from both sides of him. His heart quickened, and he wondered if there were any police officers nearby. The Rome police were ubiquitous in most piazzas, a well-governed and organized force, and he knew that if one officer was nearby, there were bound to be two or three.

He couldn't see anything indicative of police in the near vicinity, so he continued on, marching forward like the soldier he was.

Raoul's heart continued to speed up, even as people began to stand up and point in their direction. He locked eyes with the man directly across the square from him. Another Faction soldier, a man whose name he was not able to remember. To his left was John. To his right, William. No last names — The Faction kept their lower-ranking soldiers to a single first name, as declaring a surname meant declaring a lack of loyalty to the organization. He had shed his previous life — as well as his family ties and name — upon swearing loyalty to the group.

That had been a year ago, and he had been preparing and training for this moment ever since.

He wondered when it would begin. He wondered when he would get the signal.

It came a second later. A thick cloud of haze enveloped the area just past The Faction member standing directly across from him. He whipped his eyes to the left and right and saw that John and William had their backs to a similar cloud as well, and he knew then that all four sides of the piazza were covered, leaving the center area — the area he and the three other Faction men were — open.

He knew that it had begun.

The haze — particles of a powdered, aerosolized acid — were spreading out from their sources, nine strategically placed devices that had been scheduled to erupt simultaneously, at this exact moment.

He did not know what the acid was going to do, nor did he know if it would reach him here, intending to envelop him as well, but none of that mattered. He had his mission parameters and he intended to obey them.

The screams grew louder, but he sensed that they were now no longer focused on him. He heard footsteps — people running in every direction, trying to gather their things or grab their children or simply turn in circles as the world ended around them.

His smirk widened to a full smile, and it was matched by the man's across from him. To his left, John stood stoically, his rifle ready and held diagonally downward, not moving.

They all had the count — it had begun the moment he had seen the haze behind the man across from him.

Thirty seconds.

There were only twenty seconds left now, but he needed to make sure he didn't act too soon. He waited, feeling the tension growing in the piazza as the screams turned into choking gasps and the footfalls slowed, becoming plodding, lumbering steps.

And then, almost at once, it all ended. All of the sounds ceased, all of the footsteps stopped.

He knew it was time. He had no idea what he was going to see when he turned around. In his peripheral vision, he thought he saw a few people standing nearby, perhaps a family.

He turned and caught sight of the family first — the horrified looks on their faces. A father, two children, one almost a foot taller than the other. All staring directly at him.

Frozen. Unmoving. He frowned as his mind tried to parse through it, to understand what it was seeing.

He saw the old lady who must have been the screamer, the one who had spotted him as he originally walked into the square. She was also frozen, her hands locked over her mouth.

Are these people already dead?

CHAPTER 32

RAOUL

9:23 AM | March 10, 2021

Campo de' Fiori, Rome, Italy

He noticed the low-pitched sound of ignited diesel fuel lancing outward from behind him, so he lifted his own weapon and pulled the trigger. It felt strange, unnatural. He had tested and practiced his aim at a gun range a few times before the mission, but that was nothing like the real thing. Aiming at another human was nothing like aiming at an inanimate target.

And yet it wasn't entirely *unlike* shooting at stationary targets. He had expected these people to fall once hit, to collapse into themselves after being shot.

Instead, everyone he aimed for seemed to stutter a bit after impact, yet remained where they were, in place, fixed in their frozen positions, their bodies igniting, but not moving. As if they had been filled with glue and hardened.

What is happening? He was confused, but he did not let it get in the way of his job. He needed to prove to The Faction that he was serious about increasing his responsibility and role within the organization. First, however, he needed to prove his *worth* to them.

He emptied the canister, then slapped in the second one and

continued firing. He aimed for the older woman who had been screaming; he aimed for a barista who was frozen in place, leaning out over a table, the coffee in her hand still steaming upward, not bound by whatever strange ailment had frozen the young lady. The flames were already consuming the shop behind her, the fire and cloud of black smoke growing by the second.

As he emptied the second canister and reached the end of his ammunition store, he sensed that the others were nearing completion as well. John's weapon had stopped firing a few seconds prior, and William's just after Raoul's. The man across from him standing back-to-back with Raoul on the other side of the statue was still firing, and continued bursts of jetted flames for another few seconds.

When he stopped, Raoul knew it was over.

He had done his job. *They* had done their job.

He had finished his task, and he would be rewarded adequately. Perhaps not an increase in rank — The Faction didn't just toss out things like that like it was some outdated military — but certainly would receive an increase in recognition, perhaps even an increase in respect to the more senior members.

Raoul felt a surge of optimism within him, knowing he would be looked upon favorably for completing his mission without a hitch. To his knowledge, no one had been in his field of vision who would remain standing at the end of it.

He waited the necessary thirty seconds. As he did, he checked his weapon again, knowing that it was empty. He saw the flames licking at the corner of the building; would it cover his exit? Was he supposed to be trapped in here with the others?

Raoul also heard sirens in the distance, gently at first but growing louder by the second.

He wondered why they had been told to wait, wondered why they couldn't just begin to run and get back to their vehicles and back to their hotels. But he had known better than to ask questions.

When the countdown timer in his mind reached zero once again, his question was answered.

Slowly, one at a time around the square, the people he had fired into began to fall. A man stumbled backward and fell in a flaming heap, the woman seated at the table next to him collapsing forward into her cup of coffee. There were slight gasps and a couple of screams he could hear above the roar of the flames from around the piazza, but Raoul didn't turn his attention from the field-of-view directly in front of him.

The heat reached him. He wanted to leave, to get out and safe from the fires, tearing through the buildings and people in the piazza.

The barista fell forward, banging her head against the table as she collapsed toward the ground, dead. His smile disappeared and he felt the weight of what he had just done. He did not regret it — this was a necessary step in The Faction's plan — but for the first time, he felt the reality of what had just happened.

He and the three other Faction men had accomplished this together. He and the three others had just set in motion the next phase of The Faction's goal.

Charred bodies fell all around him as he moved toward the street. He walked toward the opening in the piazza, the same way he had entered. His car was parked only a block away, easily within walking distance. He sped up anyway, starting to jog and then breaking into a full run. He suddenly felt heavier, wanting to shed the weight of the flamethrower, to toss it aside and forget everything he had just done.

But he couldn't. He pressed on, reaching the vehicle in another fifteen seconds.

His next destination was the last one for the day: a hotel, many miles away. He would be led out of the city by the map on his phone and sent to the place that had been prearranged by The Faction. There, he would get a good nights sleep and wake up to a new day.

A new day in a new world.

He smiled at the repercussions he knew were coming. He smiled wider knowing that he had taken a part in it.

CHAPTER 33
BEN

6:27 PM | **March 10, 2021**
Kent, England

Ben had made it just in time. He had disembarked at London-Heathrow International Airport after the grueling eighteen hours of flight time, caught a rideshare, and told the driver he had a meeting he could not be late for. Price, therefore, was not an issue.

The driver simply laughed and reminded Ben that in the age of modern tech and ride-sharing apps, there was no such thing as price-hiking and getting somewhere faster for a higher cost.

Ben nodded silently and then handed the man a fifty dollar bill. It wouldn't be worth as much when converted to British pounds, but the driver got the hint, stopped talking, and pressed his foot to the floor.

He stepped out of the car just as a light rain began to pour. He looked up and down the quiet street, wondering what it was Baden Tennyson was hiding behind one of these walls. The street was cobblestone, but well-kept, giving the place a maintained old-London look. The streetlights were LED lamps that hearkened back to the 1800s, and the houses themselves seemed to have been pulled straight from a Dickens novel.

He smelled the air, finding it a bit briny and heavy, as if he were standing on a Liverpool pier instead of a neighborhood just outside of greater London, miles from the ocean.

He took a few steps forward, crossing the street, then stopped. He glanced at his phone and double-checked the address. *Is this right?*

The house Tennyson had sent Ben to was massive. The street view image Julie had pulled up during the flight had only showed a three-level black manor, skinny and tall, but the satellite imagery showed that the house, while sharing space with neighboring other homes to its left and right, actually backed up to a large space that had other buildings, houses, and barns on the grounds. All of the land was owned by the owner of this same house.

He wondered if Tennyson owned it. It was impossible to find anything online, at least without digging deeper, and during the plane ride the CSO team had mostly taken the time to gather their thoughts, plan their next steps, and sleep.

Julie and Sarah were back at the hotel in southeast London, researching and trying to dig up any information about Tennyson, his company EKG, or anything related. They hoped to find another link between the man who had called them here and Eliza Earnhardt, but it seemed that after the events in Switzerland, Eliza had gone quiet.

Reggie and Freddie were on their own mission tonight. Ben had sent them to London to try and dig up any leads on finding weapons and ammunition. They had taken the first and only commercial flights available that would get them all the way to London in time, so they'd had to suffer through TSA and baggage claim stations and couldn't afford to waste time, meaning they'd decided to leave their own weaponry — what little of it hadn't been destroyed in the fire — back at the hotel in Anchorage.

None of them felt safe without at least sidearms, and Reggie had some contacts in London, so they had set out directly from the airport.

Ben had decided to go it alone. If Tennyson still wanted him dead, he would have found a way to do it from afar, just as he'd sent the truck with explosives. He had obviously survived, so Tennyson must want to speak with him in person. That meant Ben was most likely not in immediate danger.

And if it meant they could save Eliza, Ben would do his part and come alone, as Tennyson had requested.

He continued across the street and found himself on the narrow path that led up two sets of short stairs to the massive front door. He paused there, then knocked.

A car, black, passed by the house slowly. He turned to look at it, but its windows were tinted too deeply. He knocked again.

Still no answer.

He waited there for another minute, knocked a third time, then looked around. *Weird*, he thought. *Is Tennyson playing with me? Why would he send me —*

"Afternoon," he heard a voice call out.

He turned fully around, then squinted into the rain to see who had spoken. A man, dressed in a long overcoat, hands in pockets. He was wearing a cabbie hat, the short bill stapled to the front side of the baggy top.

"Hey," Ben said. "You know if anyone's home?"

The man sucked his teeth for a long moment, then answered. "I suppose not. You have a meeting?"

Ben nodded, then looked down at his phone. "Yeah... I think this is the address."

"May I ask what this meeting is in regard to?"

Ben almost couldn't understand him between his southern English accent and the pattering rain, and the fact that he had lowered his voice a bit.

"No," Ben said. "Not really. May I ask who you are?"

The man smirked, then repeated Ben's answer. "No. Not really."

Ben nodded, then brought a hand over his hair and left it on the back of his neck. He put the phone back into his pocket, then pulled it out again. *Guess that's it,* he thought. *Tennyson, what game are you playing?* He opened the ride-sharing app once again and started to call for a driver. He wondered if his previous driver would return.

The man stepped up the path and began to approach the house. He walked until he was within ten feet of the front door then looked up at Ben. "May I help you with something, sir?" the man asked.

"I — I don't think so," Ben answered. "You live here?"

The man shook his head. "No, but I'm watching the house."

Ben looked behind him, tried to see where he had come from. As he did, the man sidled over into his view.

"Officer Peter Galbraith," he said.

"*Officer*?"

"Correct. Interpol, homicide specialist." He reached down and pulled out a badge. "Mind if I get that name from you, son?"

Ben's nostrils flared, his fight or flight instinct kicking in. Trouble was, he wasn't sure if either instinct would be useful right now. *Stay calm,* he thought. *You haven't done anything wrong.*

"Look," Ben began, "I'm just supposed to meet someone. I probably have the wrong —"

Officer Galbraith held up a hand. "Please, let's just start with the name, okay?"

CHAPTER 34

FREDDIE

6:59 PM | March 10, 2021
Kent, England

"You gave him your name?" Reggie asked. "Ben, come on — you told him?"

Freddie watched the exchange between the two friends with an amused confusion. He wasn't sure if these two were *actually* friends and just pretending to hate each other, or if in the last few days somehow their relationship had soured. Either way, Ben and Reggie seemed to be at each other's throat constantly.

It was an interesting power dynamic, and Freddie wondered if he'd made a mistake in wanting to join their group.

Sarah was still with Julie, working on research in the next room over. They had all met back at the hotel for late dinner, but they hadn't even had the chance to get to the restaurant yet. Right now the three of them were standing in Ben's hotel room, ostensibly to get an update on Ben's meeting at the woman's house.

"What?" Ben asked. "Was I supposed to just let him arrest me?"

Reggie's eyes looked like they were about to pop out of their sockets. "Ben, he said he was Interpol — why'd you stick around?"

"He had a badge," Ben answered.

"Christ, Ben, *I* can get a badge from any costume shop between here and Manchester. Do you even know what an Interpol badge is *supposed* to look like?"

"Look, man," Ben said, posturing and bringing his shoulders square. "He was Interpol, okay? Just get off it."

Freddie was a confident warrior, well-trained and capable enough to hold his own in a fistfight. But if things went to blows and he had to be called on to break up a fight between the two men standing in front of him, he wasn't entirely sure he could do it.

He stood up anyway, crossed the room, and took a place just by their side. "Look, guys, let's just —"

"No, Freddie," Reggie said, interjecting. "We ain't forgetting *anything*. Got it? We're in a pickle because Ben here —"

"You're *blaming* me for this mess?" Ben shouted. "You're claiming this is *my* fault?"

Reggie crossed his arms over his chest. "Tell me you weren't the one who pissed off old man Tennyson. Tell me you weren't the one who went to Switzerland to save the red-headed damsel in distress."

"You ass—"

"Enough!" Freddie said. "Cool your jets, both of you. I ain't here for a cage fight, and if I was I'd better be the one in the cage. So knock it off unless you want me to join in."

Ben and Reggie took a slight step backward, but Freddie could sense the tension in the room. Reggie's hackles were raised, Ben's fists clenched. The men were at each other's throats, and Freddie wasn't sure what to do.

To try his best to keep the peace, he spoke. "Whatever pickle you think we're in, we're still in one piece," he said. "And I hope to keep it that way. I didn't ask for a discharge just so I can get blown to smithereens in some other country."

"But Ben —"

"Ben *nothing*, man," Freddie said. "Just drop it. You guys need to figure out what to do *next*, not what's already happened."

"He's right," Ben said. "That guy knows my name. So what? It's not like he thinks I'm a suspect for anything. I'm more interested in why Tennyson called me out there. Like, what was the point of flying halfway around the world just to get stood up on a doorstep?"

Reggie was still stewing, but he was calm enough to answer. "I don't know. Maybe the girls will figure something out. Anything else from Tennyson?"

Ben shook his head, but pulled his phone out to check. Just then, Freddie heard shuffling at the door. There were three quick knocks, and then Julie's voice. "Guys?" she asked. "You in there?"

The door opened, and Julie and Sarah were standing in the hallway.

"What's up?" Freddie asked. "Hungry?"

"Yeah," Julie answered, "but that's not why we're here. Glad you haven't killed each other yet, though."

She smirked at Freddie, then shook her head as she passed between Ben and Reggie. They both seemed to deflate a bit as the women entered the room. Julie took up a spot near the desk, where Freddie's laptop was.

"Mind if I use this?" Julie asked. "I'm getting tired of staring at a phone screen."

Freddie nodded. "Sure thing. You find something?"

"Unfortunately, yes. While we were on the plane, there was a terrorist attack in Rome."

"Shit."

"Yeah. About fifty dead so far, with another fifty in the hospital."

"Do they know who did it?" Ben asked.

"Not yet, but they expect someone will come forward and take credit soon enough."

"Right," Freddie added, looking around at the others. "Thanks for filling us in."

Julie wasn't done yet, however. "That's... not actually what we found."

Freddie watched Ben's eyebrows dance up on his forehead. "No?" he asked.

"No," she said. "We were searching the address, trying to figure out who it was you were supposed to meet with, Ben."

"Yeah."

"Well, turns out the address of the house was pointing to the owner of the place, and that search was coming up empty. But the *owner* of the house isn't actually the person *living* in the house."

Ben walked over to her. "Really?"

"I think you mean *was* living in the house..." Sarah said.

"Yeah," Julie answered. "Apparently the owner is some dead guy, but he's passed it down to different family members over the years. The current owner is — *was*, I mean — a young woman named Josephine Campbell."

Ben squeezed his eyes shut. "She's dead, isn't she?"

Julie nodded. "Brutal, too. Laceration through the back of the neck, severing the spinal cord and carotid artery. Pretty quick way to go, I guess."

"Wow," Reggie said. "That is brutal. Why?"

"No idea," Julie said. "But Sarah and I have a hunch."

"Do tell," Ben said. "I'm completely ready for more bad news."

"Well, seems like she was on a trip to a place called Hever Castle, where there was an antiquities auction. She came into town to buy a gift for her husband."

Sarah jumped in. "We saw an article about her. She was found dead in her home yesterday — the *same* home you just went to and knocked on the door."

Freddie's eyes fell. *Crap, that can't be good.*

"That's... not ideal," Ben said.

"Not at all. But get this," Sarah continued. "She was at the auction to buy a very *specific* gift for her husband. See, Mrs. Campbell, through her father's side, is related to Napoleon."

"Like... *the* Napoleon?"

"One and the same," Sarah said. "And this specific gift she was trying to buy was actually something Napoleon owned. A sword, made specially for him by a Parisian smith."

"A sword..." Ben muttered. "What happened to it?"

Freddie listened, silently asking the same questions Ben and Reggie were asking. He wondered if they were also *answering* those same questions silently, as he was.

"Well," Julie said. "It *was* purchased by Mrs. Campbell, under the pseudonym Ms. Delacruz. It was boxed up and sent to her home, and then... it disappeared."

"Shit," Reggie said. "Let me guess — did it accidentally kill her, too?"

Julie nodded. "She was murdered. By a sword. The killer and the sword are missing."

"Well, the *killer's* missing," Ben said. "But I have a feeling the sword is the exact same one we saw in Eliza's video."

"Yeah," Reggie said. "The sword of Napoleon, sitting up there above her head. About to do to her exactly what it did to this other woman."

"So if we don't get to her in time, she's dead."

Ben sat down on the bed, his head in his hands. "And we have to head there soon, since Interpol is now after *us*."

Freddie watched as Julie and Sarah exchanged a glance. Julie walked over to Ben and looked down at her husband.

"Wait, *what*?"

CHAPTER 35

BEN

7:13 PM | **March 10, 2021**
Kent, England

Ben had nothing else to do but eat. He wasn't hungry, however. They were all jet-lagged from the time change after the long flights, and while they had gotten sleep and eaten in the airport and aboard the transcontinental flight, his body was still confused about exactly what he should be hungry for at the moment. The others had left to find food, and, as usual, they had decided to simply eat downstairs at the attached hotel bar and grill. It was a fish-and-chips sort of place, perfect for a simple, filling bite.

But Ben's mind was elsewhere. He was struggling with Mrs. E's death, playing back the scene in his mind in slow motion, trying to understand it. Could he have done more? Could he have saved her?

And, inevitably, the answer was always *yes*. There was always *something* he could have done: if only Reggie hadn't been arguing with him, and they had been able to get to bed, or at least get back to their own spaces in the building and cabin, Reggie or Sarah could have pulled Mrs. E out with them.

Or perhaps if Freddie was just a bit earlier, he could have seen the truck long before it was nearly on the house.

Or...

Ben pushed the thoughts away — there was nothing good to come from thoughts such as these, and he knew it. *Still...*

He thought of the flight over, how they had promised each other they would take time to process things and get their feelings out about Mrs. E's loss, and then reach out to Mr. E and try to get his take on everything. None of that had happened, of course. Instead, they had been consumed with the idea of taking on Tennyson, the man they all blamed for her death. They had decided to sleep, to try to get ahead of the jet lag that would be setting in tonight.

Then he thought of the Interpol officer, Officer Galbraith, the man who had accosted Ben at the address Tennyson had given him. Was Tennyson trying to get Ben in trouble? He had already sent a man with a truckload of explosives to his home to kill him, why stop there?

Ben felt stupid for giving the Interpol agent his name, but there had been no other reasonable play. There was nothing he could have done — the agent would only have followed him, suspecting him of foul play?

But what now? Surely the man was curious about why Ben was desperately trying to meet with someone at the house just hours after the person living inside had been murdered? And then he *had* given him his name, so the officer had something to use to track him down if they had more questions.

He shook his head quickly, trying to push all the thoughts away. *Not now,* he told himself. *Not here.*

He stood up and decided to go downstairs, where a beer and some fries might just help take the edge off a bit. His friends were there, too, and while he and Reggie seemed to be going through something, he knew they were ultimately on the same team.

As he made his way across the floor, his phone vibrated. Thinking it was Julie or Reggie checking on him, he pulled it up to his ear without looking at it.

"I'm on my way down," he said.

"Ben?" came the reply.

Ben frowned. It sounded like Mr. E, but the man had never used nicknames, always referring to them as either Harvey, Juliette, or Gareth.

"Mr. E?"

"Yes. Have I — have I caught you an inopportune time?"

He looked at his watch. He wasn't busy, but he couldn't remember what time it was back in the states. *Still morning, I think.* He couldn't remember — it must have been either very late or very early for the man. But as he thought about it, he realized he couldn't be sure Mr. E even *was* in the United States. They had always just assumed it, but now that Ben thought about it he couldn't remember the man ever telling them his actual location.

"No," Ben said. "I was just about to grab a bite to eat with the others."

"Perfect," the man said. *"Listen, Ben. I have been thinking quite a bit about the events of two days ago."*

"Of course. I'm sorry, again."

"Well, that is why I am calling now. I want you to do something for me."

Ben was sure it was Mr. E's voice, but it sounded nothing like the cold, calculating businessman that had set up the CSO long ago.

"What's that, Mr. E?"

"Something I am afraid the others will find outside the purview of what the CSO has been established to accomplish."

"Okay..."

"Something that needs to be done, but must be done with care. I need you to be subtle, Ben, and..."

Ben reached the elevator and stopped. He didn't want the call to drop before he had a chance to hear the man out. Whatever it was, it had him slipping. Whatever he needed, it was important enough to

Mr. E that it had caused him to lose his normally tight-lipped professionalism.

"Go on," Ben said. "I'm still here."

He heard Mr. E clear his throat, and then — something he never thought was possible — it sounded as though Mr. E's voice broke. *"She — she was my wife, Ben."*

Ben felt tears immediately welling in his eyes. He nodded, but didn't say anything.

"She didn't deserve it. To die, not like that. We had — well, she had always talked about a 'regal death,' whatever that means. She wanted to die fighting. In a different way I am doing, but... you get the point?"

Ben nodded again. "Yes, I mean — wait, are you saying you're dying?"

"Ben, we are all dying. That is all I meant."

"Right."

"Ben, what I need you to do. This is not a CSO task. Nor is it something I could ever ask of anyone but you. I trust you, Ben, and I know you will not take this lightly."

"Anything, Mr. E. I owe you at least that much. You have my word. Say it, and it's done."

There was a long pause, and Ben stared at the elevator as it dinged, opened, then a family got off and navigated around him.

"Ben, they took my wife. Whoever was behind this — it was a calculated attack. On you and your team, but on me as well. Now, all I care about is one thing."

Ben felt his blood cool. He had never thought he would hear this from Mr. E.

"I need you to find them. And then I need you to kill them."

CHAPTER 36

BEN

7:22 PM | **March 10, 2021**
Kent, England

Ben found the others around the table, drinks already in hand. Sarah had a soda, and Julie a tea, but Reggie and Freddie had a bottle of beer in front of them, condensation beginning to drip from their necks. Ben sat down across from Reggie and waived over the waiter. He ordered another beer, and asked for a menu.

"Everything okay?" Julie asked, as Ben sat down and tried to get comfortable.

"Yeah," he said. He didn't know if he should tell the others about his call with Mr. E, nor did he want to bring up his own insecurities and demons he was struggling with — he needed a break from heavy conversation and the emotional weight of the last couple of days. He also knew that they each had their own problems to work through, that they were each dealing with different versions of the same thing: a member of their team was gone, and they still weren't any closer to finding the person responsible.

If Tennyson were out there, Ben was going to get to him. The trouble was, he had no idea where to start. And he had been tasked this by Mr. E, who wanted to keep it from the rest of the team.

"Just needed a little bit of alone time?" Reggie asked.

He could hear the mocking tone in the man's voice, but Ben ignored it. He shrugged. "Just trying to work through it all, I guess."

There was a television on in the background tuned to one of the twenty-four hour-a-day news channels. Onscreen, sweeping shots of ambulance-riddled Campo de' Fiori were interspersed by a newscaster in a studio reading from a script. They wore a concerned expression, and in a callout box above their head was a graphic with the provocative label *A New Player in the Terrorism Game?*

He watched it for a few seconds, noticing that the death count was at sixty-four but still climbing. Police suspected four separate shooters, but there was something suspicious about the attack. Ben couldn't hear the reporter's voice, but someone near the television suddenly turned up the feed.

Two other faces joined the reporter in the shot. These two experts were claiming that the terror attack was unlike anything they had seen before. As they spoke, their voices barking out from the television's tinny speakers, the others at Ben's table listened in.

The man on the reporter's left was explaining something. *"Besides the fact that they were using* flamethrowers *for some sick reason, usually when a terrorist or shooter begins shooting, the victims around them typically have one of two reactions: they either* run *or they* collapse, *too scared to move."*

"But what are we seeing in this particular attack?" the reporter asked.

The woman on the reporter's right side spoke up. *"Well, we have no evidence that anyone was running away when they were hit by the flames. Only a few of the victims in the piazza seem to have had their backs to the attackers, but they don't seem to have been* running *from them."*

"Very interesting," the reporter affirmed. *"This confirms early reports from survivors that everyone in the square was 'frozen in place.'"*

"But how is that possible?" the first expert asked. *"How can everyone be stunned into submission?"*

"It doesn't make sense," the other expert said. *"I understand a few people, but* all *of them? No one tried to run away?"*

Before he could hear the reporter's response, the waiter returned with Ben's drink and a menu, and Julie began her own barrage of questions.

Ben shuddered. *Sick and twisted, is what that is.*

"Why was Interpol at the house, Ben? Why not the local police? And what did the Interpol guy want with you?"

"I don't know, I don't know, and I have no idea," Ben said, answering all the questions at once. "He walked up on me while I was at the door. There was no way to know it was a freaking crime scene, but I'm sure the local police and detectives were crawling around all day and will be back tomorrow."

"What did he say?" Sarah asked.

"Nothing, really. He didn't tell me anything about the crime, or anything about who was living there. He seemed suspicious of me, but he obviously didn't arrest me."

"That doesn't mean he won't," Reggie said under his breath.

Ben finally snapped. "You got a problem with me? Seriously, Reggie, none of this shit was my fault. None of what happened in the past few days —"

"Nothing was your fault?" Reggie said, raising his voice and smacking his hands down on the table, causing Sarah to jump. *"You* went to Switzerland. *You* found Eliza, helped her out. That was not a CSO mission. That was a *you* mission."

"I ran intelligence on that mission," Julie said suddenly. "And Mr. E signed off on it before anyone left the state. That's enough for me for it to be a CSO mission."

Sarah had her hand on Reggie's bicep in an effort to calm him down. "Reggie, let's just relax. There's no reason —"

"What? No reason to argue? No reason to have a discussion about this?"

"Doesn't sound like much of a discussion, man," Ben said.

"You know what your problem is, Ben? You're so damned scared you'll make the wrong call, you don't *make* the call. You sit around and worry until it's too late. I'm just saying that Ben *did* get us in this mess with Tennyson. The guy's already tried to kill us once. What makes you think he's not going to do it again? I mean, he's *already* doing it again. The explosion? Mrs. E?"

No one said anything for a moment. Ben was about to try to change the subject when the waiter came and took their orders for food. He felt his stomach lurch again, the hunger now taking center stage, and he vowed to fill it thoroughly.

After another minute, Freddie spoke. "'Cause we'd already be dead." They all looked to the newest member of their team. He nodded. "Yeah, think about it — we'd already be dead, wouldn't we? If Tennyson wanted to kill us, why would he try to blow us up, *then* invite us all the way out here?"

"He didn't invite *us*," Reggie said. "He invited Ben. We're all just waiting around to be collateral damage in whatever the *next* explosion is going to be."

"Knock it off, man," Ben said.

"What? You said it yourself — you don't give orders. You might be the leader of this team, but that doesn't make you —"

"Boys," Julie said, her voice terse. "Seriously? You're acting like teenagers."

"And Freddie has a point," Sarah said. Ben took a sip of his beer, the delicious texture almost making things right. He felt it nourishing him as soon as it touched his lips. It was ice cold, a local craft option he had never had before.

"All I'm saying is that it seems strange he would send a truck to explode and take us all out, and *then* invite you here to London."

"But he wasn't even there," Reggie said. "For all we know, Tennyson is just sending us all over the world to mess with us."

"Still," Ben said, pulling the beer bottle back away from his lips. "Freddie does have a point about the explosion being nonsurgical. It's messy, meant to cause as much damage and destruction — and death — as possible. Why would Tennyson do that, and then call me over here without even mentioning it?"

He noticed his phone sitting in front of him on the table light up. He had gotten another email. He had a feeling it was going to be something more important than spam or just an update from his fantasy football news site. Lately, the only news they had been getting was bad news.

Ben considered putting it in his pocket and just checking it later, but he noticed that Julie and Sarah had seen his screen light up as well. Neither woman said anything, but Ben knew they were wondering the same thing: *what is it now*?

"Okay," Reggie said, taking a drink of his own beer. "So what are you saying, Bennett? That it wasn't Tennyson who sent the bomber?"

Sarah turned and addressed Ben. "Ben, when you were in Switzerland, you saw Tennyson's granddaughter?"

"Yes," Ben said, nodding. "She was the younger sister of Lars Tennyson, the man who was leading the research team of the subsidiary of EKG in Grindelwald. The girl was basically on life support, but Lars thought he could keep her alive and eventually cure her."

Sarah shuttered in her chair. "That's sick. She was just a kid."

Ben remembered the scene: the tiny, frail girl, no older than a teenager, lying in the bedroom inside the laboratory. The entire space had been converted to look exactly like the girl's childhood home, down to the last detail. When he and Eliza had found her they had been stunned and shocked, but it had also led them to the final piece of the puzzle, and eventually to their success in Switzerland.

However, it had been the sort of success that brought with it the feeling of defeat. The sort of victory that sometimes felt worse than a loss. His mind churned up the memory of the face of the scientist as the apes had gotten to him...

"Tennyson is still pissed about what we did to his grandson Lars," Ben said. "He's taking revenge."

"We don't know that for sure," Julie said. "He could be —"

"No, Ben's right," Reggie said. "Tennyson said so in that article he found. Remember? He'll go to the ends of the earth to wipe us off the face of it. And he's got the resources to do it."

"So we are running from a ghost. A man who won't even show his face?"

CHAPTER 37

BEN

7:28 PM | **March 10, 2021**
Kent, England

The waiter returned with the food — steaming piles of calamari, deep-fried and golden brown, with a red ring of marinara sauce in the center of the plate. Three orders of fish and chips went around the table, Sarah's and Ben's eyes wide as they saw the size of the portions. Freddie, who had ordered the third, didn't seem at all fazed by the portion size. The waiter left after placing Reggie's and Julie's salads in front of them.

As everyone began to eat, Ben looked down at his phone once again. He opened it and found the email that had come in he clicked through and saw the first line, the subject line and sender.

His heart skipped a beat.

"What is it?" Julie asked.

"It's from Tennyson again," Ben said.

"What? Really? Read it."

Ben nodded, grabbing a piece of calamari and popping it into his mouth. He chewed, then leaned over the table and began to read the message. "It has a weird subject line," Ben began. *"The thieves are in Paris...'"*

"That's as cryptic as his first email," Sarah said. "But go on. What's the actual email say?"

"*Truly! It seems you got my message. Alas, thank you for attending to my request in such a Timely fashion; let it be true that, Indeed, we will work well together.*'"

"We will work well together?" Reggie asked. "What the hell is that supposed to mean? And why is it written so... weirdly?"

Ben shrugged and shook his head, but continued to read. "'*On that note, hear this: I have a job for you. This is related to the work you already do. There is a particular sword that wants To find its way into my collection.*'"

"A *sword*?"

"Like the one hanging above Eliza's head as we speak," Ben muttered. He suddenly felt guilty, suddenly felt like they should not have stopped to eat or rest, that they should have pushed forward and tried to find her before it was too late. But how were they supposed to do that? How would they find one individual in one specific room somewhere in the world? They simply had no clues, no leads.

He hated to admit it, but he was completely at the mercy of Tennyson.

"Keep going," Julie said. "We need to hear this."

Ben scrolled down. "There's a pretty big gap between that top section and this next one, but it's written differently. More normal, I guess. '*This sword is an exact copy of the one hanging above your friend's head.*'" Ben's mouth suddenly felt dry, but he ignored it and kept going. "'*I would very much like to have it, as well. Since you have already seen how serious I am, I know you will not take this lightly. Consider it an exchange of gifts: the sword for Eliza.*

"'*All of the clues you need are in the content of this email.*'"

"Clues?" Julie asked. "He wants us to go on a scavenger hunt?"

Ben shrugged. "Yeah, that's what it says. Verbatim."

"The sword... for Eliza?" Reggie asked, scoffing. "That's absurd.

He expects us to find a sword for him? And then just hand it over? There's no way he's going to let Eliza go. She's as good as dead."

"She's *not* dead," Julie said. "She's alive, and she's out there somewhere. Waiting for us. Tennyson is playing with us, and he's playing a very serious game — but he's not making anything up. If he says there's a sword out there somewhere, then it's something we can actually find."

"You're not really considering this, are you?" Freddie asked. He looked around the table. "I mean, like, we don't just *do* that, right? The CSO is supposed to find these sorts of things and give them to *museums*, not serial killers with a flair for puzzles who hold us ransom."

Everyone turned to look at Freddy, a massive piece of battered and deep-fried cod in his hand. He took a gigantic bite, chewed it, then swallowed. "What?"

"We do what we have to do," Reggie said. "Sometimes there are consequences."

Freddie nodded then looked back down at his basket of fish.

"Is that it?" Julie asked. "The email. Is there more?"

Ben nodded. "Yeah, one more paragraph. '*The job I need your help with is quite similar to the missions you and your team take on. Yours is an admirable little effort, but I find no need for two closely related groups like ours in existence. I have started my own team, so there will no longer be a need for yours. I am hoping that you, Harvey, will consider working with me instead.*'"

Julie let out a laugh. "He can't be serious. He wants you to work with him? For him? He's insane."

"You're right — he's playing a game. But let me finish reading it first. There's one more line." Ben cleared his throat, then looked at the others around the table. "'*I am sending a team to you in order to help persuade you of my intentions.*'"

"That sounds... sinister," Reggie said. "What's that even supposed to mean? How is he going to persuade —"

The glass wall that separated the restaurant from the rest of the hotel lobby behind Ben suddenly exploded inward. Gunshots and glass filled the air and people started to scream and drop to the floor.

CHAPTER 38

BEN

7:35 PM | **March 10, 2021**
Kent, England

In front of him, their waiter dropped an entire tray of food. It hit the ground and fell outward into a million pieces. Ben only then noticed that the waiter had a growing maroon stain on his white shirt. He had a look of shock on his face as he stumbled side to side for a moment. He looked directly at Ben, then fell to the floor.

Ben was already moving. He hit the ground at the same time as the dead young waiter, then crawled under the table. The others were doing the same thing, Reggie and Sarah finding space beneath a booth nearby.

"Reggie!" Ben shouted. "You get those guns you were looking for?"

"I'm picking them up tomorrow."

"Would have been able to make good use of them now, I suspect," Ben said to himself.

He looked around and saw other frantic patrons moving toward booths and tables to hide behind. One woman was screaming loudly about her son, but Ben couldn't see her from here. He didn't know where the shooter was, didn't know if they had entered the restaurant or were still standing in the hotel lobby and firing into it. Either way, Ben knew they needed to get out. In here, their backs were against the wall.

"Just like the day we met," Freddie said to Ben, recalling the event right before their Antarctic trip. Russian gunmen had walked into their hotel lobby and began shooting at them, killing diners and hotel staff in doing so. The CSO team had killed them then, but Ben didn't want to try his luck for a second time.

It didn't seem he would have a choice, however. He looked to the space just beyond the dead waiter's feet and saw a pair of legs step into the restaurant. Military style combat boots, black cargo pants. He didn't need to see the man's upper body to know this was the shooter.

He brought his finger up to his lips and then pointed at the guy. Freddie was already looking that direction, and he nodded. He turned to Ben and whispered, "I'm going to run to the other side of the restaurant, draw his fire that way. When I do, take him down."

Ben watched as Freddie silently counted off numbers with his fingers. When he got to three outstretched fingers, he suddenly bolted to the right and ran, half crouched, heading toward the opposite side of the restaurant. Ben saw the boots turn as the man heard Freddie moving. Ben darted forward, coming up from underneath the table. There was about ten feet of space between him and the gunmen, and he closed it in two seconds.

He stood to his full height, lunged forward the last step, and brought his arms up and around the man just as he was lifting his gun to fire again. Ben pile-drived the man and wrapped him up, both toppling sideways but not to the ground. The man dropped the pistol as he tried to keep his balance, but he crashed backward into the bar and a barstool. Ben released him then, but pulled his arm back and brought it down onto the man's face, crushing his nose. The man didn't react with any audible noise, but he brought his own fist around and smashed it into Ben's back.

Ben let out a gasp of air as the blow to his kidney landed. It felt like the man had hit him with a sledgehammer, and Ben involuntarily doubled over in pain. He heard three more gunshots, two from his left and one from his right, and only then realized that the gun men he had squared off with was not the only one.

He turned around and saw the first man's dropped pistol laying between him and the table he had just been hiding under, and he started toward it. The man behind him spat a wad of blood onto the floor and then grabbed Ben's shirt from behind. Ben felt himself being pulled backwards, but he pressed forward and tried to get away. He felt his shirt rip and with one final tug it came completely apart. He was free.

Ben reached the weapon and grasped it, rolling around and back up onto his feet all in one motion. He felt the throbbing of pain from where the man had punched him, but it was far from a wound. He'd be breathing heavy, but it shouldn't prevent him from fighting back.

The gunman was moving toward Ben, a piece of his shirt still in his hand. Ben snapped off three rounds from the man's own weapon and dropped him to the floor.

He turned just in time to see the second gunman who had entered take another shot at the tables to Ben's left.

It was the table Julie and Sarah were under.

CHAPTER 39

BEN

7:36 PM | **March 10, 2021**

Kent, England

Reggie should have been there as well, and at first Ben didn't know where the man was. He was about to fire when he saw Reggie stand up behind the man, a fire extinguisher lifted over his head. *Damn*, Ben thought. *How'd he get there so fast?*

Not wanting to accidentally miss and hit Reggie, Ben instead pulled the pistol to the right and began to aim for the third gunman. As he did, he noticed that Freddie was already there, racing toward him and aiming to take him to the ground, much like Ben had. The man couldn't see where Freddie was coming from, and was surprised when the massive bear of a man hit him on the side and together they flew through the air and landed on another table.

The woman screaming about her son was behind this table, and it nearly took her out when the two men flew onto it. She was miraculously missed by the corner of the wobbling table as it slid past her, but her screams resumed as soon as she realized she was not dead.

Ben looked over to Julie and Sarah. "Get out! Now!"

Julie and Sarah both stood and ran toward the exit just as Reggie brought the extinguisher down on his target's head. The man froze and then fell to his knees. His mouth moved a bit, but he was silent.

"Let's go! Come on!" Reggie yelled, tossing the fire extinguisher to the side, letting it clatter on the hard tile floor before rolling away behind the bar. Ben started moving toward the exit, hoping Freddie would be okay. He didn't have to wait long — as he got to the door, he saw Freddie running toward him, head up and hunched over like a linebacker.

"Bennett —" Freddie yelled. "We need to kill these guys! We have to take them out and make sure they don't —"

Ben shook his head. "No, we don't have time. And we don't need anyone thinking this was anything but self-defense."

Freddie didn't argue, but Ben did notice a menacing look in Reggie's eye as he passed by.

His heart was pounding, the adrenaline being pumped into his system skyrocketing. He forced a few long breaths, looking at Julie as he did so.

"Everyone okay?" someone called out. Ben looked over and saw the frantic, startled expressions on the faces of three hotel staffers, crouching behind the lobby desk. An older man, wearing a black vest with a manager's tag on it, was looking at Ben. "You blokes okay?"

Ben nodded. "Yeah, thanks. Two of 'em are still alive, but knocked out. If you haven't already called the police, do it."

"Already did," the manager said. "Why did they —"

"No idea," Ben said. "Just some crazies, I guess."

The old man suddenly froze and blinked a few times, as if the shock of it all had just hit him. He turned slowly and walked back toward the desk to check on his employees again.

The screaming woman from inside had finally stopped, but Ben could hear crying and wails of agony from inside. He knew the gunman had shot at least the waiter, but he didn't get a count of how many others were dead or injured. *Innocent lives,* he thought. *Unnecessary waste.*

And the truth was not lost on Ben. Somebody had sent them here to kill him. Tennyson?

"They weren't here to kill you," Reggie said. "You know that, right?"

Ben turned to his friend. "What you talking about?" Ben asked.

"Remember the email, Ben?"

Ben did remember the email, but he hadn't considered that it might be literal.

"Tennyson said he was sending a team to 'persuade you,' Ben. To persuade you to work for him. But he was *also* sending a team to kill *us*. To take out your team and take out your options."

"They were here for you," Ben said softly.

"They were. And they're in there, still alive. Probably waking up right now and wondering where we are. Freddie's right. We need to kill them. We need to make sure it's over."

"It's not going to be over with just them!" Ben shouted. He hadn't meant to raise his voice, but his emotional state was quickly reaching that dangerous and combustible mix of anger, frustration, confusion, and being scared out of his mind. "It's not going to end here, Reggie. Three guys? You think that's all he's got at his disposal? He can send an entire army of hired guns if he wants. He's trying to pick us off one by one, trying to get us scared and frantic and running, until I'm the only one left."

"It's working," Julie said.

"So we need to kill them," Reggie said again. "There's not another option."

"Reggie, think about it," Ben said. "We *can't*. How's it going to look to walk back in there and put a bullet through their heads, in front of all those innocent bystanders who are *also* trying to recover from the trauma they just experienced? The police are going to be here, which means *Interpol* isn't going to be far behind. They're already suspicious of me, so we don't have a choice. We have to leave."

Reggie looked like he was about to say something else but then stopped himself. Ben was grateful for that; he didn't want to argue anymore. He didn't want to fight.

Unfortunately, Tennyson had brought the fight to them, and fighting was exactly what they were going to have to do.

CHAPTER 40
GALBRAITH

7:36 PM **| March 10, 2021**
Chelsea, London, England

"That was all? Is there nothing else you need?" Galbraith silently cursed himself; he had not meant to sound perturbed.

There was a pause, and a crackle as the voice came back on the line. The digitized waveform was being sent through at least a dozen different private networks around the world, and then encrypted, compressed, re-encrypted, and uncompressed, all before being piped back through the phone into his ear, so it was nearly impossible to understand clearly without significant focus.

"Of course there is more," the man from The Faction said. *"There is always more. That is the job, Galbraith."*

Galbraith swallowed, then nodded quickly. He blinked a few times, still not believing his luck. *There is still work to do,* he thought. *Still work for me to do.* He could still prove his usefulness.

He could still prove his worth. The Faction was an organization he had only recently become a member of, but he was already able to serve a purpose.

"Sorry," he said. "Yes, of course. I merely meant to inquire as to whether there is more you need from me. For this mission."

"Overzealousness is the cause of many a downfall, Galbraith."

Galbraith nodded again. *But this is so exciting*, he thought. *This is so much better than my* actual *job.* "Of course, I am at your service."

"You are at the service of The Faction — no more and no less."

There was another pause, and Galbraith wondered if he should speak. Before he could, the voice returned.

"We need you to follow him."

"Do you mean Harvey —"

"Not over the phone, Galbraith. No names. But yes, we need you to continue following him, to bring him in if you can. Use whatever resources Interpol has at their disposal. He must be removed from the playing field."

Galbraith nodded once again, then confirmed. "Yes, of course. It will be done."

His mind was already racing with the possibilities. How could he do it? What was there he could use that would justify bringing in an American citizen? Could he detain the man, hold him on some charges? Could he get him thrown in prison?

As he listened for more instructions from his contact at The Faction, he scanned the triple-wide curved monitor screen sitting in front of him. Unlike at the office, where Interpol had provided him with the most basic and most cost-effective machines and monitors, at his home Galbraith had splurged on the industry's best monitor and gaming CPU, as well as the bells and whistles like a mechanical ergonomic keyboard and mouse, raised monitor platform, and water-cooled chassis. He had a few role-playing games installed on the monster machine, planning to get good at the latest and greatest first-person shooters, but he rarely found the time to play anymore.

All that aside, the machine made quick work of any research tasks or any actual work he needed to do from home.

He scanned the headlines and his attention turned to the screen on the right, where there was a transcript version of local police scanners in reverse-chronological order streaming down the page.

"The two groups are at each other's throats," the voice continued. *"We are not sure of the details, but it appears their feud is related to vengeance. Again, I remind you as I remind myself — overzealousness has been the cause of many downfalls, just like it has been theirs. Your role is to increase this agitation both parties are experiencing, but ultimately your job is to remove them from play. Do you understand?"*

"I... do," Galbraith swallowed as he spoke, and the words came out stuttered. "I do," he said again, taking the time to clear his throat. His eyes were jumping over two transcriptions on the right monitor, his mind not fully able to comprehend the coding. It was something he had never seen live. He tried to remember the list of London Police Department police codes he had memorized years ago, but he might have to look them up later. It was enough that his mind was drawing a blank yet calling his attention to them — it meant they were important.

It meant something was happening.

"Is there anything else you need from The Faction at this time, Galbraith?"

He shook his head and forced his mind clear. "Is... is there a deadline for this phase of my project?"

"Yes," the voice answered. *"Yours is tomorrow evening. We need at least one of the groups completely out of the picture, if not both. We understand that there are unforeseen variables at play, so if you fail, we will have a contingency plan available."*

"I understand, sir."

"No need for formalities, Galbraith. We appreciate your service to The Faction thus far, and I look forward to your further commitment. You will be sent a new contact number for any emergency needs; otherwise, consider this the last communication you shall have with this action until you are needed again."

Galbraith nodded, suddenly realizing what the code on the screen meant. He looked at it once again, now understanding fully. *Oh, my God.*

Something, indeed, was happening. And there was no doubt in his mind that it involved the very parties he was supposed to apprehend.

"Thank you," he said. "That will be perfect. It turns out a plan is unfolding in front of me. It seems the groups have suddenly fallen into their own traps."

"Very well, Galbraith. I eagerly await the completion of your task."

Without hesitation, the call disconnected and Galbraith heard the deadened silence on the other end of the line. He pulled the phone down and placed it on the desk in front of him. He began to breathe quickly, growing more excited by the second. More transcripts came in verifying his hypothesis. *White American male, white American female, additional undistinguished individuals* — more police radios crackled to life across London as the incident unfolded. He read through the transcripts, saw the epicenter in his mind, saw what was happening and knew this phase had just gotten easier.

He pushed back from the desk and stood up, stretching quickly before grabbing his overcoat and heading toward the front door.

CHAPTER 41
BEN

7:40 PM | **March 10, 2021**
  Kent, England

Ben and the others walked out of the hotel just as the police cars were nearing the scene. He heard the sirens of an ambulance in the distance, likely coming along to prepare for the worst. It was dark out, but there were a million lights bringing illumination down around them, bathing everything in daylight-bright color. He wished he could stay to answer questions, to help the police with the investigation and make sure everyone inside was accounted for and provided proper medical support, but he knew it was a bad idea. What he had told Reggie was true; they didn't have time to waste.

The others spilled out of the hotel behind him, trailed by the man wearing the vest. It was the manager on duty, and was probably coming out to wave down the police officers as they arrived.

"What are we doing?" Reggie asked.

"Trying to make sure there aren't any more —"

Ben cut himself off as he saw the exact thing he had been afraid to find: a van, unmarked with no windows, parked across the street and one block over. As he stared at it, it began to move, starting toward them.

"We have to go," Ben said. "We have to leave, now!"

"Ben," Julie said, coming up next to him. "What's the problem? What is it?"

Ben started walking toward one of the parked cars in front of the hotel. There were four parallel parking spaces, and each had a meter on the curb next to it. One space was empty, but the space closest to the hotel's front door had just been filled by a brand-new luxury SUV. The owner of the vehicle was exiting, obviously completely unaware of what had just taken place at the hotel, and Ben jogged over and waved him down.

"Ben, you're going nuts," he heard Reggie shout. "Slow down, let's figure this out."

Ben ignored him, focusing only on getting the attention of the owner of the car.

"Excuse me, sir?" Ben asked. The man turned and looked at Ben, gave him a once-over and suddenly bore an expression that looked to Ben like disgust. Apparently this man had more money than him and wanted him to know it.

Ben had no patience for attitude, especially right now. "Sir," he said, stepping up to the guy. "I need to ask a favor."

The man made a fuss about checking his inevitably expensive watch. "I'm late, and I won't be parked for longer than a minute."

"Actually, it is about your car. I was wondering if —"

Ben stopped. He had been tracking the van while he was talking to the driver, and he saw it approach on his left.

One of the panel doors began to slide open. *No*, he thought. *This isn't good.* He turned around and shouted at the others.

"Guys! Get down!"

They were all staring at him, not paying attention to the van. He pointed at it, beginning to form the words that would make his next sentence.

Before he could say anything, the two men inside the van began to open fire. Small semiautomatic rifles began spattering the sidewalk and front steps of the hotel.

Freddie had seen what Ben had been worked up about, and he was already pushing the others to the side, aiming for one of the parked cars in the spots on the other side of the hotel's entrance. The gunfire stopped momentarily while the men reloaded, but seconds later it began again.

Screams erupted from somewhere down the street and across from the hotel, and Ben noticed the man who had gotten out of the car next to them cowering in fear. Ben crouched down next to the rich guy and turned to make sure the others were safe. The gunshots leapt left and right, completely covering the front of the hotel, narrowly missing Freddie as he lunged for cover behind one of the parked cars, putting it between him and the shooters. The others were stacked in front of Freddie behind the car, their backs to it, sitting on the curb.

And then Ben caught sight of the manager of the hotel, the older man wearing the vest. He was on the ground, his eyes piercing through Ben, a large pool of blood growing on the pavement from beneath him. *Dead.*

"Dammit," Ben said. He turned back to the rich man who had gotten out of the SUV and grabbed his shoulder. "I need your car."

"What —" the man sputtered.

"I need your car. And I'm not asking." Ben shoved him backwards until his back hit the SUVs side and he let out a yelp of surprise. He reached for the man's hand, where he had seen the keys a few seconds before. The man clenched them tightly, not wanting to let go.

"Sir, I assure you I will return it. I just —"

The man swatted at Ben's face with his fist. It was a weak punch, but it took Ben by surprise. He let go of the man's shoulder and jumped backward onto the sidewalk. He saw the van pull to the side of the road across the street, the two men from inside stepping out. Both still holding the submachine guns.

Shit, he thought. *They're coming for us.*

Ben immediately corrected himself. *No, they're coming for* them.

He looked over to Freddie and the others and cupped his hands over his mouth. "Freddie, we need to get out of here! Look — the van!"

He saw Freddie peek up and over the rear end of the car just as the first gunman opened fire again. Bullets zinged over the surface of the car and through the glass, splinters of it shearing off and falling to the street. Freddie ducked back down.

Ben turned to the rich man. "I don't have time for this. Give me your keys." Ben stepped forward and raised his fist, but the man was already complying, a shaking hand offering Ben the keys to his SUV. Ben took them and jumped around the front of the vehicle and into the driver seat, opening all the doors on the way.

He put the key into the ignition and hit the gas without bothering with his seatbelt.

CHAPTER 42

BEN

7:42 PM | **March 10, 2021**
Kent, England

Two police squad cars raced toward him, heading directly for the hotel. They were closing the distance fast, but Ben pulled the wheel hard to the right and swerved over both lanes of the street and aimed toward the two gunmen, still walking slowly across the road. Both men had their weapons raised and were approaching the car his team was hiding behind from two different directions.

Ben aimed for the first one and hit the gas pedal harder. The car lurched and squealed but sped up and slammed through the man, sending him flying. He twisted around in the air, knocking the other gunman down and out of the way.

"Well, that worked a bit better than I thought it would," Ben said to himself. He slammed on the brakes and shouted out the open door to Freddie and the others. "Get in!"

But they had seen the entire display, and were already in motion. They jumped into the open back door of the vehicle, Freddie easily pushing all of them in as he stepped in last. Ben waited until the man's first foot was in the door and then he started off again. He ignored the others trying to get situated, instead focusing straight ahead.

He aimed the car at the same man he had hit a moment ago and sent the front right tire over his head. The car jumped a foot in the air and teetered on its side as it bounced over the gunman, but Ben didn't consider slowing down.

The second man, the one who had been knocked down by the first gunman, had recovered and begun crawling away and narrowly missed being crushed beneath the SUV as Ben swerved toward him.

"Come back around," Reggie said. "Take him out, too."

Ben shook his head. "No, no time. The police are here, and they just saw me splatter someone's head with a stolen vehicle."

"I think they would understand if —"

"Shut it!" Ben yelled. He kept his eyes on the road, speeding up and dodging other vehicles, but he directed his voice to Reggie, who had climbed over the center console and landed in the front seat next to him. "I'm tired of your bullshit, Reggie. We *are* a team, but I'm leading it. I didn't mean to get us in this mess, but I need your help getting out of it. We work together on this or we don't work at all? Got it?"

No one spoke. Ben heard the buckling of seatbelts and he pulled into the fast lane, leading toward the freeway. He had only driven on the left side of the road a few times, and he hoped he would be able to get used to it quickly enough. He navigated using the signs marking the way toward the highway, finally finding a larger road that looked like it would lead to an on-ramp. As he approached the highway, he saw a squad car in the rearview mirror.

"Dammit," he muttered. "Cops are on us. One of them must have split off from the hotel after my antics back there."

"We can't run from them forever," Julie said. "Can we lose them?"

Ben shook his head. "Not in a completely foreign country. I

don't know my way around well enough. Unless we get lucky, we're not going to shake him just by driving around."

He pushed the pedal to the floor as he hit the highway and the high-powered SUV took off like a rocket. He dodged other vehicles on the two-lane highway and was able to put a good amount of distance between him and the police officer tailing him. He knew they weren't going to give up, and that if they ran out of gas they would simply just call for more backup. Eventually, they would put road hazards in place and force them to stop.

They drove like that for fifteen minutes, Ben constantly checking the rearview mirror to see if their tail had vanished. While the officer had yet to pursue them with their lights on, they also hadn't given up the chase. Ben assumed that meant they were considered suspicious targets, but not yet confirmed as people involved with the attack.

"Who were those guys back at the hotel?" Freddie asked.

"Some of Tennyson's goons, I bet," Reggie said.

"Maybe," Ben said. "Both groups had different weapons though, and they looked a bit different from the guys who were outside the hotel."

"Two different parties?" Reggie asked. "Or just Tennyson hiring two different groups of mercenaries?"

"No idea," Ben answered. "But the second group killed the manager of the hotel. I watched them shooting at you guys, then continue shooting when you were already well out of the way. They specifically aimed for him."

"Bastards," Julie said. "You're right — Tennyson is going to have an endless stream of these guys coming after us. Who knows how many more?"

Ben nodded. "That's why we need to get to him before he gets to you guys. He meant what he said — that he'll take out the whole team, just to get to me. But he wants me alive for whatever reason."

Reggie hadn't spoken for a few minutes, but now he turned to Ben. "He's torturing you."

Ben arched an eyebrow and looked over at his friend.

"He's taking out everything you care about — your wife, your friends, and your professional career. Everything that means something. Just like you did to him."

"Bullshit," Ben said. "*We* stopped a mad scientist from hurting a lot of people and torturing those apes. If Tennyson didn't know what his grandson was doing there, then I'm *happy* to have brought it to light. But his grandson was using *his* money — *his* company — to do it. It wasn't my fault, or Eliza's."

"Doesn't matter," Reggie said. "Guys like that *need* this sort of thing. They're this tightly wound spring, ready to snap. He probably just wants to get rid of the CSO so we don't compete with whatever thing he's starting up. The fact that you're in charge of it, and you had something to do with his grandson's death is just a bonus."

Ben couldn't disagree, but he still felt like things didn't add up. Why go through all this trouble — this elaborate song and dance — just to get under his skin? If he wanted to kill his friends, why hadn't he just sent another truck to blow them all up?

"Pull off here," Sarah said, suddenly speaking from the backseat. She was pointing to the left, off the highway.

"What's up?"

"I know Rochester pretty well. Used to vacation here when I was a kid."

"What's over here?" Reggie asked.

Sarah smiled. "I have an idea."

8:00 PM **| March 10, 2021**

Rochester, England

"There's an entire strip of car dealerships coming up," Sarah said.

Ben had gotten off the highway on the exit she pointed out. The police cruiser was still chasing them, but now had its lights on, obviously now interested in bringing them in for questioning. The squad car had exited the highway shortly after them and was gaining speed. There was some distance between the two vehicles, but they were easily still within the officer's line-of-sight, and would be for a while.

They needed to get off the road, and quickly.

"This car is a Lexus," she said. "If I remember right, the Lexus dealership should be..."

"Right there!" Julie yelled, pointing from the seat next to her. Ben looked at the direction she was pointing and saw the dealership, the Lexus logo emblazoned in lights on a sign high above the front of the lot.

Ben understood the plan now. He pulled the car into the lot, the tires screeching as they left the asphalt and started onto the short concrete driveway. He knew the police officer would see them turn in here, but the plan wasn't to hide in the vehicle forever.

They just needed to buy a little time. He peeled around the long lines of smaller cars until he saw what he was looking for: three rows of tightly spaced SUVs, ones that perfectly matched the four-door version they were in now. The driver he had borrowed the car from had purchased the Lexus brand-new, and judging by the smell of the interior and the low number of miles on the odometer, he guessed it had been sometime within the past few months.

He drove around the rows of parked cars until he found an empty space. He quickly pulled their vehicle into it and parked. He immediately shut off the engine as the others were tumbling out. He looked over and saw Reggie start jogging up the rows of parked SUVs, then saw him crouch in front of a vehicle near the end of the line.

"Come on," he heard Julie say. "If we can get to the edge of the lot over there, we can snake our way back around and get out one of the side exits."

Ben saw what she was talking about — the lot was set on a slight hill, but there were no permanent walls on three sides. The perimeter was marked off by a chain-link fence, but there were a lot of gaps for entrance and exit driveways on those three sides. That meant that there were plenty of exit points available to them, they just had to first make a break for the row of cars parked against the fence bordering the west side of the property.

From there, they could probably stay hidden long enough to make their way to an exit.

Reggie returned, holding two rectangular frames made of plastic. He held them up and smiled. "Here, take one of these and stick it over the front license plate. I pulled them off of two cars facing each other, so the cops probably won't even notice they're missing."

Ben grinned and caught the license plate frame and turned it over to look at it. There was a fake plate made of paper stretched within it, featuring the dealership's gaudy logo on it, as well as a phone number. He saw that there was enough room on the back of the thing to easily snap it over the vehicle's existing license plate.

He walked over to the back of the SUV just as he saw police lights reflecting off the dealership's front windows.

"He's here," Ben said. "Let's move."

They jogged between the rows of cars, crouching and keeping their head down, and then made the short sprint across the open parking lot one at a time, making sure the officer was not nearby. The police car had turned into the lot and slowed down, just as they had suspected he would, now forced to look at every single car in the lines of SUVs, to try and find the stolen vehicle.

They weren't out of the woods yet — at some point the officer would realize that the people inside the car had gotten out and were continuing on foot.

As he thought about it, the officer sped up and turned on his brights as he rounded the corner toward the end of the lot. Ben pulled himself down farther, praying that the officer wouldn't accidentally look directly into the gap he was hiding in. He held his breath as the officer sped around the lot once more, no doubt watching the perimeter now to see if any of the carjackers had escaped.

When the coast was clear for the moment, Ben ran out and met the others at the edge of the lot, still waiting for him. Together they continued around and found a side exit. There was an empty security booth in front of a raising and lowering security arm that was currently in the down position. They could easily crouch beneath it, but there was also a gap between the chain-link fence and security booth itself that was wide enough to climb through.

They left the lot, then jogged back up the other side of the fence, staying hidden from the officer's view thanks to the tall hedges that had been planted there. They ended up in the parking lot of a small tavern.

Without hesitation, Reggie sped up and pulled the door open. Freddie and Julie ran inside, followed by Sarah, and finally Ben.

As Ben stepped over the threshold and into the dark space, Reggie grabbed his arm and pulled him back.

Ben frowned, expecting Reggie to fight, to start up their ongoing argument. Instead, the man embraced him.

"I'm sorry," Reggie whispered. "Real sorry."

Ben pulled back and looked at Reggie. "I know, man. I am too. Let's just get through this, okay? I know you've got some issues with me, but we can —"

"No, man," Reggie said, interrupting. He shook his head and looked at the cigarette-stained concrete slab. "*I've* got issues, but they're not with you. That's something for me to sort out, okay?"

Ben nodded once and saw that Reggie had outstretched his hand. Ben reached out his hand as well. Reggie pulled it in, and they shook.

"I'm here, and I'm not going anywhere. I promise. I'll follow you to the end of the earth, to hell and back, to whatever harebrained scheme you cook up, brother."

"I appreciate that," Ben said, smiling. "I really do. I need you. You know that?"

"Oh, I knew it from the day I met you, buddy. I keep saving your ass, and I'll keep doing it."

"Got it."

Reggie laughed. "Now, let's take a breath. We don't have time, but we need to *make* time. We need a plan."

"Agreed," Ben said.

"Then let's get a beer and cook up something really harebrained."

CHAPTER 44

BEN

8:08 PM **| March 10, 2021**
Rochester, England

"...Reports of a terrorist attack today at the Hilton Garden Inn in Kent are still coming in. Our on-scene correspondent is keeping us updated with things as the situation unfolds."

Ben looked up at the flatscreen TV hanging above the bar in the front corner of the room. The tavern was mostly empty, just a couple of middle-aged men playing pool in the back and the bartender himself the only others inside. Julie, Sarah, and Freddie had each ordered a beer, but Ben and Reggie had decided to go for something a bit stronger.

Ben watched as the bartender poured two fingers of scotch from a bottle behind him.

"It's cheaper here," Reggie said.

"Never liked it anyway. Now it'll just taste like cheaper stuff I don't like."

"You just need to grow some hair on your chest, man," Reggie said.

"I'm with Ben," Freddie said. "Stuff tastes like dirt. We never did get to finish our beers back at the hotel, anyway. You didn't want to try again?"

Ben chuckled. "Seems like whenever I start drinking a beer, something blows up or shoots at me," he said. "So I figured I should change it up a bit."

Ben turned his attention back to the TV and watched the surreal scene. It was hard to believe he had just been there. There were camera shots from inside the hotel, as well as the front door, where he and the others had just been thirty minutes ago. There were bullet holes covering the front wall and broken glass spiderwebbed all over the lobby doors, and in one wide, sweeping shot Ben caught a quick glimpse of a large blanket that had been placed over a mound on the patio outside.

The hotel manager, he realized.

The shot cut abruptly to a reporter holding a microphone, standing where the SUV they had taken had previously been parked. Ben recognized the rich man being interviewed by the reporter. *"You say they came and stole your car?"* the reporter asked.

The rich man nodded, his eyes wide and panicky. *"Yes — yes, one of them... he hit me and then... And then stole my keys. I — there was nothing I could do. It was all so quick. They all got in as the people started firing guns again. Then they just... left."*

"Hey, they're talking about us," Reggie said.

"Police are still searching for the car thieves, believed to have been part of the attack at the hotel. Officials are not sure to what extent they aided the terrorists, but —"

"What the hell?" Reggie yelled to the screen. "We didn't 'aid any terrorists!'"

"Keep your voice down, man," Ben said. "Don't need the bartender taking our drinks back and kicking us out."

"Doesn't matter to them," Julie said. She took a sip of her beer. "They saw us steal that guy's car. Then hit one of the gunman and kill him."

"That was just helping them out!" Reggie said. "The police should thank us!"

"Car theft, involuntary manslaughter — and what's it called when you get into a police chase and end up shaking them?" Ben asked.

Reggie shrugged. "No idea, but I'm pretty sure that's illegal, too."

"Are we hosed?" Freddie asked.

"Hosed?" Reggie asked in reply. "No, not hosed. Not yet. We're in a world of hurt, but probably not done for yet. We need to figure out where Tennyson is, and where he's keeping Eliza."

"And find the stupid sword he's talking about. If that can help us get her back —"

"We need to split up," Ben said. "He wants me — alone — so that he can take you out at the same time. But there's not a *chance* I'm going to let him do that."

"What are you suggesting?" Sarah asked. "If you don't do what he says, he could just kill Eliza."

Ben shook his head. "He could, but I don't think he will. Like we've been saying, this is all a game to him. He's *testing* me. Not to make sure I'll do things exactly the way he said to, but so I'll do things a *different* way. My own way."

"How's that?" Reggie asked.

"He said he's starting a group like the CSO, right? That means something off the books, something that doesn't really have military involvement but does things that are probably not the sort of things normal civilians should be getting themselves involved with. That tells me he wants someone who thinks outside the box, someone who's not afraid to get his hands dirty."

"But Eliza's life is on the line, man."

Ben held up a hand and cleared his throat. "I know, I know. I'm not suggesting we put her in any *more* danger, but I'm also not okay with leaving you all alone and in the same place while I go see what he wants. It would be too easy for him."

"Were not helpless little kittens," Reggie said.

"No, you're not. But you *are* far more helpful and far more safe if we split up and go about this from two different angles. I'm going to do what Tennyson wants me to do — I'm going to try to find the sword. My gut tells me it's nowhere in London, but probably somewhere in Europe. So I need to get on the plane and get to France, at least. The original smith who made it was in Paris, right?"

Sarah nodded. "If we are splitting up, I can stay back and do some research."

"That's exactly what I was thinking," Ben said. "Reggie, you're with me — if things get hairy, I don't want to have to fight my way out alone."

Reggie nodded.

"Julie, Sarah, Freddie — you guys all stay back here and figure out the next steps. Since we don't have laptops besides Freddie's, and Tennyson's men are going to keep coming, you guys might need to bounce around."

"We can do it the old school way," Sarah said. "Libraries, bookstores, online only through VPNs and never logged into any websites. If it's a treasure hunt involving something as important as Napoleon's sword, there's probably reams of published material talking about it."

"Good idea," Ben said. "But don't get comfortable anywhere. We know for a fact these guys don't give a crap about collateral damage, so you're no safer in a café or coffee shop around a bunch of other people then you are in a dark alley alone."

Ben looked back up at the TV and saw that they were now interviewing one of the young men who was working behind the counter in the lobby during the attack. He was sobbing, wiping tears from his eyes. The camera zoomed in on his face, capturing the emotional intensity of it.

Ben shook his head. He knew news agencies would milk this for every drop of advertising revenue it could. Sure, it was important that they report what had happened, but they had already made this into a 'terrorist attack' rather than what it was: a targeted attack on specific people. It hadn't been meant to cause terror, it had been meant to cleanly eradicate an enemy.

No one else was in any direct danger aside from being accidentally injured while they tried to come for him and his team. But the media would never admit that, even if they knew the truth. Crime paid far less than nationwide terrorism.

Reggie motioned with his chin up toward the TV. "This going to be a problem?"

"What? The media coverage?"

"I don't know," Reggie said. "If they have our pictures or video of us running around in there, they could send it out and get the public involved in a manhunt."

"Yeah," Ben said. "I thought of that, but there's not really much we can do. It will be harder to interact with anyone, but we still have bigger problems to worry about."

"Like Interpol?"

Ben turned and eyed Reggie. "Yeah, that is a *big* problem."

He felt his phone buzzing in his pocket, so he pulled out and looked at the screen. It was an unknown caller, but the area code signaled London.

He rolled his eyes. *Speaking of the devil...*

8:23 PM | **March 10, 2021**
Rochester, England

"You want to explain to me why you and your friends were found at the scene of a shooting thirty minutes ago?"

Ben sighed. It was the man he had met from Interpol, officer Galbraith.

"No," Ben said. "I don't really want to."

"I've got about twelve agents in the area — all looking to bring you in. On top of that, local law enforcement tells me they're looking for you, as well. Seems you borrowed a car without asking and then ditched it a little while later."

"I told the guy I was borrowing it," Ben said.

"Borrowing it or not, it really comes across like theft."

"Look, I was sent to that house by mistake; I was just trying to meet with someone and they gave me the wrong —"

"Who?" Galbraith asked. *"Who were you supposed to be meeting? And what was the meeting supposed to be about?"*

There was no way Ben was going to answer those questions. No way he would tell Interpol about Tennyson. "That's my business."

"Your business and *my* business are quickly becoming *shared*

business, Mr. Bennett," Galbraith said. Ben could hear the irritation in the man's voice. *"Tell me where you are, and I'll have someone pick you up. Just you, and we'll let your friends go. You have my word."*

"Pass."

"Mr. Bennett, this is an ugly situation for you. However you crack it, there's going to be jail time. The longer we play this out, the longer that sentence is going to be. I guarantee you that."

Ben sighed again, realizing that the others were now staring at him, listening in to the conversation. He had been keeping his voice low so the bartender wouldn't hear, but the man had gone back to the restroom. As such, he talked a bit louder. "I understand. I'm a little busy right now, unfortunately. I'm pretty sure we can work something out later, but I need —"

"No, Mr. Bennett. You do not *need anything at all, but to tell me where you are. I'm done picking around. Give me a location."*

Ben thought for a moment, weighing his options. Then he pulled the phone down and hung up the call.

"Girlfriend?" Reggie asked.

The others chuckled, but Ben shook his head. "Interpol."

"Shit," Freddie whispered. "He still suspicious?"

Ben looked at Freddie. "I'd say 'suspicious' went out the window the moment he saw our faces at the hotel."

"He was at the hotel?" Julie asked.

"No, but he heard about it from his police friends or something. Either way, he's got the hots for me right now and not in a good way."

"That change anything about our plan?" Reggie asked.

"Yeah," Ben said. "It means we need to move even faster than we were going to before. Like, *right now.*"

Ben stood up from his barstool and pulled his wallet out. Thankfully it had been in his pocket during the explosion, and there were still a couple of folded fifty dollar bills in there. "You think they take American dollars?"

The bartender still had not returned from the restroom, and Ben didn't want to wait around.

"I guess they'll have to," Sarah said.

He placed one of the fifties on the counter and the team turned to leave. The two men at the back of the tavern had stopped playing pool and were now laughing loudly over a couple of beers, still ignoring them. Neither looked in their direction when they left.

We're out of time, Ben thought. *No more running* from *this. Time to run* toward *something.*

CHAPTER 46

JULIE

9:34 PM | **March 10, 2021**
The London Library, London, England

Julie sat at the table across from Dr. Sarah Lindgren at the London Library in St. James. Dr. Lindgren had only recently joined the CSO's payroll as a part-time and temporary team member, as she had not initially wanted to commit to a full-time job with the group. She hoped to continue her role as a professor and research anthropologist at her university. The woman was brilliant, capable of just about anything the group needed her for, which meant she was a perfect fit. Her interests and expertise aligned with those often needed by the CSO, and on the missions Dr. Lindgren had taken part, she had proven to be an incredible asset to the team.

Julie hoped that for her, the chaos and terror they had experienced over the course of many of their expeditions would be overshadowed by the joy of discovery and their knack for success, and that Sarah would eventually agree to come onto their payroll in a more permanent position. Until then, they had to be satisfied with whatever time she could lend to their group.

Sarah had checked her emails, making sure there was nothing pressing at the university that might require her to return to the

United States, and then flicked her eyes up at Julie. "Ready?" she asked.

Julie nodded, staving off the post-adrenaline crash. She was still jet-lagged, and would be for the next day. In previous travels, she had done her best to stay busy, to stay active, as she had found it was the best remedy for jet lag.

After the events at their hotel in Kent, and then the near-capture with the police, she was ready for a twelve-hour nap. Unfortunately, Eliza was still out there, and Tennyson was still on their tail as well. They needed information — they needed to figure this thing out.

The group had split in half after the pub in Rochester in order to better stay incognito as they ran from Interpol, the local London police, and now the general public. While they weren't concerned that a civilian would recognize them by their faces, the news had mentioned that the team was made of five members. It seemed to be more of a risk than it was worth to continue traveling together as a group.

Ben and Reggie had decided to go get cash out at an ATM, which they would then use to catch a flight to Switzerland as well as purchase anything they would need. Julie had agreed to do the same. Since they only had credit cards to work with, there was the risk that whatever cash they could withdraw using their card would leave an easy trail to follow, but it was a necessary risk. The alternative — using their credit cards for every purchase — was a much riskier choice.

Freddie, Julie, and Sarah had caught a public bus, risking someone recognizing them, and headed north to reach the down-town London library, hoping to do enough research on the second Napoleonic sword. Freddie, at first feeling intellectually outmatched, had settled into his role as an administrative assistant, and was currently out getting coffee for the three of them.

"Ready as I'll ever be. I've already ordered a stack of books, so they should be getting here in a minute."

While Sarah had checked out a laptop from the library staff, Julie had ordered a stack of books covering the Napoleonic wars, biographies on the man himself, and any interesting historic works that seemed like it might mention Napoleon's favored sword and the Parisian smith who had created it.

"Okay," Sarah said. "First thing — we need to verify that what Tennyson is claiming is actually true. I've never heard anything about a copycat sword being made, but then again I am not an expert on Napoleon Bonaparte."

"Had you heard about the first sword? The one that was in the video with Eliza?"

Sarah nodded. "Sure, maybe a tidbit here and there. I knew there was something people referred to as 'Napoleon's sword,' and that even though he had and used many different swords over the course of his military career, there was one particular one that he called *his* sword. A favorite, one made especially for him that he carried into battle."

"What was special about it?"

Sarah clicked around on the screen in front of her and then looked up at Julie once again. "Apparently it was just a really well-crafted sword; a gift from one of the goldsmiths in Paris he used often. Gilded, made from the finest materials..." she clicked again and continued reading. "It gave it almost a bluish hue, perfectly offset by the gold lacing patterns and insets on it. It would have been an extremely expensive piece back then, and apparently it is still in perfect condition."

"And it was last seen here in London?"

She nodded again. "Yeah, sold to the woman who was buying it for her husband. At the auction at Hever Castle in Kent. It was delivered to her home — that place Ben showed up at — and that was where she was killed."

Julie shuddered, trying not to imagine the scene of the young woman being stabbed in the back of the neck by the very sword she had purchased that night. "Who would do something like that?"

Sarah shrugged. "Considering all of the people I've met and interacted with while helping the CSO, seems like there would be at least a few who would do just about anything for the right price."

"Yeah, unfortunately you're right."

"Still, it's pretty clear to me that whoever killed her was trying not to take credit for it."

"You mean Tennyson didn't want us to know he killed her?" Julie asked.

Sarah shook her head. "No, what I'm saying is that it's obvious Tennyson *himself* didn't kill the woman. He paid someone — a hired gun or mercenary or something like that — to do the job. Likely the same guys who accosted us at the hotel. But he also left some clues behind, purposefully. And, on top of that, he called Ben to London and told him to go to the exact spot she had been murdered only hours before. He set all of it up."

CHAPTER 47

JULIE

9:35 PM | March 10, 2021

The London Library, London, England

Julie nodded along, thinking of the agent who had confronted Ben at the scene of the crime. "You mean Interpol. The fact that Ben had no idea what he was getting himself into. Ben had the address, so he knew right where he was going. Anyone watching would rightfully be suspicious of him — and all of us — now."

"Right, seems like Tennyson wants us killed, but he's got more in store for Ben. For whatever reason, he basically blamed Ben for her murder, at least from the perspective of Interpol and the local police. Now they're all on our tail, and will bring Ben or us in for questioning if they catch us. Even if he can prove he didn't kill her, he's going to have a hard time explaining why he was there, and what he was hoping to accomplish."

Julie felt her skin tingle. She knew Sarah was right. Even though Ben was innocent, if Interpol or the London police wanted to make an example of him, they could certainly dredge up something from his past with the CSO that looked sinister enough to put him behind bars. "So, that means we need to get back to the task at hand: we need to find the sword, if it exists."

"Not just that," Sarah replied. "We need to find the sword, and then figure out what Tennyson wants it for. We need to understand the full picture, as much as he does. That's the only way to keep Eliza and Ben safe."

Just then, two people entered the room from opposite sides. From Julie's right side, Freddie returned with a cardboard holster and three cups of coffee in to-go cups with lids. Across the room on Julie's left, a librarian entered with a pushcart full of books. Both reached the table at the same time, and Julie couldn't help but notice each of them taking an extra-long glance at one another. The librarian, a young-looking woman with a conservative floral shirt and long black pants that accentuated a slender, short body, smiled a dainty, quaint smile.

"We're supposed to be closed already," she said. Her voice was as petite as her figure. "But I think I can hold it open for you all."

Julie smiled. "Sorry to keep you — we really won't be long. And if we can check these out..."

"Of course." She turned to the cart and started piling the books on the table.

"Oh," Freddie said. "Let me... uh... help you with those."

Julie saw the librarian blush as Freddie grabbed three textbook-sized books with one massive bear claw and pulled them up off the cart. It was amusing to watch.

"Wow," Julie said. "You're *so* strong."

Freddie made a face, but Sarah joined in before he could say anything. "So many *books*, Freddie. With only one hand. Very impressive."

At this he gave a quick shake of his head and pretended like he hadn't heard it. When the pair finished dumping books on the table, the librarian thanked them. She turned and left, pushing the empty cart away.

Julie and Sarah were staring at Freddie, who had a dumbfounded look on his face. "What?" He asked. "I was just being nice."

"Nice. Of course."

Sarah's eyebrows were raised, and Julie was grinning from ear to ear. She put on a mock Southern accent. "Ah didn't know you were so deft with them big 'ol books, Freddie."

At this, Freddie lowered his chin to his chest and tried to hide his reddened cheeks. "Fine," he said. "She was... cute. And I kind of have a thing for book chicks."

"Book chicks?" Sarah asked, her mouth open. "*Book chicks?* Seriously?"

He shrugged.

Julie thanked him for the coffee, then turned back to Sarah. "Do you think the sword is still somewhere in London?" She asked.

Sarah shook her head immediately. "No, I don't. It's pretty obvious to me that Tennyson is trying to send Ben on a world tour of sorts. The fact that the sword was last seen in London, and the murdered woman's house is in London, means that Tennyson is trying to string him along. My guess is that there will be clues that reveal themselves at certain times, and Ben needs to be keenly aware of them in order to find the next place Tennyson wants him to go."

Julie didn't like what she was hearing, but it made perfect sense. "Like a scavenger hunt," she said.

Freddie placed his hand on the table. "That's sort of what I was thinking, too," he said. "He's playing with us. Playing with Ben. A charade, all of this fun-and-games stuff. It doesn't seem like the normal way to have somebody murdered."

"Right, but we can assume Tennyson doesn't *want* to murder Ben. Tennyson wants to mess with him as much as he wants to kill *us*, but Ben's safe — for now. Tennyson wants something from him, remember?"

"He wants him to take a job," Freddie said.

"Yes, but there's more to it than that. He needs something he believes only Ben can find. It has to be that, or he wouldn't waste his own time setting this all up. I have a feeling the end goal is not going to be pretty, either."

"How so?"

"Play it out to the end," Julie answered. "There's very little chance, in my mind, that Tennyson will be perfectly happy just turning over Eliza and letting Ben go free if we can find and deliver the sword to him. We already know he wants Ben to work for him, and that doesn't sound to me like it's going to be an amicable employer/employee partnership."

"So we find the sword, we find Eliza," Sarah said. "That much is clear. But we need to do it without Tennyson *knowing* we're doing it."

Freddie nodded. "You mentioned something about clues? You think that Tennyson will reveal clues to Ben as he needs them, or something like that?"

Julie shrugged. "No idea, but I hope so. It seems to make the most sense so far in the game."

"Well, in that case," Freddie responded, "I guess we should be looking for these clues, right?"

Julie nodded again. "Yeah, that's our best bet. If we can get a jump on finding out the next place Tennyson wants Ben to go, we might be able to get a jump on Tennyson himself. You have something in mind?"

Freddie looked down at the laptop, then at both women. "You still have that video of Eliza?"

CHAPTER 48

FREDDIE

9:36 PM | **March 10, 2021**

The London Library, London, England

Freddie pulled the laptop over to him. He pulled up a chair and sat down next to Sarah, across from Julie at the library table.

Since he had been the only one who had brought along a laptop, he thought it might be smart to get a head start on research. On the flight to London, he had had a bit of time to look through some of the data and history surrounding Napoleon's sword, as well as watch the video of Eliza a few times.

While he was no professional researcher, he had hacked his way through many college essays by sheer force of will, tying together fragments of history and science in a way that at least made clear to the professor he was making a valiant effort at scholarship, even if the message was completely fabricated. In another life, he thought he might make a decent fiction author.

He had developed a few habits and interests when it came to school, and he had always had a knack for learning new things. It had made him a great soldier, able to parse information faster than his colleagues. In addition, he had some helpful talents and skills that made picking up new things a bit easier.

One such skill was that he had a near-photographic memory. While he had found it mostly unhelpful for tests during his school years, as his recall was typically very low, he had realized during his upbringing that if he saw a picture of something for at least ten seconds, there was a good chance he could describe it very accurately, even years later.

While the others had been looking at Eliza's face in the video, trying to read her angst and decipher anything they could about her mental state, Freddie had been looking at everything else: he knew that the room itself was impossible to make out, that there was nothing there useful enough to point them in a certain direction. It was blurry, out of focus. Nondescript.

Her torso was also cut off by the framing — only the upper half of her body was visible, so anything she was doing with her hands or feet was useless to them.

But he *had* gotten a very good look at the sword itself. He had been able to recreate a pretty good model of it in his mind based on the time he'd had to examine it.

When he had gotten to the hotel and had had a few minutes of downtime, he had pulled up a search and began looking for images of Napoleon's favored sword, the Sword of Austerlitz.

Sure enough, the pictures he'd seen showed the same sword he had seen in Eliza's video, the sword Tennyson had had stolen from the woman who had purchased it at auction just a few days ago, and the same sword that had been used to kill her afterward.

It was the same sword Tennyson was now threatening Eliza and the CSO with. He wanted to find a duplicate sword, one that looked exactly like this one.

"What did you find?" Julie asked. She was leaning over the table, toward Freddie and the computer. He pushed the laptop back and scooted around the corner of the table so that all of them could see what he was doing.

"Just wanted to pull up a picture of it," he said. "You've got the video here, too?"

Sarah nodded. "Ben stuck it on this flash drive," she said, pulling something out of her pocket. She revealed a thumbnail-sized disk that she shoved into one of the library computer's USB ports. "Should be the only thing on there."

Freddie nodded and double-clicked the video file when it recognized the disk. He let the video play for a few seconds and then paused it. He used the high-speed scrub bar at the bottom of the window to pull it forward and backward a few frames, until the glinting light source from somewhere out of the shot lit up the section of the hilt of the sword just right.

There.

"Seems to be a pretty high-quality video," he said. "Maybe even 4K."

"That's good," Julie asked. "If a bit overkill. Are we trying to zoom in on something?"

Freddie nodded again. "I've been wanting to see this thing close up," he said. He pulled the video window to the side and changed its size, then he pulled a browser window to the opposite side of the screen and set its dimensions so that the video and browser were side-by-side. Then, on the browser window, he found a picture of the sword of Austerlitz and enlarged it, narrowing in on the same section of the hilt he had seen in the video. He did the same on the video window, finding the best size the video would allow that was in focus enough to see the hilt clearly.

"It's the same one," Sarah said quickly. "So Tennyson *actually* stole the sword of Austerlitz. He was not lying to us."

Freddie smiled. "No, he didn't. Look closer."

Both women turned and stared at him in shock, then back to the screen. "Wait a minute," Julie said. "They're different? How?"

Freddie felt a surge of energy. This was a new feeling for him — he had never been the smartest guy at the table, usually outmatched by folks with a more cerebral or intellectual mind. He wasn't dumb, but he'd never felt at home with the big-brains in his classes. It was the reason he had turned to the military after high school — his family had a long history of military men and women, but it was really the fact that he felt more comfortable pointing a weapon downrange and clearing a room, and being a cog in the chain of command, than he did leading a strategy session.

"I saw this the other day, but I didn't know to look for it again until I saw *this* image from the web." He leaned over the computer and dragged the mouse in a circle around an area on the hilt. The gold, curved arch that formed the outer clasp where the holder's knuckles would rest was as intricately designed as the rest of the sword.

On it sat tiny, gold-covered roses, like shining orbs on the hilt. The flowers were spaced about an inch apart, five in total. "These roses — I saw them in the video. Notice anything?"

Sarah and Julie each leaned over, examining the two images. It wasn't hard to spot, now that they were side-by-side and knew what to look for.

Julie gasped. "Oh my God, there's a different number of them on each sword."

Sarah put her hand over her mouth. "You're right — Freddie, I can't believe you picked up on this."

He shrugged, and tried to hold back the blush once again. He thought of the cute librarian, suddenly wondering if she were nearby. He knew it was probably not the best time to be trying to impress a single lady.

Not to mention the fact that he wasn't even sure she *was* single.

"Freddie, you still with us?"

He shook his head and pushed the thought away. "Yeah, sorry. Anyway, I saw it without realizing what was weird about it. It got lodged in my mind as something to check into later. Didn't think it would be worth looking at again until I saw the other image and could clarify. But yeah, you can see that one of the swords — Tennyson's — has only *four* roses. The one that should be right on the spot where the clasp meets the hilt is missing, but it's there on the other picture."

"Right, according to this website, the actual sword of Austerlitz has five roses. Right there on the hilt."

"So... what does it mean?" Freddie asked.

"Well, for starters," Sarah began, "it means that Tennyson was telling the truth — there were, in fact, *two* swords made at the same time, at least one of them by that goldsmith in Paris."

"But he wasn't telling the *entire* truth," Julie pointed out. "Maybe he didn't know — or maybe he does know and wanted to test Ben — but the swords are clearly *not* identical."

Freddie nodded. "Yeah, they're pretty damn close, but I'd say these are two completely different swords. I don't think Tennyson would just pop off one of the roses. That would definitely leave an obvious mark."

"Right," Julie said. "I'm going to shoot Ben a text and let him know that we've got some information. I'll be discreet and won't tell him anything until we can figure out how to get a secure message to them. They need to know about this when they get to Paris."

Freddie recalled that Ben and Reggie had taken flight to the airport with very little explanation. Ben had a plan, apparently, but he hadn't wanted to share it with the others just yet, claiming it would only endanger them more to know about it.

He didn't like it, but Ben was now technically his boss. Julie had even let it slide, so he had kept his mouth shut.

"Julie," Sarah said, suddenly looking up and across the table. "Ben and Reggie won't be going to Paris until *after* they go to Switzerland."

"Right, but what do you mean?" Julie asked.

"It seems to me it might be in our best interest to not wait for them to finish whatever they're doing in Switzerland, right?"

Julie considered this for a moment. "But he didn't want us going anywhere — it's not safe to be out and about with Interpol and Tennyson's goons running around."

Freddie nodded, already standing up from the table and shutting the lid on the laptop. He didn't want to let Julie overrule Sarah — he felt the pressure as well, and more importantly, he didn't want to wait around and play research assistant.

He wanted to take action. "We can run back to the hotel in Kent and I can sneak in to get my laptop," he said. "It's a bit out of the way, but taking a more meandering route will only help to throw off anyone on our scent."

"What are you talking about?" Julie asked, still confused.

"I'm on the same page as Sarah," Freddie said. "We can't just be waiting around for Reggie and Ben. Eliza's out there somewhere, and the clock's ticking. I say we go on a little field trip. Let's take this stuff to Paris with us, track down someone who knows something about that old goldsmith. I'd bet a million bucks they would be *very* interested to see this."

CHAPTER 49

BEN

9:36 PM | **March 10, 2021**

London-Heathrow International Airport, London, England

Ben still felt the rush. The adrenaline hadn't yet worn off. After they'd left the tavern and after splitting up with Freddie, Julie, and Sarah, Ben and Reggie had made their way straight to the airport on the west side of London once again to catch a redeye to Switzerland. They had stopped on the way and had withdrawn their daily limit of cash, paid the absurd fee, and vowed to do so again the next day. They needed to get off the grid, to make it as difficult as possible for Tennyson — and everyone else after them — to track their movements through Europe.

Ben knew that Tennyson had sent the grunts to kill his team as soon as they had sat down for a meal at the hotel restaurant. He had waited until Ben read the email, and then sent them in. The van that had taken shots at them and killed the hotel manager had also been waiting for them to emerge — a backup in case their teammates inside had not killed all of the CSO crew.

All of those facts told Ben one thing: Tennyson was watching them, and he had eyes in all the right places. They all needed to get out of the system, and fast.

Ben wasn't sure what that meant regarding the use of their cell phones, but he would wait for Julie and her expertise on the matter regarding phones and email. However, he did know that it would be easy enough for someone like Tennyson to track them by what they purchased using their credit card, and where the transaction had taken place. If Tennyson had his fingers in the credit card companies' databases, it would be simple enough to find them.

By taking cash out here in London, it would alert Tennyson that they were on the move — that they were aware of how easy it would be to locate them — but it was still a risk worth taking. They needed cash, and there was really no other way to acquire it without raising a red flag. Besides, any bank they could use wasn't open at this hour.

Ben did not want to reach out to Mr. E again, either. He had gotten the sense that the man hoped for Ben to execute his portion of the mission in silence and isolation, without input or argument from the rest of the team, and without any further communication from Mr. E himself. Whatever the man had going on — whatever coping mechanisms the man had regarding the death of his wife — Ben would leave him to it in peace.

They had reached the airport about an hour after leaving the tavern, and Ben was pleased to discover that travel this time of the week and this time of day was relatively light. A half-hour after arriving, they had tickets booked for a flight leaving for Berne in twenty minutes.

It had been easy enough to get through security as well — neither man had a bag or carry-on items to bring — and security personnel didn't think much of it or add any extra grief to their trip. As they walked to the gate, Ben felt his phone vibrate and heard the ding of a text message. He pulled it out of his pocket.

It was from Julie.

>> *Update incoming. Filling in details now, but need to chat when you land.*

Not an emergency, Ben realized. Perhaps the first non-emergency message he had gotten in the last three days. That was a relief.

But it also meant there was new information Julie, Sarah, and Freddie had dug up. It meant they might be making progress on the Napoleon problem, or even knew where to find the second sword.

He also knew that Julie was concerned about Tennyson's ability to peer into their technological lives. If the message she needed to deliver were something completely mundane, she would have just said it. And if it were something important but she was not concerned about their phone data being intercepted, she similarly would have just explained it via text message.

The fact that she was being vague and cryptic meant she, too, was concerned. She knew Tennyson was watching them, tracking them.

He showed it to Reggie, who just nodded and continued walking. There was no reason to call her yet, no reason to freak out. It was likely the three other members of his team were simply putting the pieces of the puzzle together, and wanted to run a few things by them, to get their story straight.

When they sat down at the gate and waited for the boarding call, Reggie turned to Ben. "You finally going to tell me about this hare-brained idea you have?" he asked, a grin on his face.

Ben shrugged. "Why would I? What would be the fun in that?"

Reggie laughed, shifted in his seat to get comfortable, then looked straight ahead. "It's something *really* stupid, isn't it? You wouldn't even mention it to Julie."

Ben sighed. "What else would it be? Anything obvious is something Tennyson will have already thought of. Anything most people would do is something he will have already taken off the table."

"Like going to the police or Interpol?" Reggie asked.

Ben nodded. "Precisely. He wants to frame me for that woman's death, or at least get the authorities asking questions and honing in on me. That completely removes the option of reaching out to them for help. We can't go to them to tell them that Eliza's been taken, nor can we ask them for help tracking him down. They'll bring me in for questioning."

"Not me, though. They don't know who I am."

"They might, and it won't be hard to pull up my known accomplices. You'll be in the system, somewhere. And I didn't tell Julie or anyone else because the fewer who know about it, the safer."

Reggie shook his head and continue to laugh. He looked down at the airport carpet, the stained blue of the flattened threads. "I knew I should've stayed in Brazil. Totally off the grid, totally unable to be found unless I wanted to be found. I lived in a bunker, man. A literal, underground bunker. My walls were made of concrete!"

"Yeah, well, your wife didn't think too highly of that, did she?" Ben knew Reggie would take the joke in stride. He rarely mentioned his late wife, and Ben had never met the woman.

Reggie laughed even harder. "You know, she didn't mind. She really just didn't like that she couldn't staple crap to the walls."

"Is that how you think people decorate, Reggie? 'Stapling crap to the walls?' Have you really never hung a picture frame?"

"Look, I know how to stay alive in just about any situation I find myself in. That doesn't mean I'm a handyman. I don't know stuff like that, and I plan to keep it that way."

"Fair enough," Ben said. "Anyway, if you really want to know why we're going to Switzerland, I'll fill you in on the details of what I'm planning. I could use your input, anyway."

"Of course you should, man," Reggie said. "I am professional in hare-brained and cockamamie schemes."

CHAPTER 50
BEN

9:42 PM | **March 10, 2021**

London-Heathrow International Airport, London, England

Ben turned in the seat and faced Reggie, lowering his voice. "Look, this is... a little bit unorthodox. Something probably in the upper echelon of stupid things I've ever tried to pull off."

"Stupider than trying to prevent a volcano from erupting?" Reggie asked.

"That was a one-time thing, and I didn't really have a choice."

"You have no idea if that was a one-time thing, *and* there was a hot chick on the line."

Ben shrugged and laughed. "I did get the girl, didn't I?"

"For now," Reggie said. "Until she realizes she's married to a curmudgeonly old man, shoved inside a flabby, potato-shaped body."

Ben rolled his eyes. "Just because you know Kung Fu or whatever doesn't mean I can't just sit on your chest and smash your face with my potato-shaped fists."

"Okay, okay," Reggie said. "Why don't you fill me in on this plan of yours before you get too hot and bothered?"

"Right," Ben said. "So, Tennyson. He wants me to join his team, and he's got leverage on us. Eliza, threatening to kill her."

Reggie nodded, then stood up and started pacing. Before Ben could continue his explanation, Reggie jumped into a monologue. "Okay, so you need to find leverage on Tennyson, right? You need to get something of his that he's not okay parting with. Which means we are going to Switzerland because you learned about someone there he still cares about. A loved one, maybe? And you plan to kidnap them and use them as bait to lure Tennyson out. Or, you plan to use them as leverage when we get to Tennyson."

Ben was staring up at Reggie, his jaw on the floor. "How — what the hell, man? You just whipped that together right now?"

Reggie threw his head back and roared in laughter. A few nearby passengers waiting for the initial boarding call looked toward them, annoyance on their faces. "Ben, this was literally my first thought when I learned about Eliza. You might find this hard to believe, but I'm not just a beautiful, perfectly sculpted hero reminiscent of Greek mythology, with perfect, pure motives."

Ben rolled his eyes even harder. "Please," he said.

"No," Reggie continued. "I'm not. Inside that chiseled, amazing exterior is a dark, sinister soul. When I learned that someone you cared about had been kidnapped, my first thought was to return the favor."

"You've actually already considered this?"

Reggie nodded. "Of course, man. It's what I do. We need to get to him, just like he got to us. He played his hand when he took her. It means he understands the *human* element at play. It means he intuitively grasped the empathetic reason behind it. It means that he's not a sociopath, that he's capable of human feeling. And, it also tells me there is a similar and opposite response that can work on him, as well."

Ben nodded. "Besides Lars and his sister who died in the lab when we were there, I found out that Tennyson has at least one more granddaughter. She currently lives in Berne, with her parents.”

“Okay, that can work,” Reggie said. He looked up at the ceiling. “Yeah, that can definitely work. But how do we know he really cares about her?”

“That’s the risk we have to take,” Ben said. “She’s the only one I can find who’s close enough to the man that it might work. If he has any human decency left in him, I’m hoping he’ll do anything to protect her.”

“Or he’ll know we’re bluffing,” Reggie answered. “He’ll assume we’re not going to kill his granddaughter right in front of him.”

Ben paused, also looking up at the ceiling.

“Wait, Ben — we are *not* actually considering killing his granddaughter, are we?”

Ben made a face, raising his eyebrows and cocking his head to the side as he looked away from Reggie.

“Oh, *come on*. We can’t —“

Ben finally turned back. “No, you idiot. We’re not going to kill a kid. That’s off the table — always will be, always has been. You know that.”

Reggie let out a breath of relief. “Damn, man. You scared me. I thought you had suddenly gotten dark and twisted like me.”

“I can only wish,” Ben said with a smile. “But, you’re right: he can call our bluff. If he knows me as well as he thinks he does, he’ll know I’m not the kind of person who can do that. Not to a kid.”

“What about kidnapping one of *his* kids, then? They’re adults, so we could try that. And if it comes to it, I’m sure we can find something evil they’ve done so we don’t feel bad pulling the trigger.“

Ben waved it off. “No, won’t work. There’s still the problem of us having to murder someone who’s innocent, and it’s much more likely that a falling out happened between Tennyson and his kid, instead of Tennyson and his grandkid.”

“Right,” Reggie said. “Good chance Tennyson would just let us kill his kid if they've been distant for a while. It would only fuel his hatred for you, and possibly force his hand and get Eliza killed, as well. But there's another option: we don't have to kill anyone."

Ben felt relief wash over him. "We don't?"

Reggie shook his head. "No, we can do this a different way. We don't need to cause any harm to them, and we can come clean with our pure intentions. We tell Tennyson we have his granddaughter, and we tell him that we don't have the heart to kill her. However, we *do* have the heart to keep her from him, as long as it takes to free Eliza."

7:42 AM | **March 11, 2021**

Paris, France

Freddie's body felt crushed beneath the seatbelt and door of the small miniature sedan he was in. Julie and Sarah had crammed into the seat next to him, while the front passenger seat remained empty. They were being driven through the streets of Paris by a rideshare driver they had hired that morning.

They'd risked booking two hotel rooms upon landing in the city last night, needing the rest and knowing that no one was going to be awake when they arrived in Paris late. They hadn't heard anything from Ben and Reggie either, and Julie had told them she wanted to get a bit more information about the sword before sending anything over.

As they drove on, Freddie couldn't understand why no one had opted to sit in the front seat. He had been polite and had chosen the backseat so as to allow one of the women he was with to sit up front, and yet both of them had simply smashed their way into the back and took away all his remaining legroom.

So much for southern hospitality.

He grumbled uncomfortably but did his best to keep a good attitude. With any luck, it would only be a short drive from their hotel.

"Vingt-cinq minutes," the driver called out from the front seat. Freddie didn't speak French, but he knew the word *minutes* and he knew that the number the driver had said in front of it had had a bunch of syllables in it, which told him everything he needed to know. *We're not even close.*

"You okay?" Julie asked. She looked down and laughed as she saw his legs pressed together, his knees pointed straight forward and digging into the back of the passenger seat in front of him.

He nodded quickly, not wanting to waste any words. Any extra exertion might cause him to break out in a sweat. He was a soldier, and yet sitting with his knees touching was one of the most uncomfortable positions he could be in. He hated small spaces — not out of claustrophobia, but out of a general fear that he might not be able to get out once stuck inside. He was not a small man.

The car weaved around the streets of Paris and Freddie looked at the old, beautiful town, trying to make the best of his current predicament. They were on the left bank, which apparently meant there was a river or beach or something nearby, but he hadn't looked it up beforehand. It seemed there was a building at every turn that was older than the country he had been born in, and he couldn't help but feel impressed by the ancient feel of some of the streets they drove over.

It was simpler here — everything seemed just a bit smaller. The cars, the people, the tiny shops and storefronts and cafés. Some of the streets that shot off the main road they were on were cobblestoned, like the ones he had seen in London, and he wished for a moment that they weren't on their way to track down some dumb old sword and instead could spend a few days and nights wandering the city.

He let his mind wander back to the librarian he'd met in the library. *She was tiny too,* he thought. *She would look cute here. She would fit in well with the Parisians. And she'd fit in this car.* He started imaging that it was her, instead of Julie, smashing against him in the seat —

"We are here," the driver said. He spoke with a thick accent, but his English was easy to understand.

Has it been multiple French syllables of minutes already? Freddie wondered. He looked out the window and saw their destination, confirming. A simple brownstone that looked like it would be well-suited for a block in San Francisco or in one of the boroughs of New York. It was simple and elegant, a perfect blend of old class and modern flair, with curved wrought iron in articulate designs making up the front fence and gateway, the fence columns themselves built of stone. The gate was open, and he saw that beyond it there was a path leading up to the house. The neighboring houses on both sides of the street were similarly well-kept, all quaint and perfectly French.

They got out of the car and thanked the driver, then walked up the path and Julie knocked on the door. He knew Madame Blanchet would be expecting them, and a few seconds after knocking, the door opened.

She greeted them in French, and Sarah returned a similar greeting that was totally incomprehensible to Freddie, and then the tiny woman beckoned them into her home. She seemed to perfectly match the atmosphere and vibe of the house and the neighborhood. Everything about the woman seemed old, yet sophisticated. She carried herself with dignity, even though her torso hunched out over herself a bit as she shuffled along.

She switched to English, no doubt for his sake. "Would you like some tea? Coffee?"

Freddie was about to nod his approval for a cup of coffee when Julie butted in. "No thank you, Madame. We should be quick."

Madame Blanchet did not seem to approve of this, and she frowned and waved her hands toward Julie. "Should be quick! To be quick in conversation is to not be French. We are talking about important things, take as much time as you need."

Julie smiled. "I appreciate your hospitality, Madame. And believe me, we would love nothing more than to talk shop all day, but I am afraid we are under a bit of a time crunch."

The tiny old lady had white, wispy hair that, when in the right light, bordered on being blue. She gazed up at Julie as she offered her a seat on a plush sofa in the front room. She cocked her head to the side, quizzically. "Indeed, and most intriguing. I'll allow it. What sort of fun and games have you gotten yourself into, Mademoiselle?"

Julie thought for a moment, but Sarah answered for her. "We have another meeting later, that's all. We're — we're trying to track something down, and we thought you might be able to help."

"I hope that I may," Madame Blanchet said. "Please, you two, have a seat. The big man can sit over here if he is more comfortable."

Freddie swallowed as he realized what she was thinking. *If his fat ass sits down there, my chairs are destroyed.* He ducked his head to the left and glanced at the miniature-sized armchair sitting in the corner. It looked like a set piece from a period movie, the embroidery ornate and over the top, and the legs of the thing gilded in some kind of copper or gold.

It looked like it had been made from matchsticks, ready to implode at any moment, to just dissolve under his 'big man' weight. Even if it were sturdy, it didn't seem like he could get his entire *derrière* into it without using a pipe clamp on his hips to squeeze them together.

He quickly lunged across the room and took a seat on the sofa next to Julie. Even then, it was a tight fit. He thought of the car they'd just ridden in and almost decided to just stand the whole time. Instead, he shifted a few times and then looked back up at Sarah and the madame. "Thank you, ma'am. I'll be perfectly comfy right here."

Madame looked at him, her head a bit sideways. He wondered if she had another question for him, but if so she kept it to herself. She looked back at Julie as Sarah sat down in the armchair across from them. When they were all seated, she began. "I was the official historian for the Museum of the Army of France for the better part of a decade. Before that, I taught French history at a local college."

Julie nodded along. "Yes, your CV is quite impressive. We believe you are the perfect person to help us with tracking down this —"

"The *objet de désir*," she said with an artful flair and flick of her wrist. "What is it, my dear? The item in question?"

Freddie watched Julie from the side as she swallowed and then answered. "Well... It's — it's something that might be considered a bit... *controversial*."

"And why is that?"

"Well, perhaps not *controversial* as much as it is something that most do not believe actually *exists*."

Madame Blanchet raised an eyebrow and looked at all three of them in turn.

"You wish to find something that does not exist? A most *curious* query."

"We have reason to believe it may," Sarah said. "That's why we are here — if there is any hope it exists, you might be able to verify that."

"What is the object?"

"A sword."

She took this in and sat with it for a brief moment before responding. "A sword... Yes, these are things that certainly do exist." She winked at Freddie, and he smiled.

"A sword carried by Napoleon," Julie said.

"Of Austerlitz?"

"Yes, sort of. But not the *actual* sword of Austerlitz. A copy. A replica."

The madame shook her head quickly a few times, her brow furrowed and deep in thought. "No, I am afraid I have never heard of such a thing. It must be a modern creation, something perhaps commissioned by a museum for a Napoleonic display?"

"We don't think so," Sarah said. "We have reason to believe whoever created the Sword of Austerlitz —"

"Biennais," Madame Blanchet interjected.

"Yes, Biennais," Sarah continued. "We believe that Biennais created the Sword of Austerlitz, but perhaps also another version of the same sword. Something perhaps not designed for Napoleon but for his son?"

"But Napoleon II had not been born when the Sword of Austerlitz was forged — nor was he even a twinkle in his father's eye."

"I see," Julie said. "So what can you tell us about Biennais?"

"Well, my dear," the madame said. "Everything. You'll have to be more specific."

CHAPTER 52

BEN

7:45 AM | **March 11, 2021**

Veyrier, Geneva, Switzerland

"Okay," Ben said. "Tell me again what you need me to do."

After landing at Geneva Airport last night and booking a room at the nearest cheap motel, Reggie and Ben had rented a small sedan. They were currently navigating through the suburbs of a municipality called Veyrier, looking for the house of Baden Tennyson's granddaughter. They had tried to simplify things and get a rideshare, but apparently the service hadn't taken off in this country as much, and the wait time for a ride would have been somewhere close to forty minutes. Neither man had had patience for that, so they used some of the cash they had taken out to rent a car for the day. It would give them options, as well as a bit more freedom, so Ben was happy to make the concession.

The map app on Reggie's phone was guiding them closer to their destination, but Ben wanted to be very clear about what, exactly, his friend's plan was.

"Easy," Reggie answered as he steered the car around another turn. "We're door-to-door salesman."

"I got that much," Ben said. "But we are supposed to be *selling?* Cameras?"

"Phones, actually."

"People don't buy phones from door-to-door salesman, Reggie."

Reggie smiled, then turned on the blinker as he changed lanes and headed for the next turn. "Of course they don't — people don't buy *anything* from door-to-door salesman anymore. That doesn't mean they don't exist though, right? And you're missing the point. We don't need to sell her a phone, we just need to —"

"And why does a twelve-year-old even need a phone?" Ben asked.

"She's *twelve*, Ben," Reggie answered. "I would be surprised to learn she didn't already have one."

They had done a bit of research on the flight over, hoping that by just keeping their hunting to a small bit of research done through a VPN over the in-flight Wi-Fi network, Tennyson wouldn't be alerted to their movements, and guess their plan.

The research had been fruitful. The rabbit hole of searching for Tennyson's son's name — Bryson Tennyson — had led them to a local community website with the man's name mentioned. Her father worked nearby at a local chemical plant, and Reggie had found an article on the company's website that mentioned that he and his family lived in Veyrier. From there it was just a matter of finding anyone named Bryson Tennyson in an online white pages directory and paying a few dollars to gain access to the public records for that county.

They had ultimately discovered that the girl's name was Alexi, and that she lived with her parents — Tennyson's son and daughter-in-law — in a three-bedroom home in Veyrier.

In all it had taken less than an hour of work, but Ben still felt like they were doing something wrong. He hadn't liked the idea of kidnapping someone in the first place — especially a kid — and even though they had never planned to harm her, it felt dirty.

Ben's plan had ultimately morphed into coming up with some

way to ask her parents for permission to borrow their child. It was a long shot, and he figured there was a better chance the plan would end with getting the Swiss police called on them.

Instead, Reggie had come up with a plan that didn't involve any kidnapping or persuading parents to let their preteen daughter run around with two American men. Ben had been relieved, even though Reggie's plan seemed like a long shot as well.

He knew the pressure was getting to him. Mr. E had delivered him a directive, one he had yet to share with the rest of his team. He wanted to catch Tennyson, wanted to stop him, and he felt he would do *anything* to do that.

But he had surprised himself by even considering threatening an innocent family. He wasn't feeling quite himself, and he hated Tennyson all the more for making him feel that.

"Look, we just need to get her to take a selfie with us," Reggie said. "She's twelve, so cell phones are something she's going to care about. Right?"

"Why are you asking me? I didn't get a cell phone until after I was married."

Reggie laughed. "I think you had one a little before that, but I get your point."

"Okay, so we get her to answer the door, or at least get her to come to the door. But how do we do that? What if her mom or dad opens the door and aren't totally okay with two strapping American men calling on their daughter?"

Reggie smiled. "Easy. Already figured that out: we just need to make sure the girl is home with her nanny, or by herself."

Ben shook his head, letting out a breath. "There's no way this is going to work, man. How do you even know she had a nanny?"

Reggie shrugged as he drove down the narrow streets. They were in the suburbs now, close to their target neighborhood. "School's out right now. That was easy enough to find. And then the article that mentioned her dad works for the chemical plant, but also that her mom is a nurse, working crazy shifts. So if she's home, she's probably sleeping. I think there's an even better chance she's gone. The girl's twelve, so she's probably old enough to be at home by herself, but maybe they've got a nanny for her or something."

"Or at a friend's house by herself," Ben added.

Reggie shrugged. "So what? We can wait a little bit."

As they neared the address, Ben started to feel more and more anxious. This no longer felt like something he wanted to be a part of. He had made a mistake in even mentioning the idea to Reggie. Reggie was a good man, and Ben knew he wouldn't harm an innocent person either, but he was even more close-minded than Ben when it came to seeking vengeance for those he loved. Mrs. E had been murdered by the hand of Tennyson, and Ben knew Reggie would go to the ends of the earth to prevent it from happening again.

He wanted to call it off, to have Reggie pull over and head back to the airport, to find a different way. He wanted to consult with Julie — often his voice of reason.

But they were so close. They could at least go by the house, they could at least check and see if anyone was home...

They pulled onto Alexi's street.

He saw the house now, a cute blue thing with white trim. Two stories, but small. It was nice but not luxurious, matching most of the houses on that block in style and size.

"Should be up here on the left," Reggie said under his breath.

"Reggie, I —"

Out of the corner of his eye, Ben saw something that caused him to catch his breath. He turned his gaze toward it, trying to focus on what it was that had alerted his subconscious.

He blinked a few times, but he was sure of what he saw now, as it was rolling slowly into view.

A truck.

A *white* box truck.

"Reggie, that's —"

"I see it, man," Reggie said softly. "There's no way to know if it's anything to worry about, though. Probably just somebody delivering a washer and dryer."

Ben nodded, but he felt the turmoil in his stomach growing to a roar. He had been feeling a general discomfort before; now he simply felt terror.

"We need to get out," Ben said. "Now. We need to go over there, to knock on the door at least, to try to get her attention and —"

The truck picked up speed, then hit the brakes, squealing in front of the house just as Reggie and Ben pulled up to it. Ben locked eyes with the driver.

For a flashing second, their eyes met and Ben was confused. The face was familiar.

Then he knew.

The same eyes. The same, black curly hair. A deep complexion, almost brooding.

How the hell?

And then the man smiled.

The door opened, and the man jumped out directly onto the street, once again leaving the door wide open. This time, however, he had not come unarmed. He pulled up a subcompact machine gun and immediately pulled the trigger.

"Reggie! Get down!"

Reggie was already moving. They both ducked in toward each other, the tops of their heads nearly smacking together as they hit the center console, their arms and torsos barely below the level of the windshield.

Bullets hammered through the glass, sending chunks of plastic and glass flying.

Reggie roared in rage, but didn't move. Ben simply laid there motionless, wondering if the man would walk over to them or keep his distance.

The attacker kept firing, the bullets tearing through their headrests, sailing through the back windshield, turning everything inside the car above the steering wheel into powder and dust. He heard the pinging sound as bullets hit the engine and metal components under the hood. The car would be toast, their hope of chasing him down by vehicle were all but lost.

A few more bursts fired, and then the shots died away. Ben and Reggie sat there for an extra moment, not daring to move. Finally, Ben sat back up and peered out the now wide-open space where the windshield had previously been.

The man was gone.

"Reggie, get out. Get out, now."

Reggie nodded, already opening the door. He stepped out of the driver's side of the vehicle. Ben did the same, and both men hopped toward the back of the car and then crouched down once again. Ben didn't want to take any chances; the man was not far away, probably reloading and lining up another shot.

"You okay?" Reggie asked.

Ben gritted his teeth and nodded. "I'm just fine. But I *really* want to catch that asshole."

"Can't argue with that," Reggie said. "Ready?"

Ben wasn't sure what he was supposed to be ready *for* — they had no weapons here, no plan. Their only means of escape had just been obliterated, and it was highly unlikely that it would even start again. Even if it could turn over, there was no way it would make it all the way back to the airport.

"Sure," Ben said, knowing it was a lie.

CHAPTER 53

FREDDIE

7:46 AM | **March 11, 2021**
Paris, France

Madame Blanchet rose from her chair and walked toward the living room with small, pattering footsteps. "I'm going to prepare some tea," she called out. "Are you sure I can't get any for you?"

Freddie declined but asked for a coffee instead, and Julie accepted, with cream and sugar. As they waited, Madame Blanchet returned to the sitting room. "I can tell you everything there is to know about Martin Guillaume Biennais, born in 1764, but you have mentioned that you do not have much time. You don't seem to be with the police, and you don't strike me as private detectives — there would be no reason for all three of you to be here at once in that case — yet you *do* seem to be hesitant about explaining to me exactly why you believe *two* separate Austerlitz swords were made. May I ask why?"

Julie cleared her throat. "We do apologize for our hesitation. There has just been a lot of... activity in the last few days. Travel, hotel arrangements, flights, that sort of thing. We just got here from London, actually."

She nodded. "Yes, I remember you telling me you were in

London in your email. Terrible thing that happened there — did you hear about that other terrorist attack?"

Freddie's eyes widened a bit, and he glanced at the two women seated with him. Julie never wavered. "Yes, terrible."

"And after the attacks in Rome and Mexico," Madame Blanchet said, shaking her head. "They do seem to be increasing in frequency, do they not?"

Julie had not heard about any attack in Mexico, and she made a mental note to check into it when they left Madame Blanchet's home.

"Anyway," Sarah said, picking up the thread. "We didn't want to take too much of your time; we know you are probably busy —"

Madame Blanchet threw her head back and laughed. "Young lady, I am seventy-nine years old. I have spent most of my life studying and researching Napoleon and his impact on my country. I retired from a professional teaching job and volunteer my time when I want. I have very few friends left alive, and my husband died five years ago. If time is what you are worried about, I'm afraid your worry is wasted on me."

Sarah smiled. "Thank you. We appreciate that. To be honest, we are in a bit of a pickle because we have been tasked with actually *finding* and producing this sword, and — just like you — we did not believe it existed prior to yesterday."

"What happened yesterday that gave you reason to believe it does?"

"The person we are trying to find it for sent us a video. There is a woman in the video, but there is also a sword near her head."

"Near her head? That's odd."

"This video is indeed odd," Sarah said, quickly ensuring the conversation stayed on track and Madame Blanchet didn't get side-tracked into worrying about Eliza.

Freddie approved of her approach. No need to unnecessarily get another person worried, or wondering why Tennyson had rigged up a private guillotine using one of the world's most popular swords.

Sarah continued. "But it is *odd* because the sword in it seems to be the Sword of Austerlitz."

"Could it be a replica?"

"Of course — have there been any replicas of it made in the past?"

Madame Blanchet thought for a moment, then shook her head. "No, not that I know of. It would be a difficult thing to make a copy of this sword that is of any real value. Unless the smith had access to the sword itself, and could use it to copy its exact dimensions, they would have to be working from a picture. Not to mention the fact that it would be incredibly expensive, and I just don't see a museum wanting to invest in something like that just for display purposes."

Sarah was nodding. Freddie knew this was exactly her plan — to take all other explanations of the sword's existence off the table, so that Madame Blanchet would see the sword, then agree that it had to be what they said it was. He pulled his phone out, handing it over to Sarah.

"Freddie has a screenshot of the video, zoomed in on the sword. You can see most of the shield and hilt where the detail work was done. I'm assuming you are familiar with the sword?"

Madame Blanchet looked at her like she were a child who'd just asked if she knew how to read, but she nodded politely. "Yes, I am familiar."

She handed the phone to Madame Blanchet, who produced a small pair of spectacles from an invisible shirt pocket. She perched them on the tip of her nose and then pulled the phone toward her face and away from it a few times, eventually settling on the ideal distance from her eyes for her vision to focus. She held it in place for a few seconds, then turned the phone's screen slightly.

She looked for a few more seconds, then gasped. "Oh, my," she whispered. "Oh, this is miraculous indeed."

"Would you say that looks like the Sword of Austerlitz?" Julie asked, after a few more seconds.

Madame Blanchet stared at the image for another moment and then shook her head. "No, I would not say it looks like the Sword of Austerlitz. I would say it is, without a doubt, *the* Sword of Austerlitz."

Freddie smiled. "We thought so, too."

"So, you have just proven that the sword is real, a fact that did not need verification. So why do you believe this one is a copy?"

"Because the sword in this picture is not *actually* the Sword of Austerlitz."

No one spoke for another dozen seconds, and finally Madame Blanchet looked around at each of them. Freddie watched her eyes settling on each one in turn, knew she was trying to read them, trying to see if she were being played. "Okay," she said finally. "I'll bite. I've always liked Americans, and you three seem to be honest enough. What is it you are not telling me?"

Freddie held the phone up and showed it to her. "The hilt. The roses, or flower things. Notice anything?"

Madame Blanchet's eyes grew as she studied the image on the screen. He could see the realization in her eyes. She pulled back, then looked up at Freddie. "You — you are correct, son," she said. "This is *definitely* not the Sword of Austerlitz."

CHAPTER 54

BEN

7:49 AM | March 11, 2021

Veyrier, Geneva, Switzerland

Ben looked up over the blown-out dashboard and saw the bomber running up the street. He looked over to Reggie. "Let's go!" he yelled.

"I'm going after him," Reggie said. "You call the police for backup."

Ben shook his head. "There's no time, Reggie. Go after him, but I have to get to that truck. If it's what we think it is —"

"Are you insane?" Reggie yelled. "Ben, it's going to *explode*. There's no way you'll get there in time, and the closer you are to it, the better chance there is that you go up with it."

"Not if we're sitting here arguing about it." Ben wasn't trying to sound annoyed or frustrated, he just wanted to get the point across. "We'll meet in the woods in five minutes, no matter what."

There were some pine trees standing above the house at the end of the block, which looked like it butted up against an area of dense forest. The driver of the truck had disappeared behind that house, and Ben knew that if there were any chance of catching him, it was when he would be moving more slowly through the forest.

Ben pushed Reggie, and his friend finally shook his head and turned and began to sprint up the road. Ben could run, but he didn't have the speed Reggie had. If anyone could track down and catch the bomber in the forest, it was Reggie.

Ben turned and focused on the house, the truck still parked and running in front of it. So far, he hadn't seen anyone peek out from inside the house, but he couldn't take any chances. He had a feeling Reggie had been correct, that Tennyson's granddaughter was home, even though there were no cars parked out front or in the driveway.

He started toward the truck, hoping there would be enough time to get there before —

He was lifted off the ground and sent flying through the air backwards before he heard the sound or saw the blast. The truck in front of him simply ceased to exist, as did the house it had been parked in front of.

And parts of the two houses next door.

Windows up and down the street broke simultaneously, blasted inward from the pressure wave that had lifted Ben and thrown him back.

He landed just as he felt the heat from the blast wash over him, and his mind was pulled back to the attack on his own cabin.

He felt his head smack against grass, thankful that he had landed in a yard and not on the sidewalk or road. Still, he was less concerned for his own safety than he was for the innocent people living in these homes.

It took a few seconds of adjustment to gain his composure once again, but he blinked away the butterflies and did his best to stand up. On shaky feet, he looked over toward the space a hundred feet away. A crater sat where the road had been, which extended over the asphalt, over the sidewalk, and halfway into the yard in front of the picturesque house that had been reduced to rubble.

The house itself had just disappeared, only a few framing boards left standing, their bases mounted in the concrete slab beneath. The houses to the left and right had suffered similar damage, though there were a few walls on their far perimeter still standing erect.

He screamed, cursing the driver who had left the bomb.

If only he had not argued with Reggie — if only he had had a few more seconds.

He shook his head. *Then what, Bennett?*

Would he have had enough time to defuse the bomb? He knew it was highly unlikely. He knew very little about how to disarm a bomb, and he was pretty sure it was a little more complicated than just chopping a wire.

What should he have done? Could he have driven the truck away? It would surely have been suicide, and, besides, there were houses all the way up and down the street — there was nowhere he could've taken it that it would have been completely safe for the people living here.

He began to feel tears welling in his eyes, thinking of Tennyson's granddaughter. The man had sent a bomb to her front steps — blown up his own family — in order to stop Ben and Reggie.

The tears were quickly replaced by a feeling of rage, an anger building intensely inside him, burning hotter than anything he'd ever felt. He had seen people die — he had caused death even, killed people before — he had been tortured, tied to a chair and beaten senseless. He had been to the ends of the earth, taken down the men and women who'd deserved nothing better, but this was different.

But he had *never* seen anything like this. He had never seen someone so willing to destroy their own family in order to prove a point. Someone who could so nonchalantly send someone to kill their own granddaughter just to maintain control of the situation.

He knew then that Tennyson had known they were coming here. He had somehow known all along that he and Reggie — or at least Ben, alone — was headed here, to try to use his granddaughter for leverage.

Ben knew he should, but he no longer felt guilty. How could he?

He had changed his mind before they'd made a move on the house. The idea of kidnapping had become something far more tame — basically just snapping a picture with Tennyson's granddaughter. A task almost nearing palatable.

And even then Ben had second-guessed himself. He had not wanted to go through with it, had not been willing to cause the young woman any harm or suffering or worry.

Now she was gone. Was this actually his fault? Was it because Ben and Reggie had come here? Because Ben had not come alone, or because Tennyson did not like the idea of their gaining any leverage over him?

No. He refused to acknowledge those possibilities. He put those questions out of his mind. There was no explanation, no justification for what Tennyson had done. This was so far over the line that Ben wanted to scream. He felt his blood boiling, the rage inside him building to a level of intensity he had never known possible. As he stood there, he felt his eyes beginning to blur, his breath coming more and more rapidly.

He wondered how Reggie was getting on with his own chase. There was nothing left here for Ben, nothing he could do.

If he stayed, just watching everything burn, there would be questions to answer. The police and fire department would be here any minute, and surely neighbors would be coming outside, seeing him standing there now. There was no reason they should think him suspect, but eventually Interpol would hear of the attack — they would hear Ben's description from the neighbors. They would eventually put things together.

He needed to leave. He needed to get out, to extract himself and Reggie from this place and keep pushing forward with their mission.

Find Tennyson.

CHAPTER 55

BEN

7:50 AM | **March 11, 2021**
Veyrier, Geneva, Switzerland

He felt his neck tensing up as well, like his hackles were being raised through some force that was not his own. It was strange, and he frowned as he reached his arms up to try to loosen himself up. As he did so, he felt them tightening as well, almost like the feeling of sitting for too long in one position.

He wasn't sure what it meant, but then his back and legs spasmed and hardened. He tried to take a step forward but nearly stumbled and fell back to the grass. His foot left the ground an inch and then froze, causing him to nearly fall forward. He was barely able to balance himself again before his entire body shut down.

He could no longer move.

He could hardly breathe as well. His eyes began bulging out of his head, as far as they would go as if pushed from inside, then they too froze in place. It was the strangest sensation, but it wasn't exactly painful — the exertion of trying to move while frozen was, however.

He wondered what was happening, how this *could* be happening. He was able to sniff just before his nostrils stopped responding, holding in the sweet air for a moment, but unable to expel it from his lungs.

Ben stood there, frozen in place, noticing a few people at the end of the street running toward the scene of the explosion. They were still far away; they still had not seen him. He wanted to call out to them, to ask them to push him, to see if he were going crazy or if he had somehow been miraculously frozen by some unknown force.

Maybe this was some sort of mind game he had played on himself — something so intense the anxiety had won and his mind had just shut everything down.

Out of the corner of his eye he saw a flash of white. It stopped just out of sight, but he thought he heard the sound of a car door opening, just before his ears began to dull and the sounds became blurry, as if underwater. He saw something in front of him, but his eyes wouldn't focus right, they wouldn't adjust. He knew it was a person.

Dark hair. A darker complexion.

The driver? Was this the man who had been driving the truck? It looked exactly like the man who had taken out Mrs. E, but how was that possible? Ben had seen that man's body, dead, with a bullet in his skull. He was currently buried outside Ben's house in Alaska.

Before he could get a good answer for those questions, he felt the sensation of falling. There was no active mechanism telling him this — it just felt like his entire body had become a vase, and that vase had been toppled over. He couldn't quite feel the falling, but he felt the stiffness now, a darkness in front of his eyes. He was looking up at something, maybe laying on his back? He felt a tingling sensation in his fingers, then some of the dullness in his ears turned back into audible sound.

Another car door shut, followed by one more.

He was sure of it now. He was in the back of a van, laying on something hard. Probably the van floor, which had been cleared and the seats removed. His eyes began to focus a little bit, and he felt a bit of breath escaping his mouth.

He pushed the air out, finally regaining the ability to breathe, even though it was tense and it hurt and he wasn't sure if it was going to be enough.

When he felt his hands and arms beginning to warm up once again, he gasped for air and pulled himself over on his side in a spasmodic breath. He had no idea what had just happened, but he was now laying in the back of the van. The doors had closed, and he felt the transmission coming alive beneath him as the van sped up and drove away.

Where am I going now?

His body was still not his own, not completely, and the thoughts seemed to be from someone else. It was like he was watching this all play out, unable to speak or help or interfere.

He realized that Reggie had not been able to catch the bomber. He was in the back of the van being driven by that same man, the man that had gotten a jump on both of them.

But that left one nagging question in Ben's mind.

How the hell did he freeze my body and get me into the van?

He shifted, preparing an attack. He needed to be free, to get out of this van and find Reggie. The driver was preoccupied with the road, which meant Ben had the advantage. He needed to —

A tiny object fell at Ben's side. It was round, thumbnail-sized. A wisp of smoke or haze began falling from it.

"Too strong a dose and you would not be able to breathe," the driver's voice said. He was talking calmly, as if describing the rules of a card game. "But to weaken it, it does not last long."

Ben was shaking, furious and ready to move in on the man. He turned his head and looked around. There was a small window in the wall between him and the driver, possible large enough to get through.

All I need is an arm. I'll choke him.

He moved forward, but the man continued talking. "My brother warned you in Alaska. You will all die. Thankfully for you, we need something more from you, so today is not the end for you. But soon. Very soon."

Now.

Ben rushed forward, hoping the driver wasn't paying attention. He reached the tiny window just as he felt the back of his neck tensing up again.

No.

His arms slowed, and his legs felt like mush, then firmed up and began to slow as well. He was losing control.

Almost. There.

The van driver's hand reached up and pushed the window closed.

Shit.

Before the gap disappeared completely, the driver of the van spoke again. "The Faction gave me plenty of product, as they fully intend to keep you alive throughout the trials. Please consider staying on the floor so you do not fall and hurt yourself when the acid hits."

Ben had not been ready for that. He was halfway to the window as it slid closed, one arm outstretched, precariously leaning off-balance.

When the acid worked through his system once more, he fell. Hard.

His eyes were rigid, open, and he was facedown on the bottom of the van, staring at the cold metal subfloor.

Completely unable to move, once again.

CHAPTER 56

JULIE

7:50 AM | **March 11, 2021**

Paris, France

Madame Blanchet looked around the room, still in disbelief. Julie watched her face, trying to read any hints of what the woman might be thinking. All she could see was shock and confusion.

"You... you are sure this is accurate?"

Freddie cleared his throat. "Madame, if you are implying that the video was faked, then I can assure you it was not. I made that thumbnail image myself, and believe me — I've got zero Photoshop skills."

Madame Blanchet smiled and nodded quickly. "No, of course not that. I would not accuse *you* of such a thing. I just mean... this woman..."

"We know her, as well," Julie said. "She's a friend of ours. And we are looking for her — as we said, we need to find the *second* Sword of Austerlitz in order to find *her*. We think the key to where she is lies with the sword."

"And why do you think that?"

Julie looked at Freddie and then at Sarah, but neither offered any answer. Julie was not about to come out and explain that their friend Eliza had been kidnapped and was being held ransom over the Sword of Austerlitz. And she was not really prepared to admit to this kind old woman that they were planning to steal the sword when they found it, in order to then exchange it for Eliza's life. "Well, we have nothing else to go on," Julie said finally, taking a different tack. She had chosen to answer the woman literally — to explain why they were looking for the sword based on the only thing they had: clues in the video.

"But the *sword* is not the only clue in the picture," Madame Blanchet said.

Julie flicked her eyes toward the woman, who had finally taken a seat in the last armchair available, across from Sarah in the small dining room. She was in the middle of a sip of tea, and Julie waited for her to finish.

"Well," said Madame Blanchet, "This shirt she is wearing... a sweater, perhaps? It is difficult to completely be sure without watching more of your video, but that's a mulberry tree on it."

"A mulberry tree?"

Madame Blanchet nodded vigorously. "Yes — of course. It is a tree that has been used for centuries in the harvesting of silkworms, which in turn are harvested for their silk. It is an old tradition, one that has been used for millennia, from Asia and the Middle East to places as far west as Spain."

Sarah shifted in her seat and sat up, leaning toward Madame Blanchet. "Madame, tell us — is the mulberry tree somehow linked to Napoleon or his sword?"

The madame smiled, her warm grin inviting and reassuring. "It is one of my favorite subjects," she began. "Napoleon Bonaparte was born of a family that lived in Corsica, an island off the coast of Italy."

Julie nodded. "Yes, I've been there before, actually."

Madame Blanchet continued. "His family was not particularly wealthy, but they did have ties to the royal family, which allowed them a bit higher status and business opportunities. One of these opportunities Napoleon's father got involved with was investing in a mulberry tree farm, hoping to provide his family a consistent income stream for decades. This investment ultimately ended in failure, and caused much grief and stress — not to mention debt — for the Bonaparte family. Ultimately, Napoleon had to return home from the military academy in Paris to help them stave off bankruptcy."

"So the mulberry tree is symbolic of Napoleon's young adulthood?" Julie asked.

"I tend to think of the Mulberry incident as something that shaped Napoleon, something that gave him his cunning wit and particular knack for choosing his battles. There was no reason a boy of his age should be able to help with anything back home, but in this case, Napoleon knew he needed to be there. Most historians see this as a strong familial connection, which isn't untrue, but I tend to see a bit more in the story. The Mulberry Incident made Napoleon the man he was. It gave him his first sense of justice, his first *victory*, if you will. He would have made as cunning a businessman as he did a military commander and leader of France."

"I see," Julie said. "I don't quite understand how this is useful to us as a clue, though. Should we go to Corsica?"

Julie was searching, stretching for the truth, trying to pull any more information out of this wonderful little lady that she could.

"I wish I knew how to offer you guidance,"Madame Blanchet said. "I, too, do not understand how this could be directly connected to your search for the sword. While it leads me to believe that Corsica would in fact be a good place to search — it was Napoleon's childhood home, after all — I only think that helps to narrow it down a bit, but not enough. There are plenty of places for a tiny sword to hide on a large island."

"You have given us more than enough, Madame," Julie said. "Coming here was a long shot, and part of me hoped that you had the copy of the Sword of Austerlitz tucked into a closet somewhere."

At this, Madame Blanchet laughed. "Oh, how I *wish* to be involved in such an adventure. But, alas, if I had something so valuable, I'm afraid I would simply waste the possibility of adventure for something as mundane as donating it to a museum." She paused, turning her head to look at the ceiling for a moment, then looked back at the rest of them. "There is... one thing, however. Something that might be more helpful."

Julie felt her heart rate increase. "Anything, please," she said. "Anything that might help us — we would be very grateful."

"Yes. Well, I have always found it an interesting tidbit that Biennais was not the *only* smith of his time to work for Napoleon. He was a brilliant businessman, but not the most gifted artisan. While he was without a doubt the designer and creator of the original Sword of Austerlitz, if someone created a *copy* of it, it would most likely not have been him."

"What other goldsmiths from Paris can you tell us about?"

"There were others, particularly one other smith who had a respectable and professional feud with Biennais, particularly when it came to government projects."

"That's interesting," Sarah said. "So Biennais was not the only smith that Napoleon commissioned?"

"Oh, heavens no," Madame Blanchet said. "Napoleon had a purse of a thousand francs per year for commissioned custom gold pieces, but he often used many times more than that using gold from his own pocket. He spent this doling out commissions to Biennais, as well as a few small dealers and craftsman. But, especially later on, there was one man with whom Napoleon trusted his private commissions. A company that is still in business today, started by the goldsmith's own family in 1690. A man named Jean Baptiste Claude Odiot."

7:51 AM | **March 11, 2021**
Veyrier, Geneva, Switzerland

The forest closed in around him, pressing him on all sides, constricting him. Reggie used to love being in the forest, feeling the natural presence around him. Unfettered by human civilization, untainted yet by human greed and gluttony.

But right now he wished all of it had been razed to the ground and turned into a long, flat parking lot.

He didn't want to play cat and mouse — he didn't want to chase anyone. He wanted to catch the bastard who had shot at them, the one he had already killed at Ben's cabin just before it exploded.

This guy must be a lookalike, a twin brother of the man who had killed Mrs. E. But he was every bit a terrorist as the one from Alaska — this one had blown up a little girl's house.

He hadn't told Ben, but he had a reason for wanting to catch Tennyson.

He wanted to kill the man.

Personally. He wanted to watch him suffer. Slowly draining the life from him, drawing it out. He imagined taking a paring knife to the man's eyelids, prying his fingernails up and away from the flesh of his fingers, cutting him a thousand times and letting him bleed a slow agonizing death...

Ben would not approve, but he told Reggie himself: he was not the kind of man to give orders. The CSO was not the military. They were a group of individuals. Sure, they worked together to solve problems, but there were no written rules regarding anything like this.

It didn't matter, anyway. Ben could try to stop him, but he would fail. Reggie would fight back even his best friend in order to get vengeance for Mrs. E's death.

He turned in a tight circle, feeling his heart beginning to pound faster. His body was rigid, the only part of him not experiencing a surge of adrenaline his prosthetic arm. He needed to calm down, to slow the dopamine coursing through him. He was too excited to focus well, and he may have already missed a crucial clue.

The man had hidden his tracks through the forest well, something that would not be terribly challenging to do considering the forest floor was all pine needles and brush. A broken stick or trampled leaf would not look terribly out of place.

Still Reggie had trained for far more than just tracking a human through the woods. He had trained others how to do it, as well. He was a professional and expert tracker in every sense of the word, honing his skills over years in the military and then in Brazil, leading expeditions into the Amazon rainforest.

If anyone can find the bastard, it's me.

But it seemed the guy was a little better-equipped than he'd thought, or at least had been well-trained. So far, Reggie had not seen a single footstep in the forest, nor in the backyard leading up to it. He had seen the direction the man had been heading but hadn't actually seen him enter the woods behind the house at the end of the block.

He wondered if maybe he had been duped, if the man had doubled back and was heading along the houses by way of their backyards.

He turned around and focused his attention at the edge of the forest. He could still see the truck parked in front of the house

Without warning, the truck exploded. He saw it first, the sound reaching him a second later and the pressure wave blasting out around it. He saw the house — Tennyson's granddaughter's — as well as the two next to it suddenly flattened. He saw the truck itself disintegrate into a roiling ball of orange flames that leapt upward into the sky, saw the remnant smoke cloud billowing upward and outward.

Then he saw Ben as well, thrown backwards and into a front yard about eight houses down from Reggie's own spot in the woods.

Reggie roared in anger, then ran toward the edge of the forest. He needed to check to see if anyone was still alive in the house, though he knew it was a long shot. Ben would probably be okay — he had not gotten any closer to the truck and Reggie had seen him flailing through the air as he was thrown backward. He was fine, but he would be a bit dazed.

As he ran, he saw an older couple coming out of the house nearby. He turned left, hoping to get behind them and stay out of sight — there was no sense getting himself implicated at the scene — so he ducked behind a trash can and waited for an opportunity.

He heard the couple speaking to each other in German, but they seemed to be observing and not yet willing to go across the street and help.

Reggie swore under his breath, knowing that he was either going to have to be seen by these two or stay here and hide, allowing the driver to get farther away.

He sat there for a few more seconds, trying to weigh his options, then made up his mind. He rose, coming around the trash can and behind the couple, then began to run. He didn't turn to acknowledge them, hoping they wouldn't be able to describe him to police later since they hadn't seen his face. He aimed for a spot across the street from them and didn't slow down when the man yelled something his direction. He turned left and ran down the sidewalk toward the crater in the street. He made for the flattened house next to it, but then strange movement caught his eye.

Or, rather, a *lack* of movement.

At the other end of the street about four more houses away, he saw Ben standing, his arm half-raised, not moving. There was a van, unmarked, just like the one they had seen in the street in front of the hotel in London, the same make and model as the one the gunmen had spilled out of.

And then he caught a glimpse of the driver — the man he thought he had been chasing through the woods. He must have had the van parked somewhere nearby, planning for exactly this moment. Reggie felt sweat began to pour down his brow, felt is hands beginning to clench. He wanted to scream, but any element of surprise, any attack he might be able to pull together would be ruined.

Instead he started running again, aiming directly for the crater. If he could get down inside of it, he might be able to stay out of sight and shield his approach. Hopefully there was not still anything burning in it, and he wondered if the heated asphalt around it had melted and was still liquid enough for him to get stuck in.

He didn't bother to find out. He approached the side of the crater and jumped down into it. It was about five feet deep at its base, just enough to duck his head down but still see the van a few houses down. He watched as the driver backed the van up to where Ben was still standing.

Move, buddy. Get out of there. Reggie was shocked. Ben wasn't even trying to move — not even trying to fight back. It was like he had been frozen in place, his eyes still open but unable to respond.

What the hell am I looking at? Reggie wondered.

The driver got out, then approached Ben calmly. Reggie knew he only had a small window. He needed to get to Ben, to fight off this —

What the hell? he suddenly thought again. He watched as the driver simply pushed Ben. Ben toppled easily, then fell backward onto the empty floor of the back of the van.

The driver slammed the double doors shut, then got back in the driver seat just as Reggie pulled himself out of the crater. Reggie was at a full sprint even before his second foot out of the crater had hit the ground, aiming directly for the van.

Either the driver had seen him or was just in a hurry, because the van lurched forward, the tires squealing, then headed up the road.

Reggie knew he wouldn't catch up, but he did his best to memorize every letter and number on the license plate, in order. It wasn't hard, and he knew it would be seared into his memory for as long as it needed to be there.

Ben was gone, but the fight was far from over.

Reggie had information now — it was just a tidbit, but that would have to be enough.

No — he would *make sure* it was enough, making a silent promise to his friend.

He stopped sprinting now, knowing it was pointless. He knew the police would be here soon, followed shortly thereafter by whatever Switzerland called their SWAT teams, and — almost without a doubt — Interpol. Once the police had logged it in their systems and the question of international terrorism was raised, Interpol would come knocking. Eventually, someone on the street might describe him or Ben and Interpol would be even more interested,

He figured they had at least a day or two before that information bubbled to the surface. He had time now, but not much. The car they had rented was completely destroyed, but with any luck he could find someone willing to let him borrow a car.

He turned right and headed up the driveway of the house at the very end of the street.

Don't worry, brother, Reggie thought. *We'll get you back. We'll make this right.*

You have my word.

CHAPTER 58

JULIE

7:54 AM | **March 11, 2021**

Paris, France

Madame Blanchet smiled. "If you want more information about Odiot, you need to speak with a dear old friend of mine. It has been many years since I have heard from her, but we used to share letters two decades ago. She was just a child then, interested — like you are now — in the history of Napoleon, as well as his quirks."

"And she knows about Odiot?"

Madame Blanchet continued on but nodded. "This friend of mine believed some very fanciful things about the man, but it is her own family lineage that suggests she might be of service to you."

"She's related to Napoleon?" Freddie asked.

"She's related to *Odiot*. Hence her interest in tracking down any quirky Napoleonic information."

Julie stood up and began pacing the room. "I would like to speak with her, in fact," she said. "If she has any information at all it would be worthwhile. We don't have a lot of time, and I don't want to track down every single historian in the country."

Madame Blanchet winked. "Well, my dear, you have already saved yourself much hassle and tracked down the best Napoleon scholar there is. However, I do think speaking with Lady Catherine might help clarify your decision to visit Corsica, and perhaps more."

"You have me convinced," Julie said. Sarah and Freddie nodded along as well. "Where is Catherine?"

"I can get you her exact address," Madame Blanchet said. "She is in —"

Before she could finish the sentence, a knocking sound came at the door. Julie flicked her eyes over and saw that the deadbolt was locked, then turned back to Madame Blanchet. "Expecting someone?" she asked.

"No, but this street is full of little old ladies just like me. We drop in on one another quite often. Perhaps Greta has made me more of those god-awful cookies again, the ones with old raisins in them."

Madame Blanchet had risen from her chair and was halfway across the room. Julie saw Freddie stand up as well, no doubt intrigued by the visitor. It was probably nothing, but Julie didn't want to be too careful. She was glad Freddie was suspicious, as well. With everything that had happened to them...

Madame Blanchet unlocked the deadbolt and was moving her hand to turn the knob when the door burst open, nearly sending the frail old lady backwards down the hall.

Sarah screamed, and Freddie was making his way toward the door when Julie heard shots fired. Three, in rapid succession, all hitting Madame Blanchet in her chest and stomach. This time, the impact of the bullets *did* knock her backwards and onto her butt, where she sat on the floor and clutched at the wound closest to her heart.

Julie watched the life drain from her eyes. It only took a matter of seconds.

She had been standing there in shock, watching Madame Blanchet die on the floor, so she had missed the rest of the action.

The man who had shot Madame Blanchet from the stoop was now turning his weapon toward the rest of them. Sarah had ducked out of the way, so the man shifted his aim and was now preparing to fire at Julie.

He had not seen Freddie, however, who was still barreling toward him from the opposite side of the door. The man's arm and a leg were just inside the doorway, his hand twisted around the side of it, using the door as a makeshift shield. For that reason, he could not see Freddie at all.

Julie watched Freddie kick the door with his right foot as hard as he could, which sent the door slamming closed. That motion smacked the gun out of the man's hand and slammed into his knee. The man roared in pain and pulled his foot back from the doorway. The door closed behind him.

Freddie was there, reaching to open it. Julie ran up behind him as he got the door open again and together they both peered out.

The man was gone.

In a matter of seconds Madame Blanchet was dead on the floor, and the attacker had already vanished. Julie was confident that if Freddie had not foiled his plans, he would have put a bullet or three into each of them.

Who was it?

Julie was seething, her mind racing. Who did this? *Why* did they do this? If they wanted information — wanted something from us — they could have gotten it without killing an innocent woman.

It seemed too much, even for a man like Tennyson. To her knowledge, while he had invested in and had built a company that had no trouble engaging in research that was — at best — sadistic, she wondered if he could have been persuaded to outright *murder*.

Sure, he had had the woman who had purchased the sword killed, just as he was threatening to do with Eliza, but something about those events seemed to fit into Tennyson's game. They seemed to be in line with who she believed Tennyson to be.

But this one had been different. Calculated, cold. She couldn't shake the feeling that some of the earlier attacks and this one had not been Tennyson's doing.

But then, whose? Whose hand had pulled the trigger? Whose voice had directed it? She wanted to find everyone involved, wanted to make them pay, to do to them what they had done to this poor, innocent historian, her lifeless hand still clutching her chest on the floor.

Sarah and Freddie were at her side. Sarah's hand reached her and her fingers held for a moment, then released. Sarah didn't speak, but the slight squeeze on Julie's wrist told her that she was not alone in this.

She knew that was true, but it didn't change how she felt. She longed for Ben. She wanted to call him, to ignore her fears of Tennyson tracking them through their phones.

Ben would know what to do, she thought. *He would know how to get out of this.*

They still had a plan, however. She knew it was the only thing they could possibly do at this juncture.

Plan the work, work the plan. Something she had learned long ago in school. *And especially if you can't think of a better plan.*

"What we do now?" Freddie asked. "There are going to be cops here in a minute, and even though I hate to leave her like this..."

Julie nodded. "You're right. We don't really have a choice. We can't afford to play twenty questions, especially if Interpol gets wind of it and shows up."

"So where do we go?" Ready.

"The only place we *can* go," Julie said. "We're going to find Lady Catherine."

CHAPTER 59

REGGIE

7:55 AM | March 11, 2021
Veyrier, Geneva, Switzerland

Reggie pulled the phone up to his ear. He had been dreading making this call, for reasons he still was not aware of. If he had to guess, it was probably because he was afraid to allow himself to truly accept the loss of Mrs. E.

This call was going to remind him of that.

On the other end, Mr. E picked up after three rings. *"Gareth, is that you?"*

"Yeah... I'm sorry to call, but — I need your help."

"I am glad you called," Mr. E said. *"It has been difficult these last few days without contact from anyone. As you know, I am a solitary man. But after my wife..."*

Mr. E didn't finish the statement, nor did he need to. Reggie nodded, silently willing himself to press on.

"They took Ben."

"They what? Who is they?"

"I — I don't know. Whoever has been after us; Tennyson, maybe, but we're starting to think it's a third party. I'm not sure what the hell happened — first the house exploded, and we were trying to catch the bastard who did it. It was just like — it was like back at the cabin, and —"

Reggie had to catch himself. He wasn't sure if he wanted to continue down this path just yet. "Anyway, I ran into the woods chasing him — or so I thought — but he must have doubled back around and snatched Ben."

"Slow down. I am not sure I understand. How exactly did he snatch Harvey? Harvey is certainly not a small man."

Reggie shook his head, once again feeling the rage bubbling beneath the surface. "I have no idea. It was some sort of chemical, I guess. It's like they knocked him out, but he was still standing there. Frozen in place, like he couldn't move or something. Whatever they did to him, I'm worried about what's coming next."

There was a long pause, and Reggie pulled the phone away and examined it, checking to see if it was disconnected. It wasn't, so he held the phone back up to his ear and waited.

Finally, Mr. E spoke. *"Gareth, I know who did this. I know what they are working towards, and you do not have a lot of time."*

"Wait, you know — who they are? Who the hell was it? Tell me where they are and —"

"As I said, you do not have a lot of time."

"I have the license plate number." Reggie prepared to read it off, reciting it from memory.

"Unnecessary," Mr. E replied. *"I am going to send you directions via text message. It will come from an encrypted source and look like it is from a short code rather than a phone number. They are going to try to move Ben out of the country most likely, so you must get to him before that."*

Reggie nodded along. "Got it. I got this. Okay." He pulled the phone away and took a deep breath. "You said you knew who they were. Who?"

"It is not really a matter of who, but what. Gareth, this is a group

we want nothing to do with. Trust me. Find Harvey, and find him quickly."

Before Reggie could object, the call disconnected. He stood there in shock, staring down at the screen for a handful of seconds. He was about to place it back into his pocket but then felt it vibrate. The screen lit up.

A text message. The number of the sender was indeed a short code, but he saw Mr. E's instructions below. He read through them, trying to make sure he understood it all. If he had questions, he needed to get them answered now, before he got too far into it.

He pulled open the rideshare app on his phone and began jogging. He wanted to get a couple of streets over from the location of the explosion before giving the driver his location, just to put more distance between the growing number of police and ambulances that were still arriving. The last thing he wanted was for the driver to ask him questions about why he was hanging out at a crime scene. Two fire trucks were present in front of the house now, hooking up their hoses and hauling them in place to prepare to douse what remained of the flames.

I'm coming for you, Ben.

He picked up his pace. If Mr. E was correct, he needed to get to his friend before they took him out of the country. The address Mr. E had sent him seemed to be close to the airport, so perhaps that was indeed what they were planning.

I'm coming for you, Ben.

He repeated the mantra in time with his steps, continuing to pick up his pace until he was flat-out running.

CHAPTER 60

REGGIE

8:26 AM | **March 11, 2021**
Veyrier, Geneva, Switzerland

Reggie arrived at the destination Mr. E had sent him twenty-seven minutes later. "You sure this right place?" The driver asked in stuttered, broken English.

Reggie nodded as he opened the door and hopped out, not wanting to waste time. "Damn sure. Thanks." He had no time for pleasantries. He would close out his ride and tip the driver later using the app, but for now he wanted to get inside.

The driver muttered something under his breath, then sped away.

Reggie turned to the building. It was nondescript, no logos or lettering on any of the three sides he could see as they had approached. There was no roof visible, either, just a wide, flat top like most of the industrial buildings he had seen on the way.

There was a sidewalk that led up to a set of metal double doors, but he could not see through them. He turned to the right instead, deciding to look for a side or back entrance. So far he had seen no security.

The building was on a street in a hidden corner of the city, tucked away near the airport. His best guess was that the buildings like this one were warehouses that stored cargo before being shuffled out to their final destinations. This one was one of many similar-looking buildings that lined the street.

There were very few cars around, and he chalked that up to his guess that most of the space inside these buildings were either completely empty or only used for storage. *All the better*, he thought. If Ben was somewhere inside, he didn't want to have to lug the big man out while simultaneously fending off a bunch of guards.

He thought of Mr. E's words. *They are going to try to take him out of the country, and by then it might be too late.*

He shuddered to think what that would mean. If they wanted Ben dead, they would have already done it. That meant they had something else planned for him.

Something far worse, Reggie was sure.

And who was it, anyway? Not Tennyson — that much he was sure of. Who was trying to kidnap Ben and kill the rest of his team?

Still, they were here *because* of Tennyson. This was Tennyson's fight — one he had picked with them.

Reggie cursed Tennyson's name as he approached the rear of the building, finally seeing what he was looking for.

There was a single window, mounted on the second story above a door. He tested the doorknob, knowing it would be locked. The window would be off-limits, too. Breaking the glass would immediately alert anyone inside, and would easily set off the alarm if there was one.

But it did mean that one thing might be in his favor: the window implied there was some sort of office or meeting room inside this building, and if that were the case, it was very likely that whoever worked in there would want it climate controlled.

Perfect.

Reggie looked up higher, seeing a retracted ladder bolted onto the side of the building near the bottom-right side of the window, just out of reach. It was probably ten feet off the ground, but he knew it was his best chance at getting inside.

He backed up a few paces and then jumped forward, sprinting toward the wall. At the last moment he lunged forward, his leg up and foot flat and parallel to the building. He kicked upward with his back foot at the same time, propelling him up the wall a few extra feet. He jumped forward and caught the ladder with his hands, three rungs up.

Nice, he thought. *Room to spare.*

He pulled himself up and onto the ladder fully, soon able to climb normally when his feet reached the bottom rung. He hoped it hadn't made any noise on the inside, but the building seemed to be made of concrete — unlikely anyone in the building would hear anything from outside quieter than a train.

When he reached the top of the building, he swung his legs over the ledge. The roof was just as he'd imagined — a flat, open expanse of panels with a two-foot ledge all the way around.

And directly to his right, an air conditioning unit. The unit was small, likely a miniature industrial version meant to cool a single space, just as he'd predicted.

It also meant there would be an access panel for airflow. He approached the unit and bent down on his hands and knees. Using his thumbnail, he worked one of the two screws out. Thankfully, whoever had installed the hatch cover had not been concerned with security and had left the screws nearly loose, only to grow looser over time. He unscrewed the first and second screw and then set them aside and carefully lifted the hatch cover up.

A torrent of dust enveloped him immediately. He sat back and coughed over the ledge, careful to keep his mouth muffled beneath his elbow. When he had recovered, he looked back at the hatch and thanked God he was not claustrophobic. He wasn't even sure he would fit through the hatch all the way, or what he might do when he got to a corner. He hoped the HVAC contractor had simply installed a straight chute rather than deciding to snake the ductwork around the edge of the room.

Only one way to find out, he thought. He took a breath, braced himself above the open hole, and then lifted his arms straight above his head and dove in feet-first.

It turned out to be a straight shot, about twelve feet down to the dusty second-floor office. His feet smashed against the vent cover on the other side of the chute and it tore off its housing and fell loudly to the linoleum floor.

His feet hit the ground on top of it and he used his hands to regain his balance. It was noisy as hell, but he was in.

All told, he had made worse entrances.

He was still worried that it had made too much noise, however — anyone inside the building would now know he was here. Thankfully however, there was no one currently in the room.

He looked around. It was very clearly an office, one that had been set up quickly and hastily and then completely forgotten. A filing cabinet sat to his right against a wall, two of its doors open and empty. A heavy steel desk stood in a corner of the room, no chair behind it. There were no decorations, no notebooks or knickknacks or pictures of family laying around. The desk had been completely cleared.

Whoever works here must like keeping things simple, he thought.

He heard footsteps on a stairwell, and Reggie imagined what the outside of the office space in the building looked like. He guessed this would be the only office, and that it was set up and above the rest of the space, judging by the row of tiny rectangular windows against one wall. They were all blacked out with a poor coating of paint, so he couldn't use them to see who was ascending the stairs.

They pounded up the steps heavily and purposefully. *That means they're armed,* Reggie realized. *No one unarmed and scared of intruders marches up stairs with that sort of confidence.*

He crouched down by the door and waited. It opened, slowly.

After a pause, it opened a few inches more. Reggie waited a second longer for the shape to appear fully in the doorway, then Reggie attacked.

He lurched forward from his crouch and brought his head up, smashing his forehead into the person's chin. It took them completely by surprise, and the man wobbled and stumbled backward, crashing into the open door.

And yet they didn't fall over. Their recovery was nearly immediate, and he felt a punch to the side of his head, glancing off his ear. It hurt, but it had not been a direct blow. The attacker followed up with a blow to Reggie's side that he was able to dodge, using the defensive move to come in closer to the man. He wrapped him up in a bear hug. He jostled for positioning and brought his leg around the man's raised back foot, then pulled upward. Both men crashed to the ground.

Reggie heard a grunt, but otherwise the man was silent. In the darkness, he couldn't see any particular features, but he didn't care. He knew it was not Ben, which meant that this man was going to die.

The man, however, was *not* going to die easily. He rolled to the side and got a foot out from under Reggie, which gave him enough leverage to swing it over Reggie's back and then lift both of them off the ground. He completed the motion by twisting at his waist and throwing Reggie back down, smacking his head hard against the floor.

Reggie saw stars, realizing the man was on top of him now. His hands were working his way toward Reggie's throat.

Like hell you're going to kill me, he thought. He reached out with his right hand and felt something — the only thing available — nearby. He pulled it up and grasped it tightly, knowing he would only have one chance.

With a flick of his wrist and a swing of his arm, he flung the register cover from the vent into the side of the man's head. He had aimed it and timed it appropriately, and the sharp corner of the rectangular metal object pierced through the man's temple, lodging itself somewhere in his skull.

It was not a kill shot, but Reggie didn't need it to be. The man howled in agony and lifted his hands away from Reggie's throat, reacting involuntarily to the new appendage Reggie had given him.

It was enough to get the leverage Reggie needed. He brought his torso up and threw three punches at the man's jaw, the last one making a cracking sound. He hoped it was the guy's jaw and not his own fist that had just been broken, but he had too much adrenaline coursing through him to be able to tell.

The man loosened his grip that his legs had around Reggie's waist, and Reggie pulled himself up and away, squirming back and out of the man's reach. He tried to grab Reggie's shirt as he moved, but he was in too much pain. Reggie easily slipped the hold and turned and roundhouse kicked the man in the face, aiming for his already-smashed jaw.

This did the trick. The man sailed backwards and smacked his skull on the hard floor, out for the count. Reggie didn't want to take any chances, and he knew he had to finish the job. The man's chest rose and fell, but he did not sit back up.

Reggie looked around, not knowing how exactly to finish him off. He didn't want to have to lift his body and cradle him in his lap in order to snap his neck, and that was not an easy task to pull off anyway. He could choke him, but there would be no way of knowing how long it would take before he died. He also didn't feel like bringing him to the window and tossing him out — with Reggie's luck, the fall wouldn't kill him, and the cops would find the body five minutes after he did it.

As Reggie looked around the office, his eyes happened to glance at the man he had taken down. He got a glimpse of his face.

Reggie recoiled in shock.

He knew the face immediately. The short, Caesar-trim haircut, the dark, deep-set features.

This was the man who had blown up Ben's cabin.

This was the man who had killed Mrs. E.

Or, rather, it was a spitting image. He hadn't been wrong — this guy looked *exactly* like the man he'd killed at Ben's cabin. It must have been a twin brother.

You bastard, Reggie whispered.

Filled with a new need to rid the world of the lookalike version of the man that had already caused them so much grief, Reggie walked over to the heavy metal desk as the plan formed in his mind. He picked up the two short edges of the desk, grunting under the effort, then tilted it so he could grab it by its legs. He took a leg in each hand and allowed the desk top to rest against his belly as he carried it over to the unconscious attacker on the floor.

He pulled the desk higher and aimed for a moment, already losing his grip on the impossibly heavy object. He didn't want it to slip, but he really didn't want to miss the mark. He positioned the edge of the desk over the man's throat and then raised it up even higher, grunting at the effort.

Reggie felt no remorse whatsoever. This was not the only person he had killed, and he had a feeling it would not be the last. But he knew that this man — like a few others he had come across — deserved it.

Reggie let the desk fall, sending it the three feet straight down onto the man's windpipe, knowing it would finish the job.

CHAPTER 61

BEN

8:29 AM | **March 11, 2021**

Veyrier, Geneva, Switzerland

Ben was groggy but coming to his senses. He squeezed his eyes shut and then opened them again, noticing that his vision was not much better with his eyes open. If his sight was going to return, he wished it would happen sooner rather than later. He didn't know where the guy was who had drugged him, but he was likely to return soon and send Ben back into the strange stupor.

He stretched, feeling the muscles in his neck and back loosening. Whatever tension had been there a moment ago was gone. He swallowed next, feeling his tongue scratch against his throat. It was dry, and he tried to use saliva to moisten it again.

Whatever the hell it was, he didn't want to go through it again.

He remembered the way the strange haze had floated around him and caused him to freeze up, had caused his breath to catch in his throat. With enough pressure, enough force, he could still breathe, but it was laborious and painful. He had stayed like that the entire time, feeling his body fall onto the hard floor of the empty van. Feeling the man carrying him out of the van and roll him into this corner. As if he were a statue.

Maybe that's why my back and shoulder are killing me.

He heard a noise from somewhere above him, and he tilted his neck to try to see what it was. As he did, he felt handcuffs on his wrists and ankles pulling tight against his limbs. *Bastard trussed me, too?*

He looked around once again, but couldn't tell where he was. Some sort of storage unit or storage space, a mostly empty warehouse. It was dark inside too, the only light coming from behind blacked-out glass doors about twenty feet away. There was not enough visual stimuli to get a good feel for the space, but he thought he saw stacks of boxes across from him. He was sitting, his back against the hard metal wall.

Definitely feels like a storage locker, he thought.

The noise he'd heard was replaced by footsteps, and he worked his way up to a kneeling position, then a standing one. The handcuffs on his wrists prevented him from using his arms for balance, but at least he wasn't fastened to a pole or something. He needed to get into a standing position so he'd have a better chance of getting into a *fighting* position.

If that asshole shows his face, he's dead. He had no question he could take whoever was about step foot onto this level, even with just his feet and hands. He would hobble around a bit, but a well-placed head butt should do the trick. If not, his hands had been cuffed in front of his waist, so he could potentially swing his fists up and pummel his kidnapper.

He only hoped he was not going to be drugged with whatever potent chemical had taken him out before. There was something shockingly visceral and terrifying about being kidnapped while completely frozen, unable to speak or move. He imagined it was like drowning — knowing what was happening, yet unable to fight back. Eventually being forced to take a deep breath full of seawater.

He shuffled to a position beneath the stairs, feeling the heavy footsteps as they thundered down and onto the concrete floor. He was completely concealed now, in the dark and hopefully in a spot where he could get around the person. He just needed them to walk by, so he could slip his hands around their neck...

They stepped close. A man, large and dark, still hidden by shadows. He could sense them, seeing only a dark presence, a flicker of movement.

He worked his way forward, lifting his hands and preparing to slip them over the man's head.

Three more inches.

The man turned.

"Ben?"

Ben's mouth fell open and his hands fell back to his waist. "Reggie?"

"Jesus, Ben," Reggie said. A wide smile erupted on his friend's face and Ben could see his perfectly white teeth gleaming back at him, even in the dark.

"Damn, what took you so long?" Ben asked.

Reggie laughed. "I figured you'd want to get to know your host a little bit better. Times up though — for him and for you."

"Dead?" He asked.

"Only the best for him."

Ben shuttered. "Good riddance. You recognize him?"

Reggie nodded. "He's got to be a twin brother of the guy who took out the cabin. Killed Mrs. E."

"Yeah," Ben answered.

"Too bad we couldn't question him anymore."

Ben shook his head. "He wasn't going to talk. Whoever he's working for, it's not Tennyson. But they're definitely still after us."

Reggie's grin disappeared and his face grew dim as they walked toward the back door of the building. "We need to find the others," Reggie said. "They tracked you and me pretty easily, which means they'll be able to track the girls and Freddie, too."

Ben had already considered this. He had already come to the

same conclusion. It was not Tennyson who was after them now — at least not *just* Tennyson. Whoever these newcomers were, they were good — good enough to get the jump on Ben and good enough to track them all the way to Switzerland. Ben and Reggie had been careful to only tell Julie and the others where they were headed.

And this weapon they were using — it was terrifying. What if they had larger quantities of it? What if they could use it for...

"Reggie," Ben said, his voice dropping to a near-whisper.

"What's up?"

"This stuff they used on me... it's like a haze. An aerosol or something, and it completely shut me down. Like I was dead and rigor mortis was setting in."

"Yeah, I saw," Reggie said. "What about it?"

"I was just thinking... what if they had larger quantities of it? Or a *stronger* version of it? Couldn't they use it for taking out not just one guy, but a lot?"

"Like a terrorist attack," Reggie answered.

Exactly. Ben nodded. He was thinking of the attack in the piazza in Rome. About how the newscasters were trying to piece it together, and how they were confused as to why no one tried to run.

If the attackers there were related somehow to what had happened to Ben...

It meant they were in trouble — a lot of trouble.

CHAPTER 62

BEN

8:46 AM | **March 11, 2021**

Veyrier, Geneva, Switzerland

"Any luck?" Reggie asked.

Ben shook his head, frustrated. He had tried calling three times, dialing each of their numbers. Neither Freddie, Julie, nor Sarah had answered their phones. He knew it was too early to worry, but he couldn't help but feel like he was losing control of the situation. If none of them were answering, it meant Julie was worried about someone potentially listening in, or it meant they were traveling.

But it meant Ben was no closer to finding Eliza or the sword Tennyson had tasked them to find, and he knew he was no closer to finding Tennyson himself and completing the job Mr. E had given him. Any hope of getting information from the bomber outside Tennyson's granddaughter's house had died when Reggie had taken the man's life, but Ben still believed questioning the terrorist would have only been a dead-end as well.

Ben could tell Reggie was frustrated as well. He knew his friend almost as well as he knew himself — Reggie wanted to keep moving, to take action. Right now, they were at the airport, trying to get in touch with the rest of their team to figure out where to go next.

After the events at the storage warehouse, Reggie and Ben had decided to hike the half-mile to the small airport's front entrance, since they were already so close. At least there they would be ready to catch a flight when they did figure out their next destination.

"Any ideas about what to do next?" Reggie asked. "Where to go?"

Ben shrugged. "We have to stay ahead of Interpol obviously, and we have to stay ahead of whoever these new guys are. At least we know now there's a third party involved."

"Yeah, but we don't know a damn thing about them. Why are they after us? What do they want with you specifically, and how have they been following us?"

"I have no idea. Whatever they're doing, they're using some fancy new tech. I've never seen anything like that in my life." Ben recalled the strange sensation of his body being locked down from the inside. "It was like some sort of aerosol stuff. He squirted something around me that was like a powder, light and airy and raining down all around me. I guess I could have held my breath, but I don't know that it would've done any good. Stuff seemed to lock me down on contact."

"Yeah, that's what I saw, too," Reggie said. He let out a long sigh. "I tried to get there in time, but —"

"It doesn't matter now," Ben said. "Not your fault."

Ben felt his phone vibrate in his hand and he anxiously looked down at it. He felt a glimmer of hope; he wanted it to be a text message from Julie or any of the others. For that matter, he would even be happy if it were a text message from the Interpol agent, once again demanding Ben's location. At least then it would give Ben something to think about, something to chew on, allow him to feel as if they were still moving.

Right now he felt dead in the water. They had no leads and no contact with anyone from the outside world.

Instead, it was an email.

Ben opened the app and double-checked the sender.

"What is it?" Reggie asked.

"An email," he said. "From Tennyson."

Reggie scoffed. "No shit? What's it say this time?"

Ben could hear the intensity in his friend's voice. He was feeling the same way — he imagined what the email from Tennyson would say: *You blew up my granddaughter's house.*

Ben shook his head as he read the text of the message out loud. "'*Meet me in Elba. You will know where.*'"

"That's it?" Reggie asked again.

"That's it," Ben said. "Just wants us to meet him in Elba."

"What the hell's Elba?"

Ben was already in motion. Whatever they were going to do next, Ben had a feeling it would involve a flight.

As it turned out, he had been right. He made his way toward the ticket counter.

"Elba is an island, off the coast of Italy. If we're lucky, we can get a direct flight from here."

"Fine," Reggie said. "But *why* Elba?"

Ben smiled. "It's the island where Napoleon was exiled."

CHAPTER 63

JULIE

10:23 AM | **March 11, 2021**

Lyon, France

Madame Blanchet's contact turned out to be easy to find. The woman Madame Blanchet had called "Lady Catherine" lived outside Lyon, France, in an old, decaying castle. After running a quick search online, Sarah had found a woman named Catherine Beaulieu who matched the age range Madame Blanchet had described. She was indeed listed as a descendent of the goldsmith Odiot from Paris, and had gained some notoriety in the area by claiming that some of Napoleon's battles had been won through some sort of devine intervention. In some articles, she was called — derogatorily — *Lady*, since she had purchased a decrepit castle outside of town and was known as somewhat of a recluse.

She sounds like a quack, Julie thought. *But if she has information, we need to talk to her.*

They found a train that could reach Lyon in just over two hours, so they had each purchased a ticket and boarded shortly after leaving Madame Blanchet's house.

Armed with a mission and a bit of knowledge to go on, they had used the trip to Lyon to rest and gather their thoughts and questions. Julie tried to prepare for whatever they might find there.

She had to come to terms with the fact that it might all be for nothing — Catherine might, in fact, just be some nut job living in a dilapidated castle. According to the article he'd read, Catherine had never married or had children.

They took a rideshare after disembarking from the train, eventually reaching the outer perimeter of what used to be the castle's border wall. The land was empty out here, mostly prairies and farmland in all directions. They passed an old four-foot-tall stone wall that once would have marked the very edge of the castle's boundaries.

Julie knew that whoever had owned the castle originally would also have owned all of the nearby towns and the land they were on. In other words, everything in sight. The road leading up to the main home was as old as the castle itself, most of the gravel path now completely overgrown by tall grasses that had not been kept up in years. Trees, clearly on their last leg, bent over at their waists and hung over the road, tired remnants of a long-lost gardener's dream for a beautified driveway.

Their rideshare driver dropped them off in a circular driveway in front of a stone three-story home, and when Julie got out of the car and looked up, she got a good idea of what she might find inside.

That was because most of the *outside* had found its way *inside*.

The top story of the place had no roof whatsoever, either having fallen into disrepair long ago or simply torn off and never replaced. Stone turrets on both sides of the mansion ended abruptly, their tops also sheared off for some strange reason. From a second-story window, through a broken section of stained glass, Julie could see a tree trunk that had sprouted and been allowed to grow up through the first floor.

"Interesting place," Freddie said. "Something tells me it's probably haunted." He kicked a stick out of the way and then marched up to the front steps of the house.

Julie saw a car parked in a detached garage to her left, which reassured her. There was no way to know whether or not Catherine would be home when they arrived, and nowhere online could she find a phone number or email address to reach the woman. It had been a risk worth taking, and she was happy to see that it appeared as though someone were home. It also gave her relief that the car was a normal sedan — Lady Catherine may have had her quirks, but she at least had a vehicle.

Freddie reached the front door first and then turned to Julie, waiting for her signal to knock. She nodded, and he lifted his hand and prepared to pound on the heavy, thick wooden door. Julie examined it. At some point in the past, someone had spent a considerable amount of time and effort carving ornate floral patterns in the wood, but as the wood had aged and hardened, the organic nature of it had pressed out some of the textures, leaving it dull and flat.

Freddie's hand landed exactly one time before the door creaked open. He pulled his hand back down and took a step back.

"Bonjour?" a voice asked. A question in French followed. Julie hadn't studied French for many years, but she thought she heard the French word for reporter: *Journaliste.*

Julie rushed forward and smiled. "Are — are you Lady Catherine?" She asked.

The door opened a few more inches, and Julie saw the speaker's face. She was maybe a decade older than Julie herself, and her hair was long and pulled back into a simple ponytail. It was stark white, and seemed to have its own glow emanating from it. She was wearing a T-shirt and jeans.

Not as strange as I would've imagined, Julie thought.

"No one has called me that in quite a long time," the woman said, slipping into impeccable English. "Where did you hear that?"

Julie knew now was not the time for deception. "Madame Blanchet, in Paris. She recommended we come speak with you."

The woman's eyes squeezed together, then widened quickly. A

look of joy came over her face. "Madame Blanchet! I have not heard from her in so many years! How is she?"

Julie swallowed. *Maybe now* is *the time for a bit of deception.* "She's... uh, doing well, and had very nice things to say about you."

The door opened more and the woman made a motion for them to come inside. "I do not know why she had good things to say," Catherine said, laughing. "I was such a nuisance back then. Letter after letter, asking frivolous questions. Trying to understand every-thing possible about Napoleon."

"From what I know of the old lady," Freddie said, "that would've only endeared you to her more."

"I suppose that *is* true," Catherine said. "Please, do come in. Do not mind the mess — I live a bit of an *eclectic* lifestyle."

Julie turned around, taking in the space. The foyer of the castle was still mostly in the shape it always had been, with archways leading into deeper chambers to her left and right and directly in front of her. The one in front of her was much larger than the others and led to a lobby or wide, open seating area.

There were no seats, however, in this seating area. Instead, Julie saw a single mattress, lying on the floor with a single sheet on top of it. Next to the bed lay two cardboard boxes, both open and unla-beled. From the top of one of the boxes she saw piles of clothes poking out. On the opposite side of the bed was a line of shoes, ranging in function from elegant flat to more utilitarian boots.

There were no pictures or paintings on the walls anymore, but Julie could see rectangles of lighter stone where they must have hung for decades, or even hundreds of years. In the space to her left, she saw the tree she had spotted from outside. Not only had it been allowed to grow out of the floor, a neat pile of rocks had been arranged in a circle around its base, soil dumped inside the ring. The first of its branches shot out through a broken window near the end of the hallway, and she could see a hole in the ceiling above the trunk where the tree had pushed through during its escape to the outside.

She heard a shuffling noise from her right, and then felt Freddie bump into her. "Guys..." he said softly.

CHAPTER 64

JULIE

10:25 AM **| March 11, 2021**

Lyon, France

Julie turned to see what had Freddie so bothered. At the end of the opposing hallway stood three tiny, hooded creatures. They were all staring directly at them, not moving. The one on the left rubbed a front hoof on the stone.

"Goats?" Sarah whispered.

"Huey, Dewey, and Louie," Catherine said nonchalantly. "They should not be any trouble, they probably just want to know if any of you brought crackers."

"Should — should we have brought crackers?" Freddie asked.

"I have some in the kitchen I can bring in. They absolutely love meeting new people. Unfortunately for them, I am not much of a socialite, so they don't get to meet people very often."

"I see," Sarah said, not taking her eyes off the goats.

Julie smiled and walked toward the grand bedroom in front of her, hoping to eye more of the mysterious spaces within. She had a feeling that every single room hosted treasures as strange and juxtaposed as what she had already seen. She also got the feeling Catherine was a woman who did not appreciate art from an outsider's perspective — she had decided to turn her entire life into a work of art. Everything Julie had seen so far felt like a less surreal version of *Alice in Wonderland.*

Catherine returned a moment later with a tray of teacups, a steaming pot of tea in the center. Piled next to them was a stack of small graham crackers.

She set the tray down on some sort of twisted wooden stool that had been fashioned out of petrified branches, and then handed the cracker stack to Freddie. "Just whistle, and they will come right over."

Freddie looked at the three women around him, a confused look on his face, but then pursed his lips and let out a low, quiet whistle.

The effect was immediate and chaotic. All three of the tiny goats began stamping their hooves wildly, trying to gain purchase on the castle's smooth stone floor. The one on the left finally gained enough traction to move and began galloping toward them. The two others bleated their disappointment at coming in second and third place, but soon were speeding toward them as well. Freddie lowered himself to a knee, then stood back up quickly when he realized what was happening.

The goats were not going to slow down. Julie held a hand over her mouth, unable to control her laughter.

All three tiny mammals crashed into Freddie's knees and legs with a force that nearly pushed him back into Julie once again.

"These little guys aren't playing around," he said.

Catherine threw her head back and laughed. "Of course not — they truly love their crackers."

Freddie held the stack of graham crackers out in his right hand and prepared to peel off one from the top. Before he could, one of the goats reached their neck up, opened its mouth wider than Julie could have thought possible, and snatched a golf ball-sized chunk of crackers from the side of the stack, leaving an equally shaped divot.

"Hey, cool it little man," Freddie said, pulling the stack up out of reach. He proceeded to feed all three of the voracious animals while Julie focused her attention back on Catherine.

"I wish we were here under different circumstances, but I'm afraid our time is short. We need some help with something, and Madame Blanchet was adamant you were the person to ask."

"Something about Napoleon, I suspect?"

"Actually, it's about someone in your family tree. A man named Odiot."

Catherine's eyes grew wide once more and a large smile appeared on her face. "Of course, that is my great-great-*great*-grandfather... or perhaps a couple more *greats*. And, I might add, a much better topic of conversation."

"Why is that?" Julie asked.

"Well," she began, "I was fascinated with Napoleon as a child. I studied him in school, spent all of my spare time researching his life and his leadership. When I found out that I was a descendent of Odiot, I studied him as well. I began to develop a distaste for Bonaparte himself — he did not treat Odiot well, at least in my opinion. And I believe Napoleon was a bit of a charlatan, as well."

"That's very interesting," Sarah said. "What makes you say he was a charlatan?"

Catherine chuckled. "It does seem dubious to call him that, don't you think? After all, a man like Napoleon should be allowed at least a bit of egotism after what he accomplished. He was, without a doubt, an important figure, a fantastic leader. I just have reason to believe he was not *completely* forthcoming about some of the victories he won."

"Can you give us an example?" Julie asked.

"It — it's not important anymore," she said, her voice trailing off. "You may have read certain things about me, some of which are true. I do admit to a bit of a strange lifestyle, and I know that it makes me look like some sort of modern-day witch."

"No, not at all," Julie said. She almost immediately regretted saying it. If she were being honest, this woman seemed to have *exactly* the lifestyle she would have imagined a modern-day witch might live. Even though she was wearing jeans and a T-shirt, there was no secret that this woman lived life in the fringes of society.

"No need to be kind, my dear," Catherine said, offering a genuine smile. "I'm not clueless. I don't care about all that, anyway. But I still believe most of what they said in those articles was said just to discredit me."

Sarah interjected. "You mean about how you think Napoleon was somehow able to win his battles with divine intervention?"

Catherine nodded quickly. "Divine intervention, the Hand of God, magical spells, sorcery, whatever. I don't know exactly what it was, but I believe it was something that bolstered Napoleon's ability to fight in his battles."

Julie jumped back in, hoping to keep the conversation moving toward her end goal. "Catherine, we have a friend who is in some trouble. We need to find something and bring it to her, or we are afraid something bad will happen to her."

Catherine stood there silently, taking it in. "What is it? What is it you're looking for?"

Julie felt a flicker of hope spark within her. "A sword. A replica of the sword of —"

"The Sword of Austerlitz," Catherine said. "One moment, please."

10:30 AM | March 11, 2021

Lyon, France

Julie half expected Lady Catherine to return with the actual Sword of Austerlitz, and she felt herself a bit let down when the woman came back into the room with a simple journal. She had produced it from somewhere deeper in the house, and Julie could see that it was stuffed full of photocopied articles, newspaper clippings, photographs, and hand-written notes.

"You asked me why I believe Napoleon had a bit of help in his battles. The battle of Austerlitz is a great example," Catherine continued. She flipped through the leather-bound journal for a moment and then pulled open a section with the title *Austerlitz* at the top of it. Julie and the others leaned in, curious as to what she was going to point out.

"He was back here," Catherine said, pointing to a section of a hand-drawn map. Julie couldn't read the handwritten French labels. "But most of the intense fighting happened down here, and Napoleon himself decided to head down there and help out."

"This is historic fact?" Sarah asked.

Catherine nodded. "Oh, yes. Very much so. This battle — like just about all of the battles Napoleon had a hand in — has been picked apart by historians and military strategists for the better part of two centuries. Great minds have poured over this chain of events and just about every detail that can be known about it *is* known."

"Then," Sarah continued, "with all due respect, why have you gone through all this trouble? Much of this is handwritten, the map drawn yourself. Couldn't you just have used a pre-existing map?"

"Good question, one with a simple answer: I needed to know for myself. I needed to verify — to make sure there was nothing missed. I wanted to make sure there was not an obvious explanation."

"An obvious explanation for what?" Freddie asked.

Catherine flipped a few more pages and then revealed another map. This one was more detailed, showing a portion of the Battle of Austerlitz that she had enlarged. Julie saw a label in the center of the drawn image.

"This is Napoleon," Catherine continued, confirming what Julie read. "He rode into battle — wearing his favored sword, I might add — and joined the fray. Understand that at this point in the battle, victory was not decided yet. The Allies had taken the hill at Pratzen Heights and were putting pressure on Napoleon's forces. Any good commander would have stayed back to ensure their own safety."

"A good commander wouldn't rush into battle?" Freddie asked.

"Perhaps, within reason. But ultimately the goal of a battlefield commander, especially in this time, is to live to fight another day, no? Who would march on after a victory or defeat if the commander was killed? Anyway, a battle like this — and what all historians agree happened — is a different thing altogether. Napoleon had been with another segment of his army elsewhere, on a hill that offered him a decent vantage point over the unfolding battles around him. Yet he chose *this* battle to venture into. Why?"

Julie knew the answer; she had researched this bit of the Austerlitz battle in the library the day before. "Because it was the turning point of the battle," she said quickly. "Napoleon had to keep this hill from the Allies or he would not have had a way to ensure victory."

"Yes, indeed. That is precisely accurate. There is a nuance, however, that I'm afraid you — as well as every other historian — has missed."

Julie was intrigued, but she felt they were about to hear the true reason why this otherwise intelligent and learned historian had been ostracized from her professional community.

"Napoleon, by riding into battle, may have added a spark of morale to his team, to his men, a bit of extra edge. But that alone would not have been enough to turn the tide of a fierce battle such as this. Every report claims that the Allies were winning here, soundly beating Napoleon's forces back into submission. In movies, we all know the commander can ride in on a brilliant white horse with a flag in the air and shout great things and that is all it takes for men to suddenly remember how to fight better."

Julie smiled, and Freddie laughed. She couldn't argue with that: most battles in Hollywood period piece films featured a scene that depicted exactly that.

"Nor did he bring with him a large enough cadre of men to have made much of a difference. Three, maybe four manned horses at a minimum, possibly twice that. These would have been capable officers and loyal soldiers, but I do not believe they would have helped much at turning this around."

Freddie shifted as he stood, looking down at the Journal. "But they did," he said. "They *did* turn the tide of the battle. They eventually won the Battle of Austerlitz. What am I missing?"

The white-haired woman lifted a finger and held it out in front of her. "Exactly," she said. "What *are* we missing?"

Julie knew this was the point at which the woman was supposed to claim some sort of divine intervention that had descended upon Napoleon Bonaparte and helped him win this battle. If she continued, she would probably claim the same such intervention for other decisive Napoleon victories. "I'm so sorry," Julie said. "This is utterly fascinating, but I'm worried we don't have much time. How, exactly, does the Sword of Austerlitz fit into all of this?" She asked.

Catherine did not seem at all fazed by this, but she stopped flipping through the pages and closed the book. She set it down on the tea tray, nearly causing the porcelain teapot to crash off the side of the crooked table. The goats milling around their feet jumped at the clattering noise.

"I'll be right back once again," Catherine said.

Julie felt her exasperation growing, already having sat through one woman's Napoleonic lecture. The more time they wasted here, the more danger Eliza was in.

She thought of Madame Blanchet. *The more danger* we *are in.*

Catherine returned a minute later with another book — this one also a small, leather-bound journal — in her hand. "This is Odiot's journal," she said. She opened the front cover and read the inscription on the first page. "*The Journal of the Goldsmith Odiot, of Paris.*"

Julie's eyes grew in amazement. She was staring down at a priceless piece of history. She was stunned that it was not in a museum, being kept safe and maintained, but she suspected that Catherine had gone to great lengths to acquire it and had simply wanted to keep this relic of her family's past in a personal, private space. She couldn't fault the woman for that.

Catherine opened the journal to a spot near the middle and Julie saw a drawing of a sword. It had been rendered on all of its axes in two smaller pictures beneath it. She flipped the page over and there were more drawings of the sword on the opposite side.

"The Sword of Austerlitz," Freddie whispered.

"Well, a *copy* of the Sword of Austerlitz," Catherine said. "Odiot was given this commission — it says so right here in the pages before. I have read them many times and committed them to memory. "'Our Grand Commander has given me a special privilege this day,'" she began. "Well, that's basically what it says in French.

"But I thought Napoleon gave the commission for his sword to Biennais?" Sarah asked.

"He did. And Biennais produced that sword. Perhaps the very sword that appeared in battle by Napoleon's side."

"But you don't think so?" Julie asked.

Catherine shook her head. "No, I suspect otherwise. I suspect that the sword we see painted on Napoleon's side in the famous portrait is actually this version. The Odiot Sword of Austerlitz."

"What makes you think his was the real thing?" Freddie asked.

Catherine leaned forward, taking a moment to gaze at her willing subjects before continuing. "Well, technically they are both the *real thing*. But," she said as she flipped slowly through the pages of drawings. "After these pictures, you'll see a description of the sword, transcribed by Odiot from Napoleon's instructions."

She flipped to this page and Julie saw the fanciful, ornate calligraphy from Odiot's pen dancing across the page. She didn't understand the French lettering, and she certainly couldn't make sense of the tall, sweeping italics, so she was relieved when Catherine continued to read.

"The last sentence on this page reads, *'and on the hilt.'*" She flipped to the next page and Julie saw a single word written across it. *Avril*. She knew that meant *April* in French.

It seemed Odiot had never finished the previous sentence.

"There is a missing page," Catherine blurted out. "Look, here. If you peel back the binding just a little bit, you can see where it has been ripped from the rest of the book." Lady Catherine stretched the journal flat and held it up for the others to see. Sure enough, Julie saw the tiny, jagged edge of a piece of paper that had been ripped away.

"*And on the hilt...*" Freddie said.

Julie felt a chill. "You think Odiot was given special instructions to put something on the hilt. Something that was not in Biennais' version of the sword. And something that Napoleon could have used in battle to help him achieve his victories."

"Absolutely," Catherine said. "It is the *only* thing that makes sense. And why this particular page would have been specifically torn, ripped away and stolen, perhaps by Odiot himself...."

"Because he wouldn't want anyone else to find it," Sarah said. "If what you're saying is true, that sword had another weapon built right onto the side of it — a weapon that was either controversial or otherwise kept secret."

"It wasn't divine intervention at all," Julie said. "That's what they wrote about you, claiming that Napoleon used divine intervention or invoked some otherworldly spiritual support in his battles. But you actually believe there was a much simpler — a much more *scientific* — reason for Napoleon's success."

Catherine nodded and looked into Julie's eyes. Julie could see that the woman was being truthful. She believed that her ancestor had built a sword for Napoleon, and then kept it a secret the rest of his life.

A secret she had kept, as well.

CHAPTER 66

FREDDIE

10:35 AM **| March 11, 2021**

Lyon, France

Freddie yawned, but continued listening to Catherine's conversation with Julie and Sarah.

"I think he had some sort of explosive stored there," she said.

Julie and Sarah nodded along.

"I believe he used them like small grenades. For what he had been able to accomplish, however, they must have been very powerful and effective."

Freddie wasn't disinterested, he was just feeling the pressure of being in one place for too long. There was somebody out there, somewhere, who needed their help, and there were people out there who wanted to kill them. That combination was a serious motivating factor for Freddie to get up and *move*, and standing around talking about an old dead French guy made him feel like they were wasting time.

He yawned again, petted one of the goats who seemed to like him, then stepped back over to where the three women were talking. He interjected. "It's the little roses on the hilt. The pewter, gold-covered ones, the ones I pointed out in the picture. Something like what you're talking about could have been stored in there."

Julie nodded profusely. "That's exactly right. It *has* to be. We saw in Tennyson's video…"

"Tennyson?" Catherine asked. "Who is that?"

Freddie felt the air in the room get sucked out. He knew it was time to come clean; they had been stringing Lady Catherine along with bits and pieces of information. It was mostly to keep her interested, to keep her talking and sharing what she knew. But he had felt it, as well. The conversation was turning, and Catherine was going to be wanting to know what they knew very soon.

It seemed that time was now.

He saw a frown appear on the woman's face and she stepped back, her long white ponytail whipping around as she did. She snapped the Journal shut and then addressed the trio. "I do love talking history, but you alluded to running out of time more than once. Now you mention there is someone *else* who has a picture of this sword? Odiot's sword?"

Freddie looked at Julie. Sarah was waiting for her answer as well. Julie sighed. "Yes. Catherine," she said. "I'm so sorry we could not be more upfront with you, but the truth of the matter is that we simply do not know who to trust. We have a friend, and she was taken by a man named Baden Tennyson. We believe he is going to do her harm."

Catherine's face fell, and she took a half-step back once again. Freddie jumped in, trying to rescue the moment and get this woman back on their side. "You read about the Sword of Austerlitz's being sold at auction a few days ago?"

Catherine nodded, then dropped her head. "And then the terrible murder and theft of it afterward."

"Whoever did that was sent by this man," Julie said. "Tennyson. And he's had men following us ever since, trying to pick us off and separate us as a team."

Catherine swallowed, looking at her front door.

"We're safe," Freddie said. "For now. No one knows we came here."

"How many are you?"

"Us, plus two more. They're in Switzerland right now, trying to track down any ties to Tennyson that might tell us where he is."

"Can I see the picture?" Catherine asked. "Of the sword?"

Freddie watched Julie's face, watched her considering this. He didn't think there was any harm in bringing the woman fully up to speed, but he knew Julie and the others had been in situations like this more than he had. He trusted their judgement. He would follow their lead. If they still felt there was a reason to not trust Catherine, he'd get on board with it.

Julie relented. "Of course," she said, pulling out her phone. She flicked around on the screen and then held it out to Catherine. Catherine's eyes widened and she put her hand over her mouth. "This... this is miraculous," she said. "*Truly* incredible. This is not the Sword of Austerlitz, but the copycat one created by my ancestor."

"How do you know it is?" Freddie asked. "How do you know this isn't the *actual* Sword of Austerlitz and the one missing — the one we're trying to track down — isn't Odiot's version?"

She shook her head. "No, this is definitely Odiot's. You've probably already noticed the difference, but I pointed it out in this journal. She flipped through the pages and came to the one that showed the sword from three different sides, all hand drawn but with immaculate precision. "Look," she said. "Right there on the hilt. The page that's missing from the journal that describes exactly what these roses are made of, and what's inside them. We cannot know that answer without the missing page, but my ancestor still drew in the roses on the previous pages.

They all leaned over the journal. Immediately, Freddie saw what she was talking about. The hand-drawn hilt of this sword indeed only had four roses on it. There was a fifth rose drawn, but it was sketched in as hovering over the end of the hilt.

As if it were removable.

"Interesting," Freddie mumbled.

"It's incredible," Julie said. "It means that since the Sword of Austerlitz was put in a museum, we've all been duped into thinking that was the real one. In fact, the one stolen a few days ago — the one that had been in a private collection after being sold by the museum — was Odiot's version of the Austerlitz sword, not Biennais.'"

Sarah nodded. "So that confirms that there are *two* swords, and we now know which one is the real Sword of Austerlitz, worn by Napoleon in battle. But I'm still a bit confused as to which is which — which one is with Tennyson, and which one is still missing?"

"They're *both* with Tennyson," Freddie said.

All eyes turned to him.

"Yeah, of course they are," he said. "Remember? He's got a video with *one* sword, and he asked Ben to find the other one. But he asked him to find it as a *test*, remember? He wants Ben to help him with something, so he's sending him on this chase around the world to find the *second* sword."

Julie nodded. "So that implies he already knows where it is."

"Of course," Freddie said. "He gave Ben clues, remember? That means he knows *exactly* where the second sword is."

"And knowing a guy like Tennyson," Julie continued, "I can't imagine he'd want to leave it out of his sight."

"That's what I'm thinking," Freddie said, nodding again. "Which leads me to believe the second sword is with him. Find the sword, find Tennyson."

"And find Eliza," Sarah added.

Catherine looked confused for a moment, but Freddie was glad she didn't ask questions about that. They were getting a bit closer to their next step, and he wanted to keep moving.

He suddenly jerked his head up, feeling his stomach turning with a realization. "Catherine," he began. "You are one of the only people in the world who knew that your ancestor crafted a look-alike sword, and you are one of the only people who guessed the secret it contained."

He saw Catherine's face turn white.

"Who have you told?" he continued. "Over the course of writing about him — of studying Napoleon and his battles and his favorite sword — who else might know that you think there are multiple swords in existence?"

Julie nodded. "Yeah, Freddie's right. I didn't even think of that — you just let us in on an old family secret. *Please* tell me you haven't told anyone else."

She thought for a moment, her eyes rolling up to the stone ceiling of the foyer. "There... there was one," she said slowly. "A man, a long time ago. It had to have been thirty years ago now. He was frail, pale-looking. I thought he might have been albino, but didn't really pay close enough attention at the time."

"What did he ask about the sword?" Sarah asked.

"Not much, really. He had read one of my articles — I must have been in high school or university — and he came to my house, where I was living with my aunt at the time. She wasn't home. I let him in, not having any reason to fear a skinny little man who seemed kind enough. He asked about my work studying Napoleon, asked why I was interested, and I told him about my family ties to Odiot."

"Did he press into that?"

"A bit, if I recall. But he was definitely more interested in the sword itself. He asked me a few questions, and I could tell as I answered them that he was getting excited. I didn't feel threatened, but I also started to feel uncomfortable with it all. I just told him that I believed there was something special about Napoleon's sword, and that I didn't think it was just one sword but two. I told him I suspected my ancestor, the goldsmith, had produced a look-alike that only he and Napoleon knew about."

"Did you tell him about the journal?"

"No, I thought that would be too risky. The page had always

been missing, so I suspected someone like this would see immense value in the journal, and I didn't want to let him know I had it."

"That was smart. Did he say anything else?" Sarah asked.

She shook her head, her brow furrowing. "It was so long ago. No, I don't think so. He thanked me, then shook my hand. I told him his French was impeccable, and he laughed, complimenting me on my English. Then he left."

"What about his name? Anyway to track the guy down?" Freddie asked.

She thought for a moment, then shook her head again. "No, again. I'm sorry. I don't know that he even introduced himself. I'm sure I asked at one point, since he was so interested in a subject I cared deeply about, but he only gave me an initial."

Freddie's stomach did a backflip and he blinked a couple of times. *No way.*

He saw Julie silently gasp and then grab Catherine's arm. "An initial?" She asked.

Catherine nodded, no doubt startled by how intensely they were all looking at her right now. "Yes, just a single initial. Something like 'Mr. E.'"

CHAPTER 67

JULIE

10:41 AM | **March 11, 2021**

Lyon, France

"You are all going to Corsica, right?" Catherine asked.

Julie stopped in her tracks. They had already begun to leave, Freddie outside working to call a rideshare driver. The cost was exorbitant all the way out here, but they were not really in a position to negotiate.

And people's lives were at stake — cost was not really an issue.

Julie turned around slowly and faced Catherine. "And how... did you guess that?"

"The mulberry tree," Catherine said, smiling. "From the picture you showed me. That woman's sweater — it was a mulberry tree, wasn't it?"

Julie nodded and smiled. "Very intuitive. Yes. Madame Blanchet filled us in on Napoleon's past and his family's relationship with mulberry trees."

"It is perfect symbolism," Catherine said. "This Tennyson man who is threatening her — that is a terrible twisted thing to do — but you have to admire his cleverness and wit."

"No, I don't."

Catherine's smile faded.

Julie took another breath. "I'm sorry, I wasn't trying to be offensive."

Catherine waved her wrist. "No, that was insensitive of me. I merely meant to point out that he did a good job putting clues in place for your friend — Ben, was it? For Ben to find."

"My husband, actually."

"Oh!" Catherine said. "In that case, yes, you are a woman on a mission. Do you mind if I go with?"

Julie was taken aback. It was a strange request, and it had been so sudden. "You — you want to go with us to Corsica?"

"Yes, and I have a passport. Though something tells me you all have ways around that sort of thing." She let out a bit of nervous laughter, then straightened up again. "Look, I am probably the world's foremost expert on Napoleon's early career, if not his entire life. Yet no one takes me seriously because of a few articles I wrote decades ago, but I believe that you now know I am who I say I am."

"Catherine, your knowledge and expertise is without question. It's just —"

"It's dangerous?" she asked. "That's fine. I'm okay with that. Besides, how is it *not* dangerous for me to stay here? No offense, but you all stumbling here into my home and claiming there are people out there trying to kill you, chasing after you... it doesn't give me much confidence that I will be okay staying here by myself."

Julie had been thinking the exact thing, unable to forget the sight of Madame Blanchet's dead body on her entryway floor. *And that had happened while we were there. While we were with her.* She shuddered, then shook her head. "No, you're right. You're exactly right. I am so sorry to have put you in danger, but we..."

"You had no choice," Catherine said. "Besides — I have a car. It will take half an hour at least for a rideshare to show up way out here. By that time, we could be at the airport."

Julie nodded. "What do you guys think?"

Freddie answered immediately, taking her by surprise. "Absolutely. She's in. We can use the help."

"I agree," Sarah said. "She knows everything we don't about this sword and Napoleon, and if Tennyson is adamant that we find it, she's probably the best hope we have at this point."

Julie stuck her hand out and Catherine shook it. "Congratulations," she said. "You are now an official contractor for the Civilian Special Operations. It's not much of a title."

"And I can assure you," Freddie said with a smirk, "the actual job is *way* worse."

11:32 AM | **March 11, 2021**

France

Freddie sat with his knees almost to his chest, the cramped, tiny aircraft nearly too much for him. First it had been the taxi in Paris, smashed between a hard window and two women, but in his mind, when it came to uncomfortable and *impossibly* stupid seating, commercial flights took the cake.

The flight they were on didn't even seem real to him — where had they even gotten an airplane this small? How had it even taken off? Were there engines attached to the wings or was it a tiny little propeller up front? Did the pilot have to stand on a ladder and jump and push the propellor down to start it?

Freddie was not afraid of flying, but he certainly didn't enjoy it. He considered it a means to an end — that was it.

Although he had to admit his interest in using that means to any *particular* end had decreased exponentially after the plane crash in Antarctica.

"You okay?" Catherine asked from the seat next to him. She had, impossibly, requested a window seat.

He nodded, still incredulous that an actual grown human could fit against the window. He couldn't imagine what it would feel like for his frame being smashed against the curved wall and window. He wondered if it would stay like that if he tried it, if you would constantly have a bulging convex right side. "I'm fine," he said. "Just a little tight."

"Well, you are the size of at least two men," she said.

"That's... that's probably the most forward way I've ever been called fat," Freddie said.

She laughed, then shrugged. "Not fat. Just... large. Muscular, built like a tank. And I have never really had much interest in meandering. I much prefer direct. To the point."

Freddie smiled. "Yeah, it's sort of refreshing."

He looked across the aisle at Julie and Sarah, who were hunched over their phones, researching and studying something that he felt he had no more to contribute to. He did want to be helpful, and there still were quite a few puzzles related to the Sword of Austerlitz and Tennyson's scavenger hunt that were nagging at him, but he wasn't sure there would be enough time on this flight to even get started on a new direction. They were getting ready to depart from Lyon on a short hop to northern Italy, where they would then board a — hopefully — larger plane headed for Corsica. This leg of the journey would only be thirty-five minutes long.

In a flurry of activity, flight attendants rushed up and down the narrow aisle and the captain began to taxi the plane. Within minutes, they were airborne. Freddie was impressed at the efficiency of overseas flights, able to move much more quickly because they didn't have to explain every possible movement to a worried American public. They didn't have to deal with nearly as many strenuous regulations, either.

Finding himself already bored, and not any more comfortable than before they had taken off, he pulled his phone out and opened the forwarded email Ben had received from Tennyson.

As he read through it for the third time, he had to admit the thing was a puzzle. That had been Tennyson's intent, of course. It was very strangely worded, and the whole thing seemed off to him, like it had been written by someone on drugs, or at least a bit inebriated. He knew that Tennyson had sent them clues inside the video file, so he wondered what other clues might be in the email as well.

"What is that?" Catherine asked, her white hair suddenly swinging across his face. He pulled back a bit, but found that it didn't offer him any more of maintaining his personal bubble. He sighed, then turned the phone screen so she could see it. "It's from that guy, Tennyson. This is how he reached out to Ben to tell him to find the sword."

"It's... worded very strangely."

"Yeah, it's part of the puzzle. We're not exactly sure how though, but it's definitely a clue. Like, look at these capital letters — they're seemingly random. He didn't capitalize the beginning of sentences, or some proper nouns. I tried pulling out the capital letters and seeing if they made a word or anagram or something, but I can't figure it out."

Catherine grabbed the phone and took it out of Freddie's hand. It was like a tiny bird snatching a worm — too quick for him to react, so he just resigned himself to no longer having a puzzle to work on and looked over at her.

"It is on a very tiny screen," she mumbled. He wasn't sure if she was talking to herself or to him, but he ignored it either way as she mumbled on. "I wonder if it would look any different on a computer screen."

He thought about it, then nodded. "I'm sure it would look a little different. The text would wrap differently, right? Is that what you mean? I have my laptop; I can get it if you —"

She nodded, then cut him off. "Exactly. I wonder..." she stopped talking and flicked around his mail app, eventually finding the text settings. He watched as she changed the font size to the smallest one possible, then flicked back over to the email. "There," she said. "If we can pretend the screen size of your phone is actually the size of your laptop, that means the text would be way smaller, like this. But it should —"

"Make the text wrap and appear the same way it would show up on a laptop screen or monitor," Freddie said, finishing her thought.

"I... I recognize this," she said. Her voice had dropped a couple of decibels, and Freddie had to lean closer to her to hear over the roar of the engine.

I guess there are engines, he realized.

"What are you talking about?"

She used her finger and pointed to the first row of miniature letters on the screen. He could not see what they were from this distance, but he knew they were the same capital letters he had pointed out earlier. "These are your capital letters," she confirmed. "But now it looks a bit different. Each is on the beginning of a new line. Seem familiar to you?"

He pulled the phone back up to his eyes and nearly smashed into his eyeball before he could read anything. He blinked a few times, allowing his eyes to adjust and focus, then read the email again, this time allowing his eyes to dance over the letters and words naturally, gently lifting before the end of each line in putting emphasis on the first capital letter of each new line. "Yeah," he said. "It's like a poem."

Freddie read the screen once again.

>> *Truly! It seems you got my message.*

>> *Alas, thank you for attending to my request in such a*

>> *Timely fashion; let it be true that,*

>> *Indeed, we will work well together.*

>> *On that note, hear this:*

>> *I have a job for you,*

>> *This is related to the work you already do.*

>> *There is a particular sword that wants*

>> *To find its way into my collection.*

"It *is* a poem," Catherine said. "Albeit a terrible one. Nothing rhymes, and it is not even correct iambic pentameter, which would be the closest structure to what I am seeing here."

"So... Tennyson is a terrible poet?"

She laughed, tossing her head back. "He may be, but that's not my point. I recognize the first letters in the line. As in, I know what they're *actually* from."

Freddie frowned. "Okay," he said. "You lost me."

She closed the mail app on his phone and then went over to his web browser, apparently having no difficulty whatsoever navigating the man's device. She either had the exact same model or she was a little more intuitive than he when it came to phones and computers.

"Should be one of the top..." she began, her voice drifting off. "There!"

Catherine pointed to the screen and clicked on the second result.

He read it out loud. "*Lord George Byron: Napoleon.*"

It was a poem — a long poem, with what seemed to be hundreds of stanzas. The page scrolled as he moved his thumb, and he silently read a couple of lines.

'Tis done — but yesterday a King!
And arm'd with Kings to strive...

Freddie had never enjoyed poetry. He didn't understand it. It was too lofty, too pretentious.

"Tennyson is referencing a poem in his email," Catherine said. "He's telling us the poet, see? *'By George.'*"

"George Byron," Freddie said in a voice that was barely audible. "But how can you be sure it was this poem —"

"Because there are the same number of lines in each stanza of this poem as there are in Tennyson's terrible one he emailed. He didn't mean to write a poem, but to simply reference this one. He used the first letter of each line of his poem to tell us which stanza he's talking about."

Catherine pulled the phone back and scrolled down until she found the one she was looking for. She showed it to Freddie. Each line of the stanza she had found started with the same first letter in each of the stanzas Tennyson had written.

"Well, I'll be…" Freddie smiled. "You cracked it." *Lady Catherine had figured it out.* Whatever Tennyson wanted them to find, they should be able to find another clue — or the answer itself — in this stanza.

"Go ahead," he told Catherine. "Read it."

He watched the lines dance by as she read it aloud, noticing the first letters and how they matched Tennyson's own poem:

Then haste thee to thy sullen Isle,
And gaze upon the sea;
That element may meet thy smile—
It ne'er was ruled by thee!
Or trace with thine all idle hand
In loitering mood upon the sand,
That Earth is now as free!
That Corinth's pedagogue hath now
Transferr'd his by-word to thy brow.

"Oh, crap," Freddie said. "This ain't good."

Catherine's gray head dropped as well as she realized the implications. "No, I suppose it's not."

Freddie reached across the aisle and tapped Sarah's shoulder. She looked up, frowning, then leaned over. "What is it?" She asked. "Julie and I were just —"

"We can't go to Corsica," Freddie said quickly. His voice was in a near panic.

"What? What are you talking about?"

"She figured it out," Freddie said. "Lady Catherine. She saw it in Ben's email from Tennyson. All the weird capital letters? They line up a certain way because it's a *poem*. Or, actually, Tennyson was telling us to go *find* a poem."

Julie was now leaning over Sarah's seat so she could hear better. "What do you mean? What poem?"

"*Napoleon*, by Lord George Byron," he said. "It's right here. Read it for yourselves."

He watched as the women did just that, scanning over this phone and screen as they read the lines. When they got to the last line of the stanza, he saw it on their faces, immediately.

They would not be going to Corsica.

"'Sullen isle,'" Freddie said. "'It ne'er was ruled by thee.' Byron is talking about where Napoleon was exiled."

Catherine jumped in. "Lord Byron wrote about Napoleon a lot, actually. He knew a lot about the man, as they were contemporaries."

"At the next airport," Julie said, "We need to get off the plane and get another ticket. We need to book a flight to a different island."

Sarah nodded. "We need to go to Elba."

CHAPTER 69
JULIE

11:32 AM | **March 11, 2021**

Marina di Campo Airport, Isola d'Elba, Italy

Freddie had taken it upon himself to book an SUV while en route to Elba. Julie smiled when she saw it in the rental lot after disembarking the aircraft — it was absolutely massive, and she knew he had done it on purpose. He was tired of cramming into a seat and being at the mercy of a rideshare driver. Plus, they had now added a fourth member to their crew.

Lady Catherine had already proven to be a major asset to their search, finding the code in Tennyson's poem that pointed to Elba as Napoleon's *sullen isle.* Without her, Julie and the others would still be headed to Corsica, a neighboring island just southwest of Elba, but the wrong island altogether.

Tennyson wanted Ben in Elba, for whatever reason. Either Tennyson was here himself or this is where they would find the sword. Or, as Freddie had predicted, they would find Tennyson and both swords here.

Julie pictured the sword in her mind, then pictured the size of the island. About ninety square miles, and a population hovering around thirty thousand.

The proverbial needle in a haystack situation.

Now, Julie wondered if the mulberry tree on Eliza's sweater actually had anything to do with finding the sword. Based on Madame Blanchet's explanation, it seemed as though the mulberry tree pointed directly to Corsica, not Elba. So why were they heading toward the smaller island?

She was running through scenarios and trying to put the pieces together while they all got settled into the SUV. Since no one had any bags or suitcases to claim — and Julie didn't own any anymore, anyway — getting out of the airport after landing in Elba had been quick and smooth. It was a small victory, but Julie was appreciative that they hadn't been stopped by security or questioned about why they were now in Elba. International travel always struck her as relatively simple once she got out of the United States. No one had even bothered checking for their passports.

"Where to, boss?" Freddie asked. He seemed to be in good spirits, either sensing that they were on the right track or just excited to not have to cram into a backseat any more.

Julie had gotten into the front passenger seat, but she was still thinking through the mission, trying to put together the pieces of the puzzle Tennyson had laid out before them. She almost didn't hear his question. Freddie started to repeat it. "Oh," she said. "I have no idea. I feel like Tennyson wanted us to come here. That much is clear. But I can't figure out exactly *where* here, you know? And I've been thinking about the mulberry tree on Eliza's sweater..."

"I still don't see how that *doesn't* reference Corsica," Sarah said. "But he did make the email clear that he was referencing Lord Byron's *Napoleon* poem, and very specifically the *sullen isle*, which could only have meant Elba."

"Right," Julie replied. "So there is obviously more to it. I mean he made it a point to put her in a sweater that had a mulberry tree on it, right? So maybe there's something else about her —"

"Her clothing!" Sarah said from the backseat.

"Could be," Julie said. "But what? The video was in 4K, and Freddie mentioned that seemed like it would be overkill. I mean, sure, most phones can shoot in 4K these days, but for just something as simple as a video message like that — especially if he's going to email it — why would he have bothered with such a large file size?"

Freddie nodded from the driver's seat as they pulled out of the small rental car's parking lot, heading toward the main road that led out of the miniature airport and into what passed as the nearest town. They had agreed to stop at the first store that resembled a corner store or general store that they passed, in order to run in and get whatever hygiene items, changes of clothes, or anything else they might want or need. Julie had reminded them that they didn't have time for a full-fledged shopping trip. They hadn't even planned on booking a hotel until they had more answers — namely, until they had figured out why they had been summoned to Elba by Tennyson's clues — but she had allowed this small pitstop.

"Maybe he wanted us to see something else," Freddie said. "Something small. Maybe there's another clue somewhere else in the video."

"Her necklace?" Catherine asked from behind Julie. "Wasn't she wearing some small gold chain or something?"

Julie's eyes grew wide. "Yes, that *has* to be it. He made it a point to put her in specific clothing, so why not add a specific item of jewelry as well? I wonder if that chain wasn't hers, but something Tennyson forced her to wear."

"I think we've all got the video on our phones," Sarah said, "but I can use Freddie's laptop to get a bigger image."

Sarah handed Julie the laptop after finding the video. Julie moved the scrub tool forward frame by frame until Eliza shifted in her chair onscreen, bringing her neck and the gold chain around it a bit closer to the camera. She then dragged the corner of the window wider to fill the screen and used her thumb and forefinger on the trackpad to zoom in on it. As they had predicted, the resolution of the video was easily high enough to see in clear detail what was hanging around Eliza's neck.

It was a pendant, resting at the end of a gold chain. The pendant was small, irregularly shaped, with a jewel of some sort in the top right corner.

She frowned, not understanding what she was looking at.

Catherine leaned over her shoulder and looked down at the screen. "That's Elba," Catherine said, a hint of excitement in her voice.

"What do you mean?"

"I mean, the pendant is depicting the island of Elba. The pendant is shaped exactly like this island."

Of course. Julie pulled her phone up but left the video paused on Freddie's laptop's screen. She navigated to her map app and let her phone ping her location for a moment. When it did, she zoomed out and looked at the image filling her screen. Light blue covered all the edges, but the island they were currently on filled the center.

It was the island of Elba, and it did indeed match perfectly the shape of Eliza's pendant.

"That's it, then," Julie said. "That's the clue that confirms we needed to head to Elba. That means —"

"The jewel represents where, *exactly*, we are supposed to go."

Julie nodded. She made the map a bit smaller to try to match the size of the island on her phone with the pendant shape on Freddie's screen. When she finished, she brought her phone up and held it over the screen.

While Freddie drove, the three women looked at both images for a few seconds, then Julie pointed at a spot on her phone map. "There," she said. "That's where the jewel should be on this map."

"Anything there?" Freddie asked. "Anything noteworthy — maybe something from Napoleon's time?"

Julie saw Catherine in her peripheral vision, nodding rapidly. "Yes," she said. "Yes, I know this area. It's the Cavo region of Elba.

High, mountainous area with sharp cliffs. Beaches that stretch for miles along the coast."

"That's where we're going then," Freddie said. "Looks like there's a corner store or something up here on the right, so we'll stop first. But I think we have our destination. It's an hour away, so get some snacks."

Catherine was still nodding. "Yes, that is definitely it. It has to be our destination. And yes, there is something there from Napoleon's time. A castle, in fact."

CHAPTER 70

JULIE

12:43 PM | **March 11, 2021**
Cavo, Isola d'Elba, Italy

The castle's spires shot upward in the distance, piercing through low-hanging clouds, concealing their tops. The place seemed old enough to be from before Napoleon's time, but that was where the similarities between this castle and Lady Catherine's home ended. It appeared that this castle not only had been well-maintained over the centuries, it seemed as though more recent, modern improvements had been made.

On the way to the place, Catherine had filled them in on some details she had found online. While the castle had not been the actual location where Napoleon had been exiled, it had certainly been present on the island while he was here, though unoccupied. She found an article from three years ago stating that a rich investor had purchased the entire area and land, including the castle and grounds. That investor had spent many more millions on structural and archi-tectural improvements to the castle while maintaining its 16th-century design. It had been a boost to the local economy, and while the owner was reclusive, no one seemed to have a problem with him.

While the article did not mention the name of the investor, they had asked a local business owner at the corner store for more information and gotten the clue they needed: the owner was Swiss, if they recalled correctly.

That had further confirmed their suspicions that it was Tennyson himself who had purchased the place.

Freddie navigated the SUV up the manicured gravel path that led to the main house. It was a mile-long driveway, and while they had not yet met any interference and gates, Julie thought she noticed a few spots of light reflecting off of glass from a small structure tucked away in the trees. She stared at the spot for a few seconds as they drove past, not quite able to make out what it was, but then she saw another one on the opposite side of the road.

Guard outposts, she thought. Tennyson wanted to maintain the visual integrity of the old castle's grounds and yard, but he likely wanted some modern-day security out here.

She pointed them out to Freddie, who nodded. "Hidden surveillance is not uncommon at places like these. Rich folks want to keep an eye on people coming to visit them, but they don't want them to know they're being watched."

"The fact that there's more security than just solar powered cameras hanging on trees means that they are probably manned booths. That means guards."

"And guns," Freddie added. "You sure this is a good idea?"

Julie shook her head. "No, I can almost guarantee it is *not* a good idea."

Freddie chuckled, but he maintained speed. "Whatever we find here, it's one step closer to Eliza."

"Exactly. And I'm just hoping Tennyson's changed his mind about trying to kill us."

"We know there is a third party involved now, though" Sarah said quietly. "That could be part of the explanation for why we keep getting bombarded with people trying to stop us. Maybe they want Tennyson, too. 'Enemy of my enemy is my friend' sort of thing."

"And yet Tennyson's email was perfectly clear. 'I am sending a team to persuade you to come alone.'"

Julie and Sarah didn't argue. Freddie was right, of course. And it was a fact she had had on her mind since they had taken off from Lyon. Tennyson had been clear that he did not want the rest of Ben's CSO team helping out in the search for Napoleon's sword.

So intent, in fact, that he had tried to kill them in the hotel restaurant.

Whatever this is all about, it's probably going to get messy.

The full castle came into view a few minutes later. On either side of the main driveway Julie saw two armed security guards. Both were holding assault rifles.

"Wow," Freddie said, whistling. "Tennyson is serious about his security."

As they passed the guards, the one nearest to Julie's window lifted up his wrist and she saw his mouth moving. *Alerting Tennyson that we're here,* she realized.

That was both good news and bad. Tennyson now knew they were here — that meant there would be no element of surprise, no way to sneak into the place without being seen. She knew that ship had long since sailed anyway, knew that they were going to have to try for diplomacy rather than outright action.

But the good news was that they were still alive. Tennyson had not yet had his guards pepper their car and bodies with bullets.

She saw two more guards up ahead, both standing on Freddie's side of the road, and noticed two of the same glass booths she had seen in the woods dotting each side of a massive decorated wrought-iron front entrance gate, currently closed. Freddie pulled the car up to the gate and stopped, rolling down his window. A guard ambled over, not getting too close.

And, Julie couldn't help but notice, keeping his finger over the trigger of his gun.

"We're here for a meetin,'" Freddie said, laying on his southern drawl thickly.

"Italiano?" the man barked in response.

"Sorry, bub, I only speak proper 'Merican English."

Julie wanted to smack him. *Why are you purposefully riling him up?*

If the guard was frustrated or annoyed, he didn't show it on his face. He straightened back up and nodded his head. From behind the booth on each side of the road, two more guards walked out and began pulling the gate doors open. When they had finished, Freddie nodded and thanked the first guard with a wave and a smile, then drove the car slowly into the compound.

And *compound* was probably the best word to describe it — while the top levels of the castle structure, starting from the second story — looked every bit like the 16th-century castle that had originally been constructed, the first level of the building had been made from pure concrete. A single metal entrance door stood in front of them, two steps up, and two other low, flat, one-story concrete buildings to her right and left formed a three-sided square, the guard booths and gate itself forming the front wall. The center of the square — the part they were driving over now — was nothing but an open space covered with crushed gravel. There were two cars parked to the left and one to her right. She noticed that the one on the right was also a rental car.

"Doesn't seem like they kept up the whole 'medieval sheik' aesthetic here," Freddie said.

"It's utilitarian for sure," Sarah said. "Tennyson probably did it because he needed to, not because he was trying to win some architectural design awards."

"That begs the question," Julie said. "*Why* did he need to? What's he doing here that required him to build an ugly, industrial, well-protected facility?"

The door opened, and Julie had a feeling they were about to find out what all of the charade, all of the terrifying, death-defying country-hopping, had all been for.

She expected more guards to begin to spill out from the main castle, or at least Tennyson himself.

She was wrong.

What she saw was nowhere near what she had expected. Her eyes nearly popped out of her head when she saw the figure that had just appeared in the doorway.

Eliza.

CHAPTER 71

JULIE

12:45 PM | **March 11, 2021**

Cavo, Isola d'Elba, Italy

"I'm glad you came," Eliza said, her bright red hair tossing left and right as she spoke. She seemed surprisingly chipper. "I hope the clues were good enough for you to find your way here."

Julie and the others had entered, and she tried to contain her shock inside the castle. The guards had corralled the four of them inside, where they had exchanged brief introductions. None of them had met Eliza in person, but Julie and the others recognized her immediately from the video.

"Yes," Julie said hesitantly. "They were... Good enough, I guess." She was on edge. They weren't dead yet, but that only made her more suspicious of what Tennyson had planned.

"What's this all about?" Freddie asked. "You trying to play some sort of game with us?"

Eliza sucked in a breath. "Heavens, no," she said. "If... if it were up to me, I would never have done things this way."

"This way? You mean get kidnapped and threatened by an egomaniac?"

Her head lowered. "Yes. Tennyson *did* kidnap me, and he *did* threaten me. But — "

"Where is he?" Freddie asked. "That bastard and I need to have a word."

She held up a hand. "No, no. That's just... That's just it. I mean, I think the situation has changed. I'm not exactly sure how or why, but about four hours ago he let me out of the room he had been keeping me in and told me to change clothes, then meet him in his office. There were guards around me the whole time, just like there are now. I'm not free, but at least I'm no longer tied to a chair in a room and being kept in a makeshift jail cell."

Julie involuntarily reached out and touched Eliza's shoulder. "We're sorry we didn't come sooner. We tried. I'm glad you're okay, but I'm with Freddie — this is all really weird. Is Tennyson here?"

Eliza nodded. "Yes, I was told to welcome you." She chuckled, as if realizing how absolutely bizarre that sounded. "I believe he *was* going to try to kill you all, but something changed his mind. Probably..." Her voice fell away before she could finish, and Julie saw her twist her head around and stare at a door in the hallway to their left.

"Probably what?" Sarah asked.

Eliza shifted her gaze back to them. "It's... it's probably best for you to just come and see for yourselves."

Julie felt cold, both from the low temperature in the concrete building but also because of the growing fear that was percolating through her system. Everything was changing quickly — the status quo and her expectations for what she would find. Never in a million years would she have imagined Tennyson welcoming them with open arms through Eliza — using her as the same bait he had originally used to lure them all here in the first place.

It was all too much. She felt the urge to sit down, but fought through it.

She pulled her phone out, seeing that there was no service out here. *Great*, she thought. *One more unwelcome surprise.* She needed to get in contact with Ben and Reggie, needed to tell them —

"Come on. Right this way," Eliza said, interrupting Julie's thoughts. Eliza turned on a heel and began walking down the hallway toward the door she had been looking at, her soft flats barely making a sound as she moved.

The others followed in a line, and Julie was behind Eliza and second to reach the door. Eliza knocked and then turned the handle.

Julie noticed Freddie tensing up behind her, and she followed his silent cue to mentally prepare herself for what she might find on the other side of this door. If this were a trap, there was not much they could do. They were unarmed and still being followed by two of the assault rifle-wielding guards. Even if they had weapons, what would they be able to do here? Catherine and Eliza would only be in danger of becoming collateral damage.

If Tennyson had wanted to bring them all here for their execution, she wasn't sure they would have much chance of a fight.

The door swung open, and bright yellow light from inside the space beyond forced her eyes to adjust. She blinked a few times, then stepped into the room confidently. *No sense being timid now*, she thought.

"Jules?"

Not possible, she thought. She knew the voice — she'd know it anywhere. *There's no way —*

Her eyes finally finished adjusting and she pulled her head to the left, trying to take in all the details of the room. Her brain faltered, not allowing her to fill in any specific details other than the two massive, obvious details standing directly to her left.

Two men, standing side-by-side, one of them now moving quickly toward her.

"Ben?" She asked.

The others filed into the room. "What? What the hell, man?"

Freddie asked, flicking his eyes around to the left and right. "This thing just got a *whole lot* weirder."

Ben reached her and wrapped her in a bearlike embrace. She didn't move; she couldn't. She wasn't sure what was happening.

"This is... I don't know what..." Freddie couldn't even get a sentence out.

Julie felt like Freddie sounded. Confused, scared, angry, relieved.

Reggie smiled, then stepped forward and extended his hand out to Freddie. They shook. "Trust me," Reggie said. "You have no idea how weird this is. Come on, we're still on the clock. Tennyson wants to meet all of you, and there's not a lot of time."

Julie finally regathered her strength and hugged Ben back. She whispered into his ear. "Ben... what is this? And Mr. E —"

He whispered back. "Don't worry, Jules. I'm not entirely sure what this is, to be honest. But the situation has definitely changed. The status quo's changed. We just need to play along for a bit."

He pulled back as the others gathered around.

Reggie pulled Sarah along as he spoke. "Come on in. We'll try our best to get you up to speed."

CHAPTER 72
FREDDIE

12:50 PM | **March 11, 2021**
Cavo, Isola d'Elba, Italy

As dull as the rest of the first-floor concrete fortress seemed, the office Freddie stepped into was exactly the opposite. It wasn't lavish, but it was certainly luxurious. Smooth concrete walls stretched up to an impossibly high ceiling, and decorative furniture — arm chairs and a sofa — had been placed on a massive area rug in the center of the room. On the opposite side of the room from the door they'd entered through sat a simple, modern desk.

A bearded man stood behind it, and moved toward them as they entered the room.

Baden Tennyson.

He knew the man from the picture the others showed him. Tall, nearly six feet, with a wizened look on his face. Wrinkles, but far fewer than someone his age should be sporting. White hair, kept short and combed sideways, with a white, well-manicured beard.

He wore a smart suit as well, dark brown, with a white Oxford poking out from underneath. He strode toward them on crisp leather shoes that clacked on the concrete floor.

Freddie felt the anger inside him growing once again. This man had not only kidnapped a friend of Ben's, he had also tried to kill them. He couldn't imagine the mental torture Eliza had endured, but he knew it was probably ten times what he had put the rest of them through.

That's enough for me, he thought. *Better men have been killed for less.*

To make things worse, Tennyson had done it all through a proxy. Freddie had no problem with a fight. His beef was with a man who was too cowardly to show up to the fight in person. To take to allowing others to fight battles for them was something that bugged Freddie. It was part of the reason he had been disillusioned by — and subsequently quit — military service. Everything at one point or another came down to telling boys and girls to fight and die for a war they hadn't started in the first place, for older boys and girls who thought they were doing right by God or their country or whatever deity they prayed to.

He clenched his fists but held them at his side.

"Welcome, all of you," Tennyson said, with a powerful booming voice. The man was no-nonsense, no smile or lightheartedness, and Freddie felt grateful for that. *At least we don't have to pretend we're all friends,* he thought. *We can cut the crap and get down to brass tacks.*

"We have some matters to resolve," Tennyson continued. "I will answer your questions, but I am going to need your help."

"Bullshit," Freddie said. "Why should we help —"

"Give him a minute to explain," Reggie said, cutting in. "Trust us, we were pissed too. He's been trying to kill us. But to be fair, we all wanted to kill him, first."

"Doesn't mean he doesn't deserve to die," Freddie said under his breath.

Tennyson took the slight in stride, continuing to move toward them. When he was about ten feet away, he stopped. He didn't offer his hand or any other pleasantries. "I'm going to get straight to the point. We don't like each other, and that has not changed. I meant what I said when I emailed Ben the first time. I need his help. At the time I did not think I needed yours. It's now come to my attention that you do, in fact, work best together as a team." He turned to Julie. "You're here, which is proof enough that you are capable of putting pieces of a puzzle together."

"How did you find this place, Ben?" Julie asked.

Ben smiled sheepishly. "I wish we had figured it out, like you guys did. It was right there in the video. Eliza's necklace, right? Unfortunately, we got a bit... sidetracked in Switzerland. After Tennyson's granddaughter's house blew up, we —"

"Wait, *what*?" Sarah asked.

"I know, I know," Ben said, holding up his hands. "Trust me, we'll go through all of that later. Tennyson thought we had done it — meanwhile, we were worried Tennyson thought we were the ones who had done it... The ones who threatened his granddaughter and her family. We were there, after all, but that was not our plan, never in a million years."

Reggie jumped in. "They're okay, by the way. No one was home. But Tennyson already knew who had done it. It was the same people who have been trying to take us off the map for the past few days."

"The ones who sent a truck filled with explosives to your cabin," Freddie said.

Ben nodded, his face and solemn. "Exactly, just like the attack in Switzerland. Again, I assumed it was Tennyson."

"It wasn't?" Sarah asked. "I mean, his first email was right after the attack at the cabin. It even started with, '*now that I have your attention,*' remember?"

Tennyson's brow creased. "An unforgivable error in judgment," he said. "And I have apologized to Harvey. I was simply referencing the lawsuit that is currently being prepared against your group by my legal team."

Freddie nodded. He remembered Julie mentioning something

about that, a legal suit the team had been talking about before he'd arrived at Ben's cabin.

"Anyway," Tennyson said, "I had not heard of the destruction at your home until well after I had sent that email. I am, once again, sorry for your loss."

Freddie didn't respond. It seemed as though this man was telling the truth, but there was plenty more of that truth that needed to be told before he could even remotely start trusting this guy.

Tennyson continued. "As you can imagine, finding the second Sword of Austerlitz, the copy, has never been about fun and games. I am a collector of *people* — a connector, if you will. That is what has made me successful over the years. I own many businesses." He paused. "Some of them are, admittedly, illegitimate and in sectors that you, as you well know, operate in a bit of a moral gray zone." His eyes landed on Eliza, but she didn't respond. "I do not believe I am a *bad* person, but I am a man who is willing to do things others find distasteful, in order to further science and technology. That's it. As such, I have no time or interest in trifles such as collecting artifacts and antiquities."

"So something about this sword is important to you for reasons other than posterity?" Sarah asked.

Tennyson's voice dropped. "Yes, absolutely. Come this way, and I'll show you exactly what I mean."

They followed Tennyson over to the seating area, and Freddie noticed a stack of documents that had been laid on the low coffee table on the center of the rug. There were notebooks and folders opened and waiting there as well. Tennyson pulled out one of the folders from the stack and flipped through the loose pages inside. Finding what he was looking for, he pulled out a photocopy of another piece of paper.

Behind him, Catherine gasped. "It's the missing page!" She said.

12:53 PM **| March 11, 2021**
Cavo, Isola d'Elba, Italy

Tennyson looked at Lady Catherine, seeming to notice her for the first time, but then nodded once. "Indeed, taken from the Journal of Odiot, who created a copy of Napoleon's Austerlitz sword. It was a top-secret project at the time, and any record of it has been all but lost, if it existed in the first place."

He held out the photocopy and Catherine lurched forward to grab it, holding it up and examining every word on it. The others waited around her, and after a few seconds she held her hand up to her mouth. "It's... it's exactly as I had feared. It's exactly what I had predicted."

"Some sort of chemical compound," Tennyson said, explaining for Freddie and the rest of them. "Napoleon somehow got his hands on a special acid that, when dispersed through the air, could render subjects completely incapable of moving."

"Acid?" Julie asked.

Tennyson nodded. "When aerosolized in a powder or liquid form, it has intriguingly strong effects."

"It works, too," Ben said. Freddie and the rest of the CSO team in the room all looked at him quickly, but he didn't offer any more.

"Napoleon wanted another sword — an exact copy of his favored Sword of Austerlitz, the one created by Biennais — in order to store this acid for use on the battlefield. For this project, he needed to ensure that no one else would ever be suspicious. That no one else would ever know about it, in fact. His plan was to re-create the Sword of Austerlitz, albeit with a tiny alteration."

"On the hilt," Julie said. "He replaced the roses with little versions of whatever chemical this is."

"Precisely," Tennyson said. "They were like little pouches, essentially. Able to hold the acidic powder until he needed them."

"It is how he won at Austerlitz," Catherine whispered, still in awe over the page she was holding in her hands.

"Indeed it was," Tennyson said. "Not to mention a few other decisive victories of his. He was every bit as capable and successful a leader as history has proven him to be," Tennyson said. "Yet history has erased what exactly made him so successful in battle."

Freddie recalled Catherine's explanation back at her own castle. "So, what does all this mean?" he asked. "You pitched this to Ben as a sort of game — 'find the sword and you'll let Eliza go.' What's changed now? Why's the game over?"

Tennyson responded immediately. "Your friends Harvey and Eliza killed someone who meant a great deal to me, someone from my own family. As such, I had planned to exact revenge by taking someone he cared about. By taking his professional life away from him. Now, however, the status quo has changed."

Eliza's eyes widened a bit, but she held herself with composure.

"In a sense, it was all a game to me. Now I realize Ben was just doing what he thought was best — and I must admit he did stop my grandson from continuing with that terrible research taking place at the EKG facility."

"The facility you own and funded," Eliza blurted out.

Tennyson shot dark eyes toward her. "As I said, my research is in areas that exist in the gray space of morality."

Freddie shifted, watching the reactions of Ben and Reggie. They had stayed strangely silent for most of Tennyson's explanation, and he figured it was because they already knew most of this. He decided to follow their lead: if they weren't worked up about it, he wouldn't be.

"This third party that's in play," Tennyson said. "They are the reason I need your help. I want to keep the sword out of their hands."

"But you must already know where it is?" Sarah asked. "You have to already have it, right? Otherwise, why send Ben on this wild goose chase around the world? Why go through all the trouble? You've even dropped clues that were meant to send us looking for it — so you have to know where it is."

"Yes," Tennyson said. "The second sword is here. It has been in my possession for some time. Early on, I set up a sort of game — a scavenger hunt of sorts — for Ben to solve, but it was merely so that I could confirm my suspicions about him. It was a test. A test to see that he was good enough to find something like this, given a few inauspicious clues."

"Because you needed him to find these other people?" Julie asked. "This third group that's now after us? They want it in order to weaponize this compound. They're trying to kill us — they think we're looking for the sword because we knew about the compound and the secret it held."

Tennyson nodded. His voice was grave. "Yes, precisely. I thought Ben could help me prevent them from completing their next attack. I believed if he could find the sword that I had hidden, he would understand the importance of working with me to prevent this group from finishing their fourth and final attack."

"Their final attack?"

CHAPTER 74

BEN

12:57 PM | **March 11, 2021**

Cavo, Isola d'Elba, Italy

"Yes," Tennyson said. "What have you noticed about those terror attacks around the world?"

The group looked at each other, then back at Tennyson. Ben cleared his throat and spoke. "Well, I remember there being reports that everybody seemed to just be standing around when those guys entered the square and started lighting them all on fire. One person said on the news that it was like they were all 'too scared to move.'"

"Frozen in place," Reggie added.

Ben immediately realized the implication. Tennyson must know something they did not: that these terror attacks were all related. From the square in Italy to the strange scuba diving incident off the coast of Mexico to the mining accident — all of them had involved people all dying the same way: being frozen in place, unable to move, just before their deaths.

"Precisely," Tennyson said. "The piazza attack in Rome is the most telling. At least three gunmen, all working on their own side of the square. How did they ensure everyone would remain in place while they firebombed it? How could they make sure no one would turn and run away? With these sorts of things you usually have survivors who get away just as the attack begins. In this case, while there *were* survivors, everyone directly involved were killed or seriously injured, and reports are, indeed, that no one turned to run away."

"You think they drugged everyone with this acid first?" Julie asked.

"Almost without a doubt. They were testing it," Tennyson said. "Best we can tell, it causes the same sort of effect as rigor mortis, after the body dies — a severe buildup of lactic acid, which essentially locks the body in place. Except in this case, it is reversible — the body quickly is able to flush the lactic acid, which must end up exiting the system as urine or sweat or even as a gas, through the lungs. We don't know yet. But they were *practicing*, preparing for something much, *much* larger."

"You mentioned that before," Reggie said. "A final attack. Why do you think there's going to be another one?"

Tennyson moved over to the low set table and sat down at one of the armchairs. "Not the fourth and final attack," he said calmly. "That is too late to stop now, I'm afraid. But they are not going to be done, even after that. There will be more. There will *always* be more."

"Something *much bigger*," Ben whispered.

Tennyson pulled out another folder closer to him at the edge of the table and opened it. "I have been collecting everything I can on these attacks, following along with them from the first one. Initially, I didn't think they were related, but one of my researchers found an old webpage from two years ago. Some young radical by the name of Raoul wrote up a manifesto of sorts, claiming to be threatening the world with 'four attacks.' The manifesto was a *bit* poetic, I'll admit, but there were some elements of intelligence and concrete details within."

He pulled a printout of the webpage out of the folder. "This is it," he said. "This is the sort of thing I track at one of my companies. Right now it is just a small arm of a research company, but this is ultimately the beginnings of the organization that I was hoping Harvey would join me in starting. A group tasked with finding bits of information just like this, putting it together in meaningful ways. To find patterns around conspiratorial or simply *interesting* events — so that we might prevent these sorts of things from happening."

Ben stiffened. He hadn't heard this part of the explanation from Tennyson. *So it was true,* he thought. *Tennyson wants my help for a project similar in scope to what the CSO is trying to do.*

"This manifesto referenced two things that had stayed lodged in the back of my mind. It took some time — too much time, if I'm honest — but it finally all started to make sense. First, the writer of the manifesto invoked the memory of Aristotle at the beginning of the document. Strange God to pray to, no?"

Just then a bald man appeared in the doorway of Tennyson's massive office. "They're here," the man said. He was gone as quickly as he had appeared.

Tennyson turned back to Ben. "We'll have to finish this later — if there's time."

"Who's here?" Ben asked.

"The Faction," Tennyson said. "*They* are the reason I set this all up. I needed to get a message to you without The Faction intercepting it. The truth is, I need your help, Harvey. I need *everyone's* help. The Faction wants me dead. They're the ones who have been trying to kill you, as well. I'm afraid they've taken advantage of our little feud, caught us both off-guard."

The realization struck Ben in that moment. *The Faction was the name of the group that tried to kill us outside the hotel.*

"But *you* sent men to shoot at us in the hotel restaurant," Reggie said. "And *then* The Faction was waiting for us outside. You're not innocent in this, Tennyson."

"I was just hoping to scare you into joining my cause," Tennyson said, still addressing Ben directly. "They were never going to harm your team."

"Yeah?" Freddie asked. "Sure as hell *seemed* like they were trying to harm us. I don't think I'm going to be able to forgive you for that one, old man."

Tennyson's stoic front broke and he glared at Freddie. "Again, I apologize for my rash actions. I was angry, wanting revenge for my grandson's death. And now, I want revenge for the attack on my granddaughter's home. Your friends and I have already discussed this at length. If you want to hold a grudge, fine. But *right now*, in this moment, we have bigger problems."

"What do they want?" Sarah asked. "Why are they really here?"

"Yeah," Reggie added. "I get they want to kill us, but what do they *really* want? How did you get involved, and what is it they want from you, specifically?"

Tennyson swallowed, then looked at his watch. He muttered something, but then answered. "I stole something from them, many years ago. A page from a journal, one that detailed Napoleon's plans for the weapon inside his Odiot sword."

Ben saw Catherine's eyes go wide. "*My* journal," she whispered. "The missing page. *You* took it."

Tennyson nodded. "Yes, indeed. The journal of your ancestor, Odiot. The man who created the duplicate Sword of Austerlitz using the new chemical weapon based on the acid Napoleon was researching."

"Wait a minute," Julie said. "*Napoleon* developed this himself?"

"As far as we can tell, Napoleon was involved with an early form of this same group. The Faction. He had access to the greatest chemists in the world because of it, and due to his power in France and Europe, nothing was off-limits to him."

"And you stole the page..." Ben said.

"I was involved with The Faction back then, when we were first learning about the sword and its duplicate. Right now the understanding is that Napoleon somehow came across or was given this research and his team was able to replicate it. The Faction now has, apparently, no idea where the acid originally came from, but they *have* been able to synthesize it in a laboratory in order to create more."

"Great," Reggie said.

"It's how they have launched their previous three attacks," Tennyson said. "Again, we don't have time to discuss it all, but you'll just have to trust me."

Freddie scoffed.

Tennyson ignored him. "Please, I have a full armory. A personal collection, if you will. I need your help. Anything you want to use in there is yours to keep. Consider it an olive branch."

"Your version of extending an olive branch is conscripting us into your private army?"

Reggie smiled at Freddy's comment, but Tennyson face was once again stoic and unreadable. "They are not just here to kill *me*, I might remind you."

Ben stepped forward, glancing at the others around the room, then back at Tennyson. "We're a ragtag bunch, but if we're able to help, we will. We don't take kindly to strangers trying to gun us down. I don't like the idea of you stealing artifacts, and your research at EKG still disgusts me, but right now it does seem as though we have a common enemy."

Tennyson nodded. "The man who just came in is named Saul. He is the head of my security. You will find him a most capable ally. Go with him and get situated." He stopped and looked at his watch. "By my estimate, we have less than a minute before they arrive."

CHAPTER 75

JULIE

1:04 PM | **March 11, 2021**

Cavo, Isola d'Elba, Italy

Julie entered the brightly lit room and gasped. On every wall, stacked floor to ceiling, were weapons. To her left she saw assault rifles of every make and model, and directly in front of her was a wall of sidearms. She recognized the same model Glock that she had back home, the one she had done most of her training with at the makeshift range they had set up behind the cabin.

She felt a pang of regret when she thought about the cabin and Mrs. E. *Fire straight*, Mrs. E used to tell her. *And to fire straight, you can't anticipate.*

To her right were even more weapons, but these were of a kind far more eclectic and obscure. She noticed a medieval-era crossbow hanging next to a more traditional-looking bow and a quiver of arrows that looked like it had come straight from the movie set of *Lord of the Rings*.

"Tennyson is an avid collector," the bald man who had led them into the room said. "And in case he did not mention it, my name is Saul. I am his Director of Security. Like all of Tennyson's *collections*, he only collects what might prove actually useful, in a practical way."

That means these are all working weapons, Julie realized.

Saul continued. "We outfit our team with standardized infantry weaponry and ammunition, but this is a bit of a unique situation. Please do your best to take care of these pieces, but since ultimately they are meant for protection, anything you might feel comfortable with should be found here in perfect, working order."

Reggie and Freddie immediately walked to the left wall, searching high and low for their preferred rifle. Ben followed behind them, while Julie hung back with Sarah and Catherine.

"I must say," Catherine began, her hand over her chest. "I *am* a bit of a pacifist."

Julie smiled. "I understand. No one expects you to grab a gun and start shooting bad guys. Maybe there's a place you can stay to keep you out of harm's way?"

She noticed that the woman had started shaking, so Julie reached over and grabbed her wrist. "Look, Ben meant what he said in Tennyson's office: we *are* a ragtag group, but we *do* have a knack for getting through things alive. If you want to just sit tight, this should all be over soon, no matter how it —"

"If it's all the same to you," she said, interrupting, "I would rather stay by your side."

Julie stared at the bald man in the center of the room and then nodded. "That's perfectly fine by me."

Eliza entered the room and walked up next to the three women. "I got to spend a little bit of time with your husband in Switzerland," she said. "He was a good shot."

"I *am* a good shot," Ben said, obviously overhearing their conversation. "But she's a *hell* of a shot, and none of us come close to Reggie here. Stick with either of them and you'll be fine."

Eliza smiled and nodded, but Julie could see the fear in her eyes.

She turned her head at a new noise that broke through her concentration. It was the sound of gunfire, pounding low and deep, the sound of shots being exchanged by multiple forces outside.

They're here.

The others in the room exchanged similar glances. She knew The Faction's team would probably have come up the main road with their largest force, to earn the attention of Tennyson's security force, but also drop in smaller units somewhere along the vicinity of Tennyson's land. It was the tactical move she would make — try to get in on their flanks, while the main force was preoccupied. She wondered how many there were, what sort of weapons they would be using to attack.

In other words, what sorts of weapons would they need to *defend*?

"Anyway," Eliza said quickly. "Is that true?"

Julie was confused at first, but then remembered what Ben had said. "I'm a *lucky* shot, sure. Let's hope we've got a little bit of luck on our side today. It's never been my favorite thing to do to rush in and start taking potshots at people, but these guys deserve it."

"You ready?" Reggie called out from his corner of the room. Saul, behind him, was busy working on loading and prepping a massive assault rifle.

Julie nodded, trying to hide her reluctance. Of all the things she had done with this group, willingly rushing onto a battlefield and trying to gain purchase in a firefight had never been one of her favorites. She wasn't military trained — she barely knew her way around a gun, even if she was a crack shot. She looked over at Reggie, then at Freddie, who were both checking their magazines and making sure their weapons were loaded and ready for combat.

Ben turned and grabbed an assault rifle from the wall near the spot he'd gotten his own from, then walked it over to Julie.

He leaned in close and kissed her. "I'm not sure this is a good idea, Jules," he said.

"Nothing we've *ever* done had been a good idea, Ben," she said. Quickly, she added, "except marrying you. *That* was an okay idea."

He smiled down at her and handed her the rifle.

She took it, feeling its weight and power in her hands. "And if this even remotely makes the world a slightly better place, we need to do it. We need to end this, right here and right now."

The look on Ben's face was multifaceted. It was deep, as if trying to convey many thoughts at once.

She picked up on two of them. Reassurance — he wanted her to know that he was there, by her side. That they would get through this.

And she couldn't help but get the feeling that the *other* thing he was trying to tell her was that this was *nowhere near* the end.

CHAPTER 76

BEN

1:12 PM | **March 11, 2021**
Cavo, Isola d'Elba, Italy

Ben heard an explosion from somewhere very close by. Saul raced out of the room and he followed behind, his new assault rifle ready and waiting for a target. He wasn't sure if he believed Tennyson — that if they finished this all now it would all be over — but not finishing things here meant certain death.

He also knew The Faction, whoever they were, had more men they could call upon. More soldiers than they had sent today, but right now, they needed to stay alive. There was no other option, no other choice.

In the hallway, Ben saw out to the front atrium. The door they had walked through to enter the castle and parts of the concrete wall around it had been completely destroyed in the explosion. Smoke and dust filled the air, and two of Tennyson's guards, coughing, stumbled into the space seeking cover. As soon as they entered, both were cut down by gunfire from somewhere outside.

Saul roared something and leapt toward his downed comrades. He stopped at the edge of the gaping maw in the front of the castle and leaned out. "Come on!" he shouted to Ben and the others.

Ben found himself jogging over to where Saul had crouched. He didn't want to be a part of this; he didn't think this was his fight. But he had never been the type of man to shy away from a fight, especially when the fight came to him. The Faction was knocking at Tennyson's door, and he knew they would not differentiate between the old man, his guards, and his guests.

He turned back to Freddie and Reggie. "You two, with me."

He didn't have to explain his reasoning. He knew Reggie would want to keep Sarah out of the fight as much as Ben wanted to keep Julie out. The other woman, Catherine, was a bit of a wildcard for Ben, but he had seen everything he needed to know about her willingness to fight when she had raced out of the room with no weapon in her hands. *She's the only sane one among us*, he had thought.

Reggie and Freddie were by his side and Ben glanced down at Saul. "I'm going to the other side of the opening with them. Give us some cover fire."

Saul nodded, then began strafing rounds left and right. Ben took a breath and then jumped as far across the open space as he could. Gunfire immediately splattered the staircase and wall to his left, narrowly missing his feet and legs. He sprinted across the rest of the space and made it to the other side, sliding as if he were trying to make it to third base. He immediately shifted his weight and came to a prone position, just the end of his assault rifle poking out of the space. Reggie and Freddie followed behind, coming to a stop a few feet from Ben.

Saul's covering fire stopped and Ben saw a soldier poking his head up above one of the barrier walls in front of Tennyson's square. Ben noticed he was in a good position, the vines and growth nearly covering his upper body.

Ben backed away and spoke quietly to Reggie. "I've got one at about 2 o'clock. A bit out of reach for me unless I get lucky, but you should be able to handle it."

Reggie grinned, holding up the rifle he'd taken from Tennyson's weapons depot.

"With this thing," Reggie said, "I'm pretty sure I can handle anything from here to the edge of Tennyson's land. Let me at it."

Ben returned his friend's smile and stepped back from the opening to let Reggie take his place. Reggie copied Ben's earlier position, coming to rest on the floor of the entranceway, the end of his gun poking out. Back in the armory, when he'd joined Ben against the wall of assault rifles, Reggie had found something even more enticing than an assault rifle. It was a Brügger & Thomet APR338 sniper rifle, loaded out with NATO rounds, capable of taking out an enemy from almost a mile away.

And the edge of the square surrounding Tennyson's driveway was far less than a mile away.

Reggie took a few breaths and Ben watched him come to a complete and utter standstill. He saw Reggie's prosthetic fingers working the dial on the side of the sniper's scope.

Finally, Reggie snapped off a single shot. Ben jumped. He had no idea Reggie was about to fire. The sound was deafening, and Ben felt his ears ringing. He looked across the space to see Saul staring, open-mouthed at Reggie.

"Nice shot," Saul said. "Is he dead?"

"Well," Reggie said. "Let's just say that if he's still alive, I've rewired his brain a bit. He'll have a slightly different personality after this."

Saul flicked his eyes back out the opening. "There is another one, on your side this time. I think they sent these two forward to keep us busy while the rest of their men flank us."

"Any way they can get in from the sides or back?" Ben asked.

"Not easily, no. There are no roads to the castle but the one directly in front, and my team has positions all the way around the main compound. That said, I do not think they will be knocking on doors and asking politely to come in. Judging by what we have seen already, breaking and entering is more their MO."

Reggie shifted his position slightly while Saul continued to lay down covering fire. Ben noted that Saul was aiming slightly around the attacker's position, and Ben realized the strategy: keep the bad guy thinking they didn't know exactly where he was while Reggie lined up his shot.

Another three seconds passed, and it was over. The end of Reggie's sniper rifle smoked, and he pulled it back and slung the shoulder strap over his prosthetic arm. "He ain't going home, either," Reggie said.

"Looks like you still got it, brother," Ben said.

"*Still*? Hell, I'm better now than I ever was in the Army. Something about getting to choose my own targets makes me a better shot."

Saul ran across the open wound in the castle's front wall and joined the three men. Behind him, Ben saw Julie huddled outside the armory room with Sarah, Eliza, and Catherine on the other side of the hallway. They were discussing something, deep in thought.

"We cannot sit back and wait for them to hit us again," Saul said. "We know they have the firepower to smash through any wall here, and there is no reason to suspect they do not have enough ammunition to do it."

"What's the strategy, then?" Reggie asked.

Before he could answer, they heard the sound of another explosion, this one muffled and to Ben's right. It was deep and boomed through the castle's stone and concrete walls, vibrating everything and causing some dust to fall from cracks in the walls.

It had come from the *back* side of the castle.

"We're too late!" Saul yelled. "They are heading for the back of the building"

"You three, go with Saul," Ben said. "Try to keep them from

getting into the castle. I'm going to go with the girls and try to find somewhere to get them out of sight."

Ben hoped that The Faction didn't know exactly how many people were in Tennyson's castle. He assumed Tennyson would be their main target, followed by the men making up his security detail. Perhaps The Faction army had been informed that one or two members of another team had joined Tennyson, but he figured they wouldn't know how many. All in all, it meant Tennyson's forces — however many security guards were currently alive and still in the vicinity — as well as a few more men, would be what The Faction would expect. If there were any chance Ben could get the rest of his team tucked away safely and somewhere out of sight, he was going to try it.

"You got it," Reggie said. He glanced up at Saul. "You good with that?"

Saul nodded and then addressed Ben. "There is a basement, and the only entrance is the door across from Tennyson's office. That would probably be the best place for them."

Ben nodded. "Thanks," he said. He immediately took off across the opening on the front wall and toward Julie and the others on the opposite side of the hallway.

Reggie, Freddie, and Saul ran the opposite way, heading to a spot deeper within the castle.

CHAPTER 77
BEN

1:15 PM **| March 11, 2021**
Cavo, Isola d'Elba, Italy

"How's it going over here?" Ben asked as he reached Julie and the other women.

Julie turned to face him. "We are talking about the acid — Tennyson said it was developed by Napoleon."

"Right," Ben said. "You, uh, figure out anything useful?" He didn't want to say it, but discussing history while bullets were flying around them didn't seem like a good use of time. Hopefully, they were trying to figure out a way to stop The Faction.

Catherine spoke up. "I have pored over Napoleon's life since I was a girl. There is not much about the man that is publicly known that I'm not aware of. And yet, all of this seems like something I should have known about."

"All of this?" Ben asked. "What do you mean?"

"The swords, the weaponized acid, The Faction — if Napoleon had worked on some sort of mysterious compound like this, I feel like I should have come across something referencing it. A journal entry, a letter to one of his scientists, a cryptic note somewhere."

"Sometimes the *lack* of evidence is even more telling than the *presence* of it," Sarah added.

Catherine nodded. "Yes, that is true. And that could very well be. Perhaps he erased all record of it while he was here in exile. He would have had plenty of time to seek out those letters and references and do just that."

"Was there anything else about his life that was suspicious?" Ben asked. "I mean, did he have any weird quirks or do anything peculiar?"

Catherine thought for a moment. "That was exactly the thread I was trying to chase earlier. The only possible thing I can think of would have been his visit to Corsica while attending military college. It was abrupt, so unnatural for a young man like him. Napoleon was a very studious person, very focused, and he loved being one of the youngest kids at the school. As much of a family man as he was as well, it seems like something so mundane as helping his father with the family business just would not have been enough to call him home."

"You mentioned it was a business deal that went south," Sarah said. "Can you be more specific?"

"As far as anyone knows, that really was the gist of it. Charles Bonaparte had plans to start a mulberry farm, hoping to raise silkworms and sell their silk. It was not an unknown thing to do, but for someone of his relatively high status in Corsica and a total lack of entrepreneurial and business skill, it just seemed to come out of left field."

Ben considered Catherine's words, but he heard the more pressing matter outside. Gunshots rang out, and he thought he heard the dense impacts as they slapped into a nearby exterior wall. He corralled Julie, Sarah, Eliza, and Catherine toward the door Saul had pointed out.

"Where are we going?" Julie asked.

"Saul said there was a basement we can hide in," Ben said. "I'd much rather we stay down there and wait it out."

Eliza and Catherine seemed to perk up at hearing this news, but Julie frowned at him. "We're supposed to just hide in a corner?" she asked.

"I'm with her," Sarah said. "Reggie is out fighting with Freddie to keep us alive. The least we can do is lend a hand."

"But they're fine, they're going to hold the fort at the back of the —"

"Ben, listen to yourself," Julie said. "Now's not the time to be scared. We don't know what The Faction's capable of, and I don't want to hide somewhere while Reggie and Freddie get to figure it out on our behalf."

Ben opened his mouth to argue once again, but Sarah stopped him. "We do this together, and we're not going down without a fight." To underline her statement, she held her assault rifle up and then shook it with one hand. Nothing happened, so she tried again.

Ben and the other women stared at her. Ben raised an eyebrow.

Sarah blushed. "I... I sort of thought if I could get it to make that cool clicking sound it would let you all know I'm serious."

Ben reached out and grabbed her rifle, then flicked the safety switch off and back on. It made a minuscule clicking noise. He handed it back to her and smiled. "There, that was a click. *Now* we know how serious you are."

Everyone laughed, and Ben was happy for the brief respite. Just as suddenly, everyone's eyes fell to the floor. "So, what do we do now?" Eliza asked.

"Look," Ben replied. "I understand you two don't want to fight. We don't either, honestly, but you heard the lady, and she clicked her gun, which means she's serious. We're doing this together. But if you two want to wait in the basement —"

"We're with you," Catherine said. "I hate guns and I don't want anyone to be shooting at each other, but if they are, I'd much rather be near the people shooting back."

Ben curled his lips down his chin. "Okay," he said. "Can't argue with that." He turned around just in time to see two black-clad soldiers darting into the open space.

Shit. "Down, now!" he yelled. He didn't have time to see if the women had complied. He lifted his own assault rifle and began firing just as the soldiers' own shots rang down the corridor.

He dove to his left, hoping to draw their attention away from the others, then popped up and fired once more. He hit the lead man in the shoulder and sent him spinning, but the second soldier had begun sprinting down the hall. He reached a closed door halfway between Ben and the first shooter before Ben could readjust his aim. The soldier turned and reached for the handle, then threw the door open.

Ben tried to react, but the first soldier had already recovered his weapon and started peppering the ceiling and wall above Ben's head with wild, one-handed shots. Ben waited for a break in the barrage, taking his time to line up his next shot. He fired, sending two rounds into the man's side. The man's arm fell, his gun clattering to the stone floor, dead.

Ben stood up, jogging forward and keeping himself tight against the wall. He heard another burst of fire from inside the room. A few more seconds passed and the soldier emerged, jumping out of the doorway and across the hall while firing blindly toward Ben's previous position.

The rounds missed, but the surprise attack caused Ben to crouch down and cover his head. When he lowered his hands from his face once again and prepared to fire back, he noticed that the soldier was already aiming back at him. And his weapon was leveled at Ben's head, only twenty feet away.

Not good.

He squeezed his own trigger, not even lined up for a good shot yet, but heard the sound of gunshot ring out. He involuntarily flinched, but when Ben looked up again he saw the soldier's weapon fall out of his hands, and the man stumbled backwards.

Ben glanced over his shoulder and saw Julie standing there, her own weapon lifted up and pointed at the dead soldier.

Ben gave her a nod and a quick smile, and she winked back at him.

He stood up again and called over to her. "Guard the hallway," he said. "Use the stairwell into the basement if you need to, but I'm going in there, where that Faction soldier just came out of."

Julie frowned. "What's in there?" she asked.

Ben paused. "Tennyson's office."

CHAPTER 78

BEN

1:21 PM **| March 11, 2021**
Cavo, Isola d'Elba, Italy

None of the items inside the man's office had changed — there were still stacks of papers and manila folders on the low table in the center of the room, and everything else in the space was still immaculately placed and polished to a sheen.

The only difference Ben could see was the man lying on the rug at the far side of the room, just in front of his desk.

Ben rushed over and reached Tennyson just as the older man rolled over onto his back and tried sitting up, gasping for air.

"No, no. Stay there. I'll get help. We will —"

Tennyson's hand was shaking, but it raised up and held Ben at bay. "No," he whispered. "There's nothing you can do. Find Saul — he can get you out of here."

"We're going to take out The Faction," Ben said.

Tennyson coughed, and Ben thought he heard the man trying to chuckle. Blood appeared at the corners of his lips.

"You said you knew about the last attack," Ben said. "Something about Aristotle and what The Faction was planning. Tell me, please. If we're going to stop them, stop whatever it is they're —"

Tennyson shook his head slowly. "There... there is no stopping it now. It is far too late."

"Why do you say that?"

Tennyson gasped for air once again and Ben placed his hand over the man's gunshot wound. He knew it was in vain; Tennyson was quickly losing blood, and his injury was fatal. *But if it buys me another ten seconds of information, so be it.*

"I thought they came here for *me*," Tennyson said. "That they believed I had an antidote, a vaccine. Something to fight against the acid. But I do not."

Ben frowned, not quite putting things together. "You mean, you thought they were going to come here to kidnap you?"

A slight nod.

"That means they either know you don't have any sort of protection against the acid, or they just don't care."

Tennyson let his hand fall back to his side and Ben saw his chest lurch upwards as his lungs fought their final battle. After another few seconds, he looked Ben in the eyes and a calmness fell over the dying man. "The sword was not just a weapon for Napoleon," Tennyson said. "It was meant as a gift. A gift for his son."

Ben closed his eyes and shook his head. "No," he answered. "Catherine explained it to Julie and the others. At the time, Napoleon and Josephine had not had a child. He wouldn't ever have a child with her."

"Not Josephine," Tennyson said. "You must go to Corsica."

Ben frowned. "A mistress, then? Someone no one knew about?"

"Not an uncommon thing," Tennyson replied. "Josephine did not love him, and instead took many other men into her bed. It would have been seen as a sign of weakness for Napoleon not to do the same."

Ben shook his head. *We're wasting time talking about this.* "Why — why does that matter now? Tell me more about what The Faction is planning."

"What *Napoleon* was planning,"

"What are you talking about?" Ben asked. "The Faction has one more attack — you said there were going to be four, right? There have only been three so far, so we need to —"

"Slow down, Bennett." Tennyson coughed again, then smiled. "You will figure it out, as you always do. You have all of the pieces now. You can figure out why I needed you — *specifically* you — and no one else. It *had* to be you, and you will come to know why. You must go to Corsica, after this. You will understand why I did what I did, and the way that I did it. I could not finish the game I started; The Faction came for my family before we could finish. But follow the threads they have left throughout history. They all lead back to Napoleon himself."

Ben's mouth fell open.

But Tennyson wasn't done. "You will also find that that thread extends past Napoleon, to a time long before he was born. A plan that had been put in place by the great philosopher himself."

"Aristotle," Ben whispered. "You mentioned Aristotle before, and the writer of the manifesto invoked Aristotle's name. Why?"

Tennyson was fading faster now. Ben had so many more questions. He was no longer angry at this man, no longer wanting to kill him. No longer wanting to do as Mr. E had told him.

Ben sat back as he thought of Mr. E. *Why the strange reaction from Julie and Sarah about him?*

"Earth," Tennyson whispered. "Earth, water, fire..."

He never got to finish the sentence, but Ben knew the rest. *Earth, fire, water, air.*

He didn't understand the meaning of it. Were these just the incoherent ramblings of a dying old man? Something told Ben that was not the case, that Tennyson was trying to tell him one last thing, give him one last piece to the puzzle.

Whatever that piece was, Ben was not going to get it.

Ben suddenly heard gunfire from all sides, as well as a low deep booming sound from the back wall of Tennyson's office, then the higher-pitched, rattling sound of assault rifles in the hallway.

He picked up his own weapon he had set on Tennyson's rug when he'd entered and turned around. He jogged toward the door.

There was still a fight to fight, and his wife was leading it. No way he was going to let her go it alone.

CHAPTER 79

BEN

1:32 PM **| March 11, 2021**
Cavo, Isola d'Elba, Italy

Ben once again caught up with Julie and Sarah. They were fighting at the open edge of the driveway, the wrought-iron gate still open. Eliza and Catherine were near the side of the gate, huddled together behind one of the concrete walls. The SUV they had driven in on was still parked to their right.

Ben ran over and got a status update. "We're holding them back at the tree line," Julie said. "Looks like there are still some of Tennyson guards out there, hidden in the woods, so it's a sort of skirmish."

"Good," Ben said. "That should keep them busy for a bit. We should get to the SUV, try to swing around the backside and pick up Reggie and Freddie."

Julie shook her head. "Not yet. I can still hear gunfire back there, so we know they're still fighting it out. I think they can hold out for a few more minutes, but if we bring a target the size of the SUV around to them, it'll call too much attention to ourselves."

"What?" Ben asked, incredulous. "Why wait? We need to get out of here."

Sarah yelled across to Ben from her own perch against the concrete wall. "Over there!" she said, pointing with her gun. "Check it out — look familiar?"

Ben lifted his eyes to where her rifle was pointing and tried to make out anything abnormal about the scene. She seemed to be pointing to a field a couple of hundred yards away. It was on a slight rise to the field, a small hill sitting just higher than the ground the castle's base was sitting on. But there was nobody out there, no structures or cars that should have warranted their attention.

It took him a moment, then he noticed what it was he was supposed to be looking at.

There was a tree on top of the hill — a tree whose shape and structure matched almost exactly the tree Eliza had been wearing on her shirt.

"Mulberry," he said.

Julie nodded. "I think we're clear now. I want to go check it out. I think this was Tennyson's last clue in the video — he had the second sword all along, as we already know. He's the one who hid it and wanted you to find it, right?"

Ben smiled. "So why not hide it in plain sight? Why not put it somewhere he can keep an eye on it all the time?"

"Exactly," Julie said. She reloaded her rifle and pulled away from the wall and out past the castle grounds, already breaking into a jog. Ben had no choice but to follow her, glancing left and right to make sure she had been correct in her assumption that they were, at least for the time being, alone.

The others followed behind Ben, and the four reached the mulberry tree in another minute.

Ben couldn't help but feel the excitement. Tennyson may have had to cut his little game short on account of The Faction's interest in him, but he had nevertheless kept his word. The sword was here — it had to be.

Ben felt his heart pounding out of his chest as he stepped over to where Sarah was heading.

"Right there," Sarah said. She walked over to a spot on the other side of the tree and crouched. Ben followed along with his eyes and saw what had captured her attention. It was a long, flat stone laying on the ground, rectangular in shape and with a smoothed surface. It seemed to have been chiseled from a larger piece, as the corners were smoothed over but relatively square.

He walked over and crouched down on the opposite side of the stone, and together they pried their fingers into the dirt and under the stone and pulled. It took some shifting and wiggling, but eventually Ben felt the stone give way. It lifted off the earth, revealing a cavity inside, about six inches deep.

And, inside that cavity, laying on top of another similarly shaped stone, was an object wrapped in a piece of silk. The silk was like a blanket, wrapped tightly around its contents, a dull maroon color, the same shade as blood.

Julie gasped from over Ben's shoulder. "That's it," she said. "We found it."

Ben stood up. "*You* found it," he said. "I was too busy getting blown up and frozen in place in Switzerland. After that, Tennyson apparently ran out of time. He just called and invited me here directly."

Julie and Sarah looked at Ben strangely. "What are you talking about? Frozen in place?"

Ben shrugged. "Trust me, there's a good story there, but it will have to wait until later. Suffice it to say, I know *exactly* what it's like at the other end of that weird acid stuff Napoleon had."

"Speaking of, is there anything like that on this sword?" Eliza asked.

Ben set his assault rifle down, then crouched and picked up the object. He could feel that it was indeed a sword, and he allowed the silk scarf to billow down to the hole as he held the sword. It was extremely heavy, heavier than he imagined it would've been. No doubt the sword had been designed for display rather than combat, which only added to the intrigue as to why Napoleon had carried it into certain battles — an answer they now had.

He turned the sword over in his hands, examining the hilt and the pewter roses on it. Each was gilded with gold flakes, masterfully giving the illusion that the entirety of each rose had been chiseled from a single piece of gold.

"I don't think so," he said. "They're attached pretty good, and I don't see any protrusion that might be used to turn them on or whatever."

"That means —" Catherine said, cutting herself off. "This sword is..."

"The *actual* Sword of Austerlitz," Ben said. "Not the replica, not the one The Faction used as the basis for their chemical weapon."

Just then, Ben heard gunfire from the north. He immediately fell to the earth, hearing the others drop to the ground as they did the same. He picked up his rifle once again aimed it toward the line of trees. He saw one of The Faction's soldiers, wearing all-black and brandishing an evil-looking massive assault rifle, step out of the woods into a clearing. Ben fired three shots that direction, and the man ducked back into the trees.

"Got one to the east, too," Julie said. She fired her rifle, then turned back to Ben. "Ben, they're all around us. Trying to get us surrounded."

Ben nodded. He had noticed the same thing, seeing three other soldiers creeping out of the trees to the west. He detected movement out of the corner of his eye to the south as well, and turned his head that direction. The area was near the castle, and he saw three figures darting alongside it.

Freddie, Reggie, and Saul. Reggie was still holding the massive sniper rifle, but Freddie was running while twisted around, trying to fire shots directly behind him — no doubt being chased by more Faction soldiers from there.

"Hold your fire," Ben said. "They're heading directly for us."

"Guess this is our last stand," Sarah said.

CHAPTER 80

BEN

1:42 PM | **March 11, 2021**

Cavo, Isola d'Elba, Italy

Ben watched the three men approaching from the south, hugging the wall of the concrete first floor of the castle. As they ran, firing wildly over their shoulders, Ben and the others called to them.

Saul, in the middle of the group, stuck his head down and pumped his legs, gaining on Reggie. When he was about five feet behind the lead, he stumbled.

Shit.

Saul went to the ground, a spattering of blood misting the air behind him. Ben heard the delayed gunshots, three in a row. One must have struck Tennyson's security lead, and Saul lay on the ground, unmoving.

Freddie nearly tripped over him as he ran, but he started moving in a serpentine pattern as he made a break for the last distance to the hill.

"Wait until they're close enough to our hill," Ben said, "and then we can start firing over their heads. There are at least six guys coming out of the woods from the south side of the castle, but we can't risk hitting Reggie and Freddie."

"What about the other directions?" Julie asked.

"We'll each take a side. You've got the best shot, so you focus on keeping Reggie's and Freddie's path clear. Sarah, you focus on the east, and I'll try to nail down the north and the west."

Ben noticed about ten more Faction soldiers walking out of the woods. It seemed as though they were not scared of their group at all. They were still a long ways off, but Ben knew he could pick off at least two or three of them from his elevated position in the clearing.

Unless they're planning something else.

"On three," he said. "One... two..." He lined up his shot.

Before he got to three, he heard a thump and noticed something flying end over end, heading directly toward the tree they were using as cover.

Reggie and Freddie were halfway up the hill as the object reached the top of its arc. "Reggie!" Ben yelled. "Stay back! Something's —"

But it was too late. Reggie made it up the hill and reached the mulberry tree just as the canister came down.

Ben rolled to the side as the canister hit the tree and bounced down through the branches. It landed about five feet away from him and came to a rest.

Ben frowned. He had expected an explosion — after all, it seemed that bombs and explosives were finding their way to him quite a lot recently.

But this was no bomb. So far, nothing at all had happened.

The Faction soldiers were still advancing, but none were firing. *Weird.* Freddie was there at the top of the hill now as well, both standing near Ben and the others, trying to catch their breath. Freddie reached out and placed his arm on the mulberry tree, panting.

Just then, Ben heard a click as the canister lurched into the air. It was like a firecracker had gone off inside the canister, and air was now hissing out.

"Oh, *shit*," Reggie said.

Ben knew what it was in that moment. But this was a far larger version of the little canister that had frozen him in Switzerland. He watched as a whitish smoke started to trail out from the canister.

Ben's eyes widened. He bolted upright to a sitting position and then stood, pushing his way toward the canister. He needed to kick it, to send it down the hill back toward the soldiers from The Faction still approaching them.

But he couldn't. Even though the can was still five feet away, his body was slowing. It was not moving any longer, and this time he knew why.

He noticed Julie and Sarah in the corner of his eye, also struggling against the effects of the onset rigor mortis. He imagined their bodies, like his, pumping itself full of the newly created lactic acid, caused by the particles of acid released from the canister.

There was nothing Ben could do. The soldiers were still advancing, the canister was still spewing out its whitish contents. Ben knew this was a much higher dosage than he had been given in Switzerland — enough to knock out his entire team, easily.

And he was the closest person to it. That meant he would either be frozen longer, or perhaps hard enough that he wouldn't even be able to move.

Whatever The Faction had been planning, it seemed they had perfected their weapon of choice. It seemed as though they could put as much of the powdered acid into an object as necessary, then simply detonate it remotely, like a remotely controlled explosive device.

Ben was frozen in place within seconds, and he knew the others were as well.

The haze enveloped him completely, not dissipating or getting any lighter. His vision blurred, both from the effects of the rigor mortis locking his eyelids in place and from thick fog around him.

He could see the silhouettes of the soldiers still getting closer to them, now merely yards away. They stopped. They had all reached the base of the hill and had begun marching upward when the haze had frozen them in place, as well.

Strange, Ben thought. Did they know about the effects of it? Was it a surprise to them as well? What was the plan here?

He wondered if he would be able to breathe through it, or if he should have taken a huge breath before the effects hit him. He remembered that a smaller dose of the stuff had caused his lungs to slow, to fight against the rigidity of the rest of his body. Would a stronger dose cause a stronger effect, or would it just last longer?

He figured he was about to find out.

CHAPTER 81
REGGIE

1:46 PM | **March 11, 2021**
Cavo, Isola d'Elba, Italy

Reggie tried to blink, but his eyes were fighting against him. Every bone in his body was stiff, hard as a rock. He recognized the effect immediately — he had seen Ben get locked down by the same mechanism — in Switzerland, but he had yet to feel it himself.

Turns out, it was intense. He had never thought such a thing possible, but Tennyson had described the science briefly. It was, effectively, a temporary form of rigor mortis, a hundred-fold increase in lactic acid in the bloodstream that simply caused the body to shut down, even hardening with the stress. Every limb felt like it was on fire, and then it simply stopped feeling like anything at all.

Except, not *all* of his limbs felt that way.

As it was, Reggie only had *three* limbs. He had lost an arm about a year ago in Peru, thanks to another deranged psychopath wanting to make a point. Now he had two legs and one biological arm.

Reggie had grown up in a neighborhood where a one-armed man lived. In grade school, he knew kids had made fun of him for the fake-looking, plastic prosthesis. It wasn't something Reggie had taken part in, and he had felt bad for the old guy. The limb seemed more a nuisance than an aid, and he used to wonder why the man had bothered with getting one in the first place.

But that was thirty years ago, and apparently prosthetic technology had come a long way.

That was Reggie's silver lining. Most of the nerve endings where his arm had been severed had been replaced by surgically implanted electrical impulse machines which were fully controlled by the same thing that had controlled all of his limbs before: his mind.

All he had to do was send the same signal he had always sent — move a finger, wiggle the wrist — and his prosthetic arm and hand would move. It had taken a little bit of practice, but it had been far easier than Reggie had imagined, and within months after the surgery, he had gotten completely used to it.

These days, he could use his right arm as if it were the same arm he had always had.

So that's exactly what he did. The titanium alloy prosthetic had no bloodstream running through it. And therefore, no lactic acid that could lock it down, so his arm moved as freely as it always had. The sniper rifle would now be useless to him — he still needed two working arms and hands to operate that — so he pulled out the other weapon he had gotten off of Tennyson's armory wall: a sidearm.

More specifically, a massive, deadly looking pistol that Reggie knew from experience could put a hole through a concrete wall.

And none of these assholes are made of concrete, he thought.

He brought the pistol up with his prosthetic arm and placed it in front of his body, then locked his titanium limb in place. He didn't want to call attention to himself, not this early. Better to appear frozen, like the others, until his moment came.

He sensed movement, but couldn't turn his head to see what it was. Thankfully, the person moved into his vision a few seconds later.

It was someone from The Faction, judging by the black military outfit he had on, but the lower half of his face was hidden behind a gas mask. The man was walking through the frozen lines of his own men up the hill toward Reggie and the others. While he was dressed like the rest of his men, there was nothing in his hands — no weapons whatsoever, as far as Reggie could tell.

Reggie had to strain to breathe, but at least the rigor mortis effect still allowed his lungs to take small, gasping breaths. While his chest couldn't move, his internal lungs could still expand and contract around just enough to allow him to pull in the oxygen to stay alive.

The Faction man knew where he was going. He walked over to Ben and stood there, his hands clasped in front of him. After a few seconds, he spoke.

"Harvey Bennett," the man said. "Never in all my years at Interpol did I think something like this would be possible. See, that's why I joined, originally. I thought it would be saving the world. Stopping people like you."

The asshole from Interpol, Reggie realized. He must also have been a Faction member.

"You probably wouldn't be surprised to learn that Interpol — like most other government-backed organizations with too much bureaucracy and red tape — is mostly useless. Sure, we are good at finding bad guys and putting people behind bars, but that's not *real* change, is it? It's not actually *preventing* people like that — people like *you* — from existing in the first place. And why would it? Interpol is funded by the same governments that fund the current power structure. They have that power, and they're too afraid to lose it, so what do they do? They keep perpetuating the same lies, the same bullshit, that they always have. Setting up organizations like Interpol and the CIA and MI6 to tell the world that they will be safe.

"But *I* know better" Galbraith continued. "The Faction found me, and for once they had a goal that not only aligned with my own, but it seemed plausible. Actually *doable*. I couldn't sign my life away fast enough. And that's the difference between you and me, Harvey: you don't know who you are loyal to. You don't know who you're fighting for. But *I* do. And I'll *continue* to fight, as long as there are guys like you running around."

Reggie watched as the man looked into Ben's frozen eyes for a few more seconds, then shook his head slowly. He crouched down and disappeared from view for a second.

When he stood back up, Reggie began silently screaming in his mind.

He was holding the Sword of Austerlitz. The Interpol man, Galbraith, held the sword in his hands as if weighing it carefully, then grasped the swords hilt and pulled the metal shaft out of its sheath.

"What a meaningful and poetic way to die, Harvey," Galbraith said. His voice was muffled through the mask, and it sounded like he were talking from the other end of a phone. "I'm not sure you *deserve* such a poetic death, but I'll try to make it quick and painless for you."

He held up the sword and examined it a bit closer before speaking again. "However, I'm *not* going to extend that decency to your friends here."

Galbraith turned and examined Julie, standing near Ben. Reggie saw the Interpol agent look her up and down, sickeningly.

Now or never, Reggie thought. He twisted with his arm and brought the pistol out and up, careful to move slowly so he wouldn't draw too much attention to himself. He didn't want to pull it all the way up to his eye to aim, as he was afraid the man would see it, so he just held it out in front of him like an Old West gunslinger. He would have to just fire off the rounds and pan as he went, since there would be no moving his body to get into a better position.

It felt awkward, but he knew he wouldn't miss. He was only standing about ten feet away from Galbraith, and he was still far enough away from Julie that if he missed —

Shots rang out, the deafening sounds jolting into Reggie's stiff ears. He couldn't see who was firing, but he definitely saw what they had hit.

Galbraith stumbled backwards, immediately dropping the sword straight down. The Sword of Austerlitz sank through the earth near Ben's feet. The man fell backwards as more gunshots rang out, and Reggie knew he would be dead before he hit the ground.

What the hell?

Somebody was not frozen as they should have been. Someone had fired from just behind Reggie.

But Reggie knew who was behind him: Freddie.

He desperately wished he could turn around to see who had it had been who had fired over his shoulder, but he could not.

As if reading his mind, a figure stepped into view and closed in on Reggie's face.

CHAPTER 82

FREDDIE

1:50 PM | **March 11, 2021**

Cavo, Isola d'Elba, Italy

Freddie grinned, smacking his new friend on the shoulder. "Hey brother," Freddie said. "No idea what happened, but whatever that junk is, I don't reckon it works on me."

Freddie wasn't sure if Reggie was still completely frozen or not, but he noticed that Reggie wriggled the pistol with his prosthetic arm.

Good enough for me, he thought. Freddie waited a moment and then laughed. "Oh, yeah, I forgot. Don't say anything — I know you're all froze up and stuff. But I see you wiggling your little spider arm there, and I was hoping you'd help me pick off a few of these goons before you all unfreeze. Arrogant, too, for that Interpol guy to freeze all of us *and* all of them, right?"

Expecting no answer from Reggie, Freddie turned and jogged around the tree and down the side of the hill, getting into position.

Seeing the frozen Faction soldiers halfway up it, Freddie started to fire, taking his time to aim single shots directly to their chest. It felt wrong, dirty. It was like shooting fish in a barrel, or — as he and his brother had done so many summers growing up — like filling a barrel with fish they had caught in the lake, then tossing a few M-80s in it.

Too easy.

No matter how he felt about the brutal massacre, he knew these men — or at least their leader, Galbraith — had been about to do the same thing to his own team. Further, he had heard the Interpol guy's speech and knew *exactly* what types of people they were dealing with.

These are some of those wackos who give the deep South a bad name, he thought. The types of folks who can't see past their nose and do whatever felt best in the moment.

Including killing innocent civilians.

His mind fell back to the terrorist attacks that had happened over the past week. He now knew those had been Faction killings — trying to make some strange point he didn't quite fully grasp yet. He thought of the innocent hotel manager, bleeding out on the front steps of his own establishment. All of the innocent people they had gunned down in the streets.

He thought of Mrs. E and the fate that would have befallen the rest of his new team had he not been a bit late to Ben's house.

That motivation kept him going around the hill, taking out one soldier after another. It was especially strange that most of them didn't fall. Instead they just stood there, taking the force of the impact and lurching backwards a bit as if he had simply fired into an upright log. He saw the entry wound and knew that they would all be fatal, but he wondered if and when the contents of the canister would wear off.

He heard Reggie's pistol firing as well, but the man would only be able to fire at the few soldiers he could make out through the haze, without hitting Julie and Catherine, who were still standing in front of him and also frozen. Since Reggie couldn't turn his body around, he could only aim for what was directly in front of his face.

After another fifteen seconds and almost completing a full circle around the upper half of the small hill, Freddie heard a groan, followed by a gasp.

They're waking up.

He turned and looked up the hill as Ben forced his neck to the side, staring at Freddy, the lower half of his body still rigidly in place.

He heard a couple of shouts, a scream in agony as one of the soldiers woke up to find they only had a few more seconds to live.

He fired three more shots into the last three soldiers, then returned to the others at the top of the hill.

"That was... That was something else."

He looked at Ben and tried to smile, but it didn't feel right. He stopped, then hung his head. "I'm just glad it's over."

Ben waited for him to lift his head back up and Freddie saw the intense seriousness in the man's face. "No," Ben said. "It's *not* over yet."

CHAPTER 83

REGGIE

1:53 PM | **March 11, 2021**

Cavo, Isola d'Elba, Italy

"How the hell did you do that?" Reggie asked, coming up to Freddie's side and slapping him on the back.

Freddie shrugged. "Honestly? No idea, man. Maybe I'm like immune to it or something. Never did have chickenpox as a kid. That could be it."

Reggie watched as Freddie opened and closed his palm, noticing that it appeared to be sticky. "You get stuck in something?"

"I was leaning against the tree, trying to catch my breath. I guess I got some sap on me."

Reggie's face shot up, staring at Sarah. He hadn't had time yet to make sure she was okay, but they could decompress and debrief later. Before he could ask her something, she walked over.

"The sap," she said.

"Do you think it's a possibility?" Reggie asked.

She walked over to the tree and leaned in close, sniffing it. Then she dragged her finger across the top layer of bark and pulled it back, pinching her finger and thumb together. It, too, was now sticky. "It *has* to be," she said. "That's the only plausible solution."

"You guys want to fill me in on what's going on?" Ben asked. "I expected Reggie to be able to move his arm, but Freddie... I mean, that was insane."

"The sap," Reggie said. It's got to have some sort of magical properties to it that —"

"It's not *magic* at all," Sarah said. "It's some sort of defense mechanism. Something the tree evolved to be able to fend off predators and keep itself healthy."

"And merely touching the sap prevented the acid from having an effect on you?" Julie asked.

Sarah shook her head. "I'm not sure exactly, I would need a laboratory and probably a chemist to verify it all, but my thought is that the sap and the acid are the same thing. Different forms of it, sure, but the same core chemical composition. Sap like this has a certain pH that helps the tree's internal structure fend off sickness, like blight or worms that might burrow inside."

"Like a silkworm?"

Sarah nodded. "Yeah, exactly. In a weaker tree, the silkworm might actually be able to get inside and cause permanent damage to the tree. While the relationship is probably a mutually beneficial, symbiotic one, I'd bet that when an older mulberry tree begins to get weaker, the silkworms move in and take advantage. This sap is likely a last-ditch effort. Something the tree produces to help it fight. Like it can prevent something from getting inside the tree by literally *locking* their bodies down."

"The younger sap is safe and even has the adverse effect of not allowing the older, dryer sap to have an effect." Julie smiled. "I see how that would be mutually beneficial for a tree species that — for a while, anyway — needs the silkworms around."

Reggie nodded along. He wanted to verify this, but right now it seemed to be a perfect solution to an elegant problem. And — he now realized — it was also the perfect solution to *another* problem.

"Corsica," he said.

Ben walked over and smiled. "Corsica. Exactly. That's where Tennyson told me we should go next. Said there's someone there I should talk to. But I couldn't figure out why Napoleon wanted to go back to Corsica, just to help out with his father's failing mulberry tree business."

Reggie frowned, Julie answered anyway. "The business was failing, but Napoleon's enterprising mind was in a different place entirely," she said. "He went back to help his father, according to the history books, but when he got there he discovered something else entirely."

"The mulberry trees started producing something far more valuable than silk," Catherine said. "Something people might *kill* for."

"That's why it was always so vague, just glossed over in the history books," Ben finished. "He didn't want anyone to know why he was really going back, and his father's business was actually failing. He left school to go be with his family, but he was also working on something that would prove to be extremely useful to his future as a soldier and commander."

Reggie smiled at the rest of them. It seemed Tennyson's puzzle was finally coming into focus, and a *different* puzzle — a much larger puzzle that they were only beginning to see the edges of — was beginning to reveal itself.

And a significant portion of that puzzle seemed to still be in Corsica.

"Back to the SUV?" He asked.

Freddie laughed. "Yes, but I get to drive again. I'm tired of cramming myself into a tiny car with you, and now there's even more of us."

CHAPTER 84

CAPTAIN EDWARDS

2:45 PM | **March 11, 2021**

London-Heathrow International Airport, London, England

Captain Jonathan Edwards flicked his eyes over to his copilot. "You seeing this?" He asked his second-in-command.

Ralph Stevenson nodded slightly, swallowing a lump in his throat. "George is offline."

'George' was the commercial pilot nickname of the suite of software that commanded the aircraft once the pilot engaged it, usually after the plane hit cruising altitude. Today, however, it seemed George had decided not to come to work.

"Hey, no big deal, okay?" Captain Edwards said, calmly reassuring the man. He smiled, trying to keep the younger pilot in high spirits. It really *was* no big deal, in the whole scheme of things. He had seen things like this happen in the past — a last-minute hot-fix to the autopilot system that needed to be installed immediately.

Usually that sort of update would happen offline, well after the plane's last flight of the week. However, on long-haul flights such as this one, the update needed to happen while the plane was in the air. Since WiFi- and internet-enabled plane and flight systems could download and patch the update from anywhere in the world they had a decent satellite connection, he thought it was an ingenious solution to keeping planes up-to-date with the latest software and firmware, no matter how busy their schedules.

Still, it was a bit strange that this one was taking place in the middle of the day for most of the flights disembarking from London. Every pilot in the air was trained well enough to handle the plane at cruising altitude in their sleep, but he knew the suits running these corporations always wanted to keep things as safe as possible.

He wondered what to tell his young copilot. Not coming up with anything witty or funny to say, he resorted to the truth. "Look," he said, "these updates take maybe half an hour at most. It will patch itself and then come back online when it's ready." He finally found something somewhat witty to say. "And if it doesn't, I've got *hundreds* of hours of training — and there are two of me."

Stevenson smiled, but Captain Edwards knew it was forced. The poor guy probably was terrified. Nowhere in their training had they been told to *expect* an autopilot update mid-flight, but there was only so much he could do.

His headset buzzed and air traffic control came through his ear. *"United niner-tree-golf ground. Heading oh-niner-fife for immediate landing."*

Captain Edwards squinted out the front window of the 737-800. *What the hell?*

He sensed Stevenson staring at the side of his head, but he didn't want to add to the kids anxiety. He flicked the switch on his stick and spoke into the microphone. "Pan pan... ground, er — tower — United niner-tree-golf. George is down currently. Please repeat instruction — unclear."

Air traffic control repeated the instruction word for word, and he double checked their heading against his own flight plan. *They want us to turn around and head back,* he thought.

He had to switch again and spoke, losing a bit of the formality.

"United niner-tree-golf, please explain instruction. That's heading the wrong way, what the hell is going on down there? We've got George down here —"

There was a pause, then a crackling of activity electrostatic, then another voice picked up. *"Captain Edwards, ATC dispatcher number eight-one tango. Sorry for the confusion, but it's chaos down here. Seems something's gone haywire with our systems."*

Haywire. Systems.

"This have anything to do with George going down?"

Another pause. *"Yeah, I'm afraid it does."*

He waited for a few more seconds, then Stevenson hit his own trigger. "Care to elaborate, ATC? We are flying blind up here and would love to know why the hell we've been rerouted."

"Wish I could tell you more," came the response, *"but our system's been compromised. We're trying to regain access now. As I said, we hate to reroute you, but we've got a lot of birds in the air right now and need to drop you down into a holding pattern that won't burn up too much fuel. This is the closest we've got, but at least it's the same airport. We'll have a lot of pissed off customers, but we'll make it up."*

Captain Edwards sighed. This was something he had never encountered. Usually ATC was a bastion of confidence for pilots in the air. The seamless switching from one tower's region to another was always handled smoothly and swiftly, and no matter where he was in the world at the moment, Captain Edwards could click a button and immediately be put in contact with a live human who is tracking his plane's every movement. It added a layer of safety to the already world-class safety standards of his employer's airline.

"This will be good practice," he said to Stevenson. "You've got the stick, let's bring her around gently and hold for forty kilometers, making sure we've got her lined up well before we need to start our descent."

Stevenson did as he had been told, and Captain Edwards found himself able to relax a bit as the younger pilot proved his training and expertise. He saw their runway directly ahead another ten minutes later, and within five more Stevenson had brought their altitude down to less than a thousand feet as they approached the landing strip. "You want controls?" Stevenson asked.

"Negative, you got the stick. Light winds out of the northeast, sun behind us — couldn't ask for a better day to get some joysticking in."

While Captain Edwards enjoyed most aspects of the job, the one he knew every pilot was absolutely giddy about was — not surprisingly — *actually* flying planes. Landing was mostly a manual process, but without the help of their in-flight instrument landing system online, there was an added bonus today. Stevenson would be able to feel every little bit of draft, every little bit of wind as it kicked up at the flaps and fought against the spoilers. The beacon indicator light came on and the low tone sounding in his headset as they approached final dissent.

Captain Edward removed his hands from the controls and stuck them up above his head. "Might have to bring her nose up a few extra degrees today on this runway," Edwards said. "I believe we are heading uphill once we hit."

Stevenson nodded but didn't reply.

He reached his hand down and rubbed at the muscles on his neck, massaging out some sore spots. He hated to admit it, but he was going to be relieved to be on the ground again. He had a four-day weekend coming up, and London was as good a city as any to spend it in. He knew there were plenty of places to find entertainment in the huge city.

As he worked his muscles free from the tightness in cramps of the past few days, he felt his fingers began to tingle, and then harden. He tried to pull his hand away from his neck in order to crack his knuckles, but they wouldn't budge.

What the hell?

His right hand was still on the back of his head, so he tried to slide this down to feel around his left hand to see what was going on. It too was completely frozen. His eyes widened, but he noticed it was hard to pull them back together again. He felt his breathing begin to slow, and he found he had to suck in more and more air with each breath. It seemed like his whole body was shutting down slowly. He tried to crane his neck to look at Stephenson, but his neck wouldn't move from its position. His eyes, too, now seemed to have trouble even moving their gaze over to his copilot.

Out of the corner of his eye, he saw a whitish haze beginning to trickle toward them from the rear of the cockpit.

He felt his senses on high alert. All of the extra training he had done had so far been pointless and frivolous. Terrorism seemed every day like a smaller and smaller reality. Now, however, there was only one thing on his mind: somebody had put something into the air.

But why? And what was their plan? If they were trying to hijack the airplane, why had they waited until they were about to land?

He saw the nose of the great aircraft begin creeping upward, pulled back by Stevenson's hands. When the nosecone crested the horizon, Edwards waited for Stevenson to push the stick forward once again and bring their nose level as the plane dropped the last hundred feet to the runway.

It didn't.

He saw the horizon turn to the tops of buildings in the distance, which then turned to empty blue sky, then finally clouds.

He wanted to scream. *Stevenson we're going to stall.* At this low altitude, a stall would be an unrecoverable offense. There would be no way to pull an aircraft that size from a stall at this low of an altitude, which meant...

Captain Edwards knew in that moment that Stevenson had similarly been incapacitated. How? And again, why?

He stared up at the brilliant blue sky pockmarked with white clouds that whipped through his vision. He suddenly felt his stomach lurch. It felt odd, as if only the inside of his stomach were moving, the acid within sloshing against rigid epidermal walls. It was surreal, like he was experiencing someone else's body, inside and out.

They stalled. The nose of the plane swung quickly back down across the horizon, gaining speed as it dove toward Earth.

He heard screams from the passengers through the reinforced thick cockpit door, ringing out to his ears from the rear of the aircraft.

He felt a tingling in his hands and then felt his forefinger twitch slightly. *Finally.* Whatever had happened, it had caused both pilots to be unable to move for half of a minute.

The nose of the aircraft slammed straight down and headed for the tarmac, only this time the landing gear was not going to be the first thing to hit.

And they were gaining speed.

He saw Stevenson yanking backward on the yoke, desperately trying to fix their position. Stevenson should have known that it would do no good. He had been trained better than that, but it seemed his instincts had gotten the better of him. He was trying to recover from the low-altitude stall, pulling back instead of pushing forward to regain control. It didn't matter either way — Captain Edwards knew it was hopeless.

Finally, with his neck able to once again move side to side, he turned and looked at his copilot. He didn't have time for any more witty banter, any parting thoughts.

He nodded once just before the plane slammed into the ground.

CHAPTER 85

BEN

2:57 PM | **March 11, 2021**
Marina di Campo Airport, Elba, Italy

Ben heard about the first crash while waiting at the airport in Elba. They had purchased tickets fifteen minutes ago to hop over to the neighboring island of Corsica. It would be a short flight, but it was going to be an hour before boarding began.

He stared up at the TV monitor, the color drained from his face.

"Hang in there," Julie said. "It was an accident. It's so rare, and generally planes are safer than —"

"*Generally* I don't care," Ben snapped. "And *generally* doesn't hold up when I've already experienced a plane crash in person."

"I was there," Julie said. He heard the softness in her voice, knew she was trying to help keep him calm. The truth was, he absolutely hated flying — always had, for as long as he could remember. He couldn't take his eyes off the television, however. The plane — a 737 out of London-Heathrow had made it all the way to the runway without their autopilot system, but then, seemingly for no reason whatsoever, it stalled out and smacked onto the tarmac.

Everyone on board had perished.

"That's over two-hundred people," Reggie whispered. "Dammit."

The group was all seated in a row at a narrow, tall table in the airport's only restaurant. The table had been set up like a bar top, with stools in a line that looked out into the quiet airport gate. For the lack of people milling about, Ben had been surprised to see how many massive flatscreen TVs had been mounted, facing every direction playing multiple Italian and international news channels.

And every one of those TVs was now playing the same news segment. The newscaster was reporting in Italian, but English captions were displayed at the bottoms of the screens. The closest television was too far away for Ben to read it, so he simply watched the images.

He saw the newscaster put a hand up to her ear, frowning. She stopped talking, something Ben had never seen a newscaster on live television do. There was an awkward silence for about five full seconds — an eternity — and even some other travelers in the vicinity hushed, sensing something was amiss.

"Guess she just got more bad news," Reggie said. "All those people though, man. Two-hundred-something? Can't get much worse news than that."

Ben watched as the picture on the screen changed from a shot of the newscaster to a plane, the nose of it on the runway, on fire.

"Wait —" Freddie said, startled. He leaned forward and squinted "Is that — is that *another* plane?"

"It has to be," Sarah said. "The other one didn't look like that, it was... bigger."

And completely destroyed, Ben thought.

Ben saw a drone shot circling the plane as passengers shot out the back of it and slid down a massive yellow inflatable slide. "They're getting people off of it," he said. "People from the back, at least."

He saw in a closer shot that the front end of the plane had smashed down and crumpled in on itself, likely killing the pilots and whichever unlucky souls had been in the front of the plane. He shuddered, and he felt Julie's hand squeeze his, her fingers intertwining with his own.

"Crap," Reggie said. "Two crashes? Seems a bit fishy."

Earth, wind, water, air.

Air.

"Air!" Ben suddenly said. His voice was nearly a shout, nearly in panic.

The others leaned in and looked at him down the line.

"Air," he said again. "Tennyson said it was from Aristotle, right? Earth, water, fire, air. Guys, the flamethrower in the piazza in Italy? That weird incident off the coast of Mexico with the scuba divers?"

"And the mining excavation that killed a hundred-and-fifty people last week," Reggie said.

"This is it," Reggie said, his voice lowered to a whisper. "*This* is the last attack. The Faction's final plan."

"You think this is The Faction doing this?" Julie asked.

Ben nodded, then stood up. "It *has* to be, right? Earth, water, fire, air. Tennyson said something about finding references to those four elements at each of the attack sites. Said that the attacks would somehow loosely be based on them, that they would all represent this... thing from Aristotle's time. They're trying to make a point, but it's something more than just 'we hate the world, and we want to see it burn.'"

"Yeah," Freddie said, nodding. "Like that guy who was about to spear you with Napoleon's sword. He was on some high horse about something, about changing the world for the better."

"This could all be their way of saying Aristotle is like their God or something," Ben said. "Like they're invoking his memory or something by doing it this way."

"I'm more interested in finding out how we can stop it," Julie said.

"It's too late," Ben said. "Tennyson told me that before he died.

He said it's too late, that The Faction was too far ahead, already in motion."

As he spoke, the news cut once again to another plane, this one completely upside down and lying on the runway. Smoke was pouring from all four engines, and one was on fire already. One wing had completely broken off and was laying nearby.

There were no passengers getting out, either.

"No," Ben said, smacking the table. "*No!* We *have* to try to stop it. Whatever we can do — whatever information we can get to them — maybe there's something we can do."

The others were getting to their feet, but Ben was already in motion. He nearly knocked down a pair of travelers as he picked up speed and ran toward the only room in the entire place he thought might be able to help.

CHAPTER 86

BEN

3:04 PM | **March 11, 2021**

Marina di Campo Airport, Elba, Italy

Ben was nearly shouting, and he took a second to try to calm himself down before speaking again.

It didn't work.

"I — I need to speak with someone in air traffic control," he said. "ATC. You have that?" He pantomimed holding a radio up to his mouth and pressing the button.

The guard — the only person in the airport apparently willing to listen — didn't budge.

He sighed. *What can I do? How in the hell can I —*

"Sir?" a new voice asked. He flicked his eyes upward and saw a woman rounding the corner behind the desk in the office he'd entered. "Can I help you?"

"It's about the attacks," Ben said. "Terrorism."

The guard stiffened. *Apparently that's a word that breaks the language barrier.*

"I can help," he continued. "*Please.* I need you to listen to me. Whatever — *however* — you can, you need to reach out to the ATC stations, the communications people, whatever."

The woman didn't speak. She didn't walk away, either, so Ben took it as a good sign.

The others were there now, and Julie entered the room. He didn't even turn to look at her, hoping that by keeping his gaze locked on the woman in front of him she might understand the importance.

"I'm begging you," he said. "Those planes that are going down — they're being attacked."

"How is that possible?"

"The air, or something. I don't really know. But they released something into the air, scheduled it for the right time. It renders people completely rigid, like they're frozen in place."

"Frozen air?" the woman asked, her face telling Ben everything he needed to know about what she thought of him. The guard's own face wasn't much friendlier.

Ben took a breath, and Julie jumped in. "He's telling the truth," she said. "If you can tell someone — *anyone* — to close the vents in the cockpit, or to stop the airflow somehow..."

He heard how it sounded. It was insane, out of left field. But he turned and saw one of the televisions in the open gate area. They were talking about the attacks — three downed planes so far — and he knew that sounded even more ridiculous.

"Just call it in," he said, finally giving up. "Just... do whatever you can. It's something in the air. I can explain more, and I'm not going anywhere. I'll be right here." He motioned to a chair to his left and then collapsed down into it.

The woman and the guard looked at each other, then the woman took a deep breath. She turned and walked away.

Ben didn't want to talk. Julie and the others left the room and stood sentinel outside, waiting. He heard their hushed tones discussing things, but he didn't have the energy for any more. He just wanted to forget about all of this and fall asleep.

After five minutes, the woman returned. Ben sat straighter in the chair. "I spoke with our ATC liaison," she said. "He assured me that any crew members will check for anything strange in the —"

"That's *not good enough*," Ben said, nearly shaking. "They won't *see* it, don't you understand? It's going to be a white, hazy —"

She held up a finger and with her other hand brought up a cell phone, put it to her ear, and frowned. He hadn't heard it ring; perhaps it had been on the whole time?

She nodded, then spoke quickly in Italian.

When she hung up and met his eyes, he almost knew what she was going to say before she said it.

"Another plane went down," she said. "In Paris."

He hung his head. "I tried to tell you…"

"There were two small jets from Elba that are landing in Milan and Rome soon," she continued. "I have informed their controllers to try to shut off the air vents in the cockpits, just temporarily."

Ben shot to his feet. "Thank you," he said. He was nearly in tears. "*Thank you*. It's going to work. It *has* to work."

She put the phone back over her ear and continued discussing in Italian, offering annoyed glances up at Ben a few times. No doubt telling whoever it was on the other end of the line just how persuasive the American could be.

He waited for her to be done, and then she approached him. The guard was suspiciously close to him now, and he sensed his personal space disappearing rapidly.

"We are grounding all flights," she said. "As you can imagine, we want to end these strange occurrences as soon as possible."

He shifted.

"And we would like to keep you here to ask more questions."

"You're detaining me?" he asked.

"Are you involved in these so-called attacks, sir?"

He shook his head. "No, of course not."

"Then it is not a *detainment*, but an amicable exchange of information. Surely you would not have a problem with that?"

He looked out at the others, knowing that they weren't going anywhere anytime soon anyway. Flights would be grounded all over Europe, and likely would extend through the night until police and investigators could get a grip on the situation and isolate the cause.

"Sure," he finally said. "I'm here to help. I can tell you whatever you want to know, even though you're not going to believe half of it."

He stood up, then invited in the rest of the group. They entered single-file, and the guard suddenly seemed to realize that he wouldn't have been able to keep them all here anyway, if Ben had chosen to leave.

They lined the office, and Ben stuck out his hand to the woman. "Name's Harvey Bennett," he said. "Maybe you've heard of me. We're with the Civilian Special Operations."

CHAPTER 87

JULIE

4:18 PM | **March 11, 2021**

Marina di Campo Airport, Elba, Italy

"Ben, you did it," Julie said. She ran toward him and threw her arms around his neck. He knelt down, accepting the hug but not returning it.

"*We* did," he said. "And I just put the last piece in place."

"But the last piece was everything," Reggie added. "If you hadn't gotten up and made a stink about it, they never would have figured it out."

Ben shrugged, and Julie could see the hesitation on his face. They were gathered in the small airport. All of the flights had been canceled for the remainder of the day, and news reports were coming in that officials might move to cancel flights for at least a week in order to check every plane for traces of the acid powder.

Ben had, in fact, gotten the air traffic controllers to listen. The woman he had spoken with had kept him in the room, but once she had confirmed that his theory was true — that somehow an aerosolized version of a rigor mortis-causing acid was being released into planes' cockpits — word spread fast.

As it turned out, the European air traffic control centers were actually a tightly knit communications network, thanks to the amount of air traffic they needed to be aware of at any given time.

And since there was effectively no downside other than having a pair of uncomfortable pilots for a few minutes, just about all of the commercial planes flipped their vents closed or turned off the air circulation to the cockpit. The triggers for the acid were buried in the updated code in each plane's firmware, but only triggered at a certain low altitude — one that meant the plane was in the final approach for landing.

It meant that the twisted game The Faction was playing could be averted by closing off the air before the plane touched down.

That said, the toll was heavy.

"Over six-hundred people," Ben said. There were tears in his eyes.

Julie nodded. "It could have been more," she whispered, still embracing her husband. "It almost *was* more. A lot more."

"You can't beat yourself up, man," Freddie said, joining in. "You did a good thing, and that's that. Can't be thinking you failed."

"We didn't stop it in time," Ben said. "That's all there is to it."

Freddie dropped his head. Julie knew he didn't want to argue with Ben — no one did, especially when he was like this. She released him, and the group headed toward the front of the airport. They had returned their rental car already, but Julie wanted to get there quickly, before the tourists who now had a forced extension to their vacations beat them there.

Catherine had been on one of the planes already, heading for Lyon, and they had recently received word that she had touched down safely. Thankfully the woman had not known anything about the scare happening all around her, as she had fallen asleep upon boarding and the pilots had not woken anyone up to alert them when they had found out. If anyone on the plane had been watching the news, it apparently had not gotten to Catherine.

Julie was more than relieved to hear that Lady Catherine would be returning to her castle and be home that evening, safe and sound.

They owed the woman a debt, and Julie was not sure it could ever be repaid.

"What now?" Sarah asked, grabbing Reggie's hand as they walked through the terminal.

"Ben's getting a boat," Julie said. "Corsica is right next door, and the ferries are still running daily. I thought we could stay here for another few days, at least until flights are running again."

"We're not going to Corsica with him anymore?" she asked.

Ben shook his head. "I thought about it, but the more I did I thought it would make sense for me to go alone. It's something Tennyson told me to do — something I feel I owe him now, as strange as that sounds."

Julie heard Ben pause, and the others seemed to pick up on it.

"And there's always time to get over there and snoop around," he continued. "I know you're all dying to know more about the history and Napoleon's life —"

"To be honest, I'm pretty sick of the guy," Freddie said.

Ben laughed. "I know what you mean. And besides, Julie needs to get back to Alaska to get started on the insurance claims."

"So what about The Faction?" Reggie asked. "Are you thinking you'll run into them?"

Ben shook his head. "I don't know, but I doubt it. Something tells me this is a bit different. If The Faction wanted anything from me besides my head, I don't think they'd hide in Corsica and wait for me to stumble upon them."

They reached the rental counter, and Julie stepped forward to place a credit card on the counter and beg the young man for anything they might still have available. Hopefully, they could rent an SUV once again, something that would carry all of them to a hotel.

On the way, they would drop Ben off at a nearby marina, where the ferry would arrive in about an hour.

Julie watched as the young man behind the counter left to grab a set of keys. She turned to the group behind her and saw the tired, haggard looks in their eyes. They had not even bothered to survey the damage at Tennyson's castle, instead opting to get away from there as fast as possible. They had left their weapons where they lay, haphazardly strewn about on the ground. Catherine had taken the sword with her for safekeeping, and the plan was to touch base with her after they had all had a chance to catch their breaths.

But Ben was right, Julie knew. This was not over. Far from it.

CHAPTER 88

BEN

6:05 PM | **March 11, 2021**

Villanova, Corsica, Italy

Ben started up the path, not knowing what he would find. The trees seemed to bend away from him, pointing him along the trail. While the driver could have deposited Ben farther up the road, the dirt path that Ben was now on was far narrower than the road he'd been left at. They had wound up the hill toward the idyllic town of Villanova, near where Napoleon had been born.

He had gotten the email shortly after leaving the airport in Elba. It was from Tennyson.

Nothing but an address, and Tennyson's signature.

At first it had jolted Ben. *Tennyson is dead,* he remembered. *I watched him die.* Surely the email had to be a trick.

When he had shown it to Julie, she clicked on the sender's address in his phone's mail app, and she had pointed out that it had not been from Tennyson, at least not directly.

Instead, it appeared that Tennyson had used a forwarding service, masked behind his name, to send the email at a scheduled time. For whatever reason, Tennyson had pre-scheduled this email, with the Corsican address, to be sent to Ben.

It did not confirm that the email was, in fact, from Tennyson, but Ben had a feeling it was legitimate. He remembered Tennyson's final words. *Earth, water, fire, air.* And before that: *You must go to Corsica.*

The man had never told Ben *exactly* where in Corsica, and Ben had remembered from his and Julie's first brief trip to the island that it was a massive place.

They had run out of time in Tennyson's office, so Ben wasn't surprised that Tennyson had used an email forwarding and scheduling service like this one to prepare the email, to make sure it got sent out *after* the events at the castle that ultimately took Tennyson's life.

It was a last-ditch security effort, Ben thought. *Something important enough he had to make sure it got through.*

And there was another feature of this email, Julie had told him. Apparently Ben was not the only recipient of the email. It had been routed back through the service, ultimately landing in the inbox of another unknown person.

Intriguing, Ben had thought.

As he crested the hill over the dirt path, he saw a Tuscan-style home come into view. It was not massive, but it certainly was not small, either. It sat on picturesque rolling hills, manicured and well-kept. The white stucco walls of the main structure ended with a bright red curved-brick roof, similar to what he might find on any roof elsewhere in the Mediterranean.

And at the end of the path, in the rounded driveway of the house, sat a man.

He was in a wheelchair, seated in front of a small fountain that stood in the center of the circular drive. A man stood next to him, slightly set back, holding an umbrella over the wheelchair-bound man's head.

Ben picked up the pace, now even more curious. He assumed this man had been the other recipient of Tennyson's email and was here to await Ben's arrival.

He stepped up to the two men, standing about ten feet away. He sensed no reason to be alarmed, but he had learned to never be too careful.

"Harvey Bennett," the man said.

Ben squinted, trying to see beneath the shadow of the umbrella. The light shifted, and Ben's mouth fell open.

"Mr. E?"

The man in the wheelchair nodded slowly. "I see you have received Tennyson's last correspondence."

Ben's eyes fell to the ground. "I did. He scheduled it to be sent out automatically. He... didn't make it."

"I assumed as much," Mr. E said. "Harvey, come closer. As you can see, I am in no shape to offer you any harm, nor do I have any inclination toward it."

"But... all of this... did you *know* Tennyson?"

He nodded slowly again, this time allowing his own eyes to fall. "We were even friends once. Many decades ago. Two passionate young men, interested in seeking out the answers to life's deepest questions."

"You asked me to kill him," Ben said. "You *told* me to kill him. How could you? If he was your friend —"

Mr. E raised a gangly, thin-skinned hand and Ben stopped. Only then did he realize how frail the man truly was. On the television screens and tablets, Mr. E had appeared gaunt, but not this sickly. Whatever vivaciousness the younger version of the benefactor had was long gone now. What sat in front of Ben was a skeleton, barely alive.

Still, the man's voice worked well enough, and he continued his explanation. "We were both interested in seeking out the deepest, darkest secrets humankind has kept hidden. We each, at separate times, stumbled upon the existence of an ancient order. One that has been manipulating men and history for ages."

"The Faction," Ben said.

"Indeed. It has existed since Aristotle himself put forth the original idea, and it has morphed over the years into a twisted, macabre version of its original purpose and initiative. That is the organization I wished to stop, and now that task falls to you."

"How do I find them?"

"There is an island, off the coast of Turkey, that used be a prison complex for enemies of the state. My research suggests that this island may be hiding a Faction stronghold. My communications team has intercepted a vast array of signals originating from this area. But tread carefully, Harvey. The Faction is a well-resourced organization."

"They certainly wanted to kill us," Ben said. "Just because they thought we knew something about their terrorist attacks. Because we were looking for the Sword of Austerlitz."

He watched Mr. E swallow, the pain evident on the older man's face. "I am sure you can tell this already, Harvey, but I am dying. The pace has quickened, and I fear I have weeks left, perhaps less. As such, we are out of time."

"Why didn't you tell us sooner?" Ben asked.

"I had hoped to bring the Civilian Special Operations up to speed soon regarding The Faction's existence, but even knowing their name is a dangerous thing. You may think they are done, now that you have foiled their final attack, but I assure you, Harvey, they are only beginning."

Ben nodded. "Tennyson said as much."

"Tennyson knew the end was near. He knew far too much. Many years ago I inquired into the existence of a certain journal, one that is now owned by the three times great granddaughter of Napoleon's swordsmith in Paris."

"Odiot."

"Yes. I met with Catherine then, and asked about Odiot and his work. She was careful, and did not let it slip that she had the journal in her possession. But Tennyson had discovered this information himself, and he arranged to have a page stolen from the journal later. I warned him that it had been a terrible decision, but he kept the page hidden out of sight for nearly forty years."

"And when he started his game of cat-and-mouse with *me*, it alerted The Faction to the fact that he knew about Odiot's Sword of Austerlitz, and the page from the journal."

Mr. E smiled, a thin strip of lips, barely edging out his eyes. "Correct again. They must have feared this would interfere with their plans, so they tried to remove Tennyson. They ultimately succeeded, but at great cost to their organization."

"Because the secret got out."

Mr. E nodded again, more emphatically this time.

Ben knew what it meant, but he had to be sure. He had to hear it from Mr. E.

"They now know that *you* have this information."

BEN

6:11 PM | **March 11, 2021**

Villanova, Corsica, Italy

There it is, he thought. In that moment, he knew Tennyson had been correct. *This will not end here.*

"They are going to chase you, Harvey," Mr. E said. "You and the rest of the CSO. Until you are gone, or you can somehow find a way to defeat them. This is why I kept it secret from you, from your team. From my own wife, even."

"I — I'm sorry for — "

"It is the nature of your work, Harvey," he said. "Just as it was the nature of hers. She would not have wanted me to grieve long, and I suggest you find it within yourself to do the same."

Ben swallowed, unable to find words.

"I will miss her dearly, but I was always working toward a larger goal. The Faction *must* be brought to their knees."

"How?"

Mr. E stared at Ben, then he shook his head slowly. "I have absolutely no idea," he said.

Ben didn't want to dwell on this. He changed the subject. "Why did you want me to kill Tennyson? What would that accomplish?"

"It would make them realize you are not on Tennyson's side," Mr. E said quickly. "It will have given them pause, made them wonder who you are *truly* working for. That might have been enough to give you the upper hand."

"But now they just think I was on his side the entire time."

"I am afraid so," Mr. E said. "Although there is one last trick. One last thing we can try."

"What?"

Mr. E paused, took a deep, thorough breath, then let it out. "First, let me explain to you why Tennyson chose *you*."

"*Chose* me?"

"It *had* to be you, Harvey."

Ben felt the words hit him as hard as the revelation. *It has to be you.* Tennyson had spoken the same words to him only hours before.

It had to be you, and you will come to know why. You must go to Corsica, after this.

Here he was, about to find out why Tennyson had chosen him for this mission. "I thought it was revenge," Ben said. "Tennyson's grandson died because of me, so he was paying it back."

"It was a unique and rare coincidence that your paths crossed," Mr. E said. "But this world is full of rare and unique coincidences. While Tennyson may have entertained the idea of allowing you to believe he sought revenge, I can assure you his *real* reason for reaching out to you is far more important."

What possibly *could that mean?* Ben wondered.

The man holding Mr. E's umbrella shifted to the opposite side of his chair, catching a bit more of it in the shade. "Did Tennyson mention that Napoleon had the second sword designed for his son?"

Ben nodded. "Yes. But Catherine said that Napoleon and Josephine — his wife at the time the sword was made — had never had a son."

"That is... mostly correct."

"Was it a mistress, then?" Ben asked. This was the same line of questioning he had tried with Tennyson, but the old man had not had time to explain.

"Yes. A mistress that is not — nor will ever be — in the history books. Technically, Napoleon and Josephine were married at the time, although quite estranged. Josephine — Marie Josèphe Rose Tascher de La Pagerie — had decided to love Napoleon Bonaparte once more, but in a strange irony of Patrician society, it would be considered a faux pas to bounce from a husband to a lover to a husband again, at least in proper society. But in a brief interlude between battles, they were able to see one another once more..."

"Wait," Ben said. "Are you saying Napoleon had a mistress, but that mistress was actually his *wife*? It was Josephine?"

"Yes."

"So... Napoleon had an heir. A *real* heir, with the wife who was most likely Napoleon's true love?"

Mr. E smiled once again. "And that is not all, Ben."

Ben felt himself getting a headache. He wanted to sit down. Drink a glass of water. Or whiskey.

"Lady Josephine kept this child a secret, even from Napoleon himself. She had the child reared by a nearby orphanage, eventually entrusting its care to a family friend who promised to leave the country and raise the child in relative peace."

"Where'd they go?"

"England," Mr. E said. "The family's name was Biennais."

"That's the guy who made the *first* Sword of Austerlitz."

"Indeed it is. The family the boy was reared into was led by a nephew of Biennais himself, in fact. And when they fled France, they decided to change their name. To further hide the boy from the world. You see, The Faction was alive and well in Napoleon's time. It is said that Napoleon's chemists were members, and those would have included people close with Odiot and Biennais, who relied on their technologies for their smith work."

"So Josephine wanted to keep the boy safe, so she didn't even tell his *father* he existed?"

"Essentially, yes. But the important part is the name, Harvey. You see, when they settled in England, Biennais' nephew got a job as a clerk, and promptly changed the family surname."

Ben cocked his head sideways. It was interesting, but he wasn't sure why it mattered so much.

"The name he chose for his family was an offshoot of Biennais, to keep it in the history. He chose the name *Bennett*, and the family has been called that ever since."

Ben swallowed, feeling his eyes trying to pull him down. He opened his mouth, closed it again. *No.* "I — I don't understand, Mr. E."

Mr. E's smile returned, and this time it reached his eyes. "I believe you do, Harvey. I believe you understand everything now. Why it had to be *you* — why I started the CSO, and why *you* became its leader. Why Tennyson needed *you*, and no one else. And why *you* had to find the sword. The *second* sword. The one that is rightfully yours."

"Are — what? Are you saying the secret son of Napoleon..."

"Is your ancestor, Harvey."

"No, that's — how? That can't be possible."

"You, Harvey Bennett, are related to Napoleon himself, directly and irrefutably, through the family lineage of Biennais, a close friend and confidant of Napoleon Bonaparte. You are, thus, the rightful heir of the secret organization Napoleon lost control of when he lost power after his exile."

"The... Faction."

"Yes, Harvey. The Faction."

AFTERWORD

If you liked this book (or even if you hated it...) write a review or rate it. You might not think it makes a difference, but it does.

Besides *actual* currency (money), the currency of today's writing world is *reviews*. Reviews, good or bad, tell other people that an author is worth reading.

As an "indie" author, I need all the help I can get. I'm hoping that since you made it this far into my book, you have some sort of opinion on it.

Would you mind sharing that opinion? It only takes a second.

Nick Thacker

BOOKS BY NICK THACKER

Mason Dixon Thrillers

Mark for Blood (Book 1)

Death Mark (Book 2)

Mark My Words (Book 3)

Harvey Bennett Mysteries

The Enigma Strain (Book 1)

The Amazon Code (Book 2)

The Ice Chasm (Book 3)

The Jefferson Legacy (Book 4)

The Paradise Key (Book 5)

The Aryan Agenda (Book 6)

The Book of Bones (Book 7)

The Cain Conspiracy (Book 8)

The Mendel Paradox (Book 9)

The Minoan Manifest (Book 10)

The Napoleon Job (Book 11)

Harvey Bennett Mysteries - Books 1-3

Harvey Bennett Mysteries - Books 4-6

Harvey Bennett Mysteries - Books 7-9

Jo Bennett Mysteries

Temple of the Snake (written with David Berens)

Tomb of the Queen (written with Kristi Belcamino)

Harvey Bennett Prequels

The Icarus Effect (written with MP MacDougall)

The Severed Pines (written with Jim Heskett)

The Lethal Bones (written with Jim Heskett)

Gareth Red Thrillers

Seeing Red

Chasing Red (written with Kevin Ikenberry)

The Lucid

The Lucid: Episode One (written with Kevin Tumlinson)

The Lucid: Episode Two (written with Kevin Tumlinson)

The Lucid: Episode Three (written with Kevin Tumlinson

Standalone Thrillers

The Atlantis Stone

The Depths

Relics: A Post-Apocalyptic Technothriller

Killer Thrillers (3-Book Box Set)

Short Stories

I, Sergeant

Instinct

The Gray Picture of Dorian

Uncanny Divide (written with Kevin Tumlinson and Will Flora)

ABOUT THE AUTHOR

Nick Thacker is a thriller author from Texas who lives in Colorado and Hawaii, because Colorado has mountains, microbreweries, and fantastic weather, and Hawaii also has mountains, microbreweries, and fantastic weather. In his free time, he enjoys reading in a hammock on the beach, skiing, drinking whiskey, and hanging out with his beautiful wife, tortoise, two dogs, and two daughters.

In addition to his fiction work, Nick is the founder and lead of Sonata & Scribe, the only music studio focused on producing "soundtracks" for books and series. Find out more at SonataAndScribe.com.

For more information and a list of Nick's other work, visit Nick online:
www.nickthacker.com

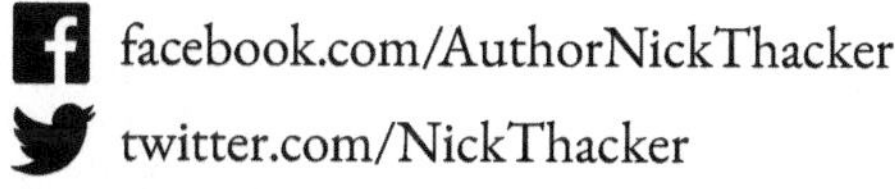

facebook.com/AuthorNickThacker
twitter.com/NickThacker